IT STARTED WITH A List

TINIA MONTFORD

This is a work of fiction. Names, characters, places, and incidents either are the product of the author's imagination or are used fictitiously. Any resemblance to actual persons, living or dead, events, or locales is entirely coincidental.

tiniamontford.com

First Edition: January 2022

Book design by Elizabeth Turner Stokes
Interior formatting by Qamber Designs
Editors: Jami Nord, Little Pear Editing Services

ISBN 979-8-9851081-1-8 (paperback)
ISBN 979-8-9851081-0-1 (ebook)

Published by 735 Emerald Press LLC

PLAYLIST

Psycho! – MASN
Separate from You – sadgods, Powfu, Indii G.
Here – Alessia Cara
Torn Apart – Eredaze
Prom Queen – Beach bunny
Hoodie – Hey Violet
Like a Radio – Keelan Donovan
Selfish – Stephanie Poetri
I Like Me Better – Lauv
I'm Yours – Alessia Cara

Interested in listening to Lazarus & Vassa's entire playlist?
https://sptfy.com/itstartedwithaList~s

Or would you like to see deleted scenes, character interviews and exclusive character art?
Sign up for my newsletter,
https://landing.mailerlite.com/webforms/landing/q4f2f5

You can also connect with me on:
My Website: https://tiniamontford.com/
Facebook | Instagram | Pinterest | Tumblr: @tiniawritesbooks

This book briefly mentions material that can be triggering for some readers. Reader discretion is advised. For a complete list of trigger warnings, please visit tiniamontford.com/trigger-warnings

To Grandma Jackie and Mom,
I'm forever indebted to you.

"Whatever our souls are made of,
his and mine are the same."
—Emily Brontë

CHAPTER ONE

Subject line: Spring Graduation

Congratulations on your upcoming graduation, Vasilisa!

Please respond "YES" if you plan to attend the May Commencement Ceremony or "NO" if you do not plan to attend the May Commencement Ceremony.

We look forward to hearing from you!
Robert Peña
Degree Audit and Graduation Adviser
Office of the Registrar

"IS THIS MAT HYPOALLERGENIC?" ASKED the customer standing in front of her.

It was simple, respond yes or no. Her concentration broken, Vassa rocked back and forth on the barstool, biting her lip. She had been about to respond to the email and now her finger hovered over the reply button as the customer stared. Life as she knew it was coming to a shrieking halt.

If she said no, her mother would kill her. She was an only child and her mother had been waiting years for this moment. Just last night, her mother ranted about her search for the best dress to show off her "perky C-cups" at Vassa's graduation.

The customer cleared her throat, and Vassa shut the device. Right, she was at work. She couldn't deal with her own life going kaput. Most of the time she was at the campus library, a slave to studying, but in her rare free time, she satisfied the nonsensical questions of San Francisco's rich and elite housewives at the yoga studio.

If Vassa wasn't a hop, skip, and a jump away from the poorhouse (with mounting student loan debt) and adamantly saving to move to New York City, she would have told this woman to shove it, but she was already on probation with her manager after the last yoga mat incident.

Vassa plastered on her intensely fake smile and perked up her voice. "I know it's a popular brand. It's slip- and sweat-resistant for our extra moist individuals."

The woman narrowed her eyes. "Are you calling me moist?"

Vassa blinked and shook her head. "No, no. I mean… I sweat. All the time. The moment I wake up, my pits are like a leaky faucet. I've put deodorant, tissue, sponges, just about anything to stop these things. Nothing, I mean *nothing*, works. Then my feet? Gosh, just when I go to do a downward dog, I'm sliding across the room…"

Vassa trailed off at the look of disgust on the woman's face. *Okay, TMI.*

"Do you have any in black?"

Vassa's eye twitched and her smile faltered, but she kept it together. Pointing to the bin of yoga mats, she said, "All our products are on display."

"I'll keep looking." The woman looked Vassa up and down before tilting her head up and sauntering away.

She opened her laptop again. The email was still there, waiting for her response. She slammed the laptop shut. Bending down, she grabbed her nearly empty pack of key-lime-pie-flavored Twizzlers. It was what she had whenever she felt overwhelmed. Tangy and sweet, light and creamy, the candy took the edge off.

Graduation was near and she had accomplished nothing *remotely* fun.

The top twenty hits mixed with chatter wafted in through the window from the restaurant next door. She worked at Vibe and Flow for multiple reasons: She could be on her laptop most of the time and do her schoolwork. It had a casual dress code. It was in the Castro neighborhood of San Francisco, Vassa's third-favorite neighborhood. There was great food and entertainment, but... You were bound to walk down the street and find some strange folks in leather or a homeless person screaming their head off. And being a receptionist at any yoga studio in the city required her to be bubbly and friendly. Something she wasn't, exactly.

I thought it would change me.

Sometimes Vassa wished she had a different life. She wished she was braver and prettier and just... happy.

Four years had passed her by, and she was still the same girl from high school. She always thought she had enough time to be someone different. *I'll go to that party next time. I'll go to the students' rendition of Cats next time.*

Graduate school was her goal. That would be completed as soon as she submitted her applications. She wanted to be Professor Vasilisa Blackwell. As a first-generation college student, her graduation and success weren't for her alone. She was achieving a milestone for her family and she didn't take it lightly. Her eyes were set on Iowa State or Harvard or Stanford. Those places weren't just letting in any Tom, Dick, or Harry off the street. She had to be competitive. So she'd put her future ahead of fun.

The Twizzlers bag crinkled as she reached for another.

Pair that soul-sucking revelation along with no play and the worst semester of her life, and she knew something needed to change. *She* needed to change.

Maybe she could start with goal she had since she was a freshman. Get totally wasted.

Who was she kidding? She was a square.

Vassa was the person who held your hair out the toilet. Took your phone away to keep you from drunk texting a mistake. It would have been easier if she had more friends. The sisterhood she had was long gone.

But hey, at least now she had access to unlimited yoga classes.

Her internal despair didn't match the Christmas decorations surrounding her. Vassa placed both arms on the table and sat her chin in her hands before she flicked the bobblehead Santa on the desk. It was mid-January, but her supervisor wouldn't let her remove any trace of Christmas in the studio.

If there was one thing she was, it was a planner.

It was an undecided plan, but she decided on a bucket list. Six things that would send her off with a bang. She had placed the list under the laptop earlier; now she read it again.

Vassa's Extraordinary Senior Send-Off

1. Get totally wasted and regret nothing.

2. See all the tourist spots in San Francisco.

3. Have an epic last Spring Break.

4. Do something completely wild.

5. Sneak into a party or event uninvited and pretend to be someone else.

6. Go on a date.

She had jotted the list down on the Greyhound back to the city. Granted she stole some ideas from her ex-best friend. They were supposed to do these things before they moved to New York.

The list seemed reasonable, but part of her wanted to rip it up and never speak of it again. To slip into her good night.

The doorbell jingled. Vassa shoved her list back under the laptop.

"Welcome to Vibe and Flow." She pasted on a smile, brushing hair behind her ears as she did a little shake to get the bad vibes off.

A group of girls entered, laughing. They were all typical San Francisco yogis: hippy, tall, and varying in expensive yoga gear. The complete opposite of Vassa's short frame and wire-rimmed glasses. *Maybe I should've put some care into my appearance today…* She looked like the Stay-Puft Marshmallow Man in a puffer jacket, sweatsuit, and scarf (it was unbearably cold and the fog was thick) but she was proud of her days-old twist-out holding up.

A girl came forward wearing a T-shirt with Vassa's university's logo. "Oh wow, no way. Vassa? Vassa Blackwell? How are you?" Her face looked familiar.

Vassa blinked and squinted her eyes for a moment. The girl smiled and nodded as if that would jog Vassa's memory. "Sophia Irvin. Alexa's friend."

Great. Right when I'm in mental and emotional anguish, here comes trouble.

"Wow, Sophia, that's crazy. It's so good to see you." *Not.* Vassa's hand slid toward the Twizzlers.

"I know, right? I feel like I never see anybody off of campus, ya know? Then you..." Sophia's ponytail bounced as she leaned on the counter. "It's still nice and... festive in here." Her lips twisted as she looked at the Christmas decorations.

"The owner has a soft spot for commercial holidays. Twizzler?" Vassa plucked another from the bag and offered it. Sophia wrinkled her nose and shook her head.

The girls behind Sophia stared at her. How much did Sophia know? Did they know? The mention of her ex-best friend's name was jarring. It'd been what... three months since she last saw her? Blowing out a series of quick breaths to gain control, Vassa aggressively gnawed off half the Twizzler.

"So, I heard about you and Alexa," Sophia whispered, widening her eyes.

"Well, you know, people outgrow each other and she thought she could be happier with a different group of friends and I am... Well, ya know. I get it. She's doing her and I'm doing me." Vassa laughed, but it was obviously fake. She finished the Twizzler and immediately went for another one.

Sophia nodded. "I mean, you both were glued at the hip. Friends since middle school, right? That's what she told me. It was wild how everything happened so suddenly and then you disappeared."

Stick the knife in deeper…

"I mean, we were all kinda hurt. I loved listening to your stories and poetry. I'm surprised you came back to campus."

Vassa felt her features turn downward. She didn't really know what to say and settled for an unconvincing murmur of agreement. It was uncomfortable to share what had really happened: that the one person closest to her in the world stabbed her in the back, posted it online, and made her seem like a villain. That taught her never to trust again.

The woman from earlier dropped the mat on the counter. "I'll take it."

Vassa began ringing up the item but listened as the girls began talking again.

"I totally need this; you know the baseball team threw another rager last night," one girl said.

They all made noises of agreement.

"Did you see Lazarus? I mean, he's so hot, I would do him in a heartbeat if I could get through the thirsty fangirls around him."

An awkward silence fell over them before Vassa cleared her throat and actually did her job. "I'm sorry, can I get you all checked in for class?"

"Right! We're here for the five o'clock vinyasa flow."

A Twizzler dangled from Vassa's mouth as she typed. The girls rattled off their names. The group congregated near the merchandise she recently stocked, oohing and ahhing loudly. The woman debating the hypoallergenic mat glared at them.

Sophia lingered near the desk. "Are you going to come back to spoken word?"

Vassa took a deep breath. She desperately wished the woman with the mat would come over here and stop this conversation.

"I have a lot of shifts here and schoolwork. Studying too, lots and lots of studying. I'm an artist too, so… You know, creativity has to hit you." Vassa shrugged before looking down at the desk.

Sophia's smile faltered before she gave Vassa a parting wave and moved over to her friends. Vassa tried not to look back at the girls, instead pretending to count the people coming into the class that day. The encounter was already on repeat in her mind.

Isn't that the reason Alexa dumped you as a friend? You're too awkward.

Alexa was more interested in partying till six in the morning. Vassa wanted to study. They'd become unrecognizable to each other, and it led to a blowout.

Vassa felt like she had lost a sister. She longed for that closeness again, but the trauma had her cowering from anybody that tried to befriend her. *What if they're another Alexa?* There was still a small fire of hope within her, that she'd find that closeness again, no matter how much she told herself she didn't need it.

Lazarus Gilbert. The one person she was glad she would never see after graduation. Vassa didn't do well with people like him or these girls: popular all-stars. He was loud, made jokes at the wrong time, and a complete pain in her ass. Lately, it seemed his favorite pastime was causing her hell if he wasn't partying. He was the type of person Alexa wanted to be around, told Vassa she should try to be like, and he reminded her of Alexa every time she saw him.

"We totally need to live it up," Sophia said.

Live it up? Vassa's mind drifted to her list nestled under her laptop.

Vassa looked over to see the girls giggling. Her heart twitched at the sight. A miniscule part of her mourned, but she quickly shoved it to the side. It was better to minimize your chances of betrayal by being alone. Vassa knew people couldn't be trusted and would always show their true colors. Alexa did. She didn't need anyone but her family and her best friend.

The woman buying the mat cleared her throat loudly, and Vassa gave her the total. The woman handed her a credit card. Her eyes drifted back to the group.

"Alexa and her boyfriend would probably come. They'll bring some other people. So, we're having the best semester ever," Sophia continued, and they all laughed. The doors to the studio opened up and as people from the class before streamed out, Sophia and the others slipped their shoes off and went inside.

Vassa offered the receipt with a fake smile. The woman snatched it out of her hand and stomped out. The buzz of the crowd started to drown out the music from the restaurant next door.

If Alexa could have a glorious end of her semester, why couldn't she?

UNSATISFACTORY ACADEMIC PERFORMANCE / ACADEMIC PROBATION: LAZARUS GILBERT

Based on Academic Policies and Procedures of the College of Business, your academic performance is unsatisfactory. You are being placed on Academic Probation for the spring semester, which may affect your status for commencement.

"Gilbert! Get in here!"

Baseball season was starting in a few weeks. For the last forty-five minutes, the team had been working hard. Lazarus had been practicing eye drills until his arms felt like they were going to fall off. He shuffled to the locker room, wincing he placed his hand on his back and stretched before he turned to his coach. His teammates laughed.

He'd hoped that he could just slide by, but judging from how red his coach's face was and the buttons about to burst off his tight button-up, that would not be the case.

"Yeah, coach?" Gritting his teeth, Lazarus straightened and sweetened things up with a smile.

Coach Maverick frowned and thrust his thumb over his shoulder. "In my office."

"Golden Boy's in trouble!"

Lazarus hung his head as more teammates hooted at him. He threw them the finger. Following him slowly into the office, Coach Maverick sat down and focused on a sheet of paper lying on the desk.

"Close the door and sit down."

Taking off his baseball cap, he sat down in the dingy seat; it creaked under his weight. The office was like a closet, with barely enough room to stretch his legs. Awards and banners from championships won before lined every piece of wall space available.

"You have something you want to tell me?"

Lazarus looked at Coach Maverick. He debated how far he wanted to play this game. By this point, he had gotten good at bullshitting people. Tell a joke or story, a bit of razzle-dazzle. It helped that he had a reputation for partying too hard, switching from girlfriend to hookup to girlfriend, and goofing off. That's who his family currently thought he was: an irresponsible wild child aimlessly drifting.

That was before. Lazarus was working hard to clean up his act, but people didn't forget easily, even if that's what he wanted the most. There were few people in his life who truly knew him, Coach being one. So, he probably wouldn't get very far with this plan, but he tried anyway.

"I think the infielders need to work more on hand-eye coordination. Wallace was all over the place today." Lazarus rubbed his nose before looking to the left at a poster.

Coach narrowed his eyes at him. The two didn't speak before he placed the sheet of paper on the desk in front of him.

"I was thinking more like this."

Lazarus leaned forward. It was the same document with blaring red letters that student services had sent him a few days earlier. He could feel Coach watching his face, and he morphed his expression into confusion.

"Wow, I can't explain this—" A grin slid in and Lazarus quickly corrected it. Confused, he was supposed to appear confused.

"What do you mean, you can't explain this? Do you know what this means for the team, Lazarus?"

"It's just one little class. I'm not failing all my classes."

"It doesn't matter if it's just one little class. It's a class you're failing. Something you told me would be fixed after that warning last semester. What happened?"

Lazarus sighed and relaxed into the chair. A grimace passed over his face as he shifted his legs as best he could. "I tried my hardest, I really did."

"Obviously not."

He rolled his eyes. "It's freaking dead dudes writing whole... poetry dissertations about the sun or dead lovers. How is it helping anyone to learn that?"

"It's a literature class, Lazarus. All you do is read and write a response. You can't even do that?" Coach Maverick rubbed his mustache as he looked at the paper and let out a long breath. "You know I'm going to have to bench you."

"No."

"Yes, you know the requirement that all athletes have to follow. You must pass all your classes in order to play."

If he didn't have baseball, he had nothing else to live for. No matter how much fun he had, he disciplined himself about his baseball. It was his only constant.

"Don't bench me, coach. This is my last season! Please!" Lazarus clasped his hands together as he leaned against the desk, ignoring the feeling of his muscles aching.

Coach Maverick twisted his lips. "You know the rules, Gilbert; I don't make them. Just enforce them."

Lazarus swallowed, clenching and unclenching his fist.

These last few months you've been out of whack." Coach's eyebrows drew together. Out of whack was saying it nicely. The crippling fear of not knowing what was next had hit him at a family dinner. Since his parents retired, taken the pet dog, and gone road-tripping cross the country, they left it up to one of his older brothers still in-state to keep up the Sunday dinners. Harvey, vice president of marketing at a fitness protein bar company and the second oldest, was the one to take up the mantle. During dinner he shot Lazarus a look over pasta and said:

"Are you done playing that game? What are you going to do next?"

Harvey didn't see what Lazarus's deal with baseball was. He told Lazarus most athletes peaked at thirty. That was in seven years. Lazarus had barely anything in his savings.

The fact was, Lazarus was torn about what to do next. He loved baseball. He would always love it, but he wanted something different. He just didn't know what that was, and with Harvey breathing down his neck to take the boring office job at his company, he had to decide fast.

What were his strengths? People. Organizing. He could throw a helluva good party. He even toyed with event management. He'd been in charge of the last three fundraising galas for the baseball team, but when he told Harvey, he shook his head and said, "Be realistic. Do something that our parents would be proud of. Party planning is just nonstop partying. Grow up."

It was hard to think of what else would impress his parents. His mother had been a scientist and his father a judge. Out of the five sons so far, they had a lawyer, doctor, VP, and a mathematician-turned-landscaper. A landscaper wasn't impressive, but his brother *owned the company*. What could he do to equal their success?

Lazarus ran a hand across his face, suddenly even more tired than before, and said, "I've just been catching up with last-minute things I want to do."

He had unadulterated respect and gratitude for Coach Maverick. He'd grown under his guidance from that immature freshman who wanted to do nothing but party to someone who was almost figuring out his life.

Coach smacked his lips as he picked up a pen and tapped it against the desk. "I hope these things were worth it. You failed last semester. You're failing again and if you don't get it right, you won't graduate."

The chair creaked under the coach's weight as he tossed the pen and leaned down to pull out a binder. Coach Maverick pointed.

"Your brother."

Lazarus glanced at the picture. Gideon, the third oldest and the reason he came to this college. He knew that jawline and those distinct bluish-green eyes all the brothers shared too well. He continued to disappoint his family by riding on the minimum passing grades. His parents never said it, but he saw it in their eyes.

"Your brother led this team, and he did it well. Now it's you. Do you really want to let this all go because you want to have fun rather than study? Real life isn't a game, Lazarus. I train my students to be talented players but I always train them to be men of substance in society."

Lazarus shrank into the chair. Disappointing Coach was something he never wanted to do. *I can never distinguish myself*, the voice in the back of his mind said. That same voice had been building in crescendo since his senior year started and he couldn't shake it off.

Instead of showing his worry, Lazarus smiled and said, "Give me a couple of weeks to show improvement. If I'm improving, then I can stay in. If I don't, then sit me on the bench until I do. I have a new tutor now."

"You have a tutor?"

It wouldn't be hard to get a tutor or someone to do his paper for him. He would do anything to stay on the team. They were playing some minor competition for their very first game. He had to play it. This was his final season. He had to leave some sort of legacy behind, like his brother did.

Coach looked at him for a long time. Reaching over into his drawer, he pulled out a sheet of paper and placed it over the academic warning paper. "I shouldn't do this for you, but I am. This is an academic check-in. You need to get it signed by your professors every two weeks and your tutor every session. A missed signature or low grade and then it's—" Coach made a slash motion across his neck. "Over. Got it?"

Lazarus nodded and took the papers.

"Don't let me down, Gilbert. You're an outstanding student and a damn dominant player. Don't self-sabotage when you're this close to the end."

"You got it."

"I mean it." Coach pointed at him. "This could set you up for the pros if you wanted too."

Lazarus stood up and shook Coach's hand. "I won't let you down."

With effort, he pushed himself up and shuffled out of the office. He read and reread the paper so many times that once he was changed and heading out of the locker rooms, he almost went past his best friend, waiting on the wall nearby.

"What took you so long, man? I was about to leave you."

Lazarus quickly shoved the paper into his back pocket. Jayden was balancing himself on his skateboard as he thumbed through a book. His long dreads were tied in a haphazard knot on the top of his head. Compared to Lazarus's old-Hollywood, Paul Newman look, Jayden was tall and slim, his skin a tawny brown contrasted with the hazel of his eyes. Brushing back the dreads that fell into his face, he closed the book and picked up the skateboard, giving Lazarus a dap as he neared.

"Sorry, I had a meeting with Coach."

They walked side by side toward Lazarus's apartment.

"I feel your energy is off. What's happenin', man?"

Lazarus focused his attention on the ground, purposely stepping on the fallen leaves. "My energy?"

"It's coming at me in enormous waves of blue and black."

"It's nothing."

Jayden placed his arm over Lazarus's shoulders and held up two fingers. "There are two types of lying. Prosocial and antisocial." Jay made sure Lazarus was paying attention before continuing.

""Prosocial is for someone else's benefit as opposed to antisocial lies. Strictly for your own gain. When you engage in antisocial lying, you're telling the universe that you don't have respect for life."

"What?" Lazarus laughed, and he wished he hadn't. He held his sore abs as he tried to minimize his laughter.

Jayden nodded. "So, in return, you benefit from the destruction of all living things. Thus making you a devil. Or demon. I don't judge."

Squinting at Jayden, Lazarus shook his head. "Just from not telling you the truth, I am the *literal* devil?"

Jayden blinked slowly, and his eyes kept wandering to the left.

"Are you high?" Lazarus stopped walking and Jayden's arm fell off.

"It's a possibility. I found a brownie under my bed and the world's been glowing ever since."

Lazarus reached into his back pocket and handed him the paper. Jayden read for a moment and then said, "Damn."

"Mmhmm."

"That is not good fortune."

"You think?"

They began walking. As they passed, students waved and said hello or gave him a high-five. He couldn't sulk right now. He switched his demeanor to a smile and waved to his friends, even though most weren't. He'd almost said fuck it, the pressure to keep up appearances was exhausting but he just had to do it for a while longer.

"I told you this was going to happen. I felt it, but you didn't listen to me, man." Jayden handed the paper back.

"Right... the frog dream?" Lazarus raised his eyebrow before rolling his eyes. Jayden had a reoccurring dream that frogs spilled out of Lazarus's bedroom closet and flooded the room until he was submerged.

Jayden tapped his temple. "The knowledge comes from the universe and our ancestors. It's up to you to drink from it."

Lazarus doubted his ancestors were speaking to him. He

had to figure out a plan quickly.

When they arrived at the fading sky-blue Victorian the campus cut up into apartments, the bare lobby gave him relief. He could get some time to himself before the craziness of the semester began.

"So, what are you going to do?"

They stopped in front of the apartment.

Lazarus looked off to the side as he scratched his elbow. "I'm sure I can find somebody to do my paper. Or hire one of those websites online."

Jayden dropped the skateboard to the ground with a thud, shaking his head as he stepped on it. "That's a mistake. They give everyone the same paper. You'll be caught for plagiarism just like that!" He snapped his fingers.

"Can you do it?" Lazarus joked, crossing his arms against his chest. He was half serious.

"My karma is aligned, and I'm not tampering with it for you. Plus, I don't like poetry. If it was a Greek tragedy or maybe about the Byzantine empire, I could help you."

That wasn't helping him, now was it?

A light bulb turned on in his head.

"*Vee.*"

His pretty downstairs neighbor who hated his guts. He knew why, but was it worth her blatant aversion? Every time he caught her in the hall, her face pinched up like she smelled shit. If they both were heading out of their apartments at the same time, she would duck back into hers and wait for him to leave.

"The sista who lives below you? That one?"

Lazarus nodded.

Jayden rubbed the back of the neck without making eye contact. "That one got some fire to her. Truth be told, Laz, you're not ready for the dark side. It's something you gotta ease into…"

He laughed, taking it all in stride. "She's a Lit major, I think."

"I don't know about that. You're better off getting a tutor

from the tutor center."

Lazarus cocked his head and then shook it. "You know why I can't go back." His last tutor relationship had crossed lines. She turned out to be a stalker in a huge social circle.

Long story short, she spun the story in her favor and he was blackballed from the tutoring center.

That's when a car door slammed shut and a voice went, "You have a good day now! Read the book before you watch the movie!"

He knew that voice. Vee's voice was smooth and raspy, like the jazz records he liked. Turning, he saw her with bags in hand and knew it was divine timing. She ran up the steps trying to hold this big coat and barreled right into him, making them both stumble. He caught himself by stepping to the side but couldn't catch her, and as she fell down the stairs, her food flew out onto the concrete.

"My Twizzlers!" she cried.

His body reacted, and he reached to help her up. She squeaked when he held her around the waist. Soft and warm under his hands, she barely made it to the center of his chest, and his eyes traced her gentle curves in all the right places. He was still curious why she was dressed to go on an artic expedition, but then he caught her smell. She smelled like fresh oranges and cranberry. Sweet and homey, like his grandparents' ranch in Tennessee.

Vee pushed her hair out of her face, and polite anger turned into annoyance. Eyes puffy and skin splotchy, she rolled her eyes and shrugged his hands away, almost sending him down the stairs as she said, "Of course, this campus is too big for me to always be running into you."

"What's with all the Twizzlers?"

Scrambling, she tried to get the contents of her grocery bag off the street. "My Twizzlers! You made me squish them!"

Was she going crazy? He bent down to help her. There were Twizzlers, lettuce, and… a diaphragm?

Lazarus picked it up and couldn't help but grin as he showed it to Jayden.

"Didn't Kirstie Alley use this in that talking baby movie and still get pregnant? Having some company tonight, Vee?"

Cutting her eyes to Jayden, Vee gave a tense smile. Lazarus froze. Her eyes were glassy, and she sniffed, wiping them briefly. Why was she sad? "Those aren't for me. They really aren't." Then she snatched it from his hand. Her almond eyes flashed fire behind her glasses.

"That doesn't explain the Twizzlers."

"For my nerves if you have to be so nosy. Would you rather I do drugs?" Lazarus saw her chin tremble before she pinched the bridge of her nose as if exhausted with their brief conversation.

"I told you, let me help your nerves."

"When pigs fly!" Vee sucked her teeth, rolling her eyes. Despite her slack expression, she was still easy to fire up.

That's what he found out freshman year when they lived in the same dorm, the first time he played a prank. Their floors had been going back and forth those first couple of weeks after move-in. He hadn't expected Vee to come out of her room and lecture him and his friends for thirty minutes about disturbing her studying time.

Their paths crossed frequently, but she never gave him the time of day. There were a few times she came to parties with her roommates and he tried to talk to her. They were night and day, but he felt something there. He wanted to figure out what, but it didn't help that she ended up in the crosshairs of his pranks more often than not, which put him on her not-so-great side.

Hands on hips, she sighed as she tapped her foot, waiting for his response. He thought she was beautiful. Those brown eyes, red right now, her round nose, and full pink lips made him want to touch. If he told her; she'd probably hang him.

"Lazarus, I don't have time for your games today. I'm busy."

With effort, he took in a full breath as that freshman crush resurfaced; he took a step back. He didn't like the lost look on her face, and decided to cheer her up the only way he knew how: by teasing.

"You know what they say about all work and no play..."

"What they say?" Jayden joined in the teasing.

"They need a handsome man like myself to unwind. I'm available. What about you?" His eyes twinkled with mischievous glee and Jayden laughed. Lazarus was enjoying the way she sucked in her cheeks and the crease in her forehead as she shifted from being annoyed to pissed off. He'd rather see her annoyed with him than sad.

"Ugh, no. Leave me alone."

Lazarus fake gasped and turned to Jayden, who did the same. "You don't mean that."

"Please, and I say this from the bottom of my heart..." She fluttered her eyes at him. Like an idiot, he stepped closer to her, his eyes tracing her lips. Her words sounded sweet, but her eyes were saying something deadly.

"Get lost and don't come back." Snatching her bag, Vee stomped up the stairs.

"See you soon neighbor!" Lazarus hollered back, and she turned to him. For a second, there was a smile. Blowing out her cheeks, she stopped herself and flipped him off.

He watched her hair whipping and hips swinging enticingly as she disappeared from view. Normally, on a good day, he'd only get the bird from her. This time, *she smiled.* Hope bloomed in his chest. He had a feeling this semester would be different.

He had to focus now. He needed to figure out how to pass his class before he failed and his family found out. He huffed out a humorless laugh; he was screwed but determined.

Jayden shook his head watching where Vee disappeared. "I think you're gonna fail, man."

CHAPTER TWO

PACIFIC GROVE UNIVERSITY WAS A prestigious school, or so they claimed. They were famous for the 1982 student sleep-in where, for forty-two days, all the students lived on the campus green in front of the president's office to protest a tuition hike. That was until the president grew tired of seeing students wash their bare asses on the lawn in front of his office and gave in. There was even a statue in their honor showed off on campus tours. Another perk was that they were minutes from the San Francisco Zoo and Ocean Beach.

Vassa wanted to get home as quickly as possible. There was a heaviness in her chest and limbs after speaking with Sophia. She cursed herself. Why couldn't things have gone differently? It seemed that wouldn't be the case when Dara, her roommate, texted her with a grocery list and a cryptic message that a mystery guest was visiting their apartment.

Considering how her day was going, she should have expected Lazarus Gilbert to be standing in the middle of the stairs. The fall was a welcome distraction from the obsessive thoughts. The entire car ride she had been gulping air, chatting absently to the driver, willing her glassy eyes not to break out in tears.

She should have ignored the way her heart speed up when his arms went around her. Or the way her eyes fluttered as she breathed in his cologne, even on the verge of a breaking down in public. Damn him for smelling so good. A long, long, *long* time ago, she had a crush on him. Hell, *all* the freshmen girls had a crush on him.

Vassa pretended she didn't feel the fire erupt across her skin as he touched her through her clothes. There was no room for new people in her life, especially not Lazarus Gilbert. Even though a tiny voice told her if she gave him the chance, he might be fun.

If she closed her eyes, Vassa could still see his blond hair casting a dark shadow, making his blue eyes look black as he stood above her to help her up. He was always flirting, and she told herself not to respond to it. He flirted with everybody.

Life was just handing her a crap sandwich because the elevators were out of service.

She thought, being a senior, she would have access to one of the modern apartments they recently built. Nope. Buena Vista Apartments is what they called it, but nothing about it was a *good view*. The elevator never worked. The paint was peeling, and the floors creaked everywhere. By the time she made it up the stairs to the fourth floor and to her door, she didn't have time to catch her breath before Dara pushed her back into the hallway.

"Don't be mad." Tucking a strand of hair behind her ear, Dara squeezed her eyes shut. "I know what you're gonna say."

Still in her pajamas from that morning, Dara wore her short black hair in two pixie ponytails sticking up like a mohawk. She looked like a beauty pageant contestant gone wrong because her skin, normally fawn, had bright red spots on her cheeks from a sunburn in Miami during winter break.

Cracking one eye open, Dara gave a small smile and Vassa's eyebrows squished together. "Did you eat my leftover Indian food again?"

A cabinet closed loudly from inside, and someone cursed. Vassa turned to Dara, who was playing with her silver septum piercing. Letting out a shaky breath, Dara confessed, "Kiki's here."

"Kiki? Kiki is in there?" Vassa pointed to their apartment and dropped the bags on the ground.

"I know. I know."

Her patience hadn't fully recovered from the last time Kiki visited. They were still on probation with the residence advisers. Plus, that stain still wouldn't come out of the white living room rug.

"I know what she did last time, but she's turned over a new leaf honestly." Dara bit her lip and looked at her hands.

"Look me in the eye when you're lying to me." Vassa crossed her arms.

Smacking her lips, Dara met her eyes. "Okay, I wasn't buying it when I was saying it, but she is my cousin. The community college isn't starting until next week and there's only so much to do in Sacramento. She's off probation now and can travel now so... yay?"

"She still hasn't replaced our rug."

"Vassa, it will be fine. I already told her we were ordering pizza and having a quiet night in. She'll pay for the rug when she gets a job."

Vassa picked up the grocery bag. "What was the purpose of me buying this food then?"

"It was a ruse to get you off the scent. We still need the diaphragm." Dara snatched the bags up.

"Fine, but I hope you let Kiki know no more picking up random people in the Tenderloin and bringing them back to this apartment. We're trying to stay under the radar of student housing."

Dara grinned, but paused before stepping into the apartment. "Were you crying?"

Vassa tugged at her hair for comfort. "I'm fine."

Dara spared her one last look before turning into the apartment. It was a basic three-bedroom apartment. Their last roommate moved out the semester before. The living room was a mix of them both. A nice cozy rug, paintings, books, and a small Buddha statue in the corner. Dara gave Vassa one last look to be nice before they entered the kitchen.

"Kiki, Vassa is—"

"Vassie girl! Look at you!"

Vassa almost fell as Kiki launched herself at her, dropping the cereal box on the counter.

"Kiki, you're here..." Vassa patted her back slowly and sent a look to Dara.

Kiara Chén was a force to be reckoned with, and best after a few stiff drinks. In her leather-on-leather ensemble paired with her thigh-high boots, she looked more ready for a club than a movie night in.

"I was bored and was like, fuck it, why not come see my cousin and her bestie." Kiki continued to squeeze and rock Vassa side to side.Peeling Kiki off her, Vassa nodded. "Sure."

"Do you like my hair? Say you like my hair. Dara said I look like a porn star." It was drug-store-platinum blond . "You do." Dara swept the cereal back into the box.

"No, I wouldn't. You're just like my mom—"

"I'm going to go change." Vassa turned as Kiki argued with Dara. Boxes still cluttered her room from her hasty departure last semester. She reached into her backpack, pulling out her bucket list. She smoothed it on her thigh and sat on the bed.

Do something completely unexpected.

The door to her bedroom burst open.

"Vassie, you're the only sane one. Tell her that leather doesn't equal slutty either."

Vassa tried to hide the paper under her thigh.

"What's that?" Kiki held the cereal box in one arm and pointed with the other.

"What? Nothing." Vassa crossed her legs.

Dara and Kiki looked at each other.

"You sure?" Kiki said.

"Positive."

The cousins gave each other a silent look before they nodded. The girls lunged at her, knowing her weakness: tickling. Dara tickled her everywhere as Kiki went for the paper. Vassa clutched her hand around the paper as much as she could until Dara tickled her armpits and Vassa yelped, using her hands to protect herself.

"It's just an all-you-can-eat flyer!" Vassa gasped once Dara released her, falling face first into her comforter.

"Well, well, what is this?" Kiki unfolded the paper. "Vassa's Extraordinary Senior Send-Off?"

Dara snatched the paper from her cousin. "Enjoy a drunken night out?" Vassa pushed herself up and tried to snatch the paper.

"That's my private property!"

Kiki took the paper back from Dara. "See all the tourist spots, epic spring break, but wait!" She let out a bark of laughter and shook her head. Kiki let Dara snatch the paper back. "Go on a date? You trying to get some regular loving, Vassie?"

Vassa grabbed the paper from Dara, folding it and placing it in her bra.

"Getting wild, I like it." Kiki stuck her tongue out and flicked it before lying back on the bed.

Vassa ignored her. "It's just an idea."

"Looks like a bucket list. Wasn't that a movie about old dudes with cancer?" Dara pushed Kiki over.

She was expecting some comments. It's what she and Alexa had started, but never got around to. Vassa thought about Alexa and Sophia and those girls going out and doing things. What was she doing besides working and eating burritos?

"It's not just for people with illnesses. You can have a bucket list at any point in your life," Vassa said.

"Sounds like a quarter-life crisis." Kiki picked imaginary dirt out of her nails.

Music started once again. She let out a huff of breath and went for the broom and hit the ceiling a few times.

"I'm not going through a crisis." Vassa set the broom down. It wasn't a crisis.

"You're not?" Dara leaned forward and cocked her head.

"I'm not."

Dara blinked several times before narrowing her eyes. "Then why do you have a bucket list?"

"Why are you in my business? Why don't you go finish your Korean drama?" Vassa got up and placed the list on her desk and sat in the chair.

"I'm your best friend. You need me judging your life decisions. Otherwise, you'll be a mess out here more than you already are."

"Isn't that the pot calling the kettle black?" Vassa snapped her fingers as if that would recall the memory. "Wasn't it just last night you woke me up in the middle of the night crying about your graphic design senior thesis? Telling me it was equivalent to 2007 Kim Kardashian?"

Dara pinched her, and Vassa yelped. "2007 Brittany."

The semester hadn't started, and Dara had finished her senior thesis three times. Vassa still could not even think of how to start hers, *and* she still needed to submit her grad school applications. Luckily for her, English masters programs had a later application deadline.

"Either way, you were a mess," Vassa said.

The music upstairs grew louder, and she got the broom and banged on the ceiling. The music immediately lowered. Dara let out a groan and threw herself back on the bed.

Vassa said, "Let's focus on your problems."

"No, let's focus on you instead." Dara closed her eyes.

"You do this every time you have an important project, Dee. Everything you create comes out perfect."

"You really do." Kiki scrolled on her phone.

"I know, but it's not coming out right! Did you know I completed my project three times over break? *Three.* It's not right."

"Did you finally tell Auntie Linh that you're not a business major yet?" Kiki grinned evilly at Dara.

Vassa's mouth dropped. "I thought you told your parents your major already."

"I was going to. Then I got sunburned, and it was a pleasant distraction."

Vassa didn't know how Dara had lied to her parents about her major. They were obviously not very supportive of the arts.

"What are you going to do? Just never show them the degree? Or just say surprise on graduation?" Vassa said.

The music upstairs grew louder. Again.

"You're too hard on yourself, Dara, you always create something great and you probably did it again." The bed dipped as Vassa sat on the other side of Dara. Grabbing her hand, Dara leaned against her. Dee was one of the most talented artists she knew. Vassa wished she could stand up to her parents and let them know she didn't want to go back to Sacramento to run their dry cleaner's, but she understood. Dara was a first-generation American, and her parents wanted her to be financially secure. Creative careers didn't offer that.

Dara still pouted, and Vassa patted her on the back. "They will be happy to know we're moving to New York. You'll have someone to watch you."

"Watch me?" Sitting up, Dara raised an eyebrow. "How about watch you? You're the one watching *Sex and the City* twenty-four hours a day."

It had been their plan since they met sophomore year of college. New York was the best place for a creative. Art, writing, music, they both could thrive and begin their careers. It was probably unrealistic considering the cost of living, but it was happening soon!

"Can I come?" Kiki laid her phone on her belly.

"No," Dara and Vassa said together, and Kiki rolled her eyes.

The beat grew dangerously loud, now with the bass, and the room vibrated. She took the broom and nearly sent it through the ceiling as she banged it.

"He's not honoring the neighborly agreement. I should report to him to the resident advisor." Vassa glared at the ceiling like Lazarus could see her.

Dara shook her head. "Let's go back to you getting desperate making bucket lists."

"Who said I'm desperate because I made a bucket list?" Vassa pinched her face. Desperate was harsh. She was just ready for something different to happen.

"Considering last semester, I think it's a good idea. We could help you with the list," Dara said.

Vassa shook her head. "No. I don't need anyone to help me. I'm probably not gonna do it honestly."

Dara sat and shifted to face her. "Vassa, people are not the plague... Well, most people aren't the plague. What's wrong with putting yourself out there and just seeing what happens? It doesn't have to be permanent."

This conversation again.

"I know last semester with you and Alexa... Well, we can agree she sucks as a person. I say if the list is going to make you happy, then do it."

Dara meant well, but Vassa had completely healed and gotten past that entire event.

The music upstairs changed to rap. Kiki danced to the beat.

"Vassa—" Dara put a hand on her arm and forced Vassa to look at her. Dara gave her a comforting smile.

"Letting someone close to you won't always result in a bad ending. Alexa changed on both of us, but you still have me and Kiki. If you let the right someone in, you'll get that thing you've been secretly hoping for all along."

Vassa smiled. "Thanks, but I'm fine. I'm totally okay."

Dara dropped the subject. "Now let's pick a movie and order some pizza." Dara slapped Vassa on the thigh and then the phone out of Kiki's hand.

Kiki gasped. "I know you're not serious. We're going out to drink."

"You're getting apple juice."

Kiki lunged toward Dara, who screamed and ran out of the room. The music turned up even louder; she felt like the speaker was in her own room. She let out a curse under her breath. Shoving her feet into her bunny slippers, she went to her window, lifted the blinds, and opened it wide.

It would be nice to go a week without doing this.

Swinging her foot out, she stepped onto the fire escape and climbed up into the lion's den.

CHAPTER THREE

THE WARMTH OF LAZARUS'S ROOM was welcomed after the temperature drop outside. She didn't have enough fingers to count the times she scaled the fire escape to deal with him and his music. Her ears were getting gnawed off by the sound of a mumble rapper with no bars. The cause of the problem was nowhere to be found.

The room was a carbon copy of hers, with various articles of clothing strewn about. Next to his closet was his miniature garden. She knew it probably violated some sort of code. Plants hung from the ceilings and sat on the floor, some small and others large. The first time she had gone up here, she thought he was growing weed. She still didn't know for sure.

Aha! Right there by the bedroom door. His speaker. Marching over, she turned it off and let out a breath.

Blessed silence.

She turned to leave, but passing his desk, she noticed a paper with red writing. It was from the student center. Academic probation.

Apparently, things weren't going well for him. Served him right.

As she made to move on, something else caught her eye. *Is that our missing door gnome?*

Vassa picked it up. It was a gnome dressed like John Travolta from *Saturday Night Fever*. She knew he stole it! Vassa didn't care that the resident advisor said not to bother her unless it was a genuine emergency. He was getting reported. This was theft. Minus the fact that she was currently trespassing.

"Isn't this a lovely surprise? What's up, Vee?"

Vassa jumped and turned. He was standing too close to her; she slammed her face into his shoulder. Groaning, she pressed a hand to her nose, hoping it wasn't bleeding, while grappling for gnome Travolta. She started to lose her balance and Lazarus grabbed hold of her arm and pulled her close to keep from falling. Her face squashed against his bare chest, she realized he wasn't wearing anything but a towel.

No… God, no. God, please no…

Swallowing down the knot in her throat, her entire body hummed with energy. Her heart knocked against her ribs and she was paralyzed with the knowledge of his near-nakedness. Peeling back again, she told her mouth not to water at the sight of his muscular flesh rippling. Who knew he was hiding that under his baseball uniform? But she would never tell him that. She tried not to think how good his hot skin felt against her body. Lazarus continued to hold her while, dazed, Vassa noticed his smell. It was her favorite scent, Irish Spring soap.

She took a step back, but he gripped her tighter. *Hormones, it's just my hormones.* She shook her head, trying to get the tendrils of lust outta her brain. His body was damp, wetting her clothing and her eyes focused on the golden skin in front of her with brown freckles across his chest. Did he take his shirt off in practice? He must have. Vassa was suddenly very hot. She pulled away again as his arms tightened.

Lazarus smiled sheepishly. "The towel dropped…"

"So, you're naked against me… and gnome Travolta?" Vassa's mouth opened and closed.

"Sorry, it fell when I caught you. At least I did this time, right?"

Vassa realized something else was pressing against her lower stomach. He wasn't wearing clothes, so that could only mean one thing. Her eyes got big as she stared up at him. Lazarus grimaced, and a blush formed across his face.

"Pick up your damn towel! What are you, some creep rubbing your junk on women? You get off like that?" Vassa yelled before she stepped back and covered her eyes. Plucking her sweater from her skin, she ignored the tingly sensation in her belly.

Vee heard Lazarus hurriedly pick up the towel and wrap it around himself. "I wasn't expecting company. Sorry, Vee."

"All the bits are covered?" She wasn't turning around until she was sure her heart wasn't going to burst out of her chest.

"Yes."

Vassa turned back around. He gave Vassa a smile that showed off his too-white teeth, which she didn't return. He looked down at her and she felt hyperaware of the tension in the room. Her palms got sweaty, her mouth dry.

"You might want to close your eyes again." Lazarus walked toward his closet and his muscles flexed as he paused for a moment to water his plants.

Vassa closed her eyes as she heard hangers clang against the metal closet bar. How did he recover so quickly? She felt the towel land on top of her face and screeched while he laughed. She tossed it to the floor.

"You can look if you dare. I'm sure you want to, so what am I saying?"

Opening her eyes, she bit her lip, clenching her hands to keep herself from running them over his sculpted chest and abs. Jeans with the fly open as he balanced himself on one leg putting on a sock. *Don't fall for the flirting...* She used to believe his teasing and flirting was genuine. She had been honored she caught the attention of the most popular guy on campus. Instead, she found out he delivered it to anyone willing to listen. So now when he complimented her, it was like a slick car salesman trying to sell her a lemon. Her dumb brain still thought it was cute how his tongue peeked out the corner of his mouth as he focused on balancing.

"I knew you stole our gnome." Vassa shook it in the air, ignoring the comment.

"That? Happened a while ago, Vee. I had a hoarder on Craigslist that was gonna pay me a pretty penny for it." Lazarus winked.

She closed her eyes and counted down from five. "Don't call me that."

Vassa remembered what she was doing up here in the first place. She pointed to the speaker. "Didn't I tell you about your music before? You're not the only one that lives here."

"Pipe down, Vee, or are you going to tell on me again?"

Maybe I will.

Vassa thrust her chin up. "You'll probably just flirt your way out of it again, so what's the point?"

He didn't seem too concerned with the anger radiating off of her, and that always pissed her off. "You know you should be nice to your neighbors. Show some respect and maybe they'll be more willing to respond to your demands."

It'll be a wintry day in hell when that happens. He stole their gnome! "You're not worthy of respect when you go around stealing innocent gnomes."

"You prefer the nickname, vicious?" He playfully snapped his teeth at her and made claws with his hands.

She didn't know whether to laugh or smack him. She settled for turning on her heels, heading back to the window.

"Keep the music down." Who knew what horrors gnome Travolta had seen? She was gonna scrub him. There was nothing she could do. She knew the politics of this university. If you weren't a student athlete, you were basically a second-class citizen.

"C'mon Vee, don't be like that." His hand circled her wrist. She hadn't heard him move.

Vassa glanced at the place he held. Her mind stumbled. Heat radiated from his hand, which circled her wrist easily. He slowly traced his thumb back and forth. She jerked away. *Damn this guy!*

"I've noticed this chasm growing between us these last few years. It really hurts the heart." Taking a step back, he picked up a T-shirt.

"Can you be serious just for once? If that's at all possible. Please buckle your jeans it's distracting."

Lazarus looked like he was considering it before he shook his head. "Don't be ashamed to admit you like what you see. You make it too easy."

Vassa continued toward the window, but he stopped her, and she stomped her foot. "I need to do my homework, Lazarus."

"You didn't come to that party before winter break. I had hoped you would."

Sorry, but my longest friendship ever was imploding.

They did this every single time. He invited her to a party or something of the like. She turned him down and then he asked her where she'd been. He wasn't sincere. Why would she trouble herself going to a party with mainly jocks and the rest of the campus upper crust?

"I'm sorry. I don't normally rub elbows with the trust funds like you do. I came to get a degree," Vassa stated.

Lazarus rolled his eyes at her. "They are really cool when you get to know them."

"When my parents become oil tycoons or I'm on a sports team bringing in money for the school, I will. Now excuse me, it's movie night."

"Why did you look like you were crying earlier?"

"Huh?" How did he notice that? The concern on his face looked genuine. That was different. Her mouth open and she almost blurted it out as his eyebrows dipped as he waited. She drew in air and shook her head to stop herself.

"I'm fine, it's nothing."

His eyes roamed her face in the silence. She had to look away because his eyes revealed he wasn't buying that. He stepped in closer once again, making her heart beat faster.

"You can trust me."

Her lips twisted. "I don't trust anyone anymore."

Lazarus frowned before he cleared his throat.

"There's a party tonight. Daly City, why don't you come?"

She mulled it over. There was reading to be done to prepare for the first day of class on Monday. She blew her cheeks out as he wiggled a paper invite at her.

Your list... this is a chance. She rocked on her heels before taking the paper from his hand and turned back toward the window. She climbed out onto the fire escape.

"Keep the music down."

His laughter followed as she climbed back into her room and slammed the window shut.

CHAPTER FOUR

"I LOVE THE SOUND OF loud music and the smell of vomit." Kiki inhaled as she stepped out of the car. It was easy to convince Kiki and Dara to go to the party instead of watching horror films all evening. It was slightly offensive they made her change multiple times until she wore an outfit they deemed sexy, and not "as if you rolled outta bed look."

"Gross." Dara scowled as she slammed the car door shut and waited for Vassa.

Vassa peered out the backseat window with dread and excitement. They were in Daly City. Close to San Francisco, but Vassa didn't find herself in this area often. The house was a dusty pink with a huge oak door and dead grass. Cars spilled out of the tiny driveway into the street. As she watched, someone stepped out of the front door, walked a few steps and collapsed face first. She winced as people around him laughed.

"Let's go. We didn't put all this work in for you to sit in the car all night." Pulling open the door, Dara raised an eyebrow and jabbed a thumb over her shoulder. "Get out."

"You're mean," Vassa mumbled as she stepped out of the car.

Fight or flight instincts were kicking in. She desired this, but she was absolutely petrified.

"Are you ready to take a step onto the wild side?" Dara hooked arms with Vassa, pulling her forward as Kiki ran ahead.

Vassa raised an eyebrow. "I take that as an insult." Thank

God she brought Twizzlers.

"The truth hurts."

She could feel the vibration of the music as they approached the house.

"I should really go home..." Vassa trailed off and turned to the car. Dara narrowed her eyes.

"You're not getting out of this, and you're not sitting in the corner like usual. C'mon Vassa, you said you want experiences."

Vassa had no business being here. The place was crawling with frat guys, athletes, popular chicks, and trust fund babies. What if Alexa was here? Negative what-if scenarios flashed through her mind. Her mouth went dry and her stomach rolled.

"Vassa, she's not here." Dara squeezed her arm.

Vassa focused on the still-unconscious individual on the front lawn.

"The situation's over," Dara continued. "She'd be stupid to try something here and most of these people are drunk and don't know who you are, anyway. Relax. If her minions are here, you know I have your back, and if we gotta fight, I'll beat a bitch ass for you."

Dara never fought in her life, but the tension in Vassa's chest lessened as she laughed. "That means a lot."

"Sisters forever."

"Are ya'll done with your little huddle or are we going to do it?" Kiki stepped outside the house and tossed her hands up.

Inside the house on the opposite wall of the entryway sat a gray couch where a group of people were squeezed together. They had pushed the coffee table in front of the fireplace. Vassa couldn't focus as she shoved through bodies. The air was tight and hot with the skunky odor of weed. She felt something crunch under her shoes and looked to see popcorn and chip fragments ground into the hardwood floor. Kiki swayed left and right to the music. Dara took off her jacket as Vassa pulled hers closer.

"If you see me mixing dark and light liquor, mind your business." Kiki pointed threateningly at them and lingered on Dara.

"Don't black out again because I will leave you here and call Aunt Nina." Dara pointed a finger in Kiki's face. Kiki slapped it away before poking out her tongue, bounding away into the crowd.

Vassa counted no less than forty people in the small space: talking, drinking, and dancing.

"I don't know. Seems like too many people in here. A fire hazard, somebody could get trampled if one breaks out. Maybe we should just go? I can try again another day—" Vassa turned to the front door.

Dara pinched Vassa, and she squeaked. "Would you stop that?"

"We haven't even been in here for five minutes. You need to loosen up, get a drink or dance with some hot guy." Dara's arm swept from corner to corner of the living room.

Vassa dug into her purse for a Twizzler. "I can barely see in front of me!"

A guy with a low-cut fade and broad shoulders approached them. "Hey, what's up?"

"Hi!" Smiling, Dara twisted her hair with a finger before walking away with him. She turned to Vassa and mouthed, *Have fun!*

Standing alone at parties was one of the worst things ever. You never looked cool standing alone. You were an obvious social reject. She couldn't even make small talk with the Migos rapping. Should she just pretend to dance along to the music? In her mind, she was a wonderful dancer, but that didn't always translate into real life. Should she force herself into the dancing crowd and maybe just pretend to have been there all the time?

Vassa slowly sidled up to a small group that had taken over the corner. They jumped up and down and she tried to do a little fist bump, one-two shuffle or something, but as she did, they dispersed. Dammit.

She tried the guy who seemed to dance to a beat in his own head, but his fist was flying so violently, she was afraid he would knock her out. Stepping back, she bumped into someone.

"I'm so sorry!"

Vassa's heart dropped into her platform boots.

The woman she bumped into was no other than Alexa.

Dara, where are you when I need you?!

Alexa's skin was a beautiful deep caramel color. Always fashionable, she looked effortless with her wavy black hair thick and luscious and mini-dress and heels. Instinct told Vassa to hug her, but she stopped herself. She was dealing with her ex-best friend. The person who, instead of rationally communicating like a normal adult, blasted her online to the entire campus because she assumed Vassa revealed her secret. It was Alexa that divided their dorm suite and forced her to leave her friends, with Dara accompanying her in solidarity. Shock crossed Alexa's features before she squinted and gave a hard smile.

"Vassa... You're here?"

Vassa had imagined this exact scenario more times than she could count in the past two months. They split with *so many* things left unsaid. She pictured snatching Alexa by her hair and dog walking her outside. Demanding she tell Vassa why. *Why did you throw our relationship out so easily over a lie?* Or Alexa groveling for her forgiveness and Vassa rejecting her just as Alexa did her. Or... Alexa and Vassa talking, possibly repairing their relationship so they could be friends once more.

That last scenario wouldn't happen. Seeing her here, just *casually* hanging out while she was so affected, Vassa was caught off guard. But she put on her big girl panties. She wouldn't let Alexa see her sweat.

"Alexa."

The music thumped as the heat of gyrating bodies and weed closed in, making Vassa feel dizzy. Her stomach churned as Alexa looked away, searching for somebody before her eyes fell back on Vassa. She nodded and her lips thinned. "So?"

So?

Every second that passed, Vassa felt suffocated. "Wasn't expecting to see you either… I guess."

They stood there, both staring at the ground, chests heaving.

"How did you get invited?"

Vassa wasn't stupid. She picked up instantly on the underlying judgement in Alexa's tone. "If you want to fit in, shed that good-girl persona." "Vassa, grow up, this is college." She had heard those words from Alexa many times before they went to out any party.

"Lazarus invited me."

"What?" Alexa asked sharply, her eyes narrowing.

Vassa knew it was petty, but it felt good to see Alexa's façade crumble. They both knew Alexa had had a crush on Lazarus since freshman year. Alexa's goal was to get him to become her boyfriend, but it never worked. Vassa did not encourage Lazarus's interest in her, out of respect for her friend, but it never stopped him from pestering and teasing her instead of Alexa. How was that her fault?

Instead of replying, Vassa shrugged and focused on the crushed napkin under her foot.

"Wow…" Alexa let out a humorless laugh. Crossing her arms over her chest, she planted her foot, cocking her hip. "I shouldn't be surprised. You're still a backstabber. First, you almost ruin me and you're still going after the guy I like? Theresa was right about you all along."

Vassa's nostrils flared. "Theresa is a liar."

At one point, they were all friends in the dorm suite. Theresa was that cool girl from New York. Alexa wanted to shed her nerdy girl persona form high school, so she clung to Theresa. There was something off about her in Vassa's gut, though. She knew Theresa thrived off of Alexa's will to do anything she wanted. Alexa mimicked the way Theresa talked, walked, and Vassa bet she even ate the same food as her. Vassa knew it was Theresa that lied and told Alexa that Vassa exposed her.

"Yeah, okay, whatever." Alexa waved her hand as if Vassa were a fly bothering her.

Vassa shook her head, "Why can't you see Theresa is bad news?"

"Why does it matter to you? We're not friends."

Alexa's iciness froze her. "Was it worth it? That's all I want to know. At least tell me why you chose her."

Vassa felt like she was about to have a heart attack the way her heart crashed against her chest, her breath increasing and she blinked several times to keep those tears of anger away, but Alexa wasn't moved.

"Yes."

Flashbacks of the good times they had flooded her mind. Riding bikes home after school to watch cartoons. Every Halloween they made their own costumes that were more rags than anything else. Sleepovers where they stayed up talking until the sun came up. Shopping at the mall, trips to the beach, eating with each other's families. Vassa was the quiet, unpopular, only child sitting alone at lunch. It was Alexa, the new kid, that just started talking to her as if they knew each other forever. Alexa was always everything Vassa wanted to be, the sister she never had. Vassa snapped back to reality. The awkward-braces-and-too-much-mascara Alexa was dead. In her place was a stranger.

They stared at one another with resentment, anger, and sorrow.

"Yes, it was worth it." Alexa screwed up her face and brushed past her.

Vassa's head buzzed, and she turned to see Alexa disappear. Inhaling and exhaling, she pushed through the crowd to find a safe place just to think. The kitchen was a safe spot. She could still give herself credit for being at a party. Pushing through the crowd, she marched to the kitchen.

There were a few people posted by the back door, revealing more guests in the backyard. On the kitchen counter were bowls of popcorn and pretzels. Absentmindedly, she grabbed a handful. She briefly thought about all the germs that could have been on it, but hunger led her to ignore that fact.

Her body vibrated with energy and her heart continued to race as she closed her eyes. Counting back from three, she tried to calm herself.

The song changed and Vassa looked into the living room. No sign of Alexa. She spotted a group of guys bump into a couple on the wall, fists pumping, causing the girl to spill her cup. . The girl started going off on the guys; they laughed and continued dancing, causing her to stomp off.

Tossing back the pretzel, she coughed and her hands flew to her throat. The rest of the pretzels fell and broke on the floor. The pretzel had gone halfway down her throat and stopped. Small, ragged gasps escaped her mouth as she felt the sharp end of the pretzel dig in.

In her anger she didn't chew her food completely. Now she would die by pretzel and Alexa would get the last laugh. She tried to cough again to drive it down. She hauled back and walloped herself in the chest, hard enough to leave a bruise.

The pressure of the pretzel and fear caused her to panic and all thoughts of the confrontation left her mind. She bent over, placing her hands on her knees. Either no one cared or it wasn't obvious enough that she was in the kitchen, dying.

"Hold on, I got you," a voice said from over her shoulder. Before she could turn around, arms circled her stomach, bringing her into contact with the hard chest of a man. Her behind went straight into his groin and she jumped, trying to pull away from him as he gave her the Heimlich.

He began sharp inward and upward thrusts to her stomach. Fear and panic clouded her logic as she fought to move about. He got a firm grip on her and the force of his fist lifted her off her toes. Spit and pretzel pieces flew.

A small drunk audience had gathered and looked on with intrigue. Her skirt was riding up, and she was gonna moon somebody while choking. Another person pulled out their camera. Tears welled in her eyes. Finally, the pretzel flew out onto the floor. The man behind her released her, and she sucked in a deep breath of air.

Pressing her hands to her knees, she wiped the drool from her mouth. She saw feet move in front of her and a beer bottle was thrust in her face. She downed it and balked at the taste, but it helped the sting go away.

"Thank you, death by pretzel would have been tragic."

"I didn't know you were going to come, Vee. Definitely didn't expect to find you choking in here."

Vassa jerked back as her eyes landed on Lazarus. *Of course he appears right now.* Vassa glanced over her shoulder for Alexa. He leaned onto the counter with his arms folded against his chest.

"I didn't think you would come. Is the world ending?" He looked out of the back window to the sky.

She let out a humorless laugh and rubbed her chest, trying to get rid of the pain. "Ha ha, funny."

Looking at the bowl of snacks nearby, she pushed it away from her. It would be a while before she could eat pretzels again. She closed her eyes and leaned back on the counter to ignore him. Alexa had ruined her mood and now she wanted to leave.

She could feel that piercing glare on the side of her face. She peeked one eye over at him.

Lazarus's gaze lingered at the point where the fleshy areas of her thighs were exposed and she cleared her throat loudly. His expression turned sheepish and he smiled as she pulled her skirt down. No doubt he felt her up during their exchange. First, he was naked against her. Now they had basically done porn in public. His eyes flew up to hers, looking not at all ashamed at being caught.

"How are you liking the party?"

She cocked her head at him. "You mean besides almost dying?"

"Yeah, other than that."

She was feeling petty and embarrassed. "It's lame and I want to go home."

Lazarus let out a laugh. "You don't mean that."

Vassa pressed herself into the counter as he approached. She stood stunned as his hand rose and cupped the back of her neck.

She held her breath as his other hand rose. Their noses were nearly touching. Her skin was flushed and her eyes fell to his lips. Her hands were flat on his chest as she watched him softly pluck something from her hair.

Her eyes crossed when he revealed a half-eaten piece of pretzel.

"You had something in your hair."

Her flush spread from her face down to her neck. Mouth opening and closing, Vassa quickly moved to the side, tucking a strand of hair behind her ear.

"You couldn't just say that?" Her voice was rough, and she cleared her throat. She grabbed her beer bottle and pressed it to her cheek.

He didn't respond and took a sip out of his red cup. Her eyes lingered on the way his Adam's apple bobbled and she averted her gaze. "Something happen?"

His words were gentle compared to the loud noise. *He is too perceptive.*

"Nothing." She cleared her throat and looked at the ground. What if Alexa walked in right now? What would she do?

"You sure?"

"I said I'm fine." The words come out harsher than she intended and she winced. She shouldn't be mean to him because of how she was feeling. "I'm sorry, it's just... I'm ready to go."

Lazarus was silent as he watched her. His fingers tapped against his cup. "C'mon Vee, you gotta let loose and enjoy life. I know what can help you feel better." Setting the cup down, he tossed his arm over her shoulder and led her to the backyard.

"Where are we going?" she grumbled, but he paid no heed to her, nodding at the people posted up by the door.

Tiki torches were posted all around, adding some ambiance to the scene. There was a plastic fold-out table by the entryway where people were playing beer pong. A beer keg was off toward the east side of the yard where Dara cheered for the poor soul trying to do a keg stand. There was a mini dance circle in the middle of the lawn. The dancers parted like the Red Sea and out came Kiki.

Kiki bounded over. "Vassa, oh my God girl, this party is outstanding!" Swaying back and forth, she grabbed Vassa's hands, trying to get her to dance too.

"I'm glad you're having a good time." Vassa moved stiffly, focused instead on her heart returning to normal after the kitchen incident. She scanned the backyard. Alexa was on the other end with a group of people laughing.

Kiki gawked at Lazarus. Pressing a hand against her chest, a slow smile played on her face. "Vassa, is this the handsome fella?"

Vassa was fixated on the ground and blinked. "Who?"

"Your boo!"

Lazarus's eyebrows shot up as his mouth parted in surprise. "Boo? I'm your boo Vee? Aww."

Kiki shot her a smug look and reached a hand out toward him like a damsel. Like a gentleman, he shook it. "She neglected to tell me about a beautiful woman like yourself. I haven't seen you on campus before." Did his voice get deeper? Was this supposed to make her feel better?

"I'm Kiara, but my friends call me Kiki. You can call me Kitty." *Did her voice get deeper?*

"All right, Kitty, let's go." Vassa broke up whatever was going on, ignoring her irritation building. She tried to force Kiki toward the door. She wasn't staying here a moment longer with Alexa in the vicinity. She knew she shouldn't have come.

Lazarus looked impressed and slightly alarmed by Kiki, but rolled with it. "Lazarus. No nicknames, I'm afraid."

Kiki gasped for air and clutched her chest like someone stole her pearls. "Vassa, why have you been hiding your side piece from me? We could have some fun with him."

Vassa squinted at Kiki.

"Side piece?" Lazarus gave Vassa an expression that screamed trouble. He would never let her live this down.

Kiki eyed him like he was the last piece of bacon on the tray.

Stepping forward, Vassa forced Kiki to move back from him. *Wait, what am I doing?*

"I thought you were dancing? Better yet, we're leaving." Anything to get Kiki away from him.

"Leaving? I thought maybe you could add 'dance the night away' to your bucket list." Vassa choked on air as she eyeballed Lazarus. "No, no, let's not. I don't want to add that."

"Bucket list?" he questioned, and Kiki smirked.

This had to be the third worst night of her life.

"You're hiding things from me, Vee?"

Kiki looked positively evil as her eyes darted between them. "*Vee?*"

"Honestly, it's nothing interesting, nothing at all." Why was she worried about what Lazarus would think? *Kiki, what happened to the girl code?*

"Yeah, didn't she tell you? She has a bucket list for her last semester. A bunch of crazy stuff. I think we can knock out at this party, amongst things..." Kiki reached into her back pocket. "I have it right here."

Vassa felt as if the entire floor dropped from under her. Her list she placed into her drawer earlier. She couldn't move as Kiki unfolded it.

"You wanna look?" Kiki handed the paper to Lazarus. Vassa lunged for the paper but Lazarus snatched it, raising it above her head so she couldn't reach it.

"That's private property!"

"You have something naughty about me?" Lazarus's arm flexed as he kept her from clawing at the paper.

Vassa was gonna skin Kiki, then him. Looking back toward Alexa, Vassa saw she hadn't noticed the scene unfurling. Lazarus's eyes ran across the list and she ducked under his arm, going for his armpits. He laughed and bent over as she snatched the paper out of his hands, placing it into her jacket pocket. He, of all people, did not need to know her business.

Kiki grinned and grabbed Vassa by the wrist as she growled in frustration. "The music sucks, but they're playing the hits. Let's go dance." She shot a look at Lazarus. "Sorry, but it's the truth."

Lazarus held his armpits and frowned at Vassa. "Jayden sucks with the music."

Vassa's embarrassment and feelings of violation were washed away in the crippling fear consuming her. Kiki led her to the opening of the circle. Overwhelmed, Vassa stopped, but Kiki dragged her in. The world moved in slow motion.

"Kiki! I said no. Let's go!"

They were in the middle of the circle. Like a deer in front of a pack of wolves, she stood there racking her brain for an escape plan as everyone watched with curiosity before cheering.

"Just move to the music!" Kiki yelled.

Vassa pulled back again, shaking her head. She walked to the wall of drunk idiots gawping at her. "Move, please let me out!"

They continued to cheer, "Dance! Dance for us, baby!"

Vassa ran to the other side. "Excuse me, excuse me!"

This was not the attention she needed. Not with Alexa here. The crowd cheered louder as Kiki put her hands on her knees, twerking. Or attempting to, because Vassa wasn't sure what was going on there, she was using her back more than her behind. Kiki pointed to Vassa.

"Go!"

All eyes were on her. This wasn't how things were supposed to go tonight. She tried one last time to escape, but it was no use.

She would not cry. That would be the last thing she did, but the crowd continued to chant and chant as she turned and made eye contact with every one of them. When they saw she wouldn't dance, the chants and cheers turned to boos.

"No fun, you suck!" someone shouted.

Vassa froze.

"Frankly, it sucked being your friend. I was just being nice to you so as not to hurt your feelings."

The words began to play over and over.

Just over the crowd, she saw Lazarus with an indecipherable expression. Huh, she thought he would enjoy her public humiliation. Maybe he was just covering it this time, so she couldn't see. Kiki was now nowhere to be seen, and now this was drawing the rest of the people in the yard over. The booing didn't cease, and everyone blurred together. She thought she heard Dara call her name. When she looked back at Lazarus, he was gone. Alexa was probably having a field day.

Closing her eyes, she counted to five. She was just going to run for it. The music changed from rap to… samba? That caused everyone to look at one another. The crowd opened and Lazarus walked in, his eyes on her. He extended his hand.

Vassa shook her head. "Lazarus, what—"

Vassa shouted as he spun her. She stumbled, catching herself before he tugged her close. Her face was squashed into his chest. She pulled back and opened her mouth to speak, but he was twirling her out again and her hair was smacking into her face.

The mob's boos turned into cheers and people clapped along to the beat. Vassa was hauled back into his arms. He moved swiftly as she clomped like a giant. His hands went down to her hips, and he twisted her back and forth in a way she hadn't moved before.

He spun her around again and pushed in closer, guiding her left, then right to match his pace, enticing another screech from the crowd.

She wasn't sure what was more embarrassing—standing like a loser in the circle or Lazarus out-dancing her. Pushing away, he took center stage. She staggered before catching her balance. Lazarus worked his hips. Some of the crowd shrilled in response. Since when did Lazarus know the samba? And why was she still standing here like an idiot?

The crowd chanted his name, and her belly dropped. He was lapping this up. If you didn't think about the crippling terror and embarrassment of the moment, it was… exhilarating?

"Ready for our finale?" His gaze was unwavering.

Vassa trembled as he took her by the arm. He performed some footwork she couldn't mimic. She realized people had their phones out.

His hands went under her chin, bringing her attention to him. "Dip."

That was the only warning she got before he pushed her backward. She didn't think that samba had dips in it, but they weren't in a crowd of ballroom dancing judges.

He straightened them up, executed another twirl, and dipped her again. As if he was in a movie, he had one hand held up and his chest heaved as the crowd went wild. She stood up and was pushed to the side by another girl asking him to dance with her. More trampled over her as they rushed him.

Lazarus beamed and chatted with the girls. "One at a time, ladies. One at a time." His eyes found hers over the crowd.

As quickly as the adrenaline came, it left, hurling Vassa physically and emotionally to the ground. Dara finally got to her, inquiring if she was all right. The others didn't care, and it didn't matter if she stayed because she wasn't important anymore. Vassa broke eye contact with Lazarus, grabbing Dara by the arm as they fled from the party.

CHAPTER FIVE

WHATEVER JAYDEN WAS COOKING, IT was awful. It smelled like rotten eggs, curdled milk, and garbage juice all rolled up into one. Closing the door of his bedroom, he took a few steps inside the kitchen, taking tiny sips of air through his mouth, but it was like he could taste it.

"Dude, whatcha got, uh… whatcha got going on there?" Lazarus's eyes watered. Jayden stood in the kitchen wearing a frilly pink apron, two large yellow gloves to his elbows, and a clothespin on his nose. On the kitchen island were boiled potatoes, butter, bread, and chopped onion.

"This is surströmming." Jayden held the can of fish out to him, and Lazarus winced as the smell grew stronger.

"Is this why your aunt kicked you out of her kitchen?" Lazarus sat at the island and shook his head. He really hoped the smell wouldn't get into the furniture. That was going to be tough to get out. "That smells, you know, kinda strong. It's gonna ruin my apartment."

Jayden popped a piece of fish in his mouth and Lazarus gagged. "Don't worry, the vendor I ordered it from off Ebay said to keep the windows open and it will carry out the smell."

It wasn't smelling like the open windows were doing anything to help the situation. They were going to need an industrial fan in here.

"Did you want some?" Jayden offered the fish again. Lazarus recoiled.

"No... My only question is *why*?" *I'm really about to pass out,* he thought.

Jayden shrugged. "I'm an adventurous eater."

"Anyway..." Lazarus opened the notebook he brought with him. "I was playing around with that business plan. What do you think?"

After the last face-off Lazarus had with his older brother Harvey, he knew that he would have to come back stronger than just telling him he wanted to be an event manager. Normally when he was frustrated, he'd lose himself in good music and dance with a cute girl. He was trying to remedy that bad habit.

"Another one? You've been working on this for months. When are you going to show him already?" Jayden plucked off the gloves and took the notebook.

Lazarus ran a hand through his hair and exhaled. "You're right, but you know Harvey." He could imagine his voice. "He's never happy or impressed."

"Are you sure he's related?" Jayden raised an eyebrow.

"You don't have any other internship experience besides working for Gideon's Landscaping." "Your first year GPA was barely past a two-point-five." "You've been acting an ass since Dad's stroke."

The thought of his father gripped him by his throat and cut off his air supply. His mother's tears in the hospital that day, the gripping fear the man he admired his whole life would just... vanish. Lazarus knew he had to be strong for his mother but he had wanted to break down. His brain was paralyzed by the thought that his father would leave the earth knowing his last son was aimless. The last few months, Lazarus had been cleaning up his act, until that damn literature class appeared.

Jayden placed the notebook down. "I think it's great, man."

"I don't need it to be great. What's wrong with it? What's missing?" Lazarus would admit that being a wild child grew old quickly. After a party, waking up with a hangover, that's when the weight of his reality always set in. His loneliness. His insecurities. The dismissive words from his brothers, and low expectations from some friends and professors.

"Why are you so paranoid over this? You should be concerned about that class you're failing. Did you ask Vee yet?"

Right, I was supposed to ask her last night.

Spotting Dara at the party, he knew Vassa would be nearby. He had rarely seen one without the other. Finding her choking on a pretzel wasn't what he expected but again, he saw sadness in her eyes. Normally she maintained an aloof manner with him, but there was always a spark behind her eyes. He could pull it out of her, but when he tried to show her he was serious, that he wasn't the jokester she saw him as, she snapped at him.

"Not yet, I'm going to ask today."

Jayden laughed. "What are you going to do when she says no?"

All he wanted was for her to see him outside his reputation. Grow past their casual acquaintanceship and really get to know him. Vee did something to him, ignited a spark he thought was long gone— he respected her smart and responsible nature. It inspired him to pull up his pants and get serious. But like with Harvey, words weren't going to cut it. He would have to prove himself to be taken seriously.

"She won't say no..." He wasn't confident about that.

"Ha! That doesn't sound confident."

Lazarus rolled his eyes. "Along with my business plan, I want to make a portfolio. Clean up my resume. Find an internship or apprenticeship... something like that. Really show Harvey."

Jayden raised an eyebrow. "You want to cram in three months everything you shoulda been doing from the jump?"

"Right."

"That might not be realistic, Laz. You're my boy and all but can you do this? I mean I know you want to get control of your money back..."

Lazarus took a moment to breathe through that reminder. He had played around so much his parents put Harvey in control of his money.

"You always tell me to listen to my ancestors. This is what they're saying." He smiled to lighten the dark mood that had fallen.

"Ah, fuck off." Jayden rolled his eyes and went back to the food. Now Lazarus couldn't even smell it.

They grinned but Jayden's words gnawed at him. He wondered if his lack of focus could be righted so late. What was the point in changing now?

He knew the answer. Chasing fleeting pleasures and distractions left him hollow inside. He needed to do it not just for his father, but also for himself.

There was a banging on the door. Thinking it was his roommate forgetting his key again, Lazarus sauntered over and peeked out the peephole.

"Shit!" Lazarus pressed himself to the door. "No, no, no. *Shit!*"

"What's wrong?" Jayden leaned over as Lazarus dashed toward his bedroom.

"Lazarus, I know you're in there!"

Jayden scratched his dreads. "Who is that?"

Hopping up and down as he tried to get his shoe on, Lazarus tripped and tumbled to the floor. "Terri… the tutor stalker."

"Oh shit!"

It was fitting. Just as he was turning things around, the past was coming back to haunt him.

"So… great party?"

Vassa glared at Kiki before stabbing her eggs. Dara opened and closed her mouth before cutting into her french toast.

"Fucking rad, I gotta say," Kiki continued and took a huge sip of her mimosa. Of course she had gone out and bought more liquor. Vassa narrowed her eyes. "Oh really, it was rad?" She stabbed the eggs again, hard, causing the fork to scrape against the glass plate.

Running into Alexa. Being humiliated in front of Alexa *and* Lazarus. There was nothing rad about the party to her. "We're speaking to one another, okay, that's progress." Dara nodded as she took a bite of food.

Every time Kiki came, something bad came along with it. Vassa continued scraping her fork across her plate before bringing the food to her mouth.

Kiki flinched at the grating noise before yawning. "I think I'm sensing some tension."

"Damn right you're sensing some tension. What the hell is wrong with you? Like seriously, I wanted to leave and you drag me into a dance mob?" Vassa slammed the fork on the table.

"Vassa, calm down. Kiki, take this seriously." Dara pressed her lips together as her gaze flitted between them.

"I helped her out. It wasn't a mob, don't be dramatic." Kiki took a sip of water.

Vassa blinked rapidly and shook her head. Kiki had to be on something other than alcohol. "You had no right to steal my list and then show it to the public."

"I got you and that hot guy, Larry, together. Dara's right, he totally wants to get all up in there." Kiki pointed her finger up and down Vassa. "It was sickening to watch you stand there like a deer in the headlights, and I pulled my good tricks out on him. A party was on *your* bucket list. I made it fun. I think a thank-you is in order."

Vassa rubbed her temples, not sure where to start. "Lazarus, his name is Lazarus."

Kiki shrugged. "Larry, Lamar, Lazarus, who cares what his name is with a face like that? How do you know him, by the way? Why have you not jumped his bones? It doesn't look like he's picky."

"There are a lot of things wrong with that sentence." Vassa's hands fell to the table.

Besides the sixth-grade formal, she hadn't danced with anyone that close. Besides the crippling fear, a tiny, small part of her, for a fleeting second, had fun. She felt this spark. A thrill of something more than what she was used to. But then seeing Alexa killed that flame.

And the way he took control and the attention from her, dammit, she was gonna have to thank him for his help.

"I'm just saying I'm leading you to water but it's up to you to drink," Kiki said.

Dara nodded, and Vassa set her sights on her. "You're agreeing to this?"

Tucking her hair behind an ear, Dara grabbed Vassa by the hands. "Vassa, while I don't condone my cousin's actions, it was from a good place. Think about it, that was a big middle finger to Alexa."

Vassa opened her mouth to argue, but Dara shook her head. "You cannot continue to shut out the world. Obviously, she's living her life and you need to as well. While I admire your tenacity to save face, you have to admit it was fun… right?"

Vassa frowned at Dara and then at Kiki.

"It was fun," she grumbled, looking at the table. Alexa seeing her with Lazarus might have felt good, but it wasn't right to take the low road.

Hours later Vassa was once again staring at a button on a screen. The TV was playing, but she wasn't paying attention. Dara and Kiki left her to go shopping in The Haight. She had two things she had to submit. Her commencement and her graduate school application.

Shutting the laptop, she picked up the list.

Vassa's Extraordinary Senior Send-Off

1. Get totally wasted and regret nothing.

2. See all the tourist spots in San Francisco.

3. Have an epic last Spring Break.

4. Do something completely wild.

5. Sneak into a party or event uninvited and pretend to be someone else.

6. Go on a date.

Kiki was right. She could cross "do something completely unexpected" off the list. She bit her lip as she reread the paper. It wouldn't hurt just to keep going and probably add some more to the list. She thought about the cruel way Alexa looked at her before she went off partying with those other people. Still, she yearned for closure. *Why throw our friendship away?*

A door slammed loud, shaking the walls. Heavy steps thundered down the stairs along with voices.

"What the hell is wrong with you, Lazarus? I saw you with that girl online!"

Vassa rolled her eyes. Looked like Lover Boy had trouble in paradise.

"You're lying to me, stop lying!"

"You're not even supposed to be here," Lazarus' muffled voice responded.

She heard a sharp *crack!* And Vassa gasped. Did the girl hit him?

"I don't care!"

Whoever she was, she was not a happy camper. She listened to them argue before she heard feet retreating. Closing her eyes, she hit the submit button for her final grad school application. *One down, one to go.*

There was a knock at her door. Pushing up from the couch and setting her laptop down, she peeked through the peephole and sucked in a breath. There was Lazarus and an unknown girl, both waiting patiently. She took a step back, not sure what this mess could be or if she wanted to be in it.

He knocked once again and said, "I can hear you breathing in there!"

Vassa jerked back. *Damn.* She opened the door slowly, peeking. "Uh, ah, how are you two doing this afternoon?"

The girl behind him was beautiful. Auburn hair, slim waist, and round hips. His type. The girl narrowed her eyes at Vassa.

"Baby, why are you acting like that?"

Baby? "Baby?" Vassa echoed. Lazarus tugged the door out of her hands. He placed his arm around her shoulders and kissed the top of her head. She looked at him and then at the girl, who looked unconvinced.

"Yes, I was just telling Terri here how I'm in a committed relationship now. She needs to *move on.*" He blinked his right eye obnoxiously before he turned to Terri. "Vassa confessed her undying love to me last night. Called me her boo and what else? Side piece? That's right, isn't it?" His eyes widened and he gave Vassa a pointed look before giving a tense smile to the girl. He must still be drunk.

Terri shook her head. "I don't believe this."

"This is real, the love between us—" Vassa's arms were plastered to her sides. She was horrified.

Lazarus grinned at Terri, scratching his head. "It's palpable, ain't it baby?"

Vassa looked at him and he nudged her.

"Oh yes, my burning desire for him was too much to spare," she said in a robotic tone, "I'm so in love… and displaying affection." To add some believability, she patted his shoulder before giving it a squeeze.

Lazarus and Vassa gazed at each other before looking back at Terri.

It was crazy, the girl looked like she wanted to burst out in tears. "You know I'll wait for you."

"I know you will. You should let me go." Lazarus took a step back into Vassa's apartment and began to close the door.

"It's time, isn't it?" Terri sniffed and wiped her face.

Vassa thought she was on an acid trip.

Lazarus let out a sigh of relief. "Yes, let me go, I wish you all the best."

Terri shot Vassa a sneer, taking a step toward her. Vassa and Lazarus stepped back. "You better treat him right, or I don't know what I'll do."

Vassa's mouth fell open as Terri turned and descended the stairs. Then she snapped out of it, shooting Lazarus a look. "What was that?"

Lazarus shrugged and went into her apartment. "My stalker. You got any chips?"

"You were not invited inside." *A stalker?*

Vassa followed him into her kitchen as he opened up the cupboards. Slapping his hand away, she pointed to the stool at the kitchen island and went to the right cabinet. "You don't deserve any chips."

She wasn't giving him her Ruffles, so she gave him the veggie straws. Nobody liked veggie straws. She tossed him the bag and he caught it with one hand.

"Really? After I saved you last night?"

Vassa sighed, leaning against the counter. He looked sleek and cozy in his university sweat suit. It made the ones she wore look frumpy. It was a good thing she got over her crush on him. Otherwise, she would've probably been crazy like Terri.

"About that... Don't let this go to your head and don't think this will happen again." Vassa pointed at him as he froze with a straw in his mouth. "Thank you... for your help. Last night. I could have handled it myself, but thank you." Her face burned as she stared at the counter and seconds passed before she glanced at him. He didn't need to know about her confrontation with Alexa.

"That took a lot out of you, huh?" He bit noisily into the straw.

"It did. I feel weird too. Like I'm in the Twilight Zone."

Lazarus laughed, and she shook her head. The way he was

smacking on those Veggie Straws made her want some. She tried to grab the bag, but he pressed it to his chest and she said, "I can handle myself. I don't need a white knight. Just information for the future."

Rolling his eyes, Lazarus stood up from the stool. "You're watching The Matrix again?" He walked into her living room and plopped onto her couch, putting his feet up on the coffee table. She leaned over, peeking at her screen and the list.

"What's that?"

"None of your business."

Lazarus's head was directly next to hers. When he leaned closer, she automatically lifted her face. There were freckles on the bridge of his nose. Interesting. She hadn't noticed it before, but she also didn't let him this close before. Her lashes fluttered, and she cleared her throat before shifting away.

"You have a place to live. Why are you still here?"

Lazarus sat back on the couch watching young Keanu Reeves kick a li'l ass.

"I came to see how you were handling it."

"Handling what?"

His eyebrows furrowed. "We went viral. You haven't seen it?"

What was he talking about? She grabbed her phone off the table and was surprised to see hundreds of red notifications. Vassa never had over twenty likes on a post before. The one she was tagged in had *five thousand.* The phone slipped from her hand and he caught it. Her muscles went slack as her brain tried to put together what happened.

Lazarus snapped his fingers in her face. "Hello? You okay there?"

Taking the phone back, she rubbed her eyes to make sure she wasn't seeing things. It was the video of him and her dancing. Someone from the crowd got the horrified look on her face front and center.

"We're not famous-famous yet. It's just around campus but

we could end up getting interviewed on *Good Morning America*." He shoved three veggie straws in at once.

She scrolled through the comments. Mostly people with laughing emojis, some saying that it was staged, and others with thirst comments for Lazarus.

"How?" Vassa gasped, trying to reaffirm what she was seeing.

He shrugged. "That's the power of the internet."

She didn't know what to say.

"I also came to just see if you were doing okay." He set the veggie straw bag on the table. Crossing his arms, his gaze lowered to her phone and back up to her eyes. It looked like he was sincere, but when had she ever seen him sincere?

"I'm fine. You don't have to pretend to care."

Lazarus frowned. "Who said I'm pretending?"

Ignoring the sharp twist in her stomach at his sharp tone, she forced a half smile. Of course he was just joking. When had he ever been serious about something? Vassa wanted to use that energy from last night to propel her forward. Not backward.

"I've never seen you serious about anything, Lazarus. The closest had to have been sophomore year when they banned rice cookers."

"I had just learned how to make great couscous in it. That's not the point, I can be serious."

Vassa raised her eyebrows and continued to scroll. "If you say so." She cleared her throat. "Is there another reason you're still here or something? More women you're dodging?"

Lazarus didn't comment immediately. He sat back in his chair before he ran a hand through his hair. "Doesn't look like you have a line waiting for your attention." He looked around the empty apartment. "What's wrong with just being in each other's presence?"

Vassa snatched the veggie sticks from him. "We're not friends."

"We can be."

"What do you want?" Vassa took off her glasses and rubbed her eyes.

"You're a lit major, right?"

She nodded.

Lazarus let out a breath and leaned back on the couch. "So you read stories and write papers?"

"That's kinda a requirement of the major."

His face went from hopeful to evil. That made her suspicious.

"I need help—"

Vassa shook her head and concentrated on her phone. "I'm not writing your paper for you."

"I need help with a literature class if I want to graduate on time. How would it look if I have to be a fifth-year senior because of one class?"

Vassa thought about the academic probation sheet she saw on his desk the other day. "I'm not a tutor. Why not just go to the tutor center?"

Lazarus made a sour face. "Terri runs the tutor center."

"Aw."

"I'll pay top dollar, and I can even help you."

Vassa set her phone face down and looked sideways at him. "You can help me? With what?"

Lazarus plucked her list out from under her thigh.

"With this. 'Get totally wasted, see all the tourist spots in San Francisco, and plan an Epic Spring Break'—"She snatched the paper from his hand, pressed it to her chest.

"I didn't get to finish reading it."

"This isn't some sign-up list." She bowed her head. Her hair hung over her face, hiding her from his view. She wished there was something to distract him with.

If she was gonna do it, she was gonna do it alone.

"I'm good company," he said.

She couldn't tutor him. She already had a part-time job, a full course load, and other things in her life.

"I'm good." Vassa shook her head.

"My brother is part of a country club in the marina. Perfect place to sneak in…"

That only piqued her interest a *bit*.

Vassa's phone buzzed with a new comment. Looking at it, she sucked in a breath.

> NotAmazonAlexa: Staged. She's stiff as a board. I could dance better than that.

Alexa commented. Vassa was both excited and pissed off at the same time.

It was an evil idea to hang out and post videos with Lazarus to piss her ex-bestie off. But it was appealing. *Maybe this will finally be the biggest middle finger to Alexa.*

"Still, is it fun to do things alone?" Lazarus scooted closer.

Vassa eyed him up and down. "It's time for you to go."

Lazarus groaned and snatched at her veggie straws. She pushed him to the door as he turned toward her bedroom. "I'll take the fire escape. I'm not sure if she really left or not."

They marched toward her window when he turned, and she bumped into him.

"You're literally my last hope." He clasped his hands together, pouted, and stuck out his bottom lip.

"There are other lit majors out there." She couldn't handle the puppy dog look. She would break. She looked at the ceiling. "I said thanks for the party. Why draw it out?"

"You're super smart. I bet you're at the top of the class." Lazarus rubbed the hands together. "I could really pimp out your last semester and let you go out with a bang. If not, you can dump me and I take my chances."

"Just help you pass the class and you'll help me end with a bang…"

A sly glint entered his eyes. "I promise."

He sounded sincere. If anything was to happen, they would just part, and she would go back to ignoring him. There could be a catch-22 in there somewhere.

"Do you know anybody at UC Berkeley?"

Lazarus ran a hand through his hair. "Tons of dudes. Why?"

"I want to go to a frat party there."

He drew back. "You? A frat party?"

"That's my only stipulation. We finish my list and we go to a party there. I help you."

He held out his hand for her to shake. "I can make it happen."

"Great, now goodbye. Be ready to study tomorrow." She pushed him toward the window.

"Don't feel up on me too much now, I like it when my girl plays hard to get."

She rolled her eyes at him. This was going to be a long four months.

"Get out of my room Lazarus."

Lazarus grinned—the sort of grin that guaranteed many mischievous things—and he might find more fun on her bucket list than she did. "This is gonna be fun."

CHAPTER SIX

THE FIRST DAY OF CLASSES was the hardest.

It wasn't even lunchtime yet and Vassa wanted the day to be over. She was trying to keep her head up as her theology professor broke down false facts about religion. Her eyes closed, and she lowered her head when she felt something brush against her.

"Looks like someone was partying hard last night." Vassa pushed her hair back from her face. Oscar, her classmate, had sat down in the empty seat next to her in the auditorium.

"Me? Never, especially on a school night. That would be preposterous even," Vassa tried to joke. Then she winced. Was that too friendly? That was too friendly.

He beamed, setting his book bag on the desk. She sat up straighter and discreetly wiped any drool from her mouth. Both English majors, they met her freshman year at Word Slam. She wouldn't categorize them as friends, but he appeared to be a nice guy and was always trying to invite her out.

In dark-washed jeans and loafers, he slid her a piece of paper. "Guess what this is."

Vassa peered at the paper. It was the Word Slam spring schedule.

"I'm in charge of Word Slam for the semester." Oscar's eyes sparkled. He took the flyer back from her before pulling out his textbook.

"Wow, really? Congrats."

"You're gonna come this semester, right?"

Vassa swallowed and focused on the professor. When was the last time she read her poetry out loud to a crowd? *Right before everything went up in flames with Alexa.* Embarrassment and panic flared in her chest as the memories came back. Shaking her head, she closed her eyes to will the memory away. Never again.

"You know I have a lot of shifts at the studio…," she started, and Oscar groaned. "You say that all the time. You were so good! I can't even compare to you. I know if people knew you were speaking, they come out in droves."

Vassa tilted her head from side to side, as if in contemplation. *Nope, never gonna happen.*

"I'm looking for talent—" Oscar began when a classmate turned and shushed them. Their professor stopped talking before switching the presentation slide. Vassa waited a few seconds before she whispered.

"How was your break?"

That was a great conversation change, and less likely to make her uncomfortable.

"Great, but I have even more glorious news."

Vassa chuckled. "You're just the gift that keeps on giving."

Several of their classmates turned back to look at her and she ducked her head, clearing her throat. "Did your piece get published in that lit magazine? I told you that the bloody hammer served as a great metaphor."

He shook his head, "A couple of us are starting a writing group."

Oh. That was nice. She tried that once with a couple of people she met online. She ended up meeting with a sixteen-year-old girl and a forty-year-old man that looked like he just rolled out of some alley. It was hard to focus while she was worried the man would steal money out of her purse. She never went to that meet up again.

"I think you will be a great fit. You should join us!"

Vassa opened her mouth to respond when the class shushed again. Professor Fernández stopped presenting. "Is this a conversation that the class can join in?"

Vassa shook her head and focused on the empty page of notes she had. Oscar cleared his throat. "No... uh, no ma'am."

Giving them the stank eye, their professor started her lecture again. Day one and she was already on a professor's nasty side. When class was over, Oscar gave her a look.

"Is she gonna make our lives hell or what this semester?" He moved out of the way for a classmate to walk by.

"Oh, definitely much hell, I see that now." Vassa finished packing her backpack.

"What do you think about joining? If you won't perform for me, at least come write with us."

It sounded like a good idea. But what if they remembered what happened? She would have to sit there with the awkward pity looks. Or if not, she could say something lame or stupid. She would be stuck in a classroom or coffee shop with no way out.

The bucket list. They made it to the exit, and he held the door open for her. Instead of saying no like she always did, she said, "When did you want to do this?"

What are you doing? she thought.

Oscar stopped. "Soon. I want to feel out if there's enough people to start it. We haven't had a poetry club for the last two years."

"You figure out the details, and I'll see if it fits with my schedule."

Leaned against a pillar was Lazarus. He straightened up when he saw her and waved. How did he know what class she had? Vassa's eyes darted to Oscar as she adjusted the strap of her bag.

"Vee, hurry or we'll be late." He sauntered to her and pinned his eyes on Oscar. "Lazarus. Nice to meet you."

Why did it feel like two worlds were clashing?

Oscar reached out to shake Lazarus's hand. "I've seen you around a lot. You play on the baseball team, right?"

"Pitcher." The guys nodded at one another and looked at her.

"Let's go, Vee." Lazarus guided her away.

"Go where? I was just talking to Oscar..." He couldn't just pop up like she was just sitting on her thumbs, waiting for him.

"We had a deal, remember. I'm upholding my end of things." Lifting an eyebrow, he shot a look at Oscar.

"Lazarus—"

"Vee."

"It's fine, we'll figure out the details at another time." Oscar smiled genuinely and began walking down the stairs.

"Are you sure?"

"You have my number, right? Also, think about Word Slam, it would be a huge favor."

She nodded, and Oscar said goodbye. With a parting wave, Lazarus and Vassa watched Oscar walk down the path before disappearing around the corner.

"You need to tell me about the guys you talk to Vee. It's not safe out here, you don't know the game like I do."

Vassa snapped her head toward him. "What is this? The eighteenth century when women need chaperones?"

"I'm just saying. You're not experienced with this stuff. I can help weed out the good-for-nothings."

"I'm experienced, even though it's none of your business," she lied. "I'm pretty sure it takes a good-for-nothing to know one." She grinned at him.

Lazarus ignored her comment. "Ready for an adventure?"

"Are we there yet?" Her fingers dug into the leather of the car seat. Peeking, she dared to look at the hill they were climbing. Old cars weren't meant for San Francisco and his jalopy sounded on the brink of death. The sputtering sound it made when he pressed harder on the gas had her sending up prayers.

"Almost. We're doing item number two on your list, if I'm correct."

See all the tourist spots in San Francisco.

"We're going sight-seeing on Monday afternoon? Right now? We aren't gonna plan it out or nothing? What about the rest of my classes? Or the proper outfit? A weekend will be better for this."

Her body was already hypersensitive to his proximity. Vassa had planned to be dressed and put together. Or at least be in the mental space of tackling her list. Not clutching the seat in something she threw on to make it to class.

They stopped at a red light. "Dara told me you only had one class today, when I ran into her in the hallway. She said grab some toilet paper, by the way."

He found a parking spot at the last second and swerved into it. Once parked, they walked for a few minutes and Vassa saw the cosmic sign of Ghirardelli Square. The smell of chocolate made her stomach growl.

"Now there's a lot of spots the blogs deem must-sees, but do you remember freshman year when you used to sneak chocolate from the building janitor?"

"How you know that?"

As a freshman, she had been really close with the janitor that cleaned the girls' floor. She was a sweet older woman from Venezuela who loved talking about her grandchildren and son who lived in the Mission district. Vassa was in first semester Spanish and wanted to show off her skills by saying "tengo mierda" proudly.

The woman laughed in her face before offering to help her practice. Her reward was Venezuelan chocolate bars.

"I noticed. You know I tried to get her to give me a bar."

"Really? How did that turn out?"

Lazarus pouted. "Not great."

It was busy. Tourists milled about, taking photos in front of the central fountain.

"First things first: ice cream." Lazarus rubbed his hands together as they exited the car.

You couldn't go to Ghirardelli Square and not get chocolate

and ice cream. The Original Ghirardelli Ice Cream and Chocolate Shop smelled heavenly as they entered. A chalkboard menu board listed ice creams and scoop prices. The whir of the blender overpowered the music, and the line was long. They took their place behind a family.

"What are you thinking? The sundae or banana split? Both have sea salt, which is good for you." His eyes roamed the menu.

Vassa mouth watered. "It's ice cream. None of this is healthy, but… I think I'll get the Land's End." It was a salted caramel brownie sundae, topped with whipped cream and a cherry.

"Going for the motherlode?" He gave her a crooked grin.

She snorted. "Nine hundred calories of pure chocolate and sugar. It's probably gonna give me the runs."

Lazarus tossed his head back and let out a bark of laughter. The couple in front of them turned around and Vassa ducked her head. Why did she say that? That was gross.

"Ignore that please." She covered her face with her hands.

He shook his head. "Nope."

Another cashier came out from the back, and the line moved quickly. Vassa ordered the sundae in a waffle cone and Lazarus changed his mind at the last minute and went with the banana split. They found a table by the window. They could see the Golden Gate Bridge. Vassa dipped her spoon in and took one bite, and let out an unholy moan. "Oh my God."

Lazarus's eyes widened. "That good?"

She was going to have to come back here. Lazarus stopped eating, watching her tongue move across her bottom lip. She closed her eyes and tipped her head back. Chocolate was her weakness. Besides Twizzlers.

Lazarus swallowed and looked down at his own ice cream. "Lemme try." Lazarus tried dipped his spoon into her sundae and she blocked him.

"Uh, uh, what are you doing?"

"I want to try some."

Vassa pulled her sundae closer to her. "You should have ordered one if you wanted to try some."

"You're going to be selfish, Vee?" Lazarus pouted.

"We both had the opportunity to order the sundae. You're gonna have to be satisfied with that sad-looking ice cream."

They looked down at the banana split. It definitely didn't look like the picture advertised. The ice cream scoops were mismatched sizes. The whipped cream was watery, the bananas dented. Vassa placed a hand over her mouth to muffle her laughter. Then she looked at his face and really laughed. He looked so sad.

"You really won't share?" His bottom lip quivered perfectly, and she knew he was acting.

Lazarus continued with the puppy dog look. She shook her head and smacked her lips. She knew what he was doing. Her brownie was nice and warm and mixed well with the vanilla ice cream. She continued to eat. Minutes passed before she looked up again. His gaze was fixed on her. *"No."*

Lazarus looked at her sundae and then her.

Sighing, she pushed her sundae forward. "Don't expect this again."

Lazarus grinned. Dipping his spoon into the sundae, she watched his eyes cross comically. He shifted his jacket off his shoulders, his muscles flexing as he got comfortable with her food. His sleeves rolled past his forearms. Veiny forearms. That multiplied his sexiness tenfold in her book.

Vassa had seen his arms before, so why did this feel more personal? Her eyes went from the wall to his pink tongue as it darted out to lick across the spoon.

He groaned, "Oh my God."

Lazarus got another scoop before she snatched it back. "No double-dipping."

The thought of his tongue sent her squirming in her seat. Within minutes, the sundae and banana split were gone. Vowing to come back, they walked around the square before descending to the pier.

The pier led them toward Fisherman's Wharf. When they made it to the famous sign, Lazarus forced her to stand in front of it for a picture, even as she refused. Next, he spotted Musée Mécanique, a museum with interactive coin-operated antique slot and arcade machines. Vassa loosened up at this point and challenged Lazarus to Asteroids. She was kicking his behind at it until he sabotaged her by using his other hand to push her to the side.

"Cheater!" She laughed and pushed back.

It didn't matter because she still won, and got to rub getting the high score on the machine in his face.

"Are you proud?" He sucked his teeth.

He was such a sore loser. She felt her lips turn up at the corners. How could he always make her smile, whether or not she wanted to? She blew out her cheeks to hide the smile, but it was too late. He saw it. "Very."

He laughed and ruffled the top of her head. She swatted his hands away, and he pinched her cheeks. The sign of affection happened so quickly, she couldn't complain because they were leaving and heading back to the pier. She wrapped her arms around herself as they looked at the boats on the water. She wasn't having that bad of a time with him.

The fog was rolling in once again, crawling over the Golden Gate Bridge. It looked like a creepy monster in the distance.

When they arrived at Pier 39, it was packed, and she didn't care too much for the crowd. She wanted to leave, but he grabbed her hand and led her. He pointed at Alcatraz off in the distance, but there was something even more important that he seemed to be taking her to. That's when she heard… barking?

They walked to the edge of the pier where people were clamoring and saw them.

"Sea lions!"

Abandoning Lazarus, she pushed through the crowd to the railing and gushed over the lazy sea lions floating on the rafts.

The sea lions were not impressed by their audience. Most slept, some cracking open an eye to watch the noisy humans. Lazarus forced his way to her as one seal let out a rancid fart, causing everyone to laugh, and Vassa covered her nose. *Cute but gross…*

"Let's take a picture." Lazarus was pulling out his phone.

He asked a nearby couple for help, and they posed by the railing. At first, she stood a few inches from him, but he put his arm around her shoulders, pulling her closer.

"Should we bark like a sea lion or say the generic cheese?" he whispered. She turned and her eyes fell to his lips. Vassa's blood hummed with excitement and a genuine smile danced in her eyes. With their heads bent close, the lingering smell of chocolate on his breath made her take a deep breath. She shivered in his arms before licking her lips and looking away.

The woman holding the phone counted down and before she could say cheese, Lazarus let out a loud bark like a seal. It triggered the other seals behind them to bark as well.

The crowd laughed. The woman handed his phone back to him and he showed Vassa the picture. Her eyes were shut as he made a funny face and used two fingers to make bunny ears behind her head.

"See, that's a great photo." Lazarus awarded her a wide grin.

She didn't want to let down her guard, but in that moment, she felt herself growing comfortable. It was sly how he wielded his normal charming passion like a weapon. It drew her in, made her excitement bubble. It was contagious, and she turned to him with a wobbly smile, and held his gaze.

Vassa couldn't help but agree.

In the next couple of hours, they walked their feet off.

Lazarus was rethinking a spontaneous adventure in the middle of the week. They walked along the Embarcadero. He pointed at Coit Tower as Vee pulled him into a tourist shop. Lazarus was obedient as she led them from product display to display. Normally, he hated shopping, but he kept a cool face.

"I'm stuck between the sea lion plushie or Golden Gate Bridge one. What do you think?" She held the overpriced items up to him.

"Get the bridge." It was much bigger and looked comfortable.

"I'm gonna get the sea lion." She put the bridge back, and he rolled his eyes. Vee liked to shop, it seemed. The wall she had early on seemed to come down as she talked his ear off about every little thing she thought was cute. She found a shirt that said "Send me to the Rock—Property of Alcatraz Penitentiary." She told him he should wear it. And he did, along with a Giants hat, sunglasses, and scarf. He looked like the quintessential tourist.

"This is *so* embarrassing." Vee ducked her head as they walked out of the store. The curious gazes from the crowd didn't bother him, and he nudged her.

"We're tourists. What's wrong with that?"

She arched an eyebrow. "You don't care about the attention, do you? You remind me of—" The name barely left her mouth in a whisper, and her eyes narrowed before she shook her head.

"Who?"

"It's nothing." Her voice was sharp, offering no explanation.

While people thought the Golden Gate Bridge was the main bridge to see, it had nothing on the Bay Bridge. It was a mammoth, a double-decker steel bridge. Lights adorned every section, making it a beacon in the night. A icy breeze came by and she shivered. He took off his jacket and handed it to her.

Vassa shook her head. "No, you don't have to."

Lazarus rolled his eyes at her and placed the jacket around her shoulders. "Don't freeze being stubborn. It's my fault you're here only in a sweatshirt."

Vassa smiled and thanked him. They found a spot to sit and look out at the setting sun.

"So, what did you think about the day? Did I deliver or what?" Lazarus asked as their shoulders brushed here and there.

"It was fun." Vassa pulled his jacket closer around her.

"That must have taken a lot to say."

She laughed. "I had a really superb time. I will cherish these memories for a lifetime. Especially when my children put me in a nursing home and I'm forced to make friendship bracelets."

Her heartfelt thanks warmed him. Finally, he was doing something right. He couldn't look away from her. From her smile. The vulnerable light in her eyes. Each brush of their shoulders brought a new whiff of her signature scent. She smelled incredible, and that laugh of hers was doing strange things to him. "Gosh, that warms the heart."

With her head turned toward the bridge, she seemed worlds away.

"This feels weird," Vassa whispered before turning to him.

He took a deep breath and forced a smile. "How?"

After a few seconds, she said, "When was the last time you and I sat for over five seconds?"

Lazarus thought about that. "Probably that one time we had to see the resident advisor. You remember? I accidentally wrapped your entire room in wrapping paper?"

"How do you accidentally wrap someone's entire room?" Her lips puckered.

"Admit it, that was a good prank."

"No, it wasn't."

Scratching his cheek, he looked at the ground. "You're right. I owe you an apology then."

"You do. Next time more groveling please." She cocked her head and studied him with an amused expression.

He scrubbed his hands over his face, trying to resist her allure. "I have a proposition."

Vassa frowned. "We made our deal already."

"Let's play a get-to-know-you game. We should get to know

each other. On a deeper level. Especially if you're going to be my tutor. And in a way... I'm your tutor."

"Tutor of what?" She stood up, placing her hands on her hips.

"Tutor of life. Of fun. Adventure, escapade, exploit, or my favorite... *romp*."

Vassa shook her head. "You know a lot of synonyms to not pass English Lit."

"I'm a master at Scrabble."

The horn of the ferry cut through the noise of the pier.

"Are you gonna play the game?" Lazarus ignored the buzzing of incoming messages on his phone in his pocket. It had been going off all afternoon. Why couldn't his brother get the hint that Lazarus wasn't in the mood to talk?

"Fine, if there's no way out of this."

Lazarus clapped his hands. "I'll start off easy, we'll play This or That."

Vassa agreed. Lazarus sat there for a minute before he snapped his fingers and sat up. "Dog or cat?"

"Cat."

Lazarus made a face. "Why cats? They're evil and lick their butts all day."

"First of all, cats are dignified creatures. Unlike dogs who roll around in feces. They are independent. They can't be bothered with people and all their issues. They only need themselves and I admire them for it."

His eyes shot to hers, his eyebrows hovering near his hairline. "Dogs give you unconditional love."

"I bet if I give a dog a piece of bread, he'll love me. If you try to give a cat bread? A smack to the face. They can't be bought with minimal efforts. They have a code even us people don't have." Vee cocked her head to the side.

"You can't be alone all the time."

He could see the indecision in her face, when maybe before she would have given him a brush off. This time, he saw the conflict in her eyes. She was trying to decide if she should tell him something.

"You'll be surprised what you can tolerate." Vee wrinkled her nose and pushed her glasses up.

He tried not to feel disappointed. They grew silent as they gazed at each other, and he tried to read the emotion in her eyes. He was confused and fascinated by Vee.

What amused him was the glimpse of the real her. Like her embarrassment at the ice cream shop about her diarrhea comment. Or the soft expression she had while watching the sea lions. The Vee in front of him wore a stony expression. That outgoing side was safely tucked back away.

He dragged his hands through his hair. "Next question. Present or future?"

"Future."

"Why?"

Vassa fiddled with the sleeves of his jacket. "The future can be talked into existence. You can create it. If you plan, then you won't make mistakes or detours. If you don't know, you'll just end up wasting time and then looking up twenty years from now wondering what went wrong."

He shoved his hands in his pockets. Wasn't that what Harvey constantly preached? His brother started out working at his company during college as an intern. Fifteen years later, he was still there, but now a vice president. Lazarus knew Harvey wanted him to come around to the idea of working for him. It would allow Lazarus to roam on a long leash, and Harvey could tolerate his momentary fuck-ups.

"I think the present is better. The future is never guaranteed." His voice came out rougher than what he intended. His old self would have agreed; *he* believed time was generous. He took a moment to breathe in that realization.

"Oh?"

Lazarus focused on a ferry chugging along through the

waves. "I think people who put more effort into the future don't want to face their unpleasant reality. They avoid and deflect, especially if their present isn't the future that they hoped for."

His phone buzzed again. Baseball was his one true love. It allowed him to escape self-awareness for a while. It's what his father taught him to relax and ease his racing thoughts. He wanted to explore more. See what made his soul race. He didn't have years to plan that out. He had to take every moment when it was given.

Text messages turned to calls and Lazarus pushed himself away from the bench. "Ready to go?" He didn't want her to see him like this. Ducking his head, he gathered his thoughts.

"Yeah." Her voice came out on a gasp. Their gazes clashed, and Lazarus found himself confronted by her eyes: warm, soft, and dewy.

The two were silent, her eyes sharp and her jaw set. He knew it wasn't the time to crack a joke. They made the long journey toward the car, both lost in their own thoughts. One thinking about the past. The other, the future.

Vassa's Extraordinary Senior Send-Off

1. *Get totally wasted and regret nothing.*
2. *See all the tourist spots in San Francisco.*
3. *Have an epic last Spring Break.*
4. *Do something completely wild.*
5. *Sneak into a party or event uninvited and pretend to be someone else.*
6. *Go on a date.*

CHAPTER SEVEN

"HEY LAZARUS, ARE YOU COMING to that party tonight?"

Lazarus was packing up from class as he turned his head to the source of the voice. It was a brunette girl. Cindy... Charlotte? He knew she was the girlfriend of someone on the team. The surrounding people turned to him.

"Yeah, are you coming?" another guy asked.

"It wouldn't be a party without you," Cindy (he settled for calling her that) said.

Lazarus gave a strained smile and shrugged, "I'm not sure..."

He wanted to badly but Coach had been riding his ass all week, his brothers too for different reasons, and he hadn't talked to Vee in a couple days. It seemed graduation was all the seniors could talk about. There seemed to be no other interesting topic of conversation. He gritted his teeth when someone asked him for the tenth time in a row, "What are your plans?"

The old him would have blown off studying and went. But he couldn't if he wanted to prove to his brothers he was responsible now. Tonight was his first tutoring session. He received a text from Vee that morning with strict instructions:

Be on time.

And BRING THE BOOK.

"C'mon, you never turn a party down," Cindy said.

Lazarus headed out the door, and the group followed him.

"I know, but I got some big plans tonight," he lied and

sucked his teeth.

"Really, what big thing?" Cindy giggled, bringing her phone out to share the exciting news.

"Yeah, what big thing you can't tell your brother?"

Lazarus froze. Cursing, he took a deep breath before he squared his shoulders. His brother Harvey was leaning against the hallway wall.

"Uh, nothing too big…" Lazarus trailed off, and he looked at the group. "I'll talk to you all later, 'kay?"

The group tossed a curious glance over at Harvey but kept insisting he come hang out tonight. He smiled and grinned, but once they were gone, he righted his shoulders for battle.

"You just show up on campus? No phone call, email, or text message? That's scorned side chick vibes, man." Lazarus placed his hands in his pockets as he squared off with Harvey.

In his expensive suit, shades covering his eyes, Harvey said, "If you don't answer my calls, what else am I supposed to do?" Height and eyes were where their similarities ended. Where Lazarus's hair was blond, Harvey's was red. "I show up when phone calls get ignored."

As the second born, their parents depended on Harvey to corral the other siblings. The brothers listened to him not out of fear, but because he would nag them to the ends of the earth if they didn't.

"Look, I'm trying to go study." Lazarus kicked a random rock on the path as he let out a deep breath.

Harvey tilted his head again. "Study? I never heard you say that before."

"A new leaf. I guess."

"A new leaf?" Harvey echoed and walked toward the exit of the building. That was Lazarus's cue to follow. His thoughts raced. How could he get Harvey off campus quickly?

"Don't you live in SoMa with your fiancée? Shouldn't you both be in a goat yoga class or something right now?" Lazarus studied Harvey's expression, but couldn't read it.

Harvey waved him off. "Nice campus, glad to see what I'm paying for."

Lazarus rolled his eyes. *Not this again.*

"I told you, you didn't have to pay for me. I could've worked or Gideon could—"

"Gideon barely has two nickels to rub together. He needs to stop playing around in dirt and go back to working for the government."

"He didn't like it," Lazarus defended their brother.

"*He didn't like it, he didn't like it.*" Harvey mocked, and he scoffed. "It doesn't matter if he didn't like it. You suck it up and do the job."

Lazarus took a deep breath and counted back from ten. "You know I'm grateful for you…"

Their father's stroke left the family with substantial medical bills. Lazarus, the last one in school, had been prepared to take out private loans until Harvey stepped in. That was selling his soul to the devil in retrospect.

Harvey said, "As you should be. Like I said before, my money comes with—"

"Strings?" Lazarus said.

Harvey sent him a sharp look. "Stipulations."

Right…

"It's your final semester. You know I want you to come work with me at the company, but imagine my hurt and shock when my brother doesn't want to uphold his end of the deal by showing up for the third interview I've set up."

Lazarus let out a sigh of relief. Harvey didn't know he was failing the class.

"Harv, you know—" Lazarus knew he didn't want to go work as a salesperson for a protein bar in some cubicle for the rest of his life.

"I know what?"

Lazarus licked his lips as he tried to find the right words.

"I know we agreed to that but I want something different. I want access to my accounts back."

Harvey did a double take before barking out laughter. "Are you serious? You want your accounts back?" He continued to laugh as if it was humorous and Lazarus's frown deepened. "Not gonna happen until you graduate and you secure a job for six months. Working for my company is a great opportunity for you, Lazarus. Get real. You need stability."

Lazarus shoulders fell as Harvey paused for a moment to answer his business phone, then continued. "Do I need to remind you that you've partied away the last four years? You were an undecided major until junior year. If I was you, I'd get my foot in the door somewhere and keep my head down…"

Lazarus went to that spot in his brain he always did when Harvey got on his soapbox. "I know."

Harvey shook his head. "You know this, but you do nothing. I'm no longer asking you. You're going to interview for my company."

His blood chilled as disbelief turned to outrage. Harvey had micromanaged every minute of his life these last four years and he had tolerated it. *Now he wants to decide my life?*

"I know you all don't trust me yet but haven't I at least proven myself this last year? I've turned my grades around; I'm not partying as much." Lazarus grabbed his brother's arm. "I wanted to wait to show you this, but I have a plan. I want to do event management. I'm fixing my résumé and getting a website. Do you remember those galas I planned—?"

"You said this before. We had that interview for the tech company set up and you didn't have the decency to show up. We're over this Lazlo. You need to grow up. Mom and Dad aren't getting younger. Emily and I want a fresh start and I'm transferring to the New York office." It was Lazarus's turn to do a double take. His brother was leaving California?

"The family is spreading out and you need to be able to

survive. I told you I'll pay for whatever you need while you're in school, but after that? You're on your own."

A stab of guilt pierced his heart, but Lazarus bit his lip, drawing blood. His parents put themselves through school, working odd jobs until they could provide a comfortable life for the family. Harvey placed his hand on Lazarus's shoulder.

"I do this because I love you. You don't have to lie about the resume, I'll pull some strings, but after this I'm done. If it was up to Gideon, he'd let you run rampant. I'm saving you, Lazarus." Harvey turned to leave but stepped back. "Oh, before I forget, I came to invite you to a party."

"My company is having a cocktail party in the Presidio in a few weeks. Come meet the staff, get a feel for everyone. Can you at least do that?"

Lazarus swallowed a roar of frustration. He didn't want to spend a perfectly good evening tied up in a room with some suits but he nodded anyway.

"Make sure you wear a suit and look presentable." Harvey's stern features softened as he patted Lazarus on the back. He reached into his pocket, pulled out some folded up bills, and placed them in Lazarus's hand. "Get something nice, on me."

Reasoning and pleading wouldn't get him anywhere with Harvey. He would hold his ground tighter than a dog with its nuts. That made Lazarus more determined than ever to prove to him he was responsible now. The money felt like fire in his hands and he shoved it in his pocket before trudging toward the library.

Thoughts of what he should have said floated in his mind and blurred his vision as he entered. He walked past the reference desk, ignoring hellos from friends, and went upstairs where the study rooms were. The second floor was buzzing with the noise of students goofing off rather than studying.

Vee had told him to meet her in study room three. He found it and knocked and the door flew open.

"You're late." Vee's arms were crossed and she turned into

the room. The lesson plan for their meeting was on the whiteboard with several bullet points. He set his bookbag on the table as he tried to force a smile.

"Have you ever thought that you're just early?"

"I made a lesson plan for you—" Vee squinted at him. "Are you okay?"

Raking his hand through his hair, he put his feet up on the desk. He was tempted to find a stiff drink, but that could lead to him losing control in public and more ammo for Harvey. The library was filled with people he knew. He couldn't risk saying how he felt to her in case of prying ears.

He shrugged and smiled. "Oh custom, I like the sound of that."

Vee shook her head before she stood up and moved the rollable white board closer to them. "Now we start with *Mac Flecknoe* by John Dryden. He's an excellent writer, by the way."

Lazarus tilted his head back and blew air out of his mouth. "Boring."

"It's a great poem."

"Really? Did his lover die from sickness or because they exiled him to the English countryside?"

She raised an eyebrow. "Neither. It's a mock epic."

"Mock epic?" He slid his feet off the table and sarcastically said, "That sounds so interesting."

"It's meant to satirize." She ignored him, passing him a paper outlining the study plan. *Imagery, metaphors, similes, themes.* He laid his head on the table. This was going to be horrible.

To his surprise she patted him on the back. "Don't worry, you'll get through this."

His head lifted and he raised an eyebrow at her. Her face flushed and she looked away, opening her pencil case to pass him a highlighter.

"The first essay you're going to do is on the poem, so we need to draft your essay early and analyze the poem…" She tucked a piece of hair behind her ear.

He studied her face and noticed the excitement. It reminded him of when he was on the field. She read the poem aloud; he placed his chin in his hand and listened. It wasn't bad since she was reading. She was adorable, with her curls pulled into a ponytail, waving her hands animatedly to get her point across. There was some impatience when he didn't understand a metaphor, but she slowed down and explained it once again. She looked up from writing and looked back down. "Am I doing too much?"

Lazarus shook his head. He respected her passion, and a dark thought popped into his brain: he wished he could show Harvey that side of him. "Can we take a break?" He needed to move, get some fresh air in his lungs.

Vee shook her head. "Read the poem again and tell me every symbol and motif in it. Then we'll take a break."

Lazarus huffed. His eyes ran over the words. His eyes ran over the words, but they all blurred together. "I can't do this anymore." Lazarus set the book down.

"It's only been an hour." Vassa leaned back in her chair.

Lazarus pouted. "C'mon Vee, there's time for a break."

"Lazarus, this is serious, your grade is at stake—"

"I appreciate you for all you've done for me so far. If I'm burned out, I can't remember the symbols and motifs." Lazarus gave her his best puppy dog expression, and she sighed.

"Fine, okay."

He was grateful to leave. Not only was he hungry, but also the fresh air would allow him to figure out how to get out of the cocktail party. He fist-bumped a few teammates and friends who passed by. Some eyed Vee with curiosity and he noticed she crossed her arms over her chest and focused on the ground. She jumped when he swung his arm over her shoulder. "You gotta loosen up. You're gonna get gray hairs early."

"Don't worry about my gray hairs. Even though there are none." But her shoulders relaxed.

The cafeteria was a five-minute walk from the library. They

entered the grab-and-go section, and he picked up a protein bar and water. He met Vee at the cash register; she had praline ice cream and pretzels.

"Praline ice cream and pretzels?" His eyebrows rose in amusement.

Vassa lifted her chin and sniffed. "Praline ice cream is the best. After Twizzlers."

"My nana eats that."

"Your nana is awesome then."

Bounty in hand, they passed the chemistry building. He stopped. "Want to see something fun?"

"Define fun." She arched an eyebrow and bit into a pretzel.

Grabbing her hand, he led her into the building as a group of students were exiting. He took the stairs two at a time, and she had to run to keep up with him. "Lazarus! Wait up!"

He slowed a bit as she huffed and wheezed. The building was quiet; the lights came on as they passed, heading for the top floor.

"What are we doing here?" Vassa looked left and right as she gripped her bag closer.

He didn't answer her, leading her down the hallway. She tiptoed behind him, expecting someone to jump out of a room. "I'm serious, Lazarus."

They made it to the end of the hallway; he went to a spot in the wall. He hit it and a hidden door opened up, revealing an emergency exit. He turned around and said, "Don't be scared. Take my hand."

She blinked and glanced down the empty hallway.

"Remember, you wanted new experiences." He offered his hand.

Vassa took a deep breath and grabbed it. Their fingers entwined and he inhaled deeply when their hands touched. Her hands were soft and just cool from the ice cream, but short and chubby. It made him laugh but felt refreshing to his bigger, rougher hand. There was barely any light, and she held onto him as they climbed up.

"Almost there." Using his shoulder, he opened the door to reveal the rooftop. Too soon, she dropped his hand and strolled toward the edge. He placed a piece of wood in the door to prevent it from shutting. They could see the entire campus center. Walking closer to the edge, he saw students riding bicycles across campus.

He sat down, hanging his legs over the side, and patted the spot next to him. "Come have a seat."

"Do we have to be on the edge?" Vee wet her lips as she eyed the spot.

"It's safe. I swear."

Vassa walked over slowly, checking the edge again. She grumbled before setting her things down and plopping next to him. "If I fall and crack my head on the sidewalk, my ghost will haunt you."

"That sounds like fun," he said with his mouth full of protein bar.

"It's not gonna be nice. I'm gonna be a poltergeist. Tear everything apart." She swung her feet back and forth and sweat erupted over her face as she looked over the edge. "I'm gonna be sick."

"Fear of heights? Just eat your old lady ice cream."

She flipped him off and reached for the carton. They were silent for several moments before she said, "You come here often?"

Lazarus shrugged and focused on a biker coming up the path. "Sometimes when I'm stressed."

"Stressed? When is Mr. Popular ever stressed?" She ate a spoonful.

He was most definitely not in the mood to replay the game tapes with Harvey today. Life as a fitness bar pusher didn't breed excitement. What Harvey and others didn't know was that last year he rediscovered a love for knowledge due to a microeconomics class. Choosing business as his major was just a random choice because of Harvey's pushing. Now he was enjoying it.

"It's a beautiful view," she said.

He cleared his throat and finished the bar. "Yes, it is." Lazarus picked up the extra spoon she had and went for the ice cream.

"Ah! No! This is my ice cream. If you wanted ice cream, you should have gotten yourself some. We're not repeating Ghirardelli." Vee held the ice cream away from him.

"Don't be like that! Share."

Lazarus reached for the ice cream and tugged. Vee refused to let go. "It's mine!"

They played tug of war for several seconds. Lazarus's vortex of thoughts on Harvey and the job ceased swirling in that moment, because maybe what Vee said was prophetic. Someone was going to tumble off the side if one didn't release the ice cream first. Smiling, he used his strength to lean them away from the edge. Who knew Vee was territorial over ice cream? She placed both hands on the carton, and with extreme effort snatched it from him.

His mouth opened to warn her, and her hands clawed the air uselessly because the cartoon went one way, and they went the other. He grabbed her by the back of her shirt, forcing her back to the roof as the carton of praline ice cream went flying over the edge of the roof.

They looked at one another before sitting up. The carton had landed inches from a professor walking out of the building. Lazarus laughed and Vee gasped as the man jumped in time to keep it from landing on his head. He looked up.

Vee squealed, and they launched themselves back to the roof. She tucked her feet under herself. "Look what you did!" She punched him softly on the arm and his belly hurt from laughing as he shook his head.

"That was all you."

Lazarus wondered what Vee would be like if she let down her guard and let spontaneity rule. He definitely wanted to see that. He sighed as he focused on the sky above them. As it darkened, tiny stars appeared.

He felt her looking at him. "When did you find this place?"

"Freshman or sophomore year? It was by accident. I couldn't sleep one night and just... found it."

The youngest in the Gilbert clan, he was often alone. There was a sixteen-year age gap between his oldest brother and himself. His other brother, Alex, was only seven years older but he was too focused on his books to play cops and robbers with Lazarus as kids. One Christmas his parents gave him a portable CD player. He would take it and lie alone in his room for hours listening to Pink Floyd and Nirvana. This spot had become his new bedroom.

"You go around banging on walls for secret doors?" He heard her ruffling in her chip bag and she handed him a pretzel.

He shook with quiet laughter as he ate it. "Should you be eating these after the last incident?" His laughter died as she hit him with some force.

He turned to her and there was a faraway look in her eyes as she stared at the sky.

"I'm sorry, that's probably too soon." He forced himself to swallow after several attempts. She turned to him. Her eyes looked bigger in the dark and, without conscious thought, Lazarus's hand rose and cupped the back of her neck. She gasped and tilted her head back. He waited for her to push him away, but when she didn't, he leaned forward and used his other hand to brush away a strand of hair that fell in her face.

He slowly traced the side of her face. She blinked rapidly, and he felt the quick pants of her breath on his hand. He wanted to kiss her. He'd wanted to since freshman year. A sigh escaped her as Vee leaned in closer, her eyes fluttering shut. He leaned back.

"Uh," he said and Vee blinked several times before she sat back on the roof. Some awkwardness rushed between them, and he blurted out, "Ever feel so overwhelmed by everything you just need to be alone?"

She was silent so long he thought she was ignoring him until she said, "All the time. Or it could be our angst. We're in our twenties."

That got a laugh out of them both. "It just feels like the closer to graduation I get, the more that feeling increases. I guess, in a way, I am a dog. I need constant attention and love." He laughed and looked at her. "You know?"

He saw her swallow, and she peeked at him before looking away. "After everything that happened—" She frowned. "Well, I'm biased. I'm so used to being alone it doesn't bother me."

"What happened?" He turned his entire body to her. Vee opened her eyes, her gaze turned forward, before she reached over for another pretzel.

"Long story that doesn't matter." Her barely audible words and sudden change of mood caught him by surprise. He could tell she was uncomfortable, so he backed down.

"There's a bonfire this weekend. You think you wanna come? It's not a part of the list, just a small get-together. You can bring Dara."

Vee rubbed her arms before nodding. "Sure."

They sat in comfortable silence, and moments later he felt Vee place her hand over his.

Ocean Beach was absolutely freaking freezing at night. It was easy to spot Lazarus and his friends. There weren't many people having bonfires in January. When was the last time she went to a bonfire? Dara, Alexa, Vassa, and a few others had snuck out one night during finals for a midnight hangout.

Lazarus saw them first, waving them over.

"C'mon Vassa." Dara's nose was running already. "This looks fun."

As they got closer to the crowd, Vassa inhaled deeply and pushed her shoulders back.

"Right?" Dara nudged her.

"Right."

Music was playing on a speaker. Some people were dancing, some sitting, and others holding a stick over the fire. Lazarus had a beer in one hand. "The girls are here. I saved you s'mores."

He led them to the fire. The people surrounding them were totally unfamiliar. There was a cooler and Lazarus reached down inside and pulled out the ingredients for s'mores. "I didn't wanna make them and ruin the experience for you. Just in case you're into that."

Vassa thanked him and raised her marshmallow over the flame. She looked up. There was a group of girls across from her. They looked at her and whispered. Vassa focused on the fire.

"Beverages at all? Beer, water, white wine? I think we have some Sauvignon Blanc for my classy folk." Lazarus looked from Vassa to Dara.

Dara nodded. "Wine sounds nice."

"Yo, Laz."

Dara cleared her throat loudly as Jayden approached and Vassa rolled her eyes when Dara stuck her chest out as he gave her a slow smile.

"Hello, have we met? I think I would remember someone with an aura like yours."

Lazarus and Vassa rolled their eyes as Dara giggled.

"What you need, man?" Lazarus broke into whatever was happening between their friends.

Jayden pointed to the parking lot. "Help me bring in more beer and hot dogs." Lazarus agreed and Jayden gave Dara another interested glance before Lazarus pushed him off toward the car.

"This *is* going to be fun." Dara bit her lip and squirmed in her seat, her eyes tracking Jayden and Lazarus.

Vassa sneezed. "I'm freezing."

"What's a little pneumonia? At least there is excitement." Dara looked around and smiled.

Vassa pulled her marshmallow out of the fire. It was half burned.

"I think they're coming back. If you'll excuse me, I'm gonna go mingle." Handing Vassa her marshmallow, Dara stood up, heading to meet Jayden and Lazarus. *Great, I'm alone again.* Vassa wasn't liking the pattern of Dara abandoning her at parties.

Vassa finished her s'more quickly. Glancing over at the other girls, Vassa thought maybe she could talk to them, but they ignored her.

Unlike at the house party, Vassa could relax. It was much more intimate. There weren't any kitchens to hide in or dance circles to distract. *Or evil ex-best friends.* This was a completely different beast.

Unfortunately for her, small talk and mingling were not her forte. To her relief, the crowd moved around the fire for warmth and she didn't have to worry about those odd girls. Someone began speaking with her and she nodded and smiled politely, relieved she didn't have to talk much.

After some time, she couldn't feel her behind on the log. Standing up, she stretched and headed for the water. Lazarus had been pulled into many conversations, and she tried not to feel some type of way he hadn't come back to her. This was his party; she couldn't expect him to baby her. Munching on another s'more, she walked to the water's edge. The only music faded as she bent down to pick up rocks. She tossed them in her hand before she got the idea to lift one and skip it across the water.

It plopped straight down and she tried again. Why was skipping rocks so hard? She picked up another rock and tossed it; it sunk.

Stomping her foot, she exhaled and threw some rocks she gathered into the ocean. She watched the waves consume them before she bent down and took off her boots, stuffing her socks into them. Rolling up her pants, she walked into the water.

She sucked in a breath as the cold hit her ankles. She grew used to it, stomping her feet in it. The water flew into the air and onto her pants. From a distance, she must look like a little kid playing in a puddle. When the wave came in, she jumped, and tried to jump back quickly when it retreated.

She turned and saw Lazarus sitting there on a blanket with her boots on it.

He took a sip of his beer. She trudged out of the water into the sand, feeling caught. As she got close, Lazarus patted the spot next to him. She took it.

"Going for a late-night dip?"

Vassa buried her feet in the sand. Her feet were already pruning. Lifting her toes from the sand, she said, "Skipping rocks."

"Skipping rocks? It didn't look like you were skipping rocks."

She showed him the leftover rocks in her hands.

Lazarus looked at the rocks and then the water. Raising the beer to his mouth, he chuckled. "You suck."

Vassa huffed out a laugh. "You don't say."

"I mean, I've skipped plenty of rocks in my lifetime. I was a Boy Scout. That's the first patch you get. You gotta work on your throwing arm, Vee."

"We can't all be baseball pitchers ." She snorted and rolled her eyes. . "You were a Boy Scout?"

He nodded, and she poked her lips out. "That explains a lot."

Lazarus flicked sand at her, and she smiled. "Are you not having fun?"

"I had chocolate and I'm freezing. I'll say I'm content."

Lazarus thrust his thumb behind him. "Doesn't look like it. You're by yourself."

"I needed to stretch my legs."

He finished his beer and stuck the bottle in the sand. "Can I ask you something?"

"You just did."

He nudged her to the side. "Smartass. I mean, I know you and Dara are close and all. What happened to you and that girl Alexa? One girl back there asked about it. I remember when you and her were together in the dorm all the time."

Vassa hung her head. "We're not friends."

Alexa continued to show up at every party she went to, it seemed. Now wasn't that a walk down memory lane. Vassa had thought things would stay the same between them when they left their hometown and came to the city... but Alexa had obviously changed and that hope had been stupidly naïve.

"We both decided it was best to go our separate ways. I mean, she's like you. Enjoys being in the crowd, parties, and what not. That's not me." Vassa pointed to herself.

He let out a short, humorless laugh. "Like me?"

"The in-crowd. We were nerds during high school. Alexa wanted to shed all that. I mean, yes, I wanted to be different, but I dunno. It didn't work out. Alexa was the only reason I went to those parties. Otherwise, you and I wouldn't have met."

A solid wall had fallen across his expression at the mention of in-crowd, but she didn't pay attention to it.

"I'll spare you the gory details, but what happened, happened. We're two different people. I'm fine just hanging out with Dara. Kiki too when she comes. I'm sure you still hang out with Alexa?"

Say you don't. Alexa had achieved the same social circle as him, even if she didn't get her claws into him. Her belly sunk. What if they were friends? There wasn't anything she could do about it, but Lazarus wasn't like Alexa. He was better than that. Or she hoped he was.

"I see her and all. It's nothing to say, really. I enjoyed talking to you more back then."

Vassa lifted an eyebrow. "You enjoyed talking to me? When you had that entire group at your beck and call?"

His cocky grin was nowhere in sight; his annoyance was palpable. "I wasn't king over them."

Vassa inspected him. It was obvious he didn't like her bringing up his popularity. There was more to him than she thought. *Why is he moody with this?*

He rolled up his pants legs and stood up. Dusting the sand off, he offered a hand to her, "Come on."

Vassa placed her hand in his. He lifted her up smoothly. She watched their connected hands as he led her closer to the water.

He bent and collected rocks. "I have to teach you how to properly skip rocks."

Vassa watched as he positioned himself like he was going to hit a ball. The waves rolled inland and dissolved into foam around their ankles.

"First, you lift high. Get a good angle." Lazarus made sure she was paying attention.

His hair looked darker in the night. Almost brown. Her eyes followed his broad shoulders and muscular arms, which strained against the confines of his jacket as he continued to explain why she needed a good stance before he tossed the rock. What was wrong with her? She had to keep some distance between them. He was partially the reason for the demise of her relationship with Alexa.

"Now you try."

He snapped her out of her reverie. Vassa mimicked his stance.

"Rotate from the hips, not the arm. That's where your power is." His expression was calculated as he bent down and moved her feet. Lightning shot up her legs where he touched and she jumped.

"Lazarus!"

"I'm sorry. Footing is important in baseball. It has to be right." He looked at her feet before he nodded. "Then you toss it."

"That easy?"

"That easy."

Vassa cleared her throat and took the rock that he held out to her. Her fingers brushed against his palms and she looked away to the water before she mimicked him. "I think I got it."

"No, no. I said swing from your hips."

"I am swinging from my hips."

Vassa tossed the rock he gave her. This one, too, sunk immediately. Lazarus groaned and rubbed his temples.

"You aren't a very patient teacher." She placed her hands on her hips.

Lazarus took the rocks from her. "Just do what I do."

He repeated the steps and tossed the rock. She did it. It sunk.

"Here, let me show you." Huffing out a breath, he stood behind her. Vassa immediately tensed when she felt his chest come flush with her back. Her eyes turned to slits.

"Don't tell me you're really trying to pull that move?"

Lazarus blinked rapidly. "What move?"

Crossing her arms, she cocked her head.

He held up his hands. "I promise no shenanigans. I'm trying to show you."

Vassa turned. *So much for keeping my distance.* She already felt mortified she thought he was going to kiss her on the roof. His body eclipsed hers, his right hand on her arm. His left hand was on her hip. His nearness made her heartbeat increase and her palms grow sweaty.

"Now swing and toss at the same time, on the count of three." She could feel his breath on her ear.

Vassa jerked her head up and down.

Once he made it to three, he forced her body to turn, and she released the rock. They held their breath as the rock skidded across the water a few times before it sunk into the water.

"I did it!" Vassa turned to Lazarus.

He smiled at her. He didn't back away. Vassa glanced up and immediately felt her heart flutter in response. She had to be strong and fight whatever this feeling was. Their faces were inches apart. He hadn't shaved, and some dark stubble was emerging on the lower part of his face. It was ruggedly sexy.

Oh my God, did I just call him ruggedly sexy?

Lazarus looked from her eyes to her lips a few times. Logic told her to move back, but her body refused. She didn't want to be embarrassed again, but why wasn't he making a joke? In an instant, her blood turned molten, and she licked her lips. She gazed at him, heart leaping out of her chest.

"Uh, thank you… for the help and whatnot. The power is in the hips and stuff…" Her soft voice trembled and she hastily turned away from him.

"Want to play This or That again?" Lazarus voice came out rough, and he cleared it.

Vassa nodded and took a step back. "Let's do something else. I want to ask this time."

Lazarus gave her a look, but let her go first. It took her a moment to come up with a question. *Who are you, Lazarus?*

"What is the strangest dream you have ever had?"

"I don't dream."

Vassa's mouth dropped. "You don't dream?"

Lazarus shook his head. "I don't."

"You're lying."

He laughed and shook his head. "I'm not!"

Who didn't dream? Even animals dreamed. "How do you not dream?"

"Trauma? The last dream I had I was six." Lazarus scratched the back of his head, a mischievous glint in his eyes.

"Six?" she gasped.

"My mom bought me a hamster. I named her Lobster—" Lazarus nodded and kicked some sand at her as she giggled,

"Lobster?"

He cut his eyes playfully at her. "It fit her personality. Anyway, I dreamed aliens came down and beamed her up. The next day, I put her in the ball next to me in bed to protect her. When I woke up, somehow she got out her ball and I rolled over on her in my sleep."

Vassa gasped and covered her mouth with her hands. He gave a sad smile and continued. "I told my brother, Gideon. He told me I was going to go to Hamster Hell, but if I gave him my allowance, he'd put in a kind word for me. I cried for days and Dad was pissed at Gideon."

She let out a low whistle. "Jesus."

"Ever since then I haven't dreamed." Lazarus shrugged, and now her heart hurt for him as a child.

Vassa's father had allergies, so she couldn't have pets. Marmalade, a dwarf hamster, had been a miracle since her fourth-grade teacher gave it to her at the end of the school year, and her dad didn't have time to argue. She grabbed his hand and squeezed. "I'm sorry for your loss."

His head tipped back, and he clutched his stomach as he laughed. "You know that was fifteen years ago?"

"A death is a death!" She huffed and crossed her arms. That's what she got for trying to be compassionate.

"I'm sorry, I'm sorry. Thank you. I know Lobster is smiling down on us from the big ball in the sky." He pointed to the sky, and they both glanced up.

She rolled her eyes. It seemed he could never stop smiling or telling a joke. She wanted to say it annoyed her, but part of her liked that. Sometimes she wished she could be like that, always a ball of energy and making people laugh.

"Now tell me yours." Lazarus kicked water at her.

"Normal stuff. Zombie apocalypse, lost in the woods, a serial killer chasing me. For a while, I dreamed I was lost in the desert with a talking snake. I had that dream almost every single day for a month. Haven't had it since."

"Hm, weird. I thought you were going to say you've had sex dreams about me." Lazarus dodged her weak hits.

"You always take things there." She kicked water at him laughing. Lazarus ducked before he bent down and splashed water on her. She screeched and ran.

No doubt this cold water would mess up her hair and her clothes were sticking to her, but it was worth it. In the past Lazarus seemed to be this one-dimensional goofball. It didn't help that she hadn't allowed herself to get to know him out of her loyalty to Alexa. That was stupid. She realized that now. Hearing about Lobster and his Boy Scout experience, she was drawn into knowing more about him. It might not be so bad tutoring him. He could teach her how to loosen up.

It was just a shame it was happening so late.

He kicked water, and it soaked her top half entirely. "My hair! I don't wanna play no more."

"C'mon Vee, don't be like that." He came closer, and she bent over, pretending to cry. Once he was near, it was too late. She pushed him, sending him into the water. His eyes bulged out of his head as he hollered. She screamed when he hopped up quicker than she expected, and she headed toward the safety of the beach. "Where are you going?" He chased her, and she laughed. It was just the two of them, splashing in the water, the music fading in the distance.

CHAPTER EIGHT

AFTER A WEEK OF CLASS and work, Fridays were glorious for Vassa because she was free from responsibility. Most of the time she slept in or studied in the library or ran errands. Today started off unusual. Her phone was ringing, and the sun wasn't up. At first, she ignored it, but it just kept going and going. Groaning, she blinked blearily at the caller ID as she answered the video chat. "Hello?"

"I guess you just don't care about your mother."

Vassa sighed and dropped her head to the bed. "Hi Ma."

"Don't *hi ma*, me. I was in labor with you for three days. You put my body through the ringer and my vagina has never been the same since."

Rubbing her temples, she sat up in bed. She wasn't going back to sleep. "We've been going over this for my entire life, Ma. I'm sorry I needed to be born."

It was Vassa's fault. She hadn't talked to her mom in over two weeks. She got ornery when Vassa went too long without phone calls.

"My body has never been the same. *Never.* Then my only child, my only daughter, doesn't call her mother for years? What did I do to deserve this punishment?"

Vassa looked at the ceiling. "I'm sorry. I got busy with class—"

"Busy with class? I'm paying for that expensive ass school and you don't call to see if I'm breathing. Do you care if your grandmother is alive? Or if your daddy's been sent to the Upper Room because a car fell on him in his mechanic shop?" Vassa's mom ranted and pointed the phone toward her grandmother.

"Eve, get that phone away from me. I'm trying to watch the news."

"Hi Grandma Laura." Vassa pouted and waved.

The connection was spotty but she could see her grandmother. Lowering her glasses, the older woman smiled. "Hi baby."

Eve turned the phone away, grumbling, and said, "Anyway, how are you, my ungrateful child? How's that bucket list coming along? Have you checked anything off of it?" Eve and Grandma Laura had encouraged her to make the list.

"I've completed two things."

"Two things? Wow." Eve's eyes widened.

Vassa stood up and placed the phone down as she made her bed. "Why'd you say it like that?"

"I just didn't think you'd do it, that's all."

Finished making her bed, Vassa rolled her eyes. "Thanks for that vote of confidence."

"I'm serious Vasilisa. I know you get touchy about it, but you haven't been the same since Alexa did you wrong—"

"*Mom.*"

"I'm just saying. You were happy. Then you became pessimistic and shut off. You know your father and I were worried about you last semester. Just a couple of days ago, I saw Alexa's mom at the grocery store. Poor thing, it seems like her husband is still a deadbeat. You know she had all those kids with her." Vassa might not care about Alexa's existence, but her mother, Sonya, was a sweet woman. It seemed like she had divorced Alexa's father, after all. "Yet you proved us wrong. Moving in by yourself, staying on top of your grades. You're about to graduate and be successful. You're getting out there again."

This was why she spaced out her mother's calls. Vassa loved her, but she was draining.

"I'm not even thinking about her, okay? She's moved on with her life." Vassa picked at the hem of her pajamas.

Eve snorted. "You may think that, but your actions tell me you aren't. I told you my colleague's niece went to your school. Grace, remember her? I gave you her number and everything. She tells me you never called or texted."

"The girl only likes pop music, likes taking selfies ninety percent of the day, and she thought Shakespeare was a fictional character. That friendship would go nowhere."

"You didn't let it. You picked one bad thing about her and cast her off." Eve sighed and Vassa fell back onto her bed.

"Mom, do we have to talk about this every time? This is old news. Let's just move on."

"Fine, I won't upset you."

Too late for that.

Eve sniffed and Vassa felt like crap. "I'm just glad you're enjoying yourself."

"I am."

"Tell me what you've done."

Vassa told Eve what she completed. Along with everything on her list and the deal with Lazarus. There was a knock on her window, and she glanced up. Lazarus was on the fire escape and pointed to the window.

"Ma, I have to go. Tell Grandma I said stay off prime time networks, it'll rot her brain. Tell Daddy I love him." She disconnected the call and rushed over to the window, unlocking it. She peered at him. "To what do I owe this unexpected visit?"

Lazarus held up the aluminum covered plate. "I made donuts. Thought you might be here."

Her stomach growled. Vassa backed out of the way so he could step inside her room. He was dressed in jeans and a band T-shirt. She stopped him and pointed. "You like Green Day?"

Lazarus looked at his shirt. "Yeah, why?"

"That's my favorite band. I had a crush on Billie Joe."

"Good information to know." He walked into the room like he owned it. Sitting on her bed, he ripped the covering off the plate, revealing donuts.

"Since when do you eat donuts, much less cook them? Bake them? How do you make donuts?" Vassa picked up one donut, inspecting it before she bit into. It was actually edible.

"I watch the cooking channel."

Vassa raised her eyebrows as she chewed. "You like the cooking channel?"

"Mom made all us boys learn to cook. She said she would be feeding into patriarchy by not teaching her sons basic housekeeping." Lazarus grinned when she grabbed another one. She had to admit, his donuts were good.

"I like the pajamas. The cartoon avocados are cute." He looked her up and down.

Vassa looked at her pajamas and reached for another donut. "Christmas present. What do you want?"

"My class got cancelled. Everyone else was busy, so I decided to see if you were here." He stretched his legs out and winked at her.

"I'm the last resort?"

He frowned. "I was saving the best for last."

Vassa cleaned the plate. A smirk was on his face and no doubt his ego was inflated. Maybe if she got desperate one day, she'd ask him to teach her how to make them.

"I have a few small errands. I haven't been to Green Apple Books in a while. I thought I'd spend the day there."

Lazarus rubbed his hands together. "That sounds like fun."

"You're not invited." Vassa passed him the empty plate.

Lazarus's mouth dropped. "You're going to dangle the carrot?"

Her Fridays were her sacred time.

"Please, can I come? Pretty please?"

Before she knew it, he had sat up on the bed. He moved the plate away and they were inches apart. His eyes slowly ran down her face to her body. Even in her dorky pajamas, he shamelessly scanned every bit of her.

She tried to be strong before he held his hands together, giving her his infamous puppy dog expression. Vassa didn't want to be affected, but she felt herself yielding. He took her hands into his own. They were still big and warm, like that night on the beach. She repressed a sigh.

"Can I, Vee?"

It's the way he said "Vee." She didn't know why, but she was nodding. He smiled and dropped her hand, breaking the spell.

"I need to change." Vassa didn't look at him as she stood, running a hand over her face. Something was wrong with her. Why was she being nice to Lazarus Gilbert?

"I'll await with bated breath. You like? That was from the poem." Lazarus stood up.

"That's corny." She shook her head as he laughed, disappearing up the fire escape.

Everything she did was interesting to Lazarus. After meeting him in the lobby with her tote bag and list in hand, she directed him to their destinations for that day. They stopped at a grocery store nearby. They battled over the cart before he won and she gave him strict instructions to not play with it in the store. With a pen in hand, they went aisle by aisle, finding everything she needed.

"I need instant coffee; I forget it every time I come in here. Dara wants plums too." Vassa's voice trailed off as she stood amid the chaos in the fruit department, her tongue poking out the side of her mouth.

"Hey look, coconuts," he said.

Lazarus placed the coconuts in front of his chest and wriggled his eyebrows. "Don't stare at my coconuts."

Vee snorted and rolled her eyes. "That's immature."

Lazarus set the coconuts down and grabbed the grapes. "What do you think? Does it accentuate my neck or my eyes?"

He held an enormous bunch of grapes at both ears. Turning from side to side, he raised his eyebrow at her. "Thoughts? Or is green not my color?"

Vee fought the smile as she rubbed her nose. "That's unsanitary. People need to eat that."

He offered her the grapes. "How about you model them?"

"No."

"Please? If not, I'm gonna be forced to do a Carmen Miranda impersonation that may or may not involve security escorting us out..."

She sighed, took the grapes from him, and held them up to her ears. "Is this all?"

"I'm gonna need a little excitement from you." He crossed his arms.

Vee cut her eyes to him before she plastered on a smile, still holding the grapes. "This enough?"

Lazarus yawned.

She huffed out a breath. Looking side to side. She wiggled and lowered the grapes. "There."

"What in the world was that?" His jaw dropped.

"Dancing."

"That was dancing?" Lazarus pointed at the grapes.

Customers streamed past them and she ducked her head. "Can we just go?"

"I need to see your best Carmen Miranda or we're not going anywhere."

She squinted and looked around them. There was an old lady at the cantaloupes, but mostly, no one was paying attention.

She frowned, and he tried really hard to hold back his laughter. Vee swung her hips from side to side. Holding the fruits, she lifted them up and down; she looked like an animatronic. It wasn't the best Carmen Miranda impression, but it would do.

Getting comfortable, she did a spin with the fruit, surprising him by finding her rhythm. She moved back and forth easily, offering him the fruit before pulling away at the last second. She even threw in a little shimmy and some footwork. Lazarus didn't know what to say. Vee turned just as the older woman began staring at them with her mouth open.

Vee lowered the grapes before she walked stiffly away. He chuckled, and she sent him a deadly look. "That was great."

"I can't believe you made me do that," she whispered.

"You liked it."

The rest of their trip went without a hitch. She struggled to make it out of the store with the bag and he stepped in, despite her complaints, and easily maneuvered the bags onto his shoulders. They sat on together on the bus. To his surprise, she pulled out her headphones and offered him one earbud. He nodded, and she placed one in his ear so he could listen.

"Have you heard of Keelan Donovan before? He's super good." She moved in closer.

He watched the way she explained her playlist. He wasn't sure what prompted her to let her guard down, but he learned that the less he teased her, the more she talked. It was tough; he loved teasing her. She always got flustered. But now it seemed he only knew one side of her. The grumpy and closed-off side. This side of her was more relaxed. He didn't want to say the wrong thing that would have her clamping up. So, he settled for nodding and smiling.

By the time they got to Clement Street where Green Apple Books was, she almost ran to the store, leaving him with the bags. There were carts of books outside for a discount price. She scanned the backs before another book called her attention. She moved inside the store and Lazarus followed.

Books lined shelves and were stacked on tables. A bestseller wall was directly to his right. The dry scent of books filled his nose, and the creaking of the wood beneath their feet filled the silence. What caught his attention was the room with music albums to the left.

Vee veered off to the stack of books. Lazarus stepped into

the empty album room. Vinyls, tapes, and CDs were stacked in boxes ranging from gospel to country. Setting the grocery bags on a nearby chair, he ventured to the nearest stack.

He flipped through the Alternative box. *Toad the Wet Sprocket, The Pretty Reckless, Deftones, Neutral Milk Hotel*... All of his favorite bands there. There was one in particular he was looking for... He held it up triumphantly and out the corner of his eye he found a listening station to listen to the album. Pulling out the record, he placed it on the stylus and sat in the chair before placing the headphones on.

The beat was eerie. Echoes of the ocean's waves and xylophones sounded before the drums kicked in. He tapped his feet to the beat before the singing began. For a moment he was back at home, in his room on a Saturday morning. It was the one authentic place he could sit and relax with no worries. No one was watching him or expecting anything.

He jumped when he felt a hand on his thigh. Opening his eyes, Vee was standing there. He took off the headphones.

"Are you okay?" she asked.

"Yeah. Amazing actually."

She held a stack of books. "You looked like you were sleeping." Vee nodded toward the vinyl. "What are you listening to?"

Faint music could be heard from the headphones as he offered them to her. "Wanna listen?"

She nodded and took his seat. He placed the headphones over her head. He watched her face as she went from confusion to neutrality to interest. He smiled when her foot tapped along to the beat.

"Who is this?!" she shouted.

He winced before picking up the vinyl cover. "Lyyke Li."

Vee took the cover from him. She ran her fingers over the album before she said, "I love her voice. It's kinda haunting and creepy but in a good way." He laughed, and Vee took the headphones off saying. "I thought actual albums were dead?"

Lazarus sucked his teeth. "Not yet. There's a small group of us who know the true way to still listen to music."

"A small group of you?" The corners of her mouth turned up.

"Yes, and I am a proud member."

Vee nodded and looked down at the cover once more. "You love music that much?"

"I only love one thing more than it. For a while I wanted to get into music producing or something like that."

"Why didn't you do that? We have a music department."

Lazarus made a face. "My brother. He said it wasn't reliable, so.... just listened to him."

"That was sucky of him to say." Vee grimaced and ran her hands along the other vinyls.

He laughed. He wasn't expecting her to be so bold in judging Harvey. "A lot of people think Harvey sucks. He's my brother and he just wants me to be successful." *No matter how flawed he is at times.*

"By crushing your dreams? If music is something you're passionate about you, do it. You know how many people told me I won't make it with writing? You follow whatever is in your heart."

Her words sat with him, could he tell her it was his fault of Harvey's deep distrust? "Even if you don't know what it is? Or rather you know but you aren't too confident about it?"

Vee didn't make a face or judge him. Her features softened. "I like to think there's something innate in all of us that leads us to our passions. We just have to be brave and follow it."

Lazarus placed his hands in his pockets. "What do you want to be?"

Vee blew out a breath. "A professor. I'm a first-generation student, so academia and stuff are pretty new to me, but I love it. I know it's for me. I love writing, as if you couldn't tell. Words, stories, and poems, stuff like that just makes me feel alive. I don't know why I always felt drawn to it." She blinked up at him with those brown eyes. It made him feel warm inside.

"I wish I could be as passionate as you." Regret crept into

the pit of his gut. If he had been smarter earlier on, maybe he would have been as passionate as her about something. Been a better student and still had his family's respect.

"What makes you feel alive?"

That made him blink. *Besides baseball, what was there?* How did he know for sure event planning was going to be his passion? Lazarus cleared his throat. After several seconds of silence, she took his hand and squeezed it. "Let's go upstairs. There're more books."

She navigated the shelves easily. He followed her, heading to the second floor to the literary fiction section. Vee squealed as she picked up a book and showed it to him.

"Haruki Murakami, have you read him before?"

Lazarus shook his head. "What does he write? Sad stories?"

Vee made a horrified face.

"Was that the wrong thing to say?"

"Yes, it was. You know, if you were with anyone else, you might have lost your life." She sniffed and flipped through the pages.

"You literary types are dangerous, huh?" He ran his hand across the other books on the shelf.

Vassa flipped through pages. "I would describe Murakami's style as magical realism. Minimalistic. Just a pinch to make you doubt reality."

"That seems… cool? Acid-trip-like."

Vassa pushed her glasses up the brim of her nose. "Cool doesn't cut it. Have a seat and let me enlighten you."

There were two bean bags nearby. They took them and Vassa pushed her hair behind her ear as she opened the book. She looked to check if he was ready before reading. Lazarus couldn't remember the last time he had been read to. His mom used to read to him all the time, but it had been years.

His world narrowed down to just Vee.

Her voice was firm. The words tumbled with ease; he held on to them. He could imagine her being a professor. He knew her students would be enamored by her. She'd probably write tons of research papers and win awards. Write a best-selling book. Everyone would know her name. He could see it now.

Him? Still a question mark. His phone buzzed again with an incoming message, but he took his phone out and placed it on silent. Vee continued to read, now seemingly more for herself than him, and finished the page, setting the book on her lap.

"What did you think?"

He scratched his cheek. "I thought it was pretty cool. Seems like it's going to be an interesting story."

Vassa's feet tapped against the floor in excitement. "Apparently the main character is looking for a cat and his wife."

Lazarus didn't know how that would be interesting, but he was sure it would be. A sad expression fell across her face. "I can only hope for this one day."

"What?" Lazarus sat up.

Vassa looked at him, then back at the book. "I probably shouldn't be telling you this. You probably don't care but…" She exhaled and closed her eyes. "Holding my book in my hands. Having other people read it? It's all I want but sometimes it just feels so far away I don't know when I will get there."

They stared at one another. Vee looked down, her fingers tracing the book. "I want to write something that will really affect people, ya know? Not just writing and then flops. No reaction, no nothing."

Lazarus could understand how she felt. That's how he felt about baseball. Each time he was out on the field, he was creating an impact. He was doing something. What would he be after it all ended?

She placed the book in her lap and clasped her hands on top of it. "Sometimes I think I'm the worst writer in the world—"

"You're not."

"You don't know that. You have read nothing of mine." Vee raised an eyebrow.

Lazarus scratched his chin. "You haven't let me."

Vassa looked down. "You're right."

"If it's okay with you, can I read something of yours one day?" he asked quietly.

She smiled and looked at the book before she nodded. Light from outside streamed into the store, illuminating her brown eyes. There was a small dimple in the corner of her mouth. He hadn't noticed before. He scooted closer to her, trying to prevent their voices from disturbing other customers, but he just wanted to be near her. She smelled amazing. It was paradise and torture at the same time.

She was the first to break contact, clearing her throat before she stood up with the Murakami book in her hand. "I'm just going to get this."

Lazarus picked up the bags. She took one of them from him to help him. "I'm going to get this." He waved his album.

"I like her, I might listen to her again sometime." Vee licked her lips and looked over at the stack of books, then back to him. They smiled, and once they bought their items, they headed to the bus stop bound for home. Vee placed her hand over his and he turned her hand over to entwine his fingers with hers.

CHAPTER NINE

"WE'RE GOING TO HAVE SAM and Vassa for workshop next week," Vassa's writing professor dismissed the class. Vassa put her notebook into her book bag but couldn't feel more despondent.

Why are there so many creative people in the world? The poems and stories she heard from her peers were amazing. One girl wrote a six-page story from the perspective of a murder weapon. Her stuff paled in comparison. It didn't help that a week had gone by and she hadn't done anything remotely creative. She was either in class, at work, or tutoring Lazarus.

"I never thought to use a flamingo to represent the loss of innocence, but it works." Oscar walked up with his bag slung over his shoulder.

Who would have thought to use a flamingo? Weren't they the only unproblematic birds of the ecosystem?

"I'm stuck trying to get any words out." Vassa shoved her books in with more force than necessary.

"You're an amazing writer, I'm not worried."

Vassa felt better. Still, compared to him, or the others, she really needed to catch up. She hoped the samples she sent for the grad program were good enough.

"I just need that to translate into an amazing story." They exited the classroom, walking side by side through the crowd of other students. They made it out of the building and headed toward the cafeteria.

"Oh, were you busy this afternoon? We could get coffee, and exchange work before workshop." Oscar glanced at his watch.

Vassa's eyes widened, and she looked up at him. He wanted to go get coffee with her? She pushed her glasses up the bridge of her nose. "Coffee?"

Oscar nodded. "There's a cool spot in the Sunset. Grinders, have you heard of it?"

She and Alexa used to go there often.

"They have great cappuccinos and pies. You should try the triple berry pie." Oscar held his stomach as he imagined it.

Vassa nodded. "Uh yeah. That sounds really good but—"

Oscar stopped her. "Don't break my heart. You already said no to Word Slam."

Vassa knew that Oscar wasn't a part of Alexa's world. He didn't think Vassa was the villain like everyone else thought she was. She must be paranoid. Oscar wouldn't take anything she said and spread it around campus and weaponize it for his own gain.

Get it together. This is supposed to be your best semester! She couldn't let the past control her anymore.

So even though it was hard, she said: "Sure, that sounds fun."

Oscar smiled and placed his hands into his pockets. "Great, let's go!"

It was a quaint coffeeshop in a residential neighborhood. The place buzzed as employees called out orders, drowning out the murmur of voices and background music.

"Thanks for inviting me," Vassa said as they sat down after ordering. Flipping open her notebook, she tried to find the pages of the poems she had written.

"No, thanks for coming. I'm just stoked you're here." Oscar relaxed in the chair and he cocked his head. "Why does it sound like a but is coming soon?"

She sipped her cappuccino. "I'm struggling with my story."

"You're struggling? You always have it so together." Oscar's eyebrows dipped.

Vassa laughed. "Me? I'm the last person to have it together. Now you? You always have it together."

"While I'm flattered, I don't have it all together. I doubt any human being in the world knows what they're doing half the time." Oscar laughed and shook his head.

"I need your secret to great writing."

Oscar smiled. "Aren't we paying for it with this English degree?" They laughed, drawing some curious looks from customers nearby. Oscar cleared his throat. "So, how are you feeling about class so far? There's been some good and... bad writing, but I think the class overall has been better than any I've had before."

"I love it. The flamingo story still has me shocked," Vassa said.

Oscar shrugged. "Is having a plan any more helpful, or is it applying pressure on ourselves?"

Vassa took another sip and set the cup down. "I think it's better."

"I think it's worse."

Vassa inspected him for a moment.

"I see that look, now hear me out." Oscar held up his hands. Vassa nodded and let him speak.

"Spontaneity is opportunity. I'm not saying don't have dreams or goals—that pot at the end of the rainbow—but plans destroy all the lovely possibilities that could be. Don't plan your way out of opportunity. Just from my own mistakes."

"Your own mistakes?"

Oscar nodded. "It's a long story, but I was angry for a long time. I'm over it now. I just know what it means to be tough. It doesn't help you."

That was all nice in theory, but theory didn't always pan out. That was a fact. She had learned life was a bit of disappointment more than anything. At least her plan would prevent it from happening again.

"I didn't know you were Dr. Phil," Vassa said.

She was partially serious about that.

Oscar shrugged. "I would say I get some sense from the women in my life."

"Women in your life?"

"My aunts, mother, sisters, and cousins. I'm the product of their hard work and sacrifice."

Vassa said nothing else. She found the poem she wanted him to look at.

"Should we begin?"

Oscar nodded before flipping to his own poem. "I can't wait to read yours."

For the next couple of hours, she and Oscar worked through their poems. They steered clear from theoretical talks of the future, and it was dark outside when they packed up their things. He held the door open for her and she thanked him as they walked to the bus stop. "I say we do this again."

Vassa nodded. She checked to see the arrival time of the bus. "Yeah, definitely." Oscar wasn't that bad. It just took her a while to relax. She didn't trust him yet, but he was a brilliant partner to get feedback from.

"Just text me and we can make another date." She could see the bus coming down the street now and she fished in her pocket for her bus pass.

"Speaking of, some classmates are having a small get together at their apartment tonight. You're welcome to come."

A jolt shot through her. Going to someone's apartment that she didn't know? That was a no from her. She couldn't do that. She wouldn't do that. That would just be so awkward, and she was not good at small talk.

Then she thought about Dara, how she was hanging out with all those people. *Why can't I do the same?*

She had opened her mouth to respond when he held up a hand.

"Think about it. I think it could be fun and you're really cool. Everyone would love you."

"This isn't that writing group you were talking about?"

Oscar shook his head. "That's something different. I swear. I'll convince you to come to that too, though, eventually."

Vassa thought about her empty apartment. She had heard nothing from Dara or Lazarus. If she didn't go, she would just go back to her room and watch reruns of *The Golden Girls*.

"I would like to come."

"I think you would like it, please…" Oscar blinked. "Wait, what?"

"I would love to come. Tonight, you said?"

He nodded. "Um, yeah, tonight. I can give you the address or pick you up—"

"Pick me up, that sounds great."

It was like ripping off a Band-Aid. She just had to do it. She had to be brave if she wanted her reality to change.

The bus arrived and Oscar waited for her to get on. She waved to him and exhaled as the bus took off. She was going to a party.

CHAPTER TEN

"IT'S MOSTLY OTHER ENGLISH MAJORS. You'll love them," Oscar said for the third time in less than a minute as he knocked on the apartment door.

He shifted the bags of alcohol he brought and Vassa stood there awkwardly, pulling on the hem of her dress. The front door opened and a redheaded girl she had seen before in classes appeared. She hugged Oscar before looking Vassa up and down and offering to shake Vassa's hand.

"It's so nice to meet you. I'm Lisa. We've had classes together before, right?"

Oscar bobbed his head as Vassa slowly nodded. He seemed to be more excited about this than she was. Lisa stepped aside to allow them in. It was a tight fit, but the place was homey, with mismatched furniture and string lights around the ceiling. They stepped into the living room to find a group of students and the smell of cigarettes and pizza. Oscar passed the alcohol to Lisa and led Vassa to an open spot on the couch. She folded her hands together in her lap, taking everything in.

The people looked mostly familiar. She was surprised to see some people who had graduated last year in the room. Vassa looked into the kitchen, and if she leaned back farther, she could see a small patio. On the coffee table in front of her was a charcuterie board and bottles of wine. Oscar reached into a bag and placed a board game on the table.

"Hope you're all ready to lose," Oscar said, causing laughter. He shifted his jacket off and turned to her, offering to help with her jacket.

"Do you drink, Vassa? I have wine, kombucha, ice coffee..." Lisa said.

"Wine, some wine would be good." Liquid courage was what she needed right now.

Oscar asked for a glass as well. Lisa disappeared into the kitchen. *Should I just turn to someone and speak?* It didn't look like anyone recognized her, so she doubted Alexa's reign went that far. After Alexa had ousted her on social media, tagging almost every person on campus, it was hard not to find someone who thought she was "Vassa the Impaler" or just a backstabbing bitch.

Oscar got up, saying he'd be back before leaving her on the couch. She had to fight the urge to pull out her phone and pretend to look busy. Stressed, she reached into her bag and opened her pack of Twizzlers. There were two guys and a girl on the opposite couch.

Oscar came back, to her relief. Plopping down, he leaned over and whispered, "Those are some of the grad students in the writing department. They're teaching assistants for some of us, but really cool. So don't worry about them ratting."

"Oscar, you're here!"

Vassa and Oscar turned to see a girl with pretty dark skin and a shaved head. A beer in hand, she cocked her hip as she smiled at Oscar.

"Melinda." Oscar grinned.

Vassa tried to hide her smile when Oscar popped up and rushed to hug her. When they pulled away, Melinda and Oscar eyed one another until Vassa cleared her throat.

"Melinda, have you met Vassa? She's a writer and poet. I'm trying to get her to join our writing group,"

Recognition passed over Melinda's face and she offered to shake Vassa's hand.

"Yes! I think I've heard you perform at Word Slam before.

Oscar talked a lot about you. Are you going to come? We could use some fresh blood. I'm tired of hearing Oscar ramble about the fog rolling in."

"Hey, I thought you said you liked that?" Oscar's eyes never left Melinda.

Vassa swallowed her Twizzler. "Um, I work a lot… so, you know how that is." Gosh, even her excuses sounded lame.

"Totally, we're starting in two weeks. Think about it, I know you're probably gonna speak at Word Slam anyway…" Melinda talked animatedly with her hands.

Melinda was nice. Lisa appeared with their wine and joined in the conversation. Vassa loosened her grip on the glass, finding herself smiling and laughing as they talked about a psycho professor they both shared.

Oscar stepped to the side to set up the game. That brought attention to her. Then the questions rolled in. What dorm did she live in or did she live off campus, how did she feel about the last semester, and what were her plans afterward? The wine definitely helped her, and she was feeling pretty nice… It might have made her too friendly because she blurted out the graduate schools she applied to.

Nina, the girl sitting across from her, asked, "You're really applying for an MFA? I thought they said those were dead. What schools are you hoping for?"

Vassa didn't think MFA degrees were dead, but she took a sip of her wine.

"NYU, Iowa, and BU. Just to name a few, and I tossed in a few Ivy Leagues for the hell of it." Vassa chuckled awkwardly before clearing her throat. She reached to snatch an olive from the tray.

"Those are top programs; you think you're good enough for that? I had a perfect grade point average, was published in multiple literary magazines, and they didn't accept me. Have you been published anywhere? Won any awards? Let me know if they let you in," the guy next to her said.

The group laughed, and the smile dropped from Vassa's face.

"Tom." Oscar looked up from setting up the board. Melinda gave Vassa a look of encouragement.

Vassa began, "I'm not published in a magazine yet but I've submitted—"

"If you want a career in academia and writing, you need a publication. Doing it yourself on some website means nothing," the guy said. Someone else laughed too before going on about the merits of not wasting money on an MFA and how writing credits were more important. Vassa took a gulp of wine.

"You know, most of the seniors from PGU applied to those places. They got rejected," Nina said.

"You have to be a really excellent writer or totally naïve to think you can just walk into those programs." Marie sipped her kombucha.

"Vassa is a dope writer. I'm sure she has this in the bag," Melinda said.

Everyone in the group looked at her.

"I… am good. Yes, I am." Vassa sat up straighter.

The group across from her gave her a doubtful look.

"Vassa's a talented writer, I know she is." Oscar placed a hand on her shoulder and gave her an encouraging smile.

Vassa wanted to get up and walk away.

"You're not supposed to be just good. You need to be great. Or you'll be in the unemployment line using up our taxpaying dollars," Tom said.

There was awkward laughter, and Vassa thought about Dara. She was passionate about her art. A few seconds passed and Vassa was surprised they just let what Tom said drop.

"I don't know how fair that is," Vassa blurted out.

No one said anything and Lisa spoke up. "You know who is good that isn't here today? Kyle. That story he wrote about the missing father and son? Totally original and mind-blowing."

"Why isn't he here?" Nina asked.

There was a murmur of agreement and Vassa sucked in a deep breath. It looked like it was going to be a rough night.

Oscar clapped his hands, calling everyone's attention to the board game. "We're doing Scrabble in teams and this round is Clabbers. So only anagrams are allowed."

Vassa wasn't in the mood to play anymore but she gave him a strained smile and nodded. Oscar explained his strategy to Vassa. He was excited about the game, but she had to admit this was one of the nerdiest and most stereotypical English major things she had ever done. Once the tiles were distributed, the game was on. Under pressure, she was having trouble thinking of words longer than three letters.

"Vassa, you start us off," Lisa said.

All eyes were on her. Taking a deep breath, she placed her tiles on the table. "Five-letter word, heart."

Tom snorted. A murmur passed through the room and she turned to Oscar. "Was that good?"

Oscar clapped and that brought her spirits up. "It's perfect."

Each team went. She had a bunch of dud words after that, but Oscar held the team down. She found herself listening to conversations around her. The more some of these people talked, the more she realized she didn't care for them. People like Melinda were nice, but most of the others were a bit snobby. That was the exact reason she kept her distance. They all appeared nice and together, but their insides were not the same.

"Chutzpah." Melinda slammed the tiles down on the board.

"That's cheating!" Oscar said.

Melinda shook her head. "No, it's not. That's seventy-seven points. Mark it down."

"Just wait a minute..." The room erupted with accusations of cheating.

Vassa used the moment to get up to use the restroom and refill her wine cup.

In the restroom, she glanced at her phone. There was no

message from Dara, but she had one from Lazarus. Her heart jumped, and she clicked the message instantly.

Came downstairs but you were gone. Where r u?

Normally, she would have given him sass, but she was grateful for his distraction.

A small get-together.

His response was instant:

Ooh party! You? Is the sky falling? Where?

I wanna come, I'll bring praline ice cream and pretzels.

Lazarus would probably make all the snobs like him.

Haha, but not your crowd.

Vassa looked into the mirror, fixing her makeup. She just needed to step out and get some air. Her phone buzzed again.

Is it yours?

Vassa exited the bathroom. There was still laughter and yelling from the living room. As she entered, they were debating if Clint Eastwood counted as an anagram for "old west action." Vassa backed into the kitchen and was topping off her glass when people stepped inside from the patio.

"Vassa, do you smoke?" Lisa lifted the cigarette box.

Vassa shook her head. "I'm more of a drinker."

Nina was next to her, lifting her cup. "Can you top me off?"

Vassa filled her cup. The brown-haired girl thanked her before the blonde said,

"Come out on the porch with us."

She really didn't want to do that, but she nodded and followed them, anyway. The patio wasn't big; it was a small area no bigger than the inside of the apartment. They had strung up some lights, and dying potted plants sat around the porch border.

Besides the girls, Tom was there with a cigarette. She groaned inwardly when he looked up and his eyebrows dipped at her.

"This is a nice patio," Vassa muttered. She looked into her wine.

"It is, isn't it?" Lisa said.

"It's a patio, what do you expect?" Tom rolled his eyes.

Vassa looked at him, and the other girls did too. Lisa cleared her throat.

"I don't think we've seen you around much. Do you come to the reading nights?"

Vassa shook her head. She had done it freshman year when it was a requirement. Other than that, she hadn't been. "I have work."

"People dedicated to writing would be there," Tom said.

Vassa looked at him.

"I'm just saying. If you want to be a writer, you need to be around other writers."

She scratched her head.

"Not necessarily, Tom—" Lisa began.

"Yes, necessarily," Tom mocked Lisa. Nina stood there drinking as he pointed his cigarette at her.

Vassa was getting really irritated with this guy. He was a total ignorant snob. *How in the hell did he become a teaching assistant?* Her heart went out to any student who had to work with him. She wanted to kick him in the face.

"Who are you to decide who's a writer and who's not? Some people have families or work to support themselves." Vassa gripped her cup tighter.

Tom looked at her. "If you're forty trying to dream about being a writer or you don't have the time to dedicate and get good at the craft, give up."

Vassa narrowed her eyes. "Are you serious?"

Tom took a drag of his cigarette, flicking the ashes onto the plants. "I am."

She looked at Lisa and Nina but neither said anything.

"Let's get back to the conversation we were having before. Commercial literature is ruining fiction. We went from Mark Twain to online teens writing vampire sagas."

Nina and Lisa agreed like robots.

Vassa thought about all the fantasy and romance books she had on her shelves. "What's wrong with commercial fiction?"

Tom looked at her like she was stupid.

"It's airport fiction. Things you pick up when you're waiting for your layover. Nothing that adds to our culture. How many more romances and witch books do we need? It's just rehashing the same plot," Tom said.

Vassa sucked in a deep breath. She *was* going to kick Tom in the face. She just knew it.

"Henry James, George Eliot, or D. H. Lawrence are what we should read, and everything else is a no."

"I agree." Lisa tossed in.

"Those stories are for the uneducated, weak-minded majority who know no better. What they enjoy reading is a danger to highbrow literature," Nina said.

The three of them laughed, and Vassa stood there feeling sick to her stomach. This was elitist behavior. Who were they to judge people that liked to read fantasy or romance? All literature was readable and should be read, whether it was about vampires or existential crises.

Vassa turned from the patio and reached into her purse for her phone.

Are you busy?

She waited a few seconds and Lazarus responded,

Listening to the Lykke Li album, what's up?

Vassa's fingers flew across the screen.

Can you pick me up?

Vassa knew it was time to go. There was no way she could stay here and pretend to like these people. So much for this party if these were the kinds of people Oscar considered friends. She should have listened to her gut and went home.

For you? Of course.

Vassa gave Lazarus her address, and he said he could be there in less than fifteen minutes. She sat in the kitchen; it was a safe spot. She was on her third cup of wine when Lazarus told her he was outside. She wobbled a bit but caught her footing and grabbed her coat as she slid by Oscar, who was absorbed in trying to figure out what Melinda was supposed to be in a game of charades. She thought about telling Oscar she was leaving, but she didn't have a chance to because he caught sight of her.

"You're leaving?"

"Yeah, I'm just tired. I have some homework to finish."

"I'll take you home. Let me get my keys."

"No, I called a ride. Thank you so much for inviting me, really. I'll see you in Professor Fernández's class on Tuesday." Vassa didn't give Oscar a chance to respond. She opened the front door, rushing down the stairs.

She didn't give Lazarus a chance to say hello before she said, "Drive. Please."

Lazarus gave her a look, but did as she asked. They drove in silence, the music low.

"You look nice," Lazarus said.

She turned to him. The streetlights cast the inside of the car in an orange glow. Lazarus's stare on her made her feel hotter, and she pulled at her dress.

"Thank you."

They pulled up to a red light when a thought came to her.

"Can we not go back home yet? Please."

Lazarus looked at her in confusion. He ran a hand through his hair, causing it to fluff up. She wanted to run her hands through it.

"Where do you want to go?"

That was a good question.

"Some place quiet."

Lazarus stared at her. In the dark, his eyes looked almost

black the traffic light turned green, and they pulled forward.

"Your wish is my command."

She clutched the seat as his car chugged up the hill.

It took her a moment to realize they were heading up to Twin Peaks. It was normally crowded with tourists but at this time of night, it was bare. The triple-pronged Sutro Tower glowed in the night, blinking slowly on and off. The farther they climbed, the more breathtaking the night skyline of San Francisco became. Vassa pulled on her thin leather jacket once they were out of the car and they strolled to the viewing area.

She embraced the cold on her exposed thighs as she sat on the concrete bench. A constellation of lights caught her eye. She thought it was Oakland.

"You come here often too?" Vassa exhaled loudly. He put on a jean jacket that shouldn't have made him look like a bad boy, but it did.

"Another getaway of mine."

Vassa nodded as she looked at the city. She felt him nudge her. "You seem upset. Something happen?"

Tom was nothing she wanted to remember and wasn't worth a rehashing. She settled for shrugging.

"That bad, huh?" Lazarus said.

"Yep."

"Is it as bad as that time you puked up chocolate milk on those cheerleaders?"

She snorted. "Possibly."

There wasn't much light up where they were. A few lamps about thirty feet apart. It made the moment more intimate and secluded. She stole a glance at him, and he was right there. She didn't understand how he could be so big, but move so quietly. Licking her lips, she swallowed. She realized they were truly alone up here. They could do anything. He could do anything to her.

"You know you can talk to me. I'm a good listener."

"You're a good listener?"

Lazarus nodded. "Trust me."

Trust. That was something she didn't do. Oh, how she wanted to, but something was screaming to keep everything to herself. No matter how much she wanted to talk to someone at the moment. She had to protect herself. What if he took what she said and blabbed it?

His blue eyes held her gaze, and she rocked in her seat. What choice did she have? Dara was off God knows where. Her mom was probably asleep. Lazarus was the only one around.

She narrowed her eyes at him. "Pinky promise?"

Lazarus lowered his eyebrows. "What?"

Vassa held up her pinky and wriggled it.

"What I say stays between us. It doesn't go anywhere. Can... Can I truly trust you? This is a lot for me right now."

He looked at her pinky. She wriggled it again, and he grinned before he held up his own pinky.

"I swear."

They entwined their pinkies and Vassa looked at him. This was frightening. She was confiding in Lazarus Gilbert. The last person she would ever expect.

She let out a breath before she fixed her gaze forward. "I was hanging out with some people in my major. Nice at first, but they turned out rude. Totally elitist snobs. I felt really uncomfortable being there, but I felt I had to stay. Oscar wanted me to come."

Vassa didn't want to add she had gotten into an argument with a few of them. Or that they had basically told her that her writing wasn't good enough to get into a top writing program. It hurt her feelings, but she wouldn't let anyone know that. She had to be tough.

Lazarus whistled. "That sucks."

"Who are you telling?" Regret immediately washed over

her. Maybe she shouldn't have said anything.

"Maybe you can take it as a lesson."

Vassa made a face and looked at him.

"Jayden's always on me about the universe sending us lessons and crap like that." Lazarus rolled his eyes. "These people sucked. Now you know not to be a snobby elitist literature writer. You can teach your students not to be like that when you become a professor. Raise a whole new generation of non-snobs."

She had to smile at his effort. That made her feel better. "I don't know. I haven't gotten into a writing program yet. What if I don't get in? Everything I've sacrificed for it will be in vain."

"When do you get decisions?"

"Late March to early April."

"That's not long. I know who you are, Vee. You're an amazing, talented, and lovable grump who's gonna do amazing things."

"Lovable grump?"

Lazarus grinned. "You know you are."

Vassa rolled her eyes. She disagreed with that. She was only grumpy with him. He was always teasing her and embarrassing her.

"Should I add life coach to your own long list of accolades? Baseball player, most popular guy, troublemaker, and life coach?"

Vassa laughed, but her smile faded when she saw him frown and shake his head.

"Those aren't my labels. Those are the boxes people put me in."

"So, you're telling me you don't like it? The privileges it gives you?"

Vassa couldn't understand. That's who he was. That's all she'd known him to be. The It guy. With all the friends and people following behind him. What genuine problems could he have? Deciding what teacher he was going to schmooze that day?

He blew out his cheeks before leaning back. He looked toward the city. "Can I be honest with you?"

She blinked. "Why would you want to be honest with me?"

"I feel like... I can just be myself. I'm not Lazarus, the baseball player. I'm just me."

Her mouth went dry. What could she say to that? She held his stare, and she saw something she had never seen in his eyes before. *Vulnerability.* There weren't any wisecracks or pranks coming. It was just him.

"I mean, if you want to. Yeah, sure."

Lazarus licked his lips. "I'm jealous of you."

"What?" Vassa recoiled.

He nodded. Why on earth would he be jealous of her? Unlimited yoga classes or her burrito meal card? Twizzlers?

"I remember freshman year when you and Alexa would come around. Your friend, she was always in our faces acting and stuff. I was acting too, but you just sat there. Trying to educate us 'heathens,' is that what you called us? About why we need to read Eric Jerome Dickey and Jane Austen. That somehow they correlate?"

Vassa laughed. She remembered that. Alexa had given her a stern talking to about being "cool" around other people. They couldn't still be the nerds they were in high school. Vassa shook her head. "You made me confess, now you buddy."

Lazarus gave her a look before he huffed out a breath. "I want to get into event management. It's a growing field and I think I could do it. I need to get an internship. Most entry-level jobs want you to have some experience but it's too late for an internship for me. I'm hoping to fix my resume and make a website..."

This shocked Vassa. He actually had plans. She hadn't heard him mention it before. Music, plants, and computers. Lazarus got more and more interesting.

"Gideon thinks it's a good idea. Harvey doesn't think it's a good idea. He says I'm just trying to party but it's not true."

Vassa bit her lip. "I thought you liked to party?"

"I mean I do." He cut his eyes at her, she could tell she wasn't getting the full story. "But that's not my entire personality anymore. I'm trying to prove to him I'm trustworthy."

"Why do you need to prove it to him?" Her brows dipped.

Lazarus opened his mouth and then closed it. "Nothing too serious. Just, he's my brother, you know. I care about his opinion." Vassa missed the way his eyes darted away and he coughed.

"No offense, but this Harvey sounds like an asshole."

Lazarus roared with laughter. "None taken. He is, but I just have to deal with it for now."

Vassa wanted to know more but the tension rolling off of him was suffocating. Obviously, something had happened with his brother, and Vassa couldn't help but feel bad for him. Harvey was punishing him for his reckless days. It was completely unfair. She wanted to comfort him.

Vassa scooted closer. He watched her as she placed her arm around him, pressing her body closer to his. She hugged him, patting his back. He stiffened before he leaned into her embrace, and she laid her head on his shoulder.

"You're a pain in the ass Lazarus, but you will be a success. I'll even help you with your resume and website. I took a coding class last semester. I'm rooting for you."

She could feel the deep rumbles of his laughter. "Was that your attempt at comforting me?"

"Take it or leave it."

They sat like that for a moment, and she leaned back to look up at him. Delight swept through her when he glanced down with a shy smile, his hands sliding farther down her back. For a second, she forgot all about the fact that she wasn't supposed to be interested in him and contemplated kissing him. He was staring at her so intensely that the blood coursing through her made her hands shake.

She swallowed, aware that she could hear both their breathing over the noise of the wind. He was so very close to her she could feel his heat through her jacket. It almost burned. How did she end up in this situation with him? He was testing her, just smiling, watching her obvious physical reaction. She shook her head, willing herself to pull it together. She needed to get up and walk around and get the blood flowing again.

She blamed the wine because, without stopping to think, she leaned closer, tilting her face up to his. He was caught off-guard, but she felt his fingers dig deeper into her back. It forced a whimper of air out of her as he leaned forward, his lips lowering to hers, his warm hands keeping her upright. Her eyes dipped to his lips and then fluttered shut. *Am I about to have my very first kiss?* Why were no alarms going off in her head? Why did it feel right?

His other hand came to rest on her cheek. His thumb traced back and forth. She let him pull her close. His breath ghosted over her lips.

Vassa cracked her eyes and saw something standing on its hind legs behind him. Her eyes widened and she opened her mouth. The raccoon lunged.

CHAPTER ELEVEN

VASSA'S SHIFT AT VIBE AND Flow was surprisingly smooth. There were only a few demanding housewives who were upset she didn't accept their out-of-date free yoga coupon. It had also been a few days of avoiding Oscar. It was childish and irrational, she knew, but regret swirled in her thoughts. She tried to step out and it landed her back in a situation just like the one with Alexa. If those were the people he hung out with, was that who he really was? He had texted her, but she hadn't decided how to respond.

February had begun and her manager ordered her to remove all the remnants of Christmas and suffocate the place in hearts and cupids. She swapped the Christmas hat that was on the large buddha in the lobby for a naked cupid instead. The front doorbell jingled and she said, "Welcome to Vibe and Flow."

"I get to see you in a new element."

Vassa jerked, hitting her head on the counter she was under. Cursing, she stood up, rubbing her head, and found herself face to face with Lazarus. "What are you doing here?"

Lazarus looked around the lobby with his backpack slung off his shoulder. He leaned on the counter and dug inside the free candy dish.

"Those are for students only." Vassa crossed her arms, ignoring how his smile widened at the red sequin headband she'd been forced to wear.

He ignored her. "It's study time. First quiz is next week. The ultimate decider if I'm playing this semester or wallowing on the sidelines..." He opened a chocolate bar, taking a huge bite.

Right, but that was in three hours, not right now.

"I feel like I should see you be domestic more often. Totally sexy stuff." Lazarus talked with his mouth full, and she shook her head.

"Don't talk with your mouth full. What's sexy about hanging a naked baby?" Vassa bent for more decorations out of the box.

They had not talked about the almost kiss that had been interrupted by the raccoon from hell. Apparently, the street life had been tough on the poor thing and the cheese and meat Vassa had snuck from the charcuterie board into her purse lured it. Lazarus did the honorable thing and blocked it from attaching itself to her face, but it ended up giving him a good ass kicking. She drove him to the hospital for a rabies shot. It was a bonding moment.

"Any signs of rabies?" She stood, untangling tinsel.

Lazarus gave her the finger, and she giggled. That's when she noticed his appearance. His gelled-back hair and nice shirt. He was dressed too nice to just study. She narrowed her eyes at him as she taped the tinsel to the counter.

"Luckily my body is intact, but the psychological trauma is alive. Don't worry, my therapist and I are working through it," he said sarcastically as he tugged the tinsel she had just hung. "I realize I've been remiss about completing your bucket list." Lazarus reached for another chocolate bar.

Vassa raised an eyebrow. "So you have been reading the poems I assigned to you."

"Did I use it correctly?"

"I applaud you this once. I understand things have been busy, it's no worries right now." She planted a heart on the wall.

"I said I would help. You're holding your end of the deal with me. It's only fair I uphold it with you." Lazarus leaned farther across the counter. Vassa's eyes fell to his hands. The thought of how they had held her made her let out a breath. A quick glance at his lips brought the night flooding back.

She ignored those rising feelings and cleared her throat. "That's your second bar."

"I have a surprise slash favor I need to ask of you." Lazarus chewed like she hadn't spoken at all.

"A favor? For what? Why does it feel like strings are attached?"

He shrugged. "There are a few here or there, depends on how you look at it."

Part of her couldn't help but notice the curve of his lips now. It wasn't the time to think about it. She was his tutor. Tutor and tutor only. *No kissing*. Thinking about kissing was bad. Bad, bad all around.

"Are you listening to me?" Lazarus snapped his fingers.

She blinked and focused on the decorations. "Uh, yeah."

"I need you to come to trivia night."

"What?"

Lazarus sighed. "Trivia night. I need a partner and you're the smartest person I know."

She stared at him. Was he trying to blow off their studying for trivia night? While educational in theory, trivia night did not trump actual studying.

"You're blowing off studying for trivia night?" She let the words roll off her tongue.

"Technically, you can call it studying because they ask book questions."

She tilted her head. "Book questions?"

He set his half-eaten bar on the counter and reached into his pocket. She huffed because she'd just cleaned the counter and he handed her a folded sheet of paper. It was a flyer for trivia night at a local bar. The prize was a hundred dollars, bragging rights, and free drinks for a month. Shaking her head, she thrust the paper toward him. "You need to study instead."

"Fifteen dollars and you keep the trophy if they have one." Lazarus rocked back on his heels and wiggled his eyebrows at her.

Vassa made a face. "You're low-balling me?"

"Fine, twenty-five dollars."

One of them had to be responsible, and it didn't seem like it was going to be him. Even if the money was slightly alluring to her empty bank account.

"Fifty-fifty, and we rotate who keeps the trophy." Lazarus leaned forward and grabbed her hands. It was warm and rough; a jolt of connection flooded her awareness.

"Lazarus. You need to study. Not have fun." *Be strong Vassa!*

"If we do this, I would have had my fill of fun and I can focus on studying. We're back on track with you. I will be less prone to mischief." Lazarus held her hands firmly. His eyes didn't leave hers for a second and she licked her lips. "Please?"

No, not the puppy eyes. Vassa peeked and there he was with the sad face. He had already won her over more times than she could count. *Be strong Vassa, say no. Say no!*

"Deal." *What was that?*

Vassa flexed her fingers when he released her hands, trying to rub away the tingly sensation in her palms as he plucked another chocolate bar. She slapped his hand away from the pile.

He pouted before snatching the chocolate bar anyway. "Let's go wipe the competition, partner."

Once Vassa's shift was over, they ordered a ride to the bar and within twenty minutes they stood outside an Irish pub. It looked like everyone from the local neighborhood was inside.

"You want something to drink? The hard cider here is good." He raised his voice so she could hear him over the noise of the bar.

Vassa stayed close to him as she looked around the room. The place was old, probably something that survived the great San Francisco fire. It had wood benches, wood tables, and wood floors that creaked when they walked. It was a total fire hazard with candles on each table.

"Laz, Vassa!" It was Jayden. Lazarus led her to his crowded table, where there were two empty seats. She didn't recognize the people except for a few from the bonfire.

"Merry meet, Vassa," Jayden said.

Lazarus's eyes went toward the ceiling and she couldn't help but smile.

"Merry meet, Jayden."

"Call me Jay, we're friends now."

Lazarus shot Jayden a look and Vassa was automatically pleased. The others at the table turned to them and she awkwardly waved when they smiled at her. Were they judging her outfit? Should she have changed what she was wearing?

Stop that. These were Lazarus's friends. They all seemed nice, but she couldn't stop the building doubt. She thought about her failed get-together. Had Lisa, Nina, or Tom said anything to Oscar? Tell him not to be her around anymore? She reached for her phone and typed Oscar a message.

Hi, how are you?

No, that was stupid.

Sorry, missed your text. What's up?

That sounded asshole-ish.

I'm fine, sorry for responding so late, busy with work.

That sounded like an excuse.

Lazarus leaned in. "Are you okay?"

Vassa jumped and placed her phone down.

"I'm fine." The message would have to wait as Lazarus shoved a piece of paper on the table toward her.

"Now, the theme for the night is pop culture. I only know about *Twilight*." Lazarus took a sip of his cider.

Vassa almost choked on the peanut she had grabbed from the nut bowl on the table. "Why do you only know *Twilight*?"

"You didn't know he loved vampire romance crap?" Jayden leaned around Lazarus. Frowning, Lazarus pushed him back, giving Vassa a sheepish look.

"I'm not into vampire romance like that. I just know it."

"Don't hide. Fly your paranormal flag high. Shame is what's stopping so many." Jayden playfully punched him. She couldn't help but laugh out loud at the blush that came across Lazarus's cheeks.

"Can I ask you for another favor?" Lazarus said.

Vassa took a sip of her cider. "No, you can't borrow my copy of *Twilight*."

Lazarus gave her a look. She laughed as he shook his head. "You finding this funny? I swear I only read the book once."

"I'm probably not gonna let this go."

Lazarus sighed and hung his head. He leaned in closer to her. She hadn't noticed how long his eyelashes were before. They curled over the ends and were a total waste on a guy like him. She would pay for those.

"Will you go to a cocktail party with me?"

Vassa's fingers circled the rim of her cup. "Cocktail party? That sounds fancy."

"It's nothing serious. Harvey wants me to come and mingle with his coworkers." Lazarus rubbed a hand across his chin.

"The same Harvey who said you should be realistic?"

"I have to go. I just think I'll have more fun if you come with me." Lazarus looked exhausted, and she pressed her lips together.

He continued, "You can also pretend to be anyone you want... That's on your list, right?"

"At an important cocktail party? I don't want to cause any problems."

"Believe me, you'll be saving me."

Vassa inhaled, and thought about their conversation the night before. There was something going on between the brothers and she wanted to find out what it was. "I'll go. Is there a dress code?"

"Formal and snobby."

Vassa rolled her eyes at the irony of it. "Great, I love snobs."

On the makeshift stage in the front of the room, the host tapped on the microphone a few times. He was a cool-looking guy with a feathered hat and red framed glasses. "All right, all right, let's start this thing, huh? The first category is Pop Culture, let's see what you youngsters know."

The crowd cheered, and Vassa felt a rush of excitement. Lazarus nudged Jayden with his elbow and turned to Vassa. "We gotta win this, I got lots of things riding on it."

She opened her mouth to question him about it when some server began passing out pencils and pens. The host interrupted again with the first question: "What is the rarest M&M color?"

Everyone in the room buzzed.

"Yellow!" Jayden slammed his hand on the table.

Vassa shook her head. "This isn't *Family Feud*. I think it's Green."

"It's not green. You see green all the time." Jayden rolled his eyes.

"You do not." She shook her head.

Vassa and Jayden argued over the colors. Then turned to Lazarus. Vassa had to swallow for a moment.

"I think it's Green," Lazarus said.

Vassa grinned and Jayden grumbled. She snatched the pen out of Jayden's hand and wrote it down.

"That's not fair. It's an obviously biased decision." Jayden shook his head.

Vassa shrugged. "You just got outvoted."

"Don't be jealous Jay, we might go with your answer next." Lazarus patted Jayden's shoulder. The guys began playfully arguing, and she took a sip of cider.

"The next question: what was the first toy to be advertised on television?" the host asked.

This started a frenzy between them as they debated about a toy older than all of them. She knew they were really supposed to be studying, but she had to admit it was fun. Lazarus shifted and rested his arm on the chair behind her. Vassa took a peek at him. He was busy debating the slinky with Jayden as his knee knocked against hers.

"Monopoly or Connect Four?" Lazarus asked.

"Bed Bugs." Jayden rolled his eyes.

Lazarus and Vassa looked at him and said in unison. "Bed Bugs?"

Jayden nodded. "Or Cap'n Crunch."

"I thought that was a cereal?" Lazarus narrowed his eyes.

"In the eighties it was a board game."

Vassa jotted down both answers. The host continued with questions. As the night flowed the questions got more difficult, rounds of cider proved to get her tipsy far too easily, and the competition got heated. When Lazarus and Jayden got into a debate with the table next to them about the Zac Brown Band, which Vassa had absolutely no clue about, he turned to her for confirmation that the best song was indeed "Chicken Fried." As she blinked slowly, the room glowed and it made a halo around his hair. The blond was golden and she wanted to touch it. Vassa giggled and nodded. He threw his arm over her shoulder and brought her close, giving the guy a smug look. "That's right, Vee!"

Like a cold bucket, her thoughts steamrolled the fun. She had to remember that it would not last. This night would end and he would go back to being her upstairs neighbor, and she would graduate. No thinking about Lazarus's eyelashes, golden hair, or how great he felt next to her. She had to stick to the deal and everything would be fine.

They lost.

By a *landslide*.

How was she supposed to know the rarest M&M was brown or the first toy to ever be televised was Mr. Potato Head? And there was no way, absolutely no way, they could ever guess that lateral epicondylitis was a condition commonly known as tennis elbow.

They left with no money or title. Just stuffed full of cheese sticks, cider, and onion rings. Lazarus said goodbye to his other friends. Vassa stood off to the side wrapping her arms around herself as the wind picked up.

"Good job in there. You gotta come back." Jayden appeared next to her. He held his skateboard in one hand.

She nodded. "Maybe next time. Of course, we have to practice. We can't let the soccer players win again."

"You're still helping Laz with his classes, right?" Jayden looked at Lazarus and then to her.

Vassa nodded.

"That's great. Stick with him if you can. I'm worried about him, actually."

That caught Vassa's attention. "What do you mean?"

"He won't listen to me."

Jayden looked over her shoulder at where Lazarus was talking. He didn't speak for a moment before he said, "It's not my place to speak on his business, but the Harvey situation? It's gonna get out of control. But maybe you can talk to him. He values what you say."

How cryptic. Vassa wanted to know why her opinion mattered the most. Looking behind her, she watched Lazarus wave goodbye to his other friends and head for them.

"I have a totally amazing idea that you're going to love," Lazarus said. There was a shine in his eyes, and his cheeks were flushed. He blinked repeatedly at her before looking at Jayden.

"What would that be other than me going home to do homework?" Vassa yawned and crossed her arms.

He ran a hand through his hair. "Do you trust me?"

Jayden shook his head. "I have my homework, ya'll have fun." He sent Vassa a look before turning down the street. They watched him disappear around the corner before Lazarus turned to her.

"Lazarus..."

He put his hands on her shoulders, forcing her to look at him. "For once in your life, don't overthink it. Just go with the flow that life is presenting to you."

"That sounds like something Jayden would say."

"He may have said that to me more than once," Lazarus said.

She sighed. It was already late. How was staying out longer going to hurt? She nodded, and he linked his arm with hers, pulling her across the street. A car nearly took them out and Lazarus tossed him the finger. They took about another two steps before they were standing in front of a building.

Craning her neck back, she looked at the sign. "Crooked Cloud Lounge. Sounds like a brothel."

Lazarus threw his hands up. "Karaoke!"

Vassa shook her head. There was no way. She wasn't drunk enough for that. She turned around when he pulled her arm. "C'mon, you can do it."

Vassa shook her head. *No, no way.* She sang off-key in the privacy of her shower. He dragged her into the establishment anyway. The place was empty. Just a bartender and a bunch of standing tables. In the corner was a couple, a sleeping security guard, and a random businessman on his phone. He brought her to the table in the middle with a thick binder.

"We're not leaving till we each do a song."

Vassa shook her head still. She was the audience. The one that clapped and cheered for the people that were obviously horrible, but had self-esteem (and liquor) through the roof.

"We should just go home; it looks like it's about to close, anyway." Vassa looked around.

"How about Smashing Pumpkins, or are you feeling Michael Jackson at the moment?" Lazarus flipped the page.

"I'll watch you do it. I need more liquid courage," Vassa said.

He frowned. "You have to live, Vee. When are you ever going to get an opportunity like this again? A nearly empty karaoke bar and me?"

She tried to ignore how he was kinda making sense.

"Let's get this over with."

Lazarus smiled. "Now we're talking."

Flipping through the binder, she felt overwhelmed by the selections. Should she pick something classic? *Off the Wall* or *Slippery When Wet*? Or something modern?

"I'll get us shots while you look."

He left and Vassa looked around the room again. At least she didn't know anyone here. They would only know her as the stranger who couldn't hold a note. She was doubly grateful Dara wasn't here to record. She tapped her hand against the table as her eyes scanned the names of the songs, but she found nothing was calling to her.

"Did you pick yet?" Lazarus sat the shots down onto the table. Six shots. Three for him, and three for her.

"Three shots at once?" Her liver was crying.

He rubbed his hands. "We can't do this sober, can we?"

"What is it?"

"Tequila."

Vassa made a face. "No vodka?"

"They were out."

She resigned herself and reached for the lime and salt. "You're going to have to pick me up off the floor."

"Someone might have to pick me up," Lazarus muttered and passed the shots to her. "Back-to-back, no stopping."

She placed the salt on the curve of her thumb and picked up the first shot. Lazarus counted down. On three, she licked the salt and took the shot. She shivered as she swallowed, the liquor burning every tastebud on the way down. She tried to ride out the burn for as long as she could before biting into the lime. She looked at Lazarus, and he looked as winded as she did.

"That was one," he gasped.

Vassa steeled herself as they tossed back the next two shots. She was feeling pretty warm at this point. They let the alcohol kick in longer before they went up.

"What did you pick?"

He closed his eyes leaning against the table. "It's a surprise."

They let the bartender, who was also serving as the DJ, know what their songs were. Lazarus grabbed another round of shots. The TV on stage turned on and the strobe lights whirled. The first chords of the song played and Vassa didn't recognize it at first, but then she looked at Lazarus, who moved toward the stage.

"No, you didn't."

He winked before jumping onstage. Vassa covered her face. No, he wasn't doing this. Peeking through her fingers, she saw him roll his shoulders back like he was getting into a fight. The beat of "I Will Survive" by Gloria Gaynor started.

Vassa shook her head at him. No, he really wasn't doing this. He pointed at her and shook his hips. *This was not happening right now.* The tequila was kicking in fast because she was hot and her body felt loose and she swayed to the beat and clapped as he hit the chorus. Lazarus pranced across the tiny stage. He gyrated his hips, pointing to the couple off to the side and then the businessman too. It was like a reject strip show.

He didn't care that he was singing off-key. The couple cheered for him. Even sleeping security guard woke up.

Lazarus worked the small crowd. He jumped down from the stage and walked around the empty tables, dancing. He looked at Vassa and made a come-here motion with his finger. She shook her head as she laughed. He came to their table and pointed the mic directly in her face.

"C'mon, sing Vee."

The music continued to play, and she shook her head again. The surrounding people chanted for her to sing.

Lazarus looked at her, and with the demand of the crowd, there was nothing she could really do. She sang a line before backing away from the mic. He said the next line and pointed the microphone back.

"Don't leave me hanging!" He wiggled his fingers.

Vassa sang. They took turns for a few more seconds before he moved on, dancing around the tables. She clapped her hands together with the rest of the crowd. When the song finally ended, he did a bow. Vassa cheered for him. He passed the couple, and they reached out to high five.

Lazarus took a shot at the table once he sat.

"I don't know what to say." Vassa blinked slowly, her hands on her face.

"There's nothing to say. You just saw a master at work."

"If baseball or event planning don't work out for you, maybe you could be a drag queen?"

They both laughed and Vassa snorted. It was embarrassing but it just made them laugh more. Vassa playfully pushed him and he tossed her another wink. Seeing Lazarus make a fool of himself made her ready to get it done and show her thing.

"What song are you singing?" Lazarus asked again.

Taking off her jacket, she rolled her sleeves up.

"You'll see with the rest of my fans." Confidence mixed with elation surged through her. Also mixed with the tequila. She was walking on clouds.

Lazarus raised his eyebrows at her and shook his head. "Your fans?"

"My fans." She took the last shot. *No more tequila for her.*

The music played, and she threw up a hand in his face as she walked past. Stepping onstage, she wasn't as much of a performer. Her last time on stage had been in the fourth grade for the Thanksgiving play, where she had been the carrot. Back then she ended up knocking the pilgrim off the stage and getting the play shot down early.

Vassa took a deep breath. "You Belong with Me" by Taylor Swift started.

Lazarus whistled and clapped loudly. The song might have made her a basic bitch but that's what she would be tonight. His energy made her laugh, and she moved side to side. No one could deny the allure of old school Taylor Swift.

She felt awkward with everyone's eyes on her. Then she just

imagined she was in the shower. She closed her eyes as she recited the lyrics she had memorized.

Opening her eyes, she connected with Lazarus. A grin on his face, he clapped and sang along, not caring about whoever was watching. It gave her a boost of confidence. She shook her hips side to side and stomped her foot to the beat, letting her inner superstar really shine. It didn't matter that she couldn't hit the note right or she screeched a little bit and ran out of breath.

What would people think of her? Why didn't she feel embarrassed? Would she regret this in the morning? She didn't care. She made a come-here motion toward Lazarus. To her surprise, he got out of his seat and came up on stage.

Sharing the mic, they sang the chorus. Then he grabbed her hand and twirled her around. They were putting on the performance of their lives. Who would have thought she would be in a karaoke bar singing Taylor Swift with Lazarus? Not her.

He moved easy, and she let his arms circle her waist as they looked at one another. They finished the song; she stared at him, her heart racing. The crowd cheered.

"Let's do another song!" she said.

Lazarus agreed and their audience was happy with an encore.

She wasn't sure how long they stayed in that karaoke bar. They went from Michael Jackson to Queen to Beyonce. They were really giving Bon Jovi their all with "You Give Love a Bad Name" when the lights to the karaoke bar went up.

"Closing time!" the bartender shouted.

Lazarus and Vassa booed and hissed, stumbling off stage. The world was spinning but somehow slow at the same time. He turned around to help her down, and she fell. He caught her in time, and she cackled as they staggered to their table to get their things.

"We have to come back, we-we… we have to come back!" Vassa slurred as she dragged her feet after him.

Lazarus shifted his jacket on. "Let's bring Jayden and Dara."

"God, she sounds like a dead cat. Especially when she tried to sing Whitney Houston."

"You sounded like a dead cat," Lazarus chortled.

Vassa flipped him off and tossed a balled-up napkin in his face. He beamed and waved to the bartender.

The cold air outside brought a tiny bit of sobriety. She felt nice and the entire night was cast in a warm glow. She rocked back and forth as Lazarus came up next to her with his phone in hand. The light from the phone made his eyes seem more cobalt in the night.

"How long till our ride gets here?"

Lazarus squinted and rocked back on his heels, almost stumbling into the wall. "Five minutes."

That wasn't bad.

She closed her eyes as the air cooled her. The weight of the day came down in that moment and she just wanted to crawl into bed.

"Did you have a good time?"

Vassa opened her eyes, and Lazarus was there. He needed to wear a bell or something. He was close. *Very* close. His eyes shimmered with that stupid smile. Why did she like that stupid smile so much? Oh God, she just said she liked his smile. She also liked his hair, and his face, and his body, and his personality. He was always so upbeat. Why couldn't she be like him?

"I did," she squeaked.

He moved closer and placed his hands on her waist. He waited, seeing if she would reject him, but when she didn't, he took another step in closer. Her world narrowed to him. Her heart was about to fall out of her chest as he lowered his face closer to hers. It must be the streetlights. His face seemed to glow.

Did her breath smell? *Oh, Lord.* She brushed her teeth twice that day. How did you kiss? Just slam your lips or pucker? He leaned forward and Vassa squeezed her eyes shut. He nuzzled his head into her neck. She blinked, surprised. He pressed a kiss to her temple. She raised her hands slowly, placing them around his shoulders. His shampoo was sweet, like apples.

He placed his hands on her cheeks, and she knew her eyes were crossed at this point. The smile was gone from his face as he stared at her before she said, "What are you waiting for?"

Lazarus looked around them. "For any raccoons nearby."

Vassa laughed, and he yanked her forward, his mouth crashing into hers. She let his lips take over hers, unsure of what to do, the shock of it making her still. He pulled back, his thumbs gliding back and forth slowly. He leaned in and her eyes fell shut as she tentatively mimicked him.

God, she hoped she was doing this right. Her lips melted into his. She twined her arms around his neck and stood on her tippy toes to deepen the kiss, his tongue sliding over her bottom lip, begging for entrance. *Woah...* She let out a nervous giggle. He took advantage, his tongue slipping in. A moan escaped her as pleasure ran from the top of her head to the soles of her feet. She ran her hands through his hair; it was so soft. She tightened her fingers in it, and his hands now moved to the back of her neck, keeping her in place.

She had never kissed someone like this before. Well, she had kissed no one period, but this was the stuff of the smut novels she kept under her bed. Never had she thought someone would kiss her so passionately. She tried his move out on him, letting her tongue run across his bottom lip. He moaned, and it thrilled her. She chuckled softly, as his teeth nipped at her bottom lip. *I'm kissing Lazarus Gilbert!*

When they finally broke apart, it took her a moment to find herself back on earth. They were still embracing, both breathing as if they had run a marathon. She didn't know what to say, but she didn't have to. A black car pulled up right in front of them and a ding went off on Lazarus's phone.

"Ride's here," he rasped.

Her eyelids fluttered at his voice as though he had awakened her from a dream. She shook her head briskly, and a veil lifted from her face. Vassa opened her mouth to respond but placed a hand over her mouth.

She couldn't move fast enough. She bent over and vomited on his shoes.

Vassa's Extraordinary Senior Send-Off

1. Get totally wasted and regret nothing.

~~2. See all the tourist spots in San Francisco.~~

3. Have an epic last Spring Break.

~~4. Do something completely wild.~~

5. Sneak into a party or event uninvited and pretend to be someone else.

6. Go on a date.

CHAPTER TWELVE

"HELLO? WHY ARE YOU ACTING like you just walked in on your parents having sex?"

Vassa looked at Dara. They were sitting inside Maki Magic Sushi Bar a few blocks from their apartment. Sushi was Vassa's favorite food. She'd kill for the salmon avocado rolls, but three floated by on the rotating sushi boats without her nabbing them. It was all-you-can-eat night, but she was barely making any damage. As for Dara, they were gonna have to butter the doors to get her out.

She was seeing Lazarus tonight. Two days after she kissed him, then vomited on his shoes. The ride home was quiet. She told him she'd buy him another pair, but he refused. He simply said he didn't care for them too much, anyway.

Vassa closed her eyes and banged her head on the table. Her first kiss. Then she went and vomited on the fellow. How embarrassing! There was no way to look him in the eye now. She was going to have to drop out and move to South Dakota. Pleasure and vomit: the memories cycled in her mind. She was in such shambles that she had forgotten to charge a woman for her yoga mat at the studio earlier.

"That's gross." Vassa's voice was muffled on the table.

"You look traumatized. That's the most traumatizing thing I can think of." Dara reached for a plate of edamame from the floating boats.

"I'm only partially traumatized."

Dara bit into the edamame. "How are you partially traumatized?"

Vassa turned her head to Dara. She sighed and closed her eyes before planting her face on the table again. "I kissed Lazarus."

"What?"

"*I kissed Lazarus!*"

Her yelling caught the attention of others in the restaurant. Dara gasped midchew. Her hands flew to her throat as she coughed and beat her chest. Their server's eyes widened and she went for the telephone, but Vassa sat up and whacked Dara on the back. The bean flew out and Dara sucked in a ragged breath. She reached for a cup of water.

"Hold up, hold up. You did what? You haven't told me this!"

Vassa pouted and looked up in time for another salmon roll coming by.

"I kissed him."

Dara blinked. "Lazarus? The guy you claim to hate. The one that annoys you so much. You kissed him."

"And vomited on his shoes."

Dara's jaw dropped and she placed a hand over her heart. "What?"

Vassa bit into her sushi and nodded. "I don't really want to go into the vomit side of things right now."

Slapping her hands on the table, Dara said, "You can't dangle the carrot. Was he that bad you threw up on him?"

Vassa sighed and picked up the other piece of sushi.

"I'm sorry. It's just the amount of shock coursing through my body is making me unnerved," Dara said.

"We went to trivia night and ended up drinking at a karaoke bar—"

"You went to a karaoke bar?"

Vassa nodded.

"Where was I at? Why didn't I get invited?"

"Do you want to hear the story or not?"

Dara pretended to zip her lips and sat back in her chair. Vassa took a deep breath and explained everything. There was no need to hide anything from Dara. From losing the trivia night to singing Taylor Swift and the subsequent kiss and disaster. By the time she had finished explaining, Dara looked ready to pass out from laughter.

"Are you serious? I mean, this is perfect that it would happen to someone like you, no offense."

"All the chocolate, tequila, and Twizzlers I ate were on his white shoes."

"Oh, my God," Dara cackled as Vassa reached for more sushi. Maybe she could eat the memories away. Or not. She didn't want to vomit again.

"So, are you dating?"

Vassa made a face. "Dating? We just kissed. That doesn't mean we're dating."

Dating Lazarus? Alexa popped into her head. If Alexa knew she was dating Lazarus, the girl might commit murder. Which was pleasing for Vassa but also startling.

"You're not the hook-up type."

Hook-up?

"Hooking up is stupid and the people who do it are crazy. We're not hooking up. It was just a kiss. We were both a little tipsy—"

"That's just a lame excuse for a decision you wanted."

Vassa frowned.

Dara poured herself tea. "I've been drunk plenty of times and I remember everything. People like to blame the alcohol for poor decisions, but it's what your heart wanted."

"We're not dating or hooking up," Vassa said firmly.

"Right now. Go get you some man-meat. You know you need it." Dara waved edamame in her face.

"What? You sound like Kiki right now." Vassa ate another piece of sushi.

Dara wiped her hands and pushed her plates away.

"We should have had this talk a long, long time ago."

"My parents gave me the birds and the bees talk when I was thirteen." Vassa focused on the sushi boats floating past.

Dara took Vassa's hands into her own. "College boys aren't just like any boys..."

"How? Because most are poor?"

Dara flicked Vassa on the forehead. "Pay attention."

Vassa hissed and rubbed the spot on her forehead.

"College guys are looking for fun. There are some that aren't, but they are few and far in between. It's best to not think of anything serious with anyone. It could be over just like that." Dara snapped her fingers. "It can also be fun and exciting. Which is what you need."

"Are you saying that Lazarus just wants to hit it and quit it?"

Now they were talking about her having sex. It was overwhelming to think about.

"I'm not saying that, but he's a man. Men suck."

Vassa just wanted to eat her sushi again.

"He's probably thinking about sleeping with you."

Vassa removed her hands from Dara's shoulders "*Dara, please.*"

"I'm just saying. You both kissed. What happens after kissing? Heavy petting, then sex. Then before you know it, Bam! You're pregnant and barefoot with three kids and a parrot."

"That's jumping the gun, isn't it?"

Dara waved a half-empty edamame pod in her face. "Don't play dumb. This wasn't on the list but... take advantage. Lazarus wants you."

"Why, thanks for that."

Dara took a sip of her tea as Vassa snatched the pitcher from her.

"At least you're coming to New York with me. I can't do adulthood without you."

Dara sucked her teeth as a pensive expression crossed her face. Tossing a glance at Vassa, she made a "hm" noise in her throat.

"You are, right?" Vassa observed her expression.

Dara's smile wavered for a second but then she nodded. . "Of course."

Lazarus's hands shook as the screams filled the stadium.

He had passed. With flying colors. He actually passed the quiz.

Full of relief and excitement, he actually kissed his professor on the cheek and screamed for joy. It startled his classmates. Now he was reaping the benefits. His team was huddled up to win the game. This was his last season. The last pitch. The last hit. The last home runs. There would be no more fall training. No more drills with Coach. It was all over after May.

This was his chance to show who he was. The best player and leader he could be.

"Let's go baby, we got this; this is our home field. They're not leaving winners," Lazarus said to his teammates.

His team cheered as they all slapped hands.

"We're about to show them what we're made of."

The team broke and the cheers reverberated in his ears, deafening him briefly as he jogged to the pitching mound. Laguna Creek, their archrival, was going down tonight.

Lazarus stood there in the center of the field trying to collect his breathing. They were leading by three points. He needed to strike this player out or set up his teammates to catch the ball. Taking a step back, he lifted his knee and pulled back his arm, and flung the ball.

"Strike!"

The crowd roared. Strike one. The catcher threw the ball back.

The whistles and cheers made him feel good. It was their first game of the season. He needed to set them on track.

"Focus, Gilbert!" Coach Maverick screamed.

Lazarus made eye contact with the opposing player. The guy readjusted his grip on the bat, watching Lazarus closely.

Glancing quickly up into the night sky, the moon was full, beaming down on him. The rival player made the mistake of following his gaze and Lazarus shifted his stance and threw the ball. The guy barely grazed the ball as the catcher caught it.

"Strike two!"

"That's right, Gilbert! Strike him out!" he heard a teammate yell.

He could hear chants of his name. The crowd began to sing the PGU chant. The blood in his veins felt like fire. Lazarus shook his limbs out, receiving the ball from the catcher easily. He tilted his head back and rotated his neck.

Let's go Hornets.

The crowd chanted. Stomping and clapping began.

Lazarus glanced at the clock; fifty seconds left. He could do this. For a second, Lazarus looked into the crowd. Where was Vee? She had been the first one he called after his quiz. He'd placed her in the best seat in the house. Front row over the players' dugout. Squinting, he tried to find her in the crowd.

The batter bared his teeth at Lazarus. His eyes narrowed and Lazarus grinned.

Let's go Hornets.

He didn't let his mind think; he let his body take over.

Lazarus threw the ball. The stadium went silent. Not a soul let out a breath as the ball careened toward the player. The runner on first base shifted and prepared to run. The basemen hit their mitts. Coach Maverick was screaming so hard spit was flying out of his mouth. Crack! The ball connected with the bat.

Lazarus cursed as he watched the ball sail. Everyone ran. Shouts to catch the ball overwhelmed the cries of disbelief. Mason, their outfielder, ran at full speed for the ball. Laguna Creek's runner went from first base to second. The batter dropped the bat and ran. Lazarus couldn't think. Jittering back and forth from foot to foot, he swiped his sweaty hand on his pants. The team members in the dugout went crazy.

The first runner made it to third base and headed to home plate. Mason missed the ball. He picked it up, running. He tossed it to a teammate. The player made it to home. The crowd groaned as it brought the score close. The batter rounded second base and headed straight for third.

The screams were uncoordinated. Cheers, boos, chants, and names were blurred into one mess he couldn't decipher. He sucked in a breath; he shifted as the ball made it to second base. The batter hit third base and headed home. The second baseman threw the ball to him. The batter was halfway home.

Lazarus threw the ball to the catcher as the batter slid into home.

The crowd went silent.

"*Out!*"

The crowd went wild and his team rushed the field.

"We did it!" Mason yelled as he hugged Lazarus. They did it. They had won. Coach Maverick entered the field as the players surrounded him.

"You made me proud, Gilbert!"

Lazarus smiled as he hugged his coach. As he stepped back, his eyes flickered to the crowd again, searching for Vee.

Eventually, the cheers died down, and they had to shake the hands of Laguna Creek.

"Not too bad for a man on his way out." An old rival patted him on the back as he walked past.

Most of the crowd was filing out to their cars and dorms. Some of his teammates suggested going out to the bar as they exited the locker rooms. Now that the game was over, the adrenaline was gone and he felt tired.

He couldn't help the grin that spread across his face at the thought of her. Minus the vomit. She was passionate and fiery; it kept him on his toes. He knew she had never been to a school game, and he wanted to know what she thought. It was almost his every thought, but he knew he had to go slow. She was easily spooked. He would follow her lead, and not rush.

"Played a helluva game out there."

Lazarus stopped as he exited the locker room and grinned.

Gideon was standing there, dressed a bit more formal than usual in a wrinkled dress shirt and pants. He opened his arms for a hug.

"Expect any less?" Lazarus said, hugging his brother.

"I shouldn't have."

Taking a step back, Lazarus eyed his brother. "Why are you dressed so nice?"

Gideon gave him a playful punch. "A business meeting with some old pals of mine. Looking into expansion."

They stepped out of the way for a group of girls giggling amongst themselves. They gave Lazarus a look before taking off.

"Looks like you have some fans." Gideon's eyes twinkled.

"It's nothing."

Gideon narrowed his eyes before scratching his beard, a smile forming. "You're up to something. Or should I say someone?"

Lazarus crossed his arms. "It's nothing."

"Don't worry, I won't steal your girl. Who is she?"

"You're immature." He rolled his eyes.

"That's rich coming from you. Now spill or I'll tell Harvey and he'll bring his uptight ass here."

Blackmail. Gideon's signature tactic.

"We're not dating yet—"

Shaking his head, Gideon groaned. "You're sleeping together? After that last girl, I thought I warned you…"

"Not that either." Lazarus didn't want to think about that situation again.

Gideon looked relieved.

"Her name is Vee—"

"Vee? Is that the same person who's tutoring you?" Gideon

placed his hands on his hips. Slowly shaking his head, he rubbed his hand across his mouth.

Lazarus exhaled. "It's fine—"

Gideon placed his hands in his pockets and whistled. "A smart one? You sure you can handle that? I thought you like them pretty and dumb?"

Lazarus punched Gideon. "I never said that, you did." He pointed at Gideon, who was grinning stupidly now.

"You never disagreed with me about it."

Lazarus rubbed his temples. "Gideon..."

Gideon looked at his brother like he was a stranger. "Since when do you act mature and not fight back? This Vee person must really have a hold on you. I have to see her for myself."

Was Vee affecting him? He wasn't sure about that. That reminded him: where was she? He told her to meet him right here so they could head back.

"She's meeting me here."

"Perfect."

Lazarus crossed his arms and shook his head. "You're not meeting her."

"Why? Are you embarrassed by your own kin?"

Out of all of his family, Gideon would be the only one that he would introduce Vee to. Lazarus ignored Gideon and placed his hands in his pockets.

"I came to see how amazing you were, but I come bearing good news."

Lazarus raised an eyebrow, and Gideon tilted his head to the side, telling him to move over to the wall and out of the way.

"What news?"

Gideon crossed his arms. "My buddy Mario out on the east coast, he's invested in a couple of businesses out there and such. I told him about you wanting to get into event planning. There's a summer internship with his company. Only if you're serious."

Lazarus didn't think he heard his brother correctly. "*What?*"

Gideon nodded. "Mario can mentor you. He's done everything in the books there is in business. He's a great guy and you should take advantage. I know how much you want your accounts back."

Lazarus felt fear and excitement. Both debilitating. This was the exact opportunity he needed to show Harvey his ambitious and practical side. He could come up with some event and spread some hype. Get local figures involved. Better yet! What if he pitched an event for Harvey's company?

"He's taking a risk, but he'll listen. It's just up to you to take it. I don't want you listening to Harvey. He means well, but he can be a piece of shit."

Could Lazarus create a career that was highly successful and afforded him the lifestyle he wanted? Gideon had done it on his own, with no help. No failures yet. Or would Lazarus fail like Harvey expected?

Lazarus shifted his bag. "Harvey was just trying to make me realistic—"

"No. Harvey was being a piece of shit. He took a safe route and now he's trying to force you into one. I know he loves you, but don't let him tell you how to live." Gideon planted his fist in his hand.

"He's trying to warn me, but it comes out wrong. Don't worry, I have a plan."

Gideon made a face. "I don't know why you get all soft with him. Yes, Harvey is looking out for you, but if you let Harvey get in your head, you'll regret it."

"I just want to prove to you guys that you can take me serious," Lazarus said, and regretted it instantly.

"Lazlo, I do. How many times do I have to tell you? We all have pasts. Don't let our family, or even me, define what success looks like for you." Gideon pressed his hand to Lazarus's shoulder and squeezed.

Lazarus opened his arms for his brother to hug him, and he did.

"Anything you do, I know you'll be great. I just want to help in any way I can."

"I'll think about it at Harvey's cocktail party."

Gideon groaned. "Why are you going to that mess? Didn't I just tell you—"

Someone cleared their throat and Lazarus and Gideon turned around. Vassa was standing there. She pushed the rim of her glasses up as she looked between the two of them.

"Sorry I'm late. There was a line in the girls' bathroom."

Gideon grinned and glanced at Lazarus and back to Vee. For Lazarus, it felt like it had been years since he last saw her. With her beat-up white high-tops and jeans and a rainbow halter top that looked painted on, all he could see was how unbelievably beautiful she looked. Soft, full lips that held a hint of gloss. Ones that he knew were fully responsive.

Pushing Lazarus to the side, Gideon ran a hand through his hair before he sized Vee up.

"No worries. Who might you be? I think I know." Gideon held out his hand.

"I'm Vassa, and you?"

"Vassa." Gideon said her name and looked at Lazarus as he held her hand. Lazarus shot him a look, which he ignored.

"Yes?"

"I'm Gideon. Lazarus's older brother. I'm the one who got the good looks in the family." He popped his collar and Vee giggled.

"Really? I've heard about you too."

"Good things I hope."

"Gideon, don't you have to go?" Lazarus stepped in.

Vee watched with wide eyes, but Gideon was eating this up.

"It's only nine o'clock. Why don't we celebrate with some drinks or food? Christie's in Florida right now for a client. The pets and I have been living on Chinese takeout and Indian for the past week. I saw a great bistro around here." Gideon continued to smile at Vee before looking at Lazarus.

"I don't want to be a bother." Vee shook her head as she observed Lazarus's face.

"Actually, we're doing something, but next time?" Lazarus gave Gideon a pointed look before turning to Vee. "Can I show you something?"

Vassa nodded, and he grabbed her hand. The lights were still on and it helped Lazarus navigate the halls quickly.

"You do this often? Are we gonna get in trouble?"

Lazarus laughed. "It's fine."

She muttered under her breath as they emerged onto the field and then gasped. "Wow."

Stars filled the sky, twinkling softly against the lights of the city. The wind blew, sending a chill through the both of them. The sky hung silent over them, forbearing and proud. It made both of them suck in their breath at its beauty. Vee looked left to right, expecting campus security to pop out. Lazarus dropped his bag to the ground, digging inside until he found his bat and ball.

"It's so different from being in the bleachers."

"It never gets old for me." He stood up with his bat and ball. He held them both in front of her.

"Ball or bat?"

Vee looked at the items and then at him before she shook her head. "I don't play."

"C'mon, give it a chance."

Vee took a step back. "I have bad luck in sports. No, thank you."

"C'mon. I'll teach you."

Crossing her arms, she cocked her hip. "Teach me?"

Lazarus nodded.

"I don't think I can learn in a night." She shook her head.

"You know you want to," he said in a sing-songy voice.

She pouted. "If I hit it once can we go?"

"Just once."

She took the bat from him and started walking to the plate. She held up one finger. "Just once!"

Lazarus took his position at the pitcher's mound.

"You're too far!" She looked awkward around the base.

"I'm not. This is fine." He tossed the ball up and caught it.

"I'm not going to be able to hit it."

"Just try." Deciding to go easy on her, he wound up slowly and tossed the ball. She screamed, dropping the bat, and ducked away from the base.

"Why are you running?"

Holding her chest, she looked wildly at the ball and then him. "It was coming toward my face!"

"It was?" He rolled his eyes as he jogged to get the ball.

"Yes, it was."

He gave her a dubious look before he returned to the mound. "Let's try this again."

"Come forward a bit and go slow," she called out.

He took a few steps forward. "Is that good enough?"

Vassa nodded and lifted the bat. It wobbled in her hands before she steadied it and placed it over her shoulder. She mimicked the stance of the players and wiggled. It made him laugh.

"Shut up and throw the ball!"

Lazarus held up a hand. "Sorry, I'm sorry."

He took a second look at her. She gave him a nod, and he took his time and tossed her the ball. She swung and missed.

"See! I told you I couldn't do it."

"You're swinging too early. It's all about timing. Wait for it to come to you."

Vassa grabbed the ball and tossed it to him. "I'll try."

Lazarus waited for her to get ready before she gave him the thumbs up. He tossed her the ball again, this time with a little more force. He held his breath as the ball sailed through the air and she closed her eyes, swinging the bat. It connected, and the ball went sailing over their heads.

"You hit it!"

"I did!" She jumped up and down.

Lazarus ran for the ball, laughing. "Let's try it again."

Vassa shook her head. "I don't know. I'm a one-hit wonder."

"That joke was lame, but c'mon, you can do it!" Lazarus said.

Vassa sighed. "Fine. You obviously don't know good humor when you hear it."

Lazarus stood on the mound. "Ready?"

"Okay."

Winding up, he tossed her the ball. Neither one of them could react fast enough. The ball careened faster than he intended in the air. He opened his mouth, calling out her name, but it was more of a broken garble. Vee's eyes were closed as she swung... just a few seconds early. The force of her swing pushed her forward and she stumbled, stepping with her right foot to steady herself and placing herself in the ball's path.

Clearing his throat, he called her name again, but it was too late. The ball clunked her in the head. She took one step back before her arms went up above her head and she fell backward.

"Vee!" Lazarus ran to her.

She landed on the ground. A gasp escaped her as he fell to his knees near her.

"*Vee!*" Her glasses lay in the grass next to her. She didn't move, and her eyes were wide as she stared at the sky, mouth opening and closing. He lifted her up and shook her.

"Vee, talk to me!"

Vassa blinked several times, her eyes rolling before they stilled and she blinked. "I think I've seen God."

Lazarus stopped shaking her, and he pushed her hair back. An ugly bruise was forming on her forehead. "I'm so sorry."

Lazarus placed his hand back on her face, looking down at her. She blinked at him, still dazed, before a grin formed on her face and she started snickering. The snickering turned into a snorting but full-blown laughter. He tried to be serious before he joined in.

"Oh my God, this has to be the most embarrassing thing

that's happened to me." Her shoulders shook in silent laughter.

"I will never forgive myself. I'm sorry Vee, I didn't mean it." The color was still drained from his face as his fingers traced the bruise.

Vassa blinked at him. "It's fine, I don't need to see, anyway."

Pushing herself up, she blinked at him with a smile on her face. He had always known that her smile could light up a room. It was a goofy smile, probably because of a concussion. Amazed and uncoordinated. Lazarus quickly dropped his lips to catch hers and she moaned happily. She arched into him as he pushed her hair back and made a deep noise of satisfaction, before a hiss of pain as he touched the bruise.

"Forgive me? I'll do anything." he groaned against her lips before he pulled back.

Vassa licked her lips, blinking a few times before she said, "Anything?"

"Anything."

"This may be crazy. Can we try again? I want to send a video to Dara to prove I hit the ball. But avoid the ball hitting my skull?"

Lazarus laughed, and he leaned in to kiss her again. "Of course."

CHAPTER THIRTEEN

"OUCH!"

Vassa hissed and shrank from where Dara was touching up her makeup. Placing a hand on her hip, Dara shook her head.

"Look, you need to keep still."

"How can I sit still when you're slapping it on like paint on a wall?"

"I wasn't the one that got hit in the head with a baseball right before a cocktail party."

The nasty bruise on her forehead had formed on the right side of her face, starting in her hairline and continuing to her ear. It was nice to have Lazarus groveling after her. It was his turn to take her to the hospital, to make sure she didn't have a concussion.

"I'm almost done. Just try to keep still."

"Try to be gentle, Ray Lewis."

Snorting, Dara continued to cover the bruise with foundation. Eyes closed, Vassa twisted her hands in the sequin material of her dress. Gosh, the heels were already killing her feet and she was sitting. Dara said the kitten heels Vassa wanted to wear were ugly and made her look like an old biddy. At least she could walk in them! Not these five-inch white stilettos she knew were gonna come off in the next hour or so.

She tried to relax but her stomach turned. She bit her lip, pressing a hand to her belly, and Dara scolded her for messing up the bold red lip she had.

"Can you just hold on for one second before you destroy my masterpiece?"

Vassa huffed. She couldn't help it. She was going to another party. This time for a major company (Vassa had seen their sports bars in the yoga studio before) and she needed to look like she belonged. Which was why she used her credit card to buy the dress, because the sweatpants she had wouldn't cut it.

When Lazarus asked her to come, she expected something simple. A restaurant or ballroom. Not for it to be at the Presidio Officers' Club. Only those with lots of money and influence rented that space out for weddings and events. She didn't want a repeat of what happened with Oscar, but she wasn't sure how she'd fit in with the rich and bougie.

"All done."

Opening her eyes, Vassa took the mirror Dara handed her.

"This is amazing, Dara." She touched her face gingerly.

Dara had pulled her curls into a chignon updo with several strands cascading and framing her face. The bruise still peeked out from under the foundation but it didn't take away from the simple smokey eye that made her brown eyes pop. Holding out her hands, Dara helped Vassa stand up. She wobbled before clasping Dara's hands tighter.

"Now, are you going to be able to walk?"

"I hope. If not, I'll pick a wall and stay there for the night."

Vassa had chosen a simple black halter neck dress. Dressed in a modest-length skirt with a tasteful slit, she felt like a sexy grown woman rather than a confused twentysomething who liked all-you-can-eat sushi. "I can't believe you're doing this." Her gaze was on Vassa's outfit and Vassa looked down to see if she had gotten deodorant stains on the dress. "Wasn't it a month ago I had to beg you to go to a party? Now you're getting dressed up for them?"

Vassa realized then she didn't have major anxiety. She was nervous. Yes, but that debilitating fear? None. No thoughts about Alexa or anyone looking at her. She was just... herself. She only hoped Lazarus liked her dress.

Lazarus.

What was happening between them? Going to her favorite bookstore and eating crepes? Kissing him not once. Not twice. Three times! Kisses she started! She was a contradiction. It was scary. She thought about him during her day. If a customer told her a dad joke at work, she wanted to tell him. She was always hoping for a glance at him in the hallway. Waiting to hear his footsteps up above so she could go up and talk to him.

He was nothing she had expected. He wasn't vain. He was humble. He had told her more about his work with Gideon. They did landscaping for nonprofits in the Bay for free. He was caring. That was proven when he brought her praline ice cream and pretzels to make her feel better. He was insightful and could appreciate the classic horror movies she forced him to watch. Yet, there was something else that rocked her to her core.

She liked his company.

He wasn't a bad person, not like she thought before. He listened to her, he could empathize, and... He made her feel comfortable.

She didn't have to put up a front or act tough. She didn't have to hide her opinion or dumb herself down like she had in the past. She could just be Vassa.

"I don't even recognize myself," Vassa said, being honest.

"That's good."

"Good?"

Dara nodded. "We get comfortable in our comfort zones. You decide to do that bucket list and look at you! Who knows who you'll be by the time we graduate?"

Who will I be at graduation?

"I'm both thrilled and crapping my pants at that revelation." She smiled.

Grinning, Dara placed the makeup brushes back in the bag. "I'm rooting you on. Just remember that—"

There was a knock on the front door.

"What? No coming down from the fire escape? He's actually using the front door?" Dara said.

Vassa stiffened and looked in the mirror, making sure everything was in place. "Can you answer that? I'll just be a minute."

Dara bowed. "Take your time, Cinderella."

Flipping Dara off as she went to answer the door, Vassa gave herself one last look. For the first time in a while, she liked what she saw. She saw someone living and not sitting watching the world go by. Even if it pained her heart to think of leaving this all behind.

Dara called her name, and she sucked in her gut and stuck out her chest. It was show time.

Vassa heard Dara and Lazarus talking as she slipped on her jacket. The clicking of her heels slowed their conversation by the time she got to the front door.

"Are you ready?"

She froze before a big grin went across her face, and she covered her mouth with her hand. She had never seen Lazarus in anything other than jeans or sweatpants. *Now?* He took her breath away.

He was handsome. His thick blond hair was slicked back with his sculpted cheekbones and chiseled jaw, if any of his fan girls saw him now, they would all pass out in awe. His tall, muscular body filled out the black suit to perfection. One hand was in his pocket, and the other held a bouquet. His bowtie was crooked and his eyes widened when he saw her.

"You look great Vee."

"You actually clean up nicer than I thought you would." She looked him up and down and swallowed.

They both grinned as Dara looked between the two of them with an amused expression. Vassa glanced at the floor before taking a glance at him, then at his tie. "Here, let me fix that."

Righting his tie, she got a whiff of his cologne. It wasn't his normal Irish Spring. This scent was darker, more oak. Manly.

Lazarus pinned his eyes to her face as she fixed the tie, brushing imaginary lint off the shoulders of his jacket. His eyes darkened and a flush crept up his neck as her body brushed against him. Dara cleared her throat loudly.

Vassa stepped back and looked at the flowers in his hand. When Dara cleared her throat again, Lazarus sprang into action and forced the flowers onto her.

"For you. They're almost as beautiful as you but not quite."

Pressing a hand to her chest, she took them. "Look at you with the pickup lines. You mean that?"

"Absolutely."

She grinned as she brought them to her face to smell. They were sweet and fruity. Turning to Dara, she handed them to her. "Can you put this in water?"

"It's not like I'm going to a cocktail party. Have her back at a reasonable time, mister. Or I'm calling campus security and her mom." Dara pointed a finger at Lazarus. He grinned and nodded.

"Don't come home early," Dara whispered to Vassa before she disappeared into the kitchen.

Vassa and Lazarus stood there for a moment before he extended his arm to her. "Are you ready?"

Vassa wrapped her hand around his arm and sucked in a deep breath, setting her shoulders back. This was it. She was more ready than she had been in a while.

"As I'll ever be."

"That's my girl."

Vassa started to leave but turned to the kitchen. "Dara, are you going to be okay by yourself?"

Dara's head peeked out the kitchen. "Don't worry. I'm hanging out with a friend."

Vassa was about to ask who when Lazarus tugged on her hand again.

"Don't be nervous, Vee. It'll be easier for you and much

more soul crushing for me."

She wanted to ask him what he meant by that but he changed the subject, leaving her to wonder what she was getting into tonight.

Any confidence Vassa had fled as they entered the ballroom.

Harvey's Company, *Fit Energia*, rented out the entire Officers' club in the Presidio. Both halls and the courtyard. There had to be almost two hundred people there.

Vassa held tight to Lazarus. Servers with white gloves carrying hors d'oeuvres and wine on silver platters glided past. A live band played smooth jazz that filled the room and the singer sang either in French or another language. Conversation filled the air and Vassa was grateful she had bought the dress. The women looked straight out of magazines and the men looked like models.

Swallowing, she snagged a flute of champagne as a server passed as they stood inspecting the scene.

Lazarus's eyes scanned the room quickly. "What do you think?"

"I thought this was a small get-together?"

The place dripped money. Vassa looked at Lazarus. She couldn't help but think he fit in with the group.

"That's what Harvey said, but this is a small get-together for him," Lazarus said.

She took a sip of her champagne. Harvey sounded less and less like a person she wanted to meet.

He rocked on his heels. "So, time for another item off the bucket list?"

Vassa snapped her head to him. "That would be?"

Was this a date? Vassa was hoping for something more romantic than this…

"Go to a party and pretend to be someone else."

Her mouth dropped and looked around. "You want me to do that here?"

Lazarus laughed. "This is as good a time as any."

She hadn't thought through that task clearly. This was an important cocktail event. Vassa and Lazarus looked to be the youngest ones there. They wouldn't appreciate a college student mucking the party up.

"I don't know—"

"I thought we'd been through this, Vee? No backing out. Now tell me, who are you going to be?"

"Right now? Like on the spot? I was hoping, you know, to do a little research or something beforehand."

She could watch a few action movies like James Bond or something. See how the secret spy agents pretended to be people during their mission. Obviously, she wasn't a spy, but she could translate that energy into a persona.

"So, who are you? What's your life story?" Lazarus crossed his arms.

Vassa's mouth opened and closed.

"You're supposed to be a writer and you can't think of something on the spot?" Lazarus sucked his teeth. "Not looking good, Vee."

"Hush! You caught me off guard, okay? Lemme think."

Her mind raced as she thought of every movie, book, and character she'd seen or read about in her life.

"Got it! My name is Natalia Tubbs."

Lazarus made a face. "What?"

"Natalia Tubbs. I'm a long-lost cousin of Rico Tubbs."

He blinked.

"*Miami Vice*? Crockett and Tubbs, you haven't seen it?"

"Why is that the first thing to come to your mind?"

"I dunno, you put me on the spot! Plus, Grandma and I watch it all the time. She thinks young Don Johnson is gorgeous." Vassa downed the rest of her champagne.

"Well, Natalia Tubbs, I'm going to look for Harvey. You mingle." Lazarus gave her a thumbs up before he disappeared into the crowd.

Taking a deep breath, she had to remind herself that no one here knew her. She most likely wouldn't see them ever again. That gave her some more courage. Champagne would give her more courage and also the buffet table of treats.

Making a beeline for the food, she grabbed another flute of champagne. The food looked too pretty to touch. Fancy deviled eggs with pickled radish, prosciutto ricotta rolls, and finger sandwiches. Looking around, Vassa piled her plate with food. She might have to stuff some in her pocket to take home. She had just spotted the mini fruit tarts and went for them when her hand collided with someone else's.

"I'm sorry," she said.

It was an older woman in her late fifties with graying hair. She blinked as she gave Vassa a smile.

"No worries, dear."

The older woman looked at Vassa's plate stuffed with food.

"Oh, uh, this is for a friend." She held the plate closer.

The woman looked around before she leaned in. "I understand. These parties can be a bore. I came to stuff more eggs in my purse."

They laughed, and the woman extended her hand. "I'm Adrienne Stiller."

"Vas—Natalia Tubbs."

Vassa pursed her lips. She couldn't believe this was actually happening.

"Oh, that sounds familiar."

"Does it?" Vassa blinked rapidly.

Taking another sip of her drink, Vassa felt a twinge of fun.

Adrienne placed more food on her plate. "What do you do?"

"Oh um… Well, I work of course." Vassa mind raced for a lie. "I'm a private detective in Miami."

Adrienne's eyes widened. "Really?"

Vassa bit into her deviled egg. Gosh, it was fantastic.

"It's family business. My cousin was a detective. Got really famous for it. My dad to my granddaddy. We're big on... catching criminals. The bad guys, you know? Gotta keep the streets safe."

Adrienne nodded, totally intrigued, and she pointed to Vassa's forehead. "Is that how you got *that mark*?" She whispered the ending and Vassa's hands flew to her forehead.

"Oh yes. My family has tons of enemies. My cousin Vinny, has this arch enemy, Calderone. He tried to take Vin out and put a contract on him. Well, Calderone's men wanted to come back ya know, finish the rest of the family off." Adrienne looked horrified, but Vassa kept rolling. "I had to crack a couple skulls. One guy got the best of me and clunked me in the head, but don't worry, see how he looks!"

Laughing, Vassa took another bite of food as Adrienne's eyes widened.

"You know this is like the last case I had—"

She leaned on the table. Or what she thought was the table.

It was the platter of deviled eggs.

Vassa's champagne flute went one way and her plate of goods went the other. Trying to catch herself, she fell onto the table as twenty deviled eggs went straight for Adrienne. She could only watch in horror as the older woman closed her eyes and egg yolk landed on her face and dress. People around them turned and gasped. Vassa placed her hands over her mouth as it Adrienne's clothing was streaked with yolk and paprika.

"Oh my God, I'm so sorry!"

Ripping off the first cloth she saw, she pulled the other platters to the ground. Silverware clanged, and servers rushed to see what the commotion was. She attempted to wipe the yolk off of Adrienne, but it smeared even more into her outfit, which probably cost more than Vassa could ever afford.

"Please stop!" Adrienne cried.

"I have to help you." The smears got worse. They were drawing a crowd when she heard a deep voice say, "What is going on here?"

Vassa froze. She turned her head slowly to see a tall man with red hair in a suit, glaring at her. Jumping up, she bumped into the server behind her, causing him to land in the pile of food. "Oh, my God!"

"Who are you and why are you here?"

Vassa looked at the angry guy. He raised an eyebrow, waiting for her to respond. He looked familiar, but she knew she never met him before.

"Uh, I... Well, what happened was—"

"Vee, what happened?" Lazarus appeared, and she felt relieved.

He looked at the food on the floor. Adrienne was covered in egg yolk and the mean guy was still glaring at her.

"Uh, I mean Natalia," Lazarus corrected himself.

"You know her?" the man asked.

Lazarus said, "Yeah, it's my friend. I invited her."

"Lazarus, this isn't some party you can bring any stray off the street in." The man pointed to her, and she flinched at his tone.

Who was he calling a stray?

"I think most places have a plus one, Harvey."

Harvey.

Vassa now saw the resemblance between them. Harvey continued to frown as he looked at her, like she had just pissed on his parade. This was the guy Lazarus had to answer to? If she had a brother like him, she'd take her chances with the streets.

"Most plus ones are not responsible for smearing deviled eggs on the vice president of sales."

Oh. She may have made a mistake.

"She needs to go. I'll escort her out." Harvey made a step toward her and Lazarus blocked him.

"She stays with me."

Harvey tilted his head and narrowed his eyes at Lazarus before turning to Adrienne. "I'm so sorry, Adrienne. I'll reimburse you for the dry cleaning,"

"Oh, it's no problem."

Harvey took Adrienne's hand and led her away. "I take full responsibility for my brother and his… friend's nonsense. Let's have our meeting at a better time. Can I escort you to the bathroom?"

Adrienne shook her head before she gave them all a shaky smile and headed for the bathroom. Harvey watched her go before he turned on them. "I can't believe you did this Lazarus."

"C'mon, it was an accident."

"A mistake that could cost you a job! Adrienne is in charge of hiring; do you know I talked you up to her? Your job could have been secured right now!"

Vassa gripped the back of Lazarus's jacket. Harvey's face was red as he hissed at them. She hadn't meant to cost Lazarus a job. She didn't know the woman was vice president of sales when the eggs flipped.

"Harv—"

"I apologize Mr. Gilbert. It was an accident. I did not mean to ruin any previous business that was planned." Vassa stepped from behind Lazarus.

Lazarus gave her a quick smile before frowning at his brother. Harvey looked her up and down. "Are you a new girlfriend?"

"No."

Gideon raised an eyebrow. "Hook-up?"

"Harvey." Lazarus voice simmered with anger.

"I'm Natalia. I mean, *Vassa.* My name is Vassa. I'm Lazarus's friend and tutor,"

"Tutor?" Harvey looked at Lazarus. "Tutor for what? Is there something wrong with a class?" Harvey's eyes turned to slits.

Vassa swallowed. "Well—"

Lazarus cut her off. "You can never study enough for classes. Vassa's just helping me stay on top of things." He gave her a look.

"This doesn't change the fact you ruined plans in the making," Harvey told her.

Swallowing, she looked at Lazarus. Her anger was rising and she felt suffocated between the men.

"You better hope Adrienne wants to talk to you after this. The amount of groveling I'm going to have to do for you, you'll owe me more than you already do."

Vassa frowned at that. Lazarus said nothing, but she saw his fist clench.

"This isn't over Lazarus," Harvey said. Sending another look Vassa's way, he disappeared into the crowd.

Letting out a shaky breath, she looked at Lazarus. His jaw was clenched, and his cheeks were stained red with his anger. But he gave her a reassuring smile and grabbed her hand. He led her to the exit, ignoring the looks from attendees. "Let's just go."

"I'm sorry again about the deviled eggs."

Lazarus and Vassa had arrived back at their apartment. Standing outside her door, she turned to him. Hands in pockets, he shrugged and grinned.

"It was kinda funny. How did pretending to be someone else turn out?"

Vassa scratched her head. "I was getting into the vendetta Calderone had on my family before the mess happened."

"I think I need to watch Miami Vice now." He let out a humorless laugh and his eyes looked dull.

Her heart pulled. She wanted to comfort him, but he kept a distance between them. Twisting her hands, she tried to smile. "It's a good show, but there's something else I want to ask you."

It had been pressing on her for the entire car ride home.

"Why doesn't Harvey know about your probation?"

Lazarus ducked his head. Vassa didn't know the full scoop on Harvey and Lazarus's relationship. There was something there that didn't sit right. She planted her feet firmly as she waited for him.

His voice was cold and businesslike. "It's a long story."

"I like long stories."

Lazarus closed his eyes and exhaled. He looked at the floor before he faced her. "Harvey pays my tuition. After my dad had his stroke, Mom had to pay the hospital bills and his physical therapy. She even had to downsize our house. Harvey stepped in to help us."

Her body softened and opened in response, her mind racing. "I'm sorry that happened. Family is supposed to look after one another."

His eyes were molten onyx, filled with frustration. "If he found out it… Let's just say it would be better if he didn't. I just go along with what he says. He means well, and it saves me loads of trouble."

Vassa's lips puckered like she was sucking on a lemon. "So, he's manipulating you through money?"

They hadn't discussed any specifics about his family drama in their deal. Graduation would happen and she would move to New York. That night she met him after the game, he had looked to be in deep conversation with Gideon. How did Gideon play into this dynamic?

The silence stretched on between them as his gaze bore into hers with an intensity that stole her breath.

"He's not manipulating me."

She shifted on her heels to ease the pain. "That's what it sounds like to me. I mean it's in your face, Lazarus."

"You don't know Harvey or my family enough to comment with an uneducated opinion, do you?"

The distance between them seemed to stretch out endlessly. He was right; she didn't know everything. They only had their deal. He watched, not offering any further information, and she composed her face into neutrality. They didn't have long left, just two months, and she wanted it to go as smoothly as possible.

"You're right. I won't comment again."

"Vee—"

Vassa turned to unlock the front door. She went to close it but Lazarus was able to block it because she was focused on getting to her bedroom.

She stopped in the living room as Dara and Jayden jumped apart from each other, a pan of lasagna and wine in front of them. Vassa furrowed her eyebrows. "What's going on here?"

Dara set her plate down before making more room between herself and Jayden. Vassa narrowed her eyes on the two. Lazarus came up behind her and she moved away from him.

"We're uh, just planning for spring break."

Jayden had a dumb look on his face and Dara elbowed him. "Yeah."

Grateful for a distraction from Lazarus, she didn't ask anything else.

"What do you think, Cabo or Miami Beach?" Dara asked Vassa.

Jayden shook his head. "That's overplayed, Texas is where it's at."

Vassa frowned. Both of those places sounded less than ideal. Drunk college students, staying up all night, and more drinking than sightseeing. Not her cup of tea. Why couldn't they go somewhere nice, like Virginia?

"Los Angeles is nice." Lazarus made eye contact with Vassa, and she gave a curt nod.

"I say we do Vegas." Jayden leaned back on the couch, purposely avoiding eye contact with Dara.

Vassa just wanted to kick her shoes off and go to bed. "We? We're a group now?"

"Like literally, yes." Dara clapped and bounced on the couch.

"My parents have discounts at a few hotels," Jayden tossed in.

Vegas for spring break? Vassa could already imagine the chaos.

"Kiki's gonna love it." Dara reached for her wine.

Vassa groaned. "Please don't bring Kiki. That's a nightmare waiting to happen."

"She'll bring the party!"

"Trouble, too." Vassa kicked her shoes off, not caring that she wasn't in her room.

Everyone talked at once. It seemed Vegas was their destination. Vassa stood up, glancing at Lazarus as he was staring at her. He took a step toward her and she shook her head, giving him a curt smile, and headed to her bedroom. He was right. It wasn't her place to comment on his family. She'd never make that mistake again.

<u>Vassa's Extraordinary Senior Send-Off</u>

1. Get totally wasted and regret nothing.
2. ~~See all the tourist spots in San Francisco.~~
3. Have an epic last Spring Break.
4. ~~Do something completely wild.~~
5. ~~Sneak into a party or event uninvited and pretend to be someone else.~~
6. Go on a date.

Mission Dolores Park was packed with people there to lounge, play with their dogs, and enjoy the view of the city's skyline. Oscar was the reason she was here. A last-minute invite to Shakespeare in the Park was just the icebreaker she needed to finally talk to him about the party.

Vassa approached Oscar and waved. "I hope you didn't wait too long." He wore dark shades to block out the sun.

"I'm just glad you could come last minute. I brought wine and pupusas." Oscar wiggled a bag of food.

She smiled. "How do you know I need food?"

They fell into simple conversation as they climbed the hill and watched some dogs chase a frisbee. There was a small stage at the base of the hill. Oscar directed them to a suitable spot between the stage and the park. He laid out a blanket, and they sat. "This is from a restaurant. I can't vouch for the goodness of it but I know the soul is there."

"I just need it to be fresh and hot for me to eat it," Vassa said.

"Have you had pupusas before?"

"No," She shook her head. "Have you?"

Oscar grinned. "Prepare to be amazed."

There was an enormous platter of thick fluffy pancakes stuffed with meat, cheese, and beans, along with bowls of rice, lettuce, fresh cheese, and cream.

"I had them when I went to El Salvador to visit my abuelos on my father's side. The best thing I ever had."

Her stomach growled. "It smells delicious."

"You're going to love them. Now tradition says eat it with a side of curtido and salsa, but you don't have to." He ripped off part of the pupusa and scooped the salsa and curtido on it. "Bon appetit."

Vassa dug into the food, the flavors exploding on her tongue. She needed to get this restaurant on speed dial. It was so good she went for a second.

"I'm glad you said yes to today," Oscar said.

Vassa nodded as she swallowed. "Yeah…"

"Did I do something wrong before?"

"Of course not." She ripped apart her pupusa. "I'm stupid and overthink but I actually thought you would be mad at me."

Oscar blinked before he laughed. "Why?"

Taking a sip of her wine, she swallowed before saying in a rush, "You know… Tom and the other girls? I didn't know what to say. Those were your friends. I assumed they would tell you and then you would hate me…"

Oscar started laughing and threw his head back.

"What's so funny?"

He shook his head. "Everyone argues with Tom."

Vassa chewed aggressively on her food. "I'm serious. That guy was a jerk. I wanted to punch him."

"Everyone wants to punch Tom. He's a dick."

"Why are you friends with him, then? You should have told me! I thought I fucked up or something—"

"Politics? The English major is small, and that group is even smaller in the city. I should have said something." Oscar took a sip from his cup. "I apologize for not prepping you for them."

"I just thought back to a bad time I had and I don't know. I panic. I just… I'm sorry." Vassa tucked a strand of hair behind her ear.

The crowd clapped as an ensemble began setting up on the stage.

"It takes a little time to get used to the crowd. No biggie, I just thought we could use someone like you." Oscar sighed, and she could see the wheels turning in his brain.

"I know what happened last year with you and Alexa. I don't want you to think I'm doing this out of pity or whatnot, but I just want to say it was wrong how she made that fake page pretending to be you. It could've gotten you kicked out of school."

Right. They had to go back there. Her instincts had been right. Oscar was doing this out of pity.

"That's just me trying to relate. I lost my best friend in a nasty situation. I don't think you should hide. You're a talented writer and we lost something when you stopped coming to Word Slam and department meetings. I understand if you don't want to do it anymore, but I just want to let you know."

Vassa traced the rim of her cup with her finger and nodded.

Oscar continued, "So after spring break next week, come by Word Slam. It would be outstanding." He pushed his sunglasses up and she could see he was being sincere.

She finished her wine and reached for more. "Well, I hope the rest of the night went well."

Oscar nodded. "It did. We might do another one. Hopefully, you can come to that. I'll make sure not to invite Tom."

"Please don't invite Tom."

They laughed. He wiped his mouth and pushed the small pile of pupusas closer to her. "Want some more?"

She did, she really did, but she didn't want to look too greedy. "I'm good. I'll take some home if that's okay?"

The curtain on the stage opened and performers stepped out.

She sat up straighter. "What are they going to perform?"

An actor in a Victorian costume came out as Oscar whispered, "The Merchant of Venice."

Vassa settled down to watch the performance. In the back of her mind Vassa wondered if she should go to Word Slam. If she went, she would have to confront Alexa. Was she ready for that?

The play was amazing. Oscar ended up giving her all the pupusas. Setting the container to the left of her bed, she stared at the ceiling as her food coma kicked in. She probably shouldn't have munched on them on the bus ride back.

There was a knock on the window and it opened. Lazarus had an SF Giants cap on with the matching jersey.

"You just choose not to wait anymore?" Vassa sat up and observed him.

She still felt some type of way from their… argument? Was it an argument? More like disagreement.

"We've grown past that, haven't we?" Lazarus asked.

He spotted the plastic bag of food and snatched it before she could. He picked up a pupusa, inspecting it before taking a bite.

"This is good, what is it?"

Vassa got up and snatched the container back. "Do you normally eat food you don't know?"

They stared at one another. Then they spoke at the same time and laughed before she allowed him to speak.

He blew out a breath. "I'm sorry for snapping at you. I shouldn't have done that—"

"You don't need to apologize. I was out of line. It wasn't my business." Vassa peeled the polish off her nails before setting her shoulders back.

He grabbed her hand again and gave it a squeeze. She gave him a tentative smile before he took her container of food again. "You're going to be thrilled when you hear what news I have."

"What is it?"

"I have tickets to a Giants game and I want you to come with me."

Vassa opened her mouth to give a smart retort when she closed her mouth. "A baseball game? Like a date?"

Vassa licked her lips as she rocked back on the bed. He smiled and nodded. "Only if you're free. It's something everyone living in San Francisco should do at least once. So, you can either add this to the list or tack it on to the first item we finished."

"That sounds good, but I have to clean the microwave. Dara exploded eggs in there again and I have some homework and we can work on your studying—" Vassa listed them one by one on her fingers.

"Be like every other underachieving college student for once in your life and do it five minutes before class like everyone else."

She sighed. Her responsible nature was fighting this. Another part of her had no interest in doing her boring tasks.

"I'll get you whatever you want, even the baseball helmet nachos." Lazarus reached for a pupusa.

She eyed him. It would be nice to get out again. Homework could wait for tomorrow. "I'll go."

He grinned and reminded her to dress warmly, taking her container as he walked to the front room. When she was dressed and ready to go, he plopped a baseball hat on top of her head.

"Now you're truly ready."

"You didn't get this from the lost and found, did you?" Vassa frowned, poking at the hat.

"Let's go, so no one takes our seats."

They took the MUNI downtown before transferring to the train. As they emerged from underground, Vassa's heart raced. The crowd was a sea of orange and black. She tugged his hand, pointing when she saw a baby in full-on orange sports gear.

"Aren't you glad you said yes now?" He guided them through the crowd.

Vassa kept a grip on Lazarus's hand. The crowd grew thicker as they piled into the stadium. Colognes, sweat, and fried foods made a nauseating mix as they climbed the stairs. She got distracted by people selling glowing sunglasses and stuffed plushies and he had to circle back twice for her.

As they hurried to their seats, she could see their reflection in the glass panels of the stores. They looked like a couple.

She could see herself getting attached, and then what would happen? They would end up in a long-distance relationship. What if Lazarus didn't want a relationship? What if he was looking for hook-up like Dara said? Should she hook up with him? Gosh, she was overthinking now. Who said this was going there? She should just enjoy his company for as long as it lasted.

They made it to their seats in the nosebleed section. Oracle Stadium was beautiful at night so it made up for their seats. They could see the city, and the boats floating in the bay. Lazarus nudged her and pointed. "They have dogs to catch any of the balls that go into the water."

Vassa tried to glimpse the dogs on the boats. "Really? That's so cool."

The players ran drills with one another and kids shouted at the players to catch their attention.

Lazarus leaned over and said, "I'll go get us something, okay?"

She nodded, and he stood up and headed to the concession stands. Sitting there by herself, she watched the players as the music changed to the infamous "Are you ready for this?" song and people appeared on the big jumbo screen. She noticed a man holding a stick with cotton candy walking down the aisle. Vassa hadn't had cotton candy since she went to the circus. She called out to him and asked for two bags.

Lazarus found her munching on pink and blue cotton candy with her feet up on the railing, her lips stained by the dye of the candy. He took a photo with his phone. "I never thought I'd see the day when you would relax."

"Delete that." She pointed, but the gesture lost its threat since her fingers and lips were artificially purple.

He snickered and handed over a helmet of nachos before passing her a beer.

"I'm not gonna be able to eat this. Not after the pupusas." She held her stomach, gazing at all the food but already preparing room for it.

Lazarus put his legs up. "Eat it. It's a behemoth portion of stale chips and suspicious florescent cheese, questionable ground beef, and twenty-year-old jalapenos, salsa, and guacamole. A staple for a baseball virgin." He waved a chip at her and took a bite.

Vassa frowned, sniffing the nachos. "Food poisoning? Is that what you're telling me to expect?"

"It's all part of the experience."

She sighed before doing a Hail Mary: biting into a chip gingerly, she chewed slowly before nodding. It was actually good. She paused for a moment for her stomach to reject it, but when her guts didn't bubble, she went for another. Alternating between cotton candy, beer, and nachos, Vassa found herself leaning into Lazarus as the game began.

Licking her fingers, she pointed at the players. "Who's in the blue again?"

"The Dodgers." Lazarus's eyes didn't leave the field.

"We don't cheer for them?" She glanced at him and he shook his head.

"Absolutely not."

Vassa scratched her head. "How long is an inning?"

He clapped and cheered when the Giants struck the opposing player out, then said, "About twenty minutes. It depends."

"Depends?"

Lazarus cut his eyes at her. "There's early and late innings."

She didn't even know what that meant. When she watched his baseball game, she had been more focused on watching him play than on the logistics of the game. Vassa munched on another chip. "Now who is that player again? I think I've seen him in an insurance commercial."

Lazarus groaned, and she tossed her hands up. "I'm sorry I don't know what's going on!"

Rubbing his temples, he inhaled slowly. Lazarus explained the roles, players, and rules of it all and unspoken rules as well. She felt competent enough to cheer when one player hit a home run. When they struck out, she booed with the rest of the fans. When a player hit the ball and it went out of the stadium and into the water, she screamed, trying to see the dogs.

Baseball was definitely more interesting in person than on TV and with someone else. And she knew she was into it when Lazarus's arms went around her and she laid her head on his shoulder. She looked at him from under her lashes, but he was focused on cursing as the crowd as the playerstruck out. He squeezed her shoulder. "That better?"

She felt safe and comfortable, and he grinned back. The crowd roared and Vassa leaned closer, shouting for him to hear her. "Is this why you love baseball?"

"What exactly?"

Vassa lifted her hand and pointed to everything, "The people, noise, energy, and whatnot."

He was quiet and shifted in his seat, then he leaned forward, his mouth grazed her ear. "Only partially."

"Partially?" Vassa looked at him. She watched Lazarus's eyes take everything in. She could feel his body stiffen, and he punched the air as the player hit the ball.

"As you know, it was five of us boys in the house. Dad tried to go pro, but he never made it." Lazarus took a sip of his beer. "None of my brothers took to it. Then I came along. We would play catch in the backyard at first."

Vassa plucked another piece of cotton candy as his eyes followed the players.

"I just enjoyed hanging out with my dad. Having all of his attention and stuff—"

"Baby of the family syndrome." Vassa smirked.

He squeezed her side, making her laugh. "Yeah, maybe that. I grew to love baseball. Dad put me in the local league. I got better. You know, I wanted to make him proud. He would sit in the stands during practice and games. In about a year, I could run and steal a base."

"So even as a kid, you enjoyed having all the attention?"

Lazarus laughed at her. "The power was intoxicating." Then he shifted in the seat before taking a sip of beer. "Dad wanted me to get better. I think he believed his dream had hope again. So, he trained me. Hard. I got upset when I didn't make plays. When Dad was at work, I would play by myself."

She watched his face soften, and he sniffed, rubbing his nose. Here she was thinking he'd been some trust-fund baby since the cradle. "I felt like baseball was finally something only I could do. None of my brothers could do it. I thought I could stand out to my parents by being good. Not that they didn't love me, but all my brothers were special at something besides me. For a long time I used it as an excuse to fuck up."

Vassa placed a hand on his thigh as his face fell.

"As a freshman I was wild, you know that. Coach didn't take me seriously, and I wasn't the star player anymore, and I couldn't handle it. I knew Dad was upset. I didn't care but he sat me down and eventually it clicked. I tried to clean up. Dad and I worked night and day practicing again. Mom was worried about us out in the yard day and night, but we shrugged her off. This was our thing."

Lazarus eyes watered and he rubbed his jaw. "I remember last year, it was a normal day. We were at the field and I threw the ball toward Dad. But he collapsed." His foot tapped rapidly as he took another drink of his beer. "He had a stroke. I dragged him through the field to the car. I got him there in time, but the damage was done. His throwing hand was gone."

Vassa sighed and squeezed his thigh. "Lazarus."

"It's fine. I focused on helping Dad in recovery. The nerves in his hand were severely damaged. That just did something to me I can't explain. Since Dad couldn't practice with me anymore, I felt like it was my responsibility to fulfill the dream for him. Not let all his hard work go down the drain." Lazarus's head ducked and he sniffed. Vassa's heart broke and she circled her arms around his waist and hugged him tight. "He still jokes about me getting into the league one day but sometimes I don't know."

"You don't know what?" Vassa lifted her head from his chest.

He cut his eyes toward her. "Sometimes he'll get this look in his eye as he watches me play. He wants me to go big but I don't want to go to the MLB. I'm drawn to something else but I don't want to let him down. That's why I tolerate Harvey. Why I'm considering taking the job because I know I'll disappoint him by not getting in the league, he'll be impressed I'll have stability after so long. I just want to make him proud of me."

The crowd cheered as they hit another home run. Lazarus looked back at the field. Vassa bit her lip. Blinking back her own tears, she could only realize how dumb she'd been about him. All this time, he'd been changing and for his father. Who knew he could be so compassionate? "I'm sorry Laz—"

Lazarus stiffened and turned. "What did you call me?"

"Your name?"

Lazarus's grin threatened to break his entire face. "You called me Laz."

"I said Lazarus." She pulled back and crossed her arms.

"No. You said Laz. You called me *Laz.*" He nudged her, laughing.

She turned and focused on the field. He was staring, and she smiled, even though she didn't want to. "I swear I said Lazarus."

His arm came back over her shoulder and he placed a brief kiss on her temple. "Not so mean anymore, Vee?"

When the game ended, it was freezing outside. They made it to the train with the rest of the crowd, collapsing into the seats. She was full from the nachos, cotton candy, and beer. She closed her eyes and listened to the chatter. Lazarus nudged her shoulder. "The night is still young. Don't tell me you want to go in just yet?"

Vassa groaned and held her belly. "The nachos did me in."

"Well, before you fall asleep over there, I have one more thing for us to do."

"We're here."

Golden Gate Park at night wasn't the best place to be, with many critters and the unsavory of society. A few streetlamps gave a light, but it didn't shake the feeling they were being watched. She hoped for no more rabid raccoons.

Vassa was going to demand that they go back when they emerged through the thicket and she stopped in her tracks at the sight of a crowd of skaters with ultrabright glow sticks and neon flashing sunglasses. Music played and everyone glided in a circle on a makeshift skating rink. "What's this?"

There were a few people doing spins and tricks, some skating backward, some small children and couples holding hands.

Lazarus nudged her forward. "Skating after dark. The Church of 8 Wheels comes to the park every week. You can skate right?"

Vassa sputtered and held her stomach. She was regretting eating the nachos and cotton candy. He dragged her to the sign-up table. He paid for them and before she knew it, she was strapping the skates onto her feet and he was pulling her toward the make-shift rink.

"I can't do this!" she cried and pulled back, but she was deathly afraid of falling and when she lost her stance, she clung to him, allowing him to pull her forward with him.

"You can do this. Don't be afraid." He released her.

That was easier said than done. Holding her arms out, she called for him, people rushing past her. She looked like a baby trying to walk for the first time. She called him when he drifted too far and he came back as she lost her footing and grabbed him. "I can't believe you got me out here doing this."

He laughed at the baby steps she took. "You can say you roller skated in Golden Gate Park at night with the geriatric population."

Skaters breezed past, making her wobble and clutch him. She didn't think she would ever do this, much less with him. Much less with a smile on her face. They made it around and she grew confident. Releasing him, she swatted him away when he offered to hold her. The Bee Gees played. Imagining she was John Travolta in his white suit, she swayed left and right. Her mistake was trying to do the dance. It was not in the cards for her.

Lazarus reached out, but he was one second too late. She felt her center-of-gravity shift and her heart shoot into her throat. Her legs went up and her body went down. The world rushed by in a blur. Just lights and glowing bands. Faces appeared and disappeared as she waited for the pain she knew was coming.

The fall felt forever. Slow, almost suspended, then… impact.

A rush of air left her as pain radiated from her back up her spine to her head. Her bones moved when they shouldn't, jangled and scraping before settling on the cold concrete. Her eyes rolled around in her skull and she looked up into the night sky. Lazarus appeared above.

She blinked a few times to get only one of him to appear. "Please tell me nobody saw."

He looked around before he nodded. She groaned, closing her eyes as she felt him pull her up to a sitting position.

"A few, but I'm sure we can pay them off," Lazarus said.

She was no longer in the mood for skating. He dusted off her back and helped her up and to a bench. "Are you going for the world record of most concussions in the shortest span of time?"

Looking at the skaters, she saw that some fell and got back up, giggling. Others split and came back together, avoiding those on the ground.

Lazarus stared at her and she put her hand to her face. "What? Is something on it?"

"I like you Vassa. I always have."

Opening her mouth, she closed it. He liked her when she was a freshman? Awkward and pessimistic? When she thought she still looked good in her Y2K style and braces?

"That's good you like me. I don't think you woulda stuck around if you didn't."

He shook his head and leaned forward. "I mean I had a crush on you."

Air escaped her lungs as sirens rang in her brain. Vassa pointed to herself and he nodded.

"Huh." She looked back at the skaters.

They were silent before she said, "That makes me feel bad. I tried to make a voodoo doll of you once before..."

Lazarus and Vassa laughed. Her hands shook from adrenaline. Licking her lips, she turned to him.

"I admit I was a dick in the past with the pranks. I apologize. You seemed out of my league."

Now it was her turn to be surprised. Out of his league? She had to admit when she was a freshman she had wanted his attention. All the girls wanted his attention. She had thought she would be happier if she was a part of that popular group. It had made Alexa happy, but it never brought the joy Vassa expected. It went deeper and, as a freshman, she hadn't been ready to do that soul-searching. She told herself she didn't need people like that. She accepted the title of being a loner and made it who she was.

Vassa rolled her feet back and forth as her head pounded. She would probably regret confessing this, but she did it, anyway. "In some ways, I was jealous of you. I wished I could be one of the popular kids everyone liked and wanted to be around. You were just able to talk to everyone so easily. I never knew how you did it."

He had to get all sentimental on her and tell his secrets. Now she was airing out her dirty laundry. The soul crushing, panicky feeling of revealing herself with no response from him made her want to get up and go. The music changed to Etta James. That slowed the atmosphere down and the children left the rink, and more adults piled on.

"How about we start over with a clean slate? All judgments and appearances aside?" He stood up, holding out his hand.

There would be nothing wrong with starting over. He had proven himself to be someone reliable. It would be wrong for her to keep expecting him to be some past self.

"I've been sometimes rude and judgmental to you in the past. I mean it when I say I'm sorry."

She took his hand, and he squeezed it with a grin. She took his hand and let him lead her back onto the rink. They held hands, and she tried not to fall face first. When she looked up at him, his eyes seemed to glow in the dark. Squeezing his hand, she held tight. She wasn't sure if it was the beers and nacho combination, but the moon and her emotions swirled together, and she never felt so glad that Kiki had given him her bucket list. Lazarus was so much more than she thought. Strangely enough, they had many similarities. There wasn't anyone else she would want to accomplish the list with other than him.

CHAPTER FOURTEEN

"OH, MY GOD WE'RE REALLY in Vegas!" Dara gushed as they stepped out the taxi.

It was amazing how the weeks flew past. Between work, school, and studying, the entire campus was bursting with excitement for spring break. Fun and fun only.

"I know a few clubs we could hit. They have the best music and drinks." Kiki took a picture of the hotel's entrance.

"Stop sulking. We're here. You should be happy!" Dara linked her arms with Vassa as the boys went for their luggage.

She caught Lazarus's eyes, and he gave her a slow smile. Vassa blushed and looked away. They had fallen into a comfortable routine since their *date.* He would come by the yoga studio and walk her home after her shift. They had even gone back to her sushi place a few times. Had there been more kisses? Yes.

"Are you paying attention to me? Why do you have that silly look on your face?" Dara said.

Vassa blinked. "I'm listening."

The bags were distributed, and the guys paid the driver. Dara pulled her out of the heat into the air-conditioned lobby of the hotel. It was nearly eight in the morning, but already a crowd mingled near the slots and blackjack tables.

"This place is really nice. I'm liking this Jayden guy," Kiki said. Vassa missed the glare Dara shot her cousin. Jayden had hooked them up with a spot at the heart of the strip.

The LINQ hotel was as impressive as the pictures online. Classy, sleek, and the receptionists stood behind the counter in suits. No doubt without Jayden's parents' discount and splitting the cost of the rooms, they probably would have never set foot inside. Vassa's stomach growled as servers walked by with drinks and food, and guests passed dressed in everything from swanky attire to Hawaiian T-shirts and flip-flops.

Jayden booked the rooms and had to be the one to check them in. He nudged Lazarus to follow him but he hesitated for a second, giving Vassa a look before Jayden pulled him to the concierge line. Kiki looked between the both of them with interest as Dara oohed and aahed at the things in the lobby.

"Should we have a mimosa now?" Dara took out her phone and took pictures of the lobby.

"Yeah, that sounds like fun," Vassa muttered and Kiki squinted at her. Across the lobby there was a room leading into the casino area. A group of guys yelled as the dealer flipped the cards over at the blackjack table.

Dara continued to snap pictures. "Or should we walk the strip first? I know of a store—"

"What's going on with you?" Kiki interrupted Dara, pointing at Vassa.

It was best to play dumb. Kiki was a blabbermouth, and she didn't need all of Sacramento to know her business.

Vassa scratched her head. "What are you talking about?"

Dara looked between them as Vassa and Kiki stared-off. Vassa shook her head. Nope. Nada. Zilch. Kiki wouldn't get it out of her. She wasn't telling. A few seconds passed and when Vassa peeked over at Kiki but Dara joined in with the knowing look. *Traitor.*

"I swear it was only a kiss," Vassa blabbed.

Kiki squealed and launched herself at Vassa, spinning her around. They drew the attention of the people around them and Vassa gave them an apologetic smile as she tried to shush Kiki.

"That's old news," Dara said.

Kiki gasped. "She kissed Lazarus?"

Dara and Kiki's voices babbled happily. Vassa touched her temples as she closed her eyes when suddenly pain flared in her right arm and she realized Kiki had pinched her. "Ow!"

"Why didn't you tell me this? You've been sitting on this information the whole time?!" Kiki pinched Dara and she hollered.

Vassa rubbed the pain away. "It may have happened once or twice—"

Kiki pinched her again.

"Would you stop pinching me?" Vassa was losing the feeling in her arm.

"He's not a bad-looking guy. If you didn't have him, I would have made my move this time." Kiki looked Lazarus up and down like he was a full-course meal and Vassa exhaled.

She wasn't dating Lazarus yet but she just didn't like the idea of him being with another girl in front of her. Especially Kiki. That was a combination that could never be.

"I don't have him," Vassa said, seriously regretting opening her mouth.

"Then it's okay if I talk to him?" Kiki said.

"No."

"So, you are with him." Dara raised an eyebrow.

"I wouldn't say that." Vassa poked her lips out.

"Then what are you two? You don't look like the hooking up type." Kiki eyed Vassa.

"Why do people keep saying that?" It wasn't like they were planning on heading down to the chapel to get married. She didn't really know what to call them. They were friends… yes? A kiss didn't mean that they were committed, and she definitely wasn't gonna act like the clingy chick because he took her out on her first date. Even if they were, she didn't want to talk about it in a public place.

"We're just having fun. Does that satisfy the grapevine?" Vassa looked from Kiki to Dara. Kiki crossed her arms while Dara pouted, but they let it go. The guys had made it to the concierge desk now and she was grateful a bed would be coming soon. Now she needed a nap.

"How's the bucket list coming along?" Kiki asked.

That was a safe conversation. Vassa smiled. "I'm almost done, just three things left on the list."

The men from the blackjack table let out another roar of excitement, making them jump. More people moved in closer to the table, probably hoping their luck would rub off.

"Oh, what's left?" Kiki asked once the men's noise died down.

"Get wasted. Technically I accomplished that a while ago but I don't want to go into details about that night—"

"Don't worry about that. We'll get that done tonight. Who comes to Vegas to be sober? You know what they say, what happens in Vegas…" Kiki wriggled her eyebrows as the guys joined the group.

Jayden said, "Do you want the good news or plain news first?"

"Do you mean bad news?" Vassa asked.

"Bad is a man-made concept to force the population into socially acceptable forms of action." He raised an eyebrow.

Vassa narrowed her eyes in confusion as Dara stepped forward. "What did you do?"

"Why did I have to do something?" Jayden pressed a hand to his chest.

"If we have to fly back to San Francisco, I'm going to be upset and I will blame you." Dara poked him in the chest and he hissed.

"We can't go back yet. We haven't been to Fat Tuesday yet. I want to get that huge foot long tube of daiquiri!" Kiki stomped her feet.

"Don't tell me you booked it for a different day?" Vassa started to panic. Where would they sleep? The streets? It was too hot to be out on the streets.

"Y'all are taking this way out of context," Jayden said and

turned to Lazarus. "Help?"

Lazarus shook his head as the girls talked at once. Taking two fingers, Jayden whistled and silenced them.

"Good news is Laz and I have our double room. Ya'll don't."

Kiki, Dara, and Vassa began talking at the same time again and he cut them off.

"They didn't have another double on the floor so they gave us two single rooms so battle amongst yourselves on who gets a room to themselves."

Kiki started to speak but Dara cut her off. "Kiki and I will share. Vassa, you can have the room."

Kiki opened her mouth to object but Dara shook her head. "Aunt Nina told me to monitor you and my eye is not leaving you for this entire trip."

It was decided. Since they had arrived so early their rooms weren't ready. Leaving their bags with the bellhop, they walked down the strip to Denny's for breakfast. Once seated at a booth, they flipped through the menu.

"I think I'm going to get the salted caramel and banana cream pancakes with a chocolate shake," Lazarus said as he pointed to the picture on the menu.

He sat on the other side of Vassa and she leaned over his shoulder to see what it was.

"You're going to have the runs after eating that."

"We're in Vegas." He shrugged.

"You don't want to come back fifty pounds heavier than how you left." She flipped the page, then tapped it in triumph. "Here's something healthy. The senior breakfast. Egg whites with fresh spinach and turkey bacon strips."

Lazarus rolled his eyes. "I don't need to control my cholesterol."

"You will thank me when you're a sixty-year-old man and the doctor says he's never seen arteries as clear as yours."

"Aww, looking out for each other? You both are too cute," Kiki said.

Vassa gave subtle headshake. She should have never told her anything.

"Lazarus, how are you lately?" Kiki twirled the spoon back and forth in her hand.

"I got a good grade on my English quiz, thanks to Vee right here." He nudged her.

"Is that so?"

Kiki went to ask another question when Vassa shot her foot out and kicked Kiki in the shin. She yelped, reaching under the table to rub her leg as she shot Vassa a sharp look.

"Are you okay?" Lazarus asked.

Nodding, Kiki winced. "Hit my shin."

Their server took their orders. When the food was brought out, Dara hit her orange juice glass with her fork. Clearing her throat, she dug into her fanny pack and pulled out a folded sheet of paper.

"I've taken the liberty of forming an itinerary. I found all the free, cheap, and discounted things along with some pricier things if the need should arrive. After this we have exactly twenty minutes to—"

Jayden snatched the paper. He pushed her away easily when she tried to snatch it back.

"We're on spring break. You want us on a schedule? We should move with the energy of the group."

Dara snatched the paper back from him and rolled her eyes. "If we plan nothing, we're going to waste time."

Kiki leaned over and snatched the paper. "You even scheduled meals. This is Vegas. We should get drunk, throw up, and do it all over again."

"I don't want to throw up," Vassa said.

Vassa took the paper from Kiki and read it. Lazarus leaned over her shoulder to get a peek.

"I see nothing wrong with a little structure," Vassa said.

Dara snatched the paper from Vassa. They finished their

meals, and the server placed the bill down. Vassa was slouched in the booth with her eyes half closed when Kiki clapped and forced her to sit up.

"Now that we've eaten, I propose a nap, and then we party." Kiki looked around the table before she leaned forward and whispered, "Let's dine and dash."

Vassa's eyes went wide. "No!"

"Yes."

Jayden raised an eyebrow at Kiki. "You're wild."

She winked at him. "Thank you."

"That's a crime." Vassa leaned forward.

Lazarus scratched his chin. "I bet people do it all the time."

Vassa narrowed her gaze at him.

Dara shook her head. "You want to dine and dash? Don't you have enough criminal charges?"

"I mean, this place is crowded. They'll make their money back, and it's Vegas. Let's get wild!" Kiki grabbed her purse and moved to the edge of the booth.

"What about the server? He was nice and gave me extra bacon." Vassa began breathing rapidly, her palms sweaty.

"This will mess with my karma. I've perfectly aligned spirituality at this moment," Jayden said.

"Your karma's been shot for a while now, pal," Dara said, and Jayden narrowed his eyes on her.

Kiki was already rising from the booth. "We're being wild this week. Just do it. Get up one at a time, meet me in the lobby and walk out." She stood up and walked toward the entrance.

The rest of the table looked at one another. Dara got up next. Jayden followed.

"You ready?" Lazarus asked her.

"This is wrong. Why are we doing this? Why are none of you fighting back?" Vassa took a quick sip of her water. Her heart pounded in her ears and all those bible lessons not to steal came rushing to the forefront of her mind.

"Add this to your bucket list."

"Crime?" she hissed.

Lazarus stood up and waited for Vassa. Her heart was beating a mile a minute as she stood up. They were walking out when she realized she left her phone on the table. Lazarus wanted her to leave it, but she told him to wait. Running back to the table, she picked up her phone.

"Hurry," Lazarus hissed.

Vassa tried to shove it in her pocket as he pushed her forward. "I don't want to leave it. I need to call my mom later."

"Hey!"

Lazarus and Vassa looked at one another. Taking her hand, he yanked her through the crowd, knocking into families waiting by the host stand.

"Hey!"

The rest of the gang was waiting, but once they saw Lazarus and Vassa sprint past, they all descended the escalator, tumbling over one another down to the strip. Vassa looked back and the server and the manager were on their ass.

"They didn't pay!"

"Run!" Kiki said.

Vassa gasped as Lazarus pulled her down the escalator. She thought her face was going to meet the metal and she barely caught her footing as they made it to the bottom and took off into the crowd.

"I'm going to jail!" Vassa cried.

"Not if you keep running!" Lazarus dodged people easily, pushing an older couple to the side. Vassa didn't dare look back.

"Hey!"

The voice was close. They definitely broke safety laws. The gang split, rushing through the throng of people, running across the street when it was a green light. Taxis and cars honked their horns loudly. Some people watched with curiosity and cheered for them. Vassa didn't dare look behind her. This was the longest and farthest she ever ran since high school P.E. class. The thought of getting booked into the jail and her parent's disappointed faces had her moving faster than Lazarus. They ducked into an open casino, catching their breaths.

"Vegas, right?" Kiki tried to catch her breath. Vassa closed her eyes as she leaned forward, placing her hands on her knees.

Welcome to Vegas.

CHAPTER FIFTEEN

"YOU SHOULD HAVE CALLED ME the moment you got there!"

Vassa sighed, sitting on the edge of the bed as her mother lectured her. She had gotten out of the shower when she heard her phone ringing. Now she had to listen how her mother rant about sending the cavalry after her.

"We ate and then took a nap. I just woke up about thirty minutes ago." Vassa picked up the remote and turned the TV on.

"I didn't suffer in labor for five days to lose you to the drug mules in Vegas. You know, I was watching on the news that Vegas is the number one place for drugs, sex trafficking, and other lawlessness. It's getting worse by the day! I was talking with Tanya from next door too, she said her daughter went there and stayed at mobster's hotel! Just drugs and death! Tanya's girl watched the mob kill someone at dinner and bury them in the desert. You want that? To be buried in the desert? Then you had your poor grandmother over here losing her mind. Tell her mom, how you were losing your mind."

Vassa flicked dirt from under her nails. "I thought you were in labor with me for three days?"

They were video chatting and her mother turned the phone toward Laura, Vassa's grandmother, and told her to lecture Vassa on respecting her elders. "Eve, leave me alone. I'm trying to read here."

"Hi grandma," Vassa said.

The older woman looked at the phone. Squinting, she

pushed her reading glasses up and smiled. "Hi baby, having fun?"

The camera turned to her mother and she grumbled, "I'm a mother. I just want to know you're safe."

Vassa mumbled some sort of acknowledgement and flipped through the channels. It was a black and white movie with cowboys riding on fake horses. "For the fifth time, I'm sorry."

Eve seemed satisfied now, but that would not last long. "How is everything going?"

"Fine, all we've done is eat and sleep." It was best not to include dining and dashing.

Eve shifted the camera. "Are you being nice? Putting yourself out there to make friends?"

"Mom, please. Let's not start that. I'm having fun. These are my friends."

That was the truth. No matter how annoying or law-breaking they were. She had formed a tiny community without even realizing it. She didn't want to talk about her faults or anything of the like. She had moved on.

"I know large groups of people aren't your thing."

Her mother meant well but this wasn't the time to bring up the past game tapes. Vassa knew why she acted the way that she did and she didn't need a reminder. She didn't want one right now at this moment.

"Thanks, but I'm fine. You'll be proud of me lately. I've hung out with Oscar. Lazarus isn't so bad now. Kiki is here—"

For the first time in a long time, she felt a part of something again.

"Oh? Isn't that the foul mouth girl I met? Be careful with her. She'll get you into trouble,"

Too late for that.

"Lazarus? The same one from before? Now honey, I think it's about time that we had the talk—"

"Mom!"

"I've been waiting for this moment for so long. Now honey,

you're gonna get… feelings. In your groin. Be smarter, though! Don't let her lead you into unpleasant situations because the guy can slang some sausage—"

"*Mom!*"

"I told you before. Don't bring home no babies. If you gonna be out there acting like a grown woman, wrap it up. That's all I ask. I'm an old woman now. I can't take any surprises."

Vassa rubbed her temples. Her mother was too much right now. "Please stop trying to be hip with words you heard off reality TV."

"More than anything, I just want to say, I'm proud of you."

That made Vassa sit up. "For what?"

Peering into the phone, Vassa saw her mom's eyes sparkle with unshed tears. That made her heart drop. She never liked to see her mother cry. She would do anything in this world to keep her happy. "Mom, what's wrong?"

Eve shook her head and wiped her eyes. "It's just after that entire ordeal. You shut down, baby. You didn't want to eat, go outside, pretty much anything that involved getting out that bed. You don't know what it's like to see your child in pain and not be able to help."

Vassa had never heard her mother say this before.

"Besides wanting to kick that little girl's ass for making you cry, I felt weak. It took months for you to be normal again and when you did, you never talked to us about it. It was like it was done and over. I didn't want to push you, but you were never the same. This underlying anger and hurt you just couldn't let go, most likely because of the closure you never got. But now? Baby, there's a brightness around you. I hope it's not because of sex—"

Vassa groaned but Eve continued.

"It's because you're healing. Learning to trust and live life again. We can't avoid pain, betrayal and heartache, Vasilisa, especially if it comes from the ones we trust the most. We can only control if we let it beat us to our knees or get up and continue to live."

Picking at her fingernails, Vassa closed her eyes so the tears wouldn't fall out.

"You may never get the closure you want from Alexa, but realize sometimes you don't need it. You living and learning to trust again is closure. You understand me? So, no matter what I say about mobsters and drugs, you better have a damn good time in Vegas because you more than deserve it."

Sniffing, Vassa wiped a tear that had escaped and sat back on the bed. "Aw Mom."

"I know, I know. We both about to be crying on this phone and that wasn't my intentions. What's the plan tonight?"

"We're going out dancing."

Someone knocked on her door. Pulling the towel closer to her body, she stood up from the bed and scurried over, looking through the peephole.

"Can I call you later?"

"Remember, watch your drinks and stay together."

"All right, I love you."

Vassa opened the door and Dara came in. "What are you doing? You're supposed to be ready!" Dara's hair was pressed and her makeup done flawlessly. She wore a leather skirt and fitted blouse that was serving up all the cleavage.

Vassa wolf whistled. "When have I ever seen this side of you? Pulling out the big guns to get a high roller?"

Vassa went to her suitcase to pull out her dress for the night.

"I'm just trying to fit the part," Dara said.

Vassa laughed. It didn't take Vassa long to get her dress on and rarely did she straighten her hair, but it was a special occasion tonight.

"I'm ready for your makeup magic." Stepping out of the bathroom, she held her arms out. "Do I look totally bad?"

She wore a minidress. Sexier than what she had worn to the cocktail party, it was pink with sequins, backless, and strappy. It hugged every curve, was flattering to her angles, and hid her tummy just right.

Dara's eyes were watery and Vassa rolled her eyes at her. "Don't get all sappy."

"I can't help it."

Once the makeup was complete, she slipped on her shoes. Dara linked her arm with Vassa's.

"We're going out with a bang? Thelma and Louise?"

Vassa squeezed her arm. "Always."

They stepped into the hallway as Kiki opened her bedroom across the hall, and Vassa gasped. She was wearing tight leather pants and a see-through mesh top. *With no bra.* Vassa's hands covered her eyes as Dara groaned. "Do you have to wear that? Your nipple piercings are out."

Kiki waved them off. "I look good. Now come on, everyone's ready!"

They stepped into Lazarus and Jayden's room. Kiki and Dara sat on the closest bed as Vassa walked to the other bed. Lazarus stood at the desk by the window with several bottles of liquor varying in sizes and shapes. He held red plastic cups in both hands and he turned and smiled. "Just in—" Lazarus's mouth fell open as he looked at Vassa.

She looked at herself and then back to him. "Too much?"

Shaking his head, he handed her a cup, still staring. Jayden chuckled as he nudged Lazarus to give him the other cup. Vassa sat on the other bed and her stomach began to turn slightly when she saw the tequila in his hand.

"I don't have good memories of tequila," she said.

Jayden took the chair from the desk and fell back into it. "Who does?"

"Not me," Kiki said.

Another cup was in front of her face. It was filled with orange juice and she looked up to see Lazarus raising an eyebrow. "I like my memories with tequila."

Blushing, she snatched the cup from him muttering a thanks.

"Let's make a toast," Lazarus said.

Jayden grinned as Dara and Kiki crowded onto the bed with Vassa. They raised their cups as Lazarus spoke.

"To all of you. You're all my friends." He looked around the room, his eyes lingering on Vassa a little bit longer. "Here's to a night we won't remember with the best people in the world, now let's get to drinking!"

They cheered and clinked their cups before tossing back the drinks. Vassa balked at the taste as she chased it with the orange juice.

"Let's do another," Kiki said.

Vassa groaned as Lazarus went for the bottle to pour more shots. It wasn't even ten o'clock yet.

The world was spinning.

It wasn't spinning, maybe she was spinning, or the world had lost gravity and she was floating. She wasn't sure at this point. After pre-gaming they decided to walk the strip in order to kill some time before the clubs really got jumping. She had about three or four shots, probably, before stopping at Fat Tuesday for Kiki. They ended splitting the daiquiri tube. Vassa had forgotten that rum wasn't kind to her either.

Vassa trudged behind the group, mentally telling herself to stay upright as they strolled the promenade. Someone bumped into her, jarring her. She hissed and squinted at the lights from the oncoming restaurants and stores. Kiki and Dara hollered at the Chippendale dancers passing by.

She felt something warm press against her side and she blinked lazily. "Hi."

"Hello to you." Lazarus's face was flushed and his eyes twinkled.

They passed a street performer dancing to "Thriller." Lazarus tossed a few bills into her hat as Vassa grabbed his shirt and pointed. A candy store. Her mouth watered at all the candies she could see through the glass. She hit his shoulder multiple times as she pointed. "Look, look at that. *Look, look*…"

"What?" Lazarus squinted at the store.

"Do you want some? Do you want me to buy you some?" She was pulling him toward the store.

Lazarus blinked and allowed her to guide him. "Yeah."

They were greeted by the sweet smell of sugar and chocolate. Candy lined the walls and counters in vibrant shades. Customers walked by with plastic bags filled to the brim with treats. Lazarus and Vassa grabbed a bag and recklessly stuffed it with candy. Her mouth watered at the sugar-covered fruit jellies, licorice, sour candies, and gum drops. It all went in, along with a handful of chocolate pralines. Lazarus appeared, munching on cotton candy.

Vassa gasped. "Nooo, they have… They have cotton candy? Where?"

"Yes." Lazarus smacked his lips not answering.

"I want some." She reached over for his bag and he blocked her.

"You… You, you have more than enough candy." Lazarus pulled her back.

Pouting, she didn't fight him as he led her to check out. They found a bench and sat down with their bounty. Lazarus stole a peanut butter cup, and she looked around.

"I uh… I think we lost the group." Vassa spun around and it made her head spin.

Lazarus blinked. "I think we have."

Vassa bit into a chocolate and moaned at the taste. She was going to have to come back to get some more. "Have we ever been drunk together?"

Lazarus leaned over and flicked her forehead. "Didja forget karaoke night?"

Vassa gave a loopy grin. "Oh."

Lazarus snatched another chocolate. Licking her lips, she

tried to ignore the tingly feeling that rose as his tongue grazed his bottom lip. It was totally unfair that he was unaware of the reaction he was causing as he smacked loudly. Looking away, she tried to blink some sobriety into herself.

Lazarus swayed, "I didn't tell you then, but I feel like… like I can tell you now. It could just be the alcohol."

Vassa looked at Lazarus and he sucked his teeth. "You suck as a singer."

"I suck? What!"

"You suck. I just didn't want to hurt your feelings, so I went along with it." Lazarus reached for another candy.

Vassa slapped his hand, making him drop the chocolate. "I guess I should tell the truth too. When you hit that high note with "I Will Survive," I thought you should just let Gloria Gaynor sing it."

They both laughed as the crowd continued to rush by.

The slight breeze ruffled his blond hair, and he looked dashing against the blacktop. It made him look really sophisticated and mysterious. His blue eyes took in everything in front of him and when he looked at her, she could see the deeper flecks of green in his irises. She had to tell him. Especially if she wanted to move forward into whatever was happening between them. It made her feel happy, and it made her feel sad.

"Why do you look sad?"

Vassa didn't answer right away. She stole his cotton candy. "You remember when you told me I could trust you? When I was ready?"

Lazarus nodded. A group of guys walked by whooping and hollering. "Well… I don't know how to say this or where to start."

"Whatever you want to say." He grabbed her hand and squeezed it.

Vassa's eyebrows drew together, and she snacked on a few more pieces of cotton candy.

"You're the reason Alexa and I aren't friends."

Lazarus blinked and leaned back on the bench. He opened

his mouth and closed it, squinting at her as his brain fired off. "What?"

She licked her lips. "Well, *part* of the reason."

He didn't say anything and Vassa took a couple of deep breaths, feeling the fog lift from her brain slightly. "Alexa and I met in middle school. Typical outsider story, she was new and I was a loner. Over time, it grew into a real sisterhood. I got accepted to PGU, and convinced her to come with me."

Vassa twisted her fingers. "I was so excited. We were going to be roommates and be college girls and just have fun believing all the lies they tell you about what college is going to be like."

Lazarus watched her. As the memories flooded back.

"We took the same classes and were in the same clubs. We were the Goody Two-shoes nerds in school. Alexa wanted to shed that when we got to college. I didn't care about that." She felt like an eighteen-year-old freshman again. Adulthood was intoxicating, being on your own for the first time. For Alexa it had been overwhelming.

"It was little things that caused issues. She would be out late into the night and come back to our dorm, loud and smelling like alcohol. Or not clean up the room from things like that. It caused some tension, but I let it go because she was my best friend." Vassa took the bag of cotton candy from him, ignoring his protest.

"I didn't know she was having suicidal thoughts again. She had them in high school, but she had said nothing to me." It still bothered Vassa to this day. Even after everything that transpired between them, the awkward meeting at the party, she wanted nothing horrible to happen to Alexa. "She confided in me at dinner that she was considering taking a bunch of pills."

Vassa felt Lazarus's shocked look and nodded.

"By that time, grades had come out. She was failing. Her parents were furious and threatened to cut her off and bring her back home. She hated her major, but all the friends she made were in there. It was a terrible combination at the wrong time. I told our resident advisor, who told other people. They admitted her to the hospital." Vassa closed her eyes, imagining the sterile walls of the psych unit.

"I visited her every day. Eventually they released her, but when she got back, she was mad at me. Told me I overreacted. That she didn't want me to tell anyone because it could ruin her reputation. Things got really rocky between us." Vassa passed Lazarus a chocolate from his bag when he motioned for one.

"Only then?" Lazarus muttered.

Vassa nodded. "She was on academic probation, and I even did her homework for her. When we'd hang out, she told me to act normal around her other friends. Then she told me what to wear and how to talk. I walked on eggshells around her: trying to avoid conflict, trying to remain encouraging." This was the part of the story that made her blood boil with anger.

"Do you remember the house party in Oakland you invited us to?" Vassa asked.

Lazarus nodded.

"I didn't want to go, but I went to be supportive. Alexa had a major crush on you at this point. Being the friend I was, I wasn't going to make a move on you or anything, girl code, ya know? She wore this yellow dress to get your attention." Vassa sat up and ran her hand over her own dress. "With the shoulders cut out and low-cut. I guess you said you liked yellow, and she thought it would get you to notice her."

He made a face, and she shook her head. Men were so oblivious sometimes.

"Well... you didn't. You came straight for me. It pissed her off, but she saved face. I tried hard to get you to pay attention to her. I went to the bathroom, and she followed me. I didn't make it out of the stall before she told me straight up: 'You know I like Lazarus. If you're my friend, you won't talk or smile at him, at all.' And she left." Vassa chewed the candy aggressively as her foot tapped rapidly on the ground.

"I stood on the wall but you came back again and again

asking me to dance. Eventually you just pulled me off the wall and made me dance with you—"

Lazarus gave a low laugh. "I remember that."

"Accusations from Alexa became normal and she started hanging out with this girl Theresa more than me. The accusation was that I thought I was better than her because my grades were good, my parents sent me money, and I made friends with my professors. I coulda ignored it but Theresa… She called Alexa and asked had she been online." Vassa felt cold, hard.

"Someone posted about Alexa's psych visit. She accused me of posting it online. I told her I didn't do it, that it was Theresa. For some reason Theresa never liked me and I could see through her bullshit. But the campus is small and gossip gets around. She insisted that I betrayed her." Vassa ground her teeth as heat filled her body. "After all the times I had supported her, she sacrificed our entire friendship over an accusation. And one that wasn't even true."

Vassa had to force herself to continue the story.

"She publicly outed me online. Everything I ever told her. She even made a fake page about me and posted some problematic stuff. You know we planned to go to New York together? Alexa, Dara, and I. That was obviously over but I'm glad that Dara believed me through the whole mess. Dara insisted on changing apartments with me. Alexa and I hadn't spoken in a month or so, until the party in Daly City."

Lazarus said nothing. Vassa's heart beat fast as she remembered the awful feeling of that night. Wanting to cry, scream, hit something, and tear her hair out all at once. Why did Alexa have to do that to her? Weren't they sisters? They were supposed to be each other's maid of honor at their weddings. Godmothers to their unborn children. New York had been what they'd dreamed about since middle school.

Lazarus placed his arms around her and she let him hold her. Planting her face in his shirt, she let the Irish Spring comfort her. "I think what makes it so hurtful is that after all the support I have given her, she wasn't able to give me the benefit of the doubt. Once she was gone, it's like everyone saw me differently. This monster. That's when I told myself I rather be alone than with people. No matter how good you are to them, they will turn on you." Vassa believed that with full certainty. "I've been keeping to myself and just focusing on graduating."

"What about Dara?" Lazarus asked.

Vassa laughed. "Dara didn't give me a choice. She's been herself since the beginning and forced me out of the funk after Alexa. She's not like Alexa, but… I keep my guard up. I can't help it. I'm always thinking, when am I gonna be alone again?"

She looked at Lazarus. She couldn't read the look on his face. There weren't any looks of pity, which she was grateful for. "I'm sorry you had to hear that long, drawn-out story. I don't want any pity or whatnot, I was just—"

"You don't have to explain anything to me."

Vassa stared at him and he cupped her cheek with his other hand. She closed her eyes briefly as she leaned into it.

"Thank you for trusting me. You don't have to worry," Lazarus whispered.

Vassa smiled and sniffed before he pinched her cheek. "Getting soft on me, Vee?"

She punched him. "It seems like I'm like that a lot with you lately."

Lazarus sighed, and he finished another candy. She held onto his hand, scooting over to rest her head on his shoulder. His hands were rough yet gentle and constant. He had always been constant, even when she was difficult. He tugged her close, leaning in. She licked her lips and swallowed, wondering if his lips tasted as sweet as the candy now. His other hand came to push her straightened hair behind her ear.

"Did I tell you how fantastic you look tonight?"

Vassa shook her head.

"You're beautiful. I love your hair like this. It's different. I like the curls more but this? Did it take a long time?" He ran his hand through her hair, twisting the strands.

"Not too long."

Their lips met and her mind went blank again. She hoped after kissing him so many times, it wouldn't turn her into a potato anymore. She was learning to crave his kisses like she needed air. They energized her. Brought her into the present moment and didn't let her hide away in her shadows. Placing another soft kiss on her lips, he pulled back, giving her a big grin before kissing her again. She laughed against his lips as he continued his soft pecks.

Someone screamed from above. Pulling back, Vassa's mouth dropped open, and she laughed as she watched people come down on zip lines above them.

"Let's do that!" Vassa stood up and her eyes followed the line.

Lazarus looked up. "We're tipsy enough for it."

She felt raw and exposed and she tried hard not to close up. What she needed was something to cut this raw feeling.

Five minutes later, they were standing at the edge of the platform. Helmets on, they put her bags and candy into a little pouch that was attached to the harness she was in. Now that she was way up here, she was sober and shook her head.

"We should come back with the others."

The employee strapped Lazarus in, and he choose to lie suspended like Superman. "Too late to back out now. Think about your bucket list."

Think about your bucket list, think about your bucket list...

She nodded but remembered that in a movie she watched, a girl went ziplining and got stuck halfway down the line. Then she peed on the crowd of people below her. She prayed that didn't happen because she felt the urge for the bathroom.

They strapped her in and pointed to a bar above her she could hold onto. As she looked over the edge, her stomach turned dangerous, and she felt her mouth water. *Don't puke!* She wasn't afraid of heights. *I'm not afraid of heights.* She repeated it like a prayer.

"Relax, it'll be fun," Lazarus said.

Safety instructions explained, the employees backed off. She was doing this for bragging rights only. A countdown began. The people in line snickered in anticipation, and she squeezed her eyes shut.

Lord, don't let me hit the ground.

There was a snap! She jumped and opened her eyes, then shut them as they moved. Everyone cheered as they picked up speed, heading down the line. Vassa screamed as the wind whipped past her face and she clutched the bar above her.

"Open your eyes!"

She didn't want to do it, but she did. People below looked up, pointing and waving at them as went by. The High Roller glowed in the distance. She screamed in excitement instead of fear. She let go of the bar, arms spread out like she was flying, the wind slipping through her fingers.

"I can't believe I'm doing this!" she screamed. And in the seconds that followed, she was filled with emotions like nothing she had felt in a very long time.

The employees on the other side caught them as they slid in. Her heart was racing, and she rocked on her heels as she waited for them to unstrap her.

"Oh my God, let's do that again!" she told Lazarus when he was out of the harness.

"Let's go!" His hair was wild and he swayed.

He went to kiss her but she blocked him with her hand.

"Excuse me," she muttered and clutched her stomach. This time, she had practice. Slipping through crowd, she found the nearest trash can and puked out her guts. All while the drunk crowd cheered her on.

Vassa's Extraordinary Senior Send-Off

~~1. Get totally wasted and regret nothing.~~

~~2. See all the tourist spots in San Francisco.~~

3. Have an epic last Spring Break.

~~4. Do something completely wild.~~

~~5. Sneak into a party or event uninvited and pretend to be someone else.~~

~~6. Go on a date.~~

CHAPTER SIXTEEN

"CHECK OUT THE BELLAGIO WHILE you're there. I won ten thousand on a table there before." Gideon laughed as Lazarus balanced his phone on his shoulder and pulled up his pants.

"Did you forget we're poor college students?"

"You still have the credit card I gave you. I told you to go wild."

Lazarus zipped his pants and looked for his shirt. "Then I would owe you." That was one thing Lazarus didn't want to do. Leech more money off his family when his own was right there in front of him. All he needed was to hear back from that place he'd applied to.

"Rather me than Harvey."

After Vee's confession, everything made sense. He could she see still felt uncomfortable with telling him. He hadn't thought she ever would, but it was humbling knowing she trusted him. He didn't want to do anything to ruin that.

"I have my money," Lazarus said.

The bathroom opened and Jayden came out with a towel. "You have a razor?"

Lazarus reached into his bag and tossed him one.

"What are you doing tonight?" Gideon asked, and Lazarus could hear a dog barking in the background.

"Supposedly gambling and a show. I'm hoping that's all. I haven't drunk this much since Amsterdam." Lazarus reached for his shoes.

"Amsterdam was a good time." Gideon chuckled.

Someone knocked at the door. He opened it to find a tipsy Kiki pushing past him. "Hello to you."

The girls were right behind and Dara sent him an apologetic smile. He inhaled sharply and a smile broke on his face as Vassa emerged. He was definitely grateful for the Vegas trip. His eyes soaked up the cheetah print dress. It made her thighs and ass look delectable.

"Lovin' the cheetah," he told her.

She playfully slapped his chest. "It's leopard."

"That was my second guess." His eyes fell to her swaying hips as Gideon cleared his throat.

"Are you still there?"

Lazarus had forgotten his brother was on the phone. Closing the door, he spotted Kiki pouring shots. "I am, but I have to go."

"If you need the card, it's there."

"Thanks, but don't worry." Lazarus had his fingers crossed that he would hear something soon. He ended the call and noticed Dara sitting on the edge of Jayden's bed with a pinched expression.

"Oh, my God! I forgot the chaser," Kiki said. Turning to Vee, she set the alcohol bottle down and grabbed her hand. "Come with me."

Vassa didn't have a chance to complain as Kiki rushed out of the room. Music thumped from Jayden's speaker in the bathroom as Lazarus sat on his bed, tying his shoes. Glancing at Dara, she glared at the bathroom door.

"Wanna talk about it?" Lazarus asked as Dara's knuckles turned white.

"There's nothing to talk about."

Lazarus raised an eyebrow.

Dara glanced at him. "He told you, he didn't he?"

Lazarus shrugged as he crossed his legs on the bed. "It's easy to pick up."

"Don't tell Vassa." Dara sat forward on the bed.

"Why?"

Dara looked at her hands before letting out a sigh. "She's judgey about hook-ups and stuff like that. So can you just keep it to yourself until I tell her?"

"Okay." Lazarus paused before he grinned. "Was it good?"

Instead of replying, Dara flipped him off. The music blasting through the speakers couldn't drown out Lazarus's diabolical laugh. The bathroom door opened and Jayden stepped out fully dressed and shaved. He froze when he saw Dara sitting there. Then he looked at Lazarus.

"I'm not even going to go there," Lazarus said.

Banging came from the front door as Kiki demanded to be let in. Jayden answered the door. Oblivious to the awkward situation occurring, Kiki frowned and threw her hands up. "Can we go now?"

They headed to Fremont Street. The crowd grew thicker and Vee took his hand and pressed in closer to avoid getting trampled by the loud drunks. Binion's Gambling Hall sign glowed high above as Kiki led them inside. The ringing of winning slot machines overpowered them alongside rows of tables with dealers dressed as cowgirls. They had every game you could think of: craps, roulette, poker, and more. He spotted a live poker tournament going on.

"Slots or craps?" Jayden said.

Lazarus looked to Vee. "What do you suggest?"

He loved her brown eyes under the twinkling lights.

"Penny machines first. I read one woman won ten thousand dollars off it."

"I say we try the table." Kiki miraculously had a drink in hand.

The group split, Lazarus, Vee, and Dara heading for the slots, while Kiki and Jayden headed for the tables. Lazarus saw Dara and Jayden exchange looks before they split. He was going to get the full story from Jayden later.

They found an open row of slots and sat. An old woman sat in the slot next to him with an oxygen tank in one hand, a drink in the other. She alternated between feeding two slot machines. Lazarus nudged Vee and whispered, "How long do you think she's going to last?"

Vee gasped and hit his shoulder. "That's rude. That's going to be you one day."

"Oh, I plan to look this good till the grave." Lazarus smirked.

"So, you're going to die casket sharp, huh?"

Lazarus nodded and slid his money into the machine. "Totally, just make sure they don't put funny makeup on me."

"Who said I'm going to be planning your funeral when you're ninety?" Vee watched his slot machine and laughed when it was a whammy.

Lazarus gave her a long look. He grabbed her chin and placed a peck on her lips. "You know we're going to be together for life, Vee? Can't get rid of me."

The machine buzzed; she had won nothing. At that moment, Vee glanced over at him, her brown eyes wide and beguiling. He had to kiss her—to taste those sinful crimson lips. Lazarus dipped his head to do just that when Dara shouted, "Ew, get a room!"

Sliding his money into the slot, he pulled the lever. Now he realized why the slots were so addicting. He needed three lemons to win the jackpot. Sometimes he got one, and other times he got two. He came so close to winning, but the spinning stopped between the symbols. Lazarus wasn't sure how much time passed. They put more and more money in and got squat back.

Dara got bored and left. Eventually, Vee threw in the towel and Lazarus tried to hang on. After the next five flops, he, too, gave up.

"I thought I would win big. Guess that was a lie, huh?" Vee said.

"Let's keep hope alive."

As they were leaving, the old lady leaned over, putting a penny in Lazarus's machine. She pulled the lever and instantly the lights and sirens went off.

Lazarus's mouth dropped open. "You gotta be kidding me."

The old woman hollered as the pennies poured out onto the

floor faster than she could catch.

"C'mon, let's go." Vee pulled him by his shirt.

"I can't believe it!"

Jayden and the others were at the roulette table. Lazarus and Vee squeezed through the crowd to the table. To his left was an Elvis impersonator and the guy was obviously drunk. Elvis reached out a hand. "Hi, I'm Eddie."

"Dammit." Jayden threw his hands up as the dealer took his chips. Apparently, the stakes were high. Lazarus shook the impersonator's hand. Kiki tried to calm Jayden down as she took a sip of her martini.

"I should have blown on the dice." Kiki gripped her hair.

"You should have blown the dealer." Dara downed the rest of her drink, flagging a server.

"New shooter!" the dealer said.

Kiki looked at Vee and Lazarus. Vassa moved out of the way before he could comprehend what was happening and Kiki forced him to the table. "I got a new shooter here!"

They shoved dice into his hand.

"What?" he asked.

Jayden kept his head on the table, his shoulders shaking slightly. Dara patted him on the back.

"Just roll! Don't stop until we're driving home in a new Escalade," Kiki said.

To his left, Eddie the Elvis impersonator gave him a big thumbs up. Vassa even squeezed his arm. Lazarus tossed the dice carelessly, waiting to hear the bad news when the dealer said, "We have a winner!"

The entire table roared as Kiki shook the life outta him and screamed in his ear.

Vee leaned over his shoulder. "You did it!"

Kiki was on him. Licking her lips, her eyes ran over the table before she said to him, "Roll! Roll until we're in a new tax bracket. Dara, are you seeing this?"

Jayden thumped his head on the table. Lazarus held the dice again and tossed it.

"Winner!"

Someone placed a drink in his hand and slapped him on the back. Eddie the impersonator sang and the surrounding crowd joined in.

Lazarus continued to roll and roll. By this time, a crowd had gathered. He held the dice in front of Vee. "Blow?"

"Why are you smirking? Don't get comfortable with this," she told him before she blew. He laughed and let the dice go.

"Snake eyes!"

The entire table gasped.

"You cursed him!" Dara said to Vee.

"I didn't curse him!"

"You did! Someone get security and get this woman from the table." Kiki looked around the room.

Eddie sang "I'm So Lonesome I Could Cry."

"Eddie, please." Sweat was pouring from Lazarus's brow. An older man had walked up. He looked like Pinky from *Friday After Next*, whiskey in one hand and a cane in the other. Three women surrounded him, all in varying stages of undress. Jayden blinked as he looked the girls up and down one by one. Dara hit him.

The older man ignored Lazarus to get a look at Vee. Clearing his throat loudly, he caught her attention and her eyes widened at him. The man licked his lips, bringing his pinky and thumb to his mouth. He licked them before pressing them to both of his eyebrows. "Hi."

Lazarus stopped what he was doing and looked at the man.

"Hello?" Vee looked at the man and then back to the table.

"Roll the dice, Lazarus!" Kiki hit her fist on the table.

The man continued to talk to Vee. "How are you doing tonight?"

"I'm fine. Lazarus, roll." Vee nudged him.

Lazarus tossed the dice and the dealer said, "Craps!"

The table booed. Jayden put his head back on the table with a groan.

"I've been checking you out for a while now, and I have to say. I like your style," the old pimp said.

Vee lowered her eyebrows. "Thank you?"

"Nice hair too."

She pressed closer to Lazarus. "I'm sorry, who are you?"

Lazarus frowned at the man.

"Toss the dice, man!" Jayden yelled.

"Call me Smooth Mike."

"Smooth Mike? Is that your legal name?" Vee squinted.

"Cool ass name if it's legal." Dara eyed the man up and down.

Lazarus tossed the dice and the dealer said, "Craps!"

"Get your head in the game, man!" Jayden shouted in his ear.

"I just saw a nice young filly, and I thought I better go up to her. Add her to my stable." Smooth Mike licked his lips.

Vassa pursed her lips. "Stable? Like a horse stable?"

Smooth Mike snapped his fingers and the girls surrounded him nodded.

Dara's mouth fell open. "I don't know how to respond to that."

"I run a pleasant business with beautiful girls. I'm sure you could make some money."

Lazarus felt it was time to step in. He tossed the dice and didn't care how they landed. The dealer called out a winner as Lazarus looked the older man up and down. "She needs nothing."

Smooth Mike looked Lazarus up and down in return. "So, you have a white man? Turned your back on the brothas?"

The entire group looked at Smooth Mike in shock.

"You're out of line." Lazarus took a step toward him.

Vassa frowned. "Completely."

Smooth Mike shrugged. "I call it as it is. Not too late to come back to the light."

"If this is your recruiting speech, it needs some work," Vassa said.

The girls around Smooth Mike frowned. Just then, Eddie the Elvis impersonator sang "Can't Help Falling in Love" at the top of his lungs.

"I'm her boyfriend. She's fine." Lazarus took another step toward the guy.

Lazarus had at least a good four or five inches on the guy, not to mention thirty or forty years fewer. Smooth Mike had a greasy jerry curl and a potbelly.

"You're my boyfriend?" Vassa asked.

Jayden nudged Lazarus. "Your turn to roll."

"Yes, I'm your boyfriend," Lazarus told her.

Vee grinned at him, but it was short-lived because Smooth Mike cleared his throat.

"I'm not talking to you, young blood. I'm talking to your girl here."

"I'm talking to you," Lazarus said.

Jayden hit Lazarus on his shoulder. "Roll!"

Lazarus tossed the dice and the crowd went wild.

"Winner!"

Eddie the impersonator continued to sing.

"She's not available. There's no need to talk to her." Lazarus ignored the waitress who passed by with drinks. Vassa, on the other hand, flagged her down.

"Oh, so you're already working her? Then let's partner buddy." Smooth Mike reached out to touch Vee.

At first, Lazarus and Smooth Mike were simply standing. Jayden snatched the dice from Lazarus. Kiki swayed as she downed the rest of Jayden's drink. Lazarus hauled his hand back and lofted it toward Smooth Mike. Pain radiated in his hand as it collided with Smooth Mike's face. The surrounding girls screamed and one launched herself at Lazarus. Vassa blocked her and she and the girl went over onto the table, making the crowd part.

"Oh, shit!" Jayden said.

Lazarus went to pull the girl off Vassa. Smooth Mike recovered and headed for Lazarus, punching him in the face.

It was a brawl.

The girls around Smooth Mike went for Lazarus and Vassa. Kiki, Jayden, and Dara dove in to help as Lazarus handled Smooth Mike. Eddie the impersonator began to sing "Jailhouse Rock" Lazarus hadn't been in a fight since he was in middle school and that was when Billy O'Kelly stole his lunch. It had been sloppy joe day. Screams came from the crowd and dealer as they dove out of the way to avoid being trampled on. His heart pounded in his ears as he tussled on the floor with Smooth Mike, his jerry curl grease getting into his eye.

He heard his friends tussling, and blocked a hit from the pimp. A couple of phones flashed light on them, recording, and he prayed that no one important saw him online. Lazarus landed a few more punches on Mr. Smooth Mike when he heard the stampede of guards coming. He dropped Smooth Mike by his shirt.

"Guards!"

Everyone froze before Lazarus got up and said, "Run! Run!"

Grabbing Vee from the table, he ran to the door with the rest of the gang following them.

"Oh well, we're going to jail for real this time!" Vee cried.

Lazarus pushed any and everyone out of his way. The doors were in sight, but guards came in, blocking the exit. He dipped to the side and Vee stumbled as he knocked into a server carrying drinks. He tossed back a "sorry!"

He had no intentions of sitting in a Las Vegas jail.

He found a door leading back to Fremont Street and powered ahead. The crowd exclaimed as they burst onto the street. He didn't stop there. They ran and ran until they made it to a safe place down the street next to a drugstore. That's when Vee placed her hands on her knees trying to breathe. "I'm not athletic enough for this crap."

Lazarus looked behind them. "Where's everyone else?"

"You don't think…" Vee's eyes widened.

Welcome to Vegas, indeed.

CHAPTER SEVENTEEN

KIKI HAD MANAGED TO TALK the police out of arresting them for disorderly conduct. Her attire probably had something to do with it, but they received a slap on the wrist and were sent on their way.

The brawl wore everyone out, and the gang opted to go back to the hotel to shower and sleep. Lazarus and Vassa decided on breakfast, but before they left the hotel, Vassa noticed a rack filled with brochures. She stuffed some into her purse.

They headed south down the strip to the Mirage. The smell of cigarettes drifted out of the casinos they passed. The fun never stopped. Older gamblers focused on their machines. They sat back and drew deeply on cigarettes as they played. Lazarus and Vassa went inside The Venetian for the Grand Canal Shoppes. A beautiful mural of a clear sky had been painted on the building's ceiling. The clouds looked almost airbrushed and soft; she wanted to touch them.

Once seated with their orders placed, she watched the gondolas pass by filled with couples and families.

"Are you sure you don't want to take a ride?" Lazarus asked.

"I want to talk about my list." She waved the paper in his face.

"Not the brawl?"

"Let's save that for the airplane ride back." She took a sip of water. "I didn't know you could fight."

"I'm more of a lover but I defend when necessary."

She grinned and tucked a strand of hair behind her ear. "It

was nice… seeing you all manly. Tough and stuff."

Lazarus raised his eyebrow. "Oh really?"

Clearing her throat, she had to look away from the provocative look Lazarus sent her. Instead, she reached into her purse for the list. "The list is almost done. I just have a few things left."

"What are those things?"

"Have an epic spring break—"

"That's in progress." Lazarus thanked the server who refilled their glasses.

Vassa twisted her lips. "That's debatable. I've thrown up and run from security twice in three days."

Lazarus chuckled. "The next one?"

"It's getting close for me to hear back from my graduate school applications. I know I'm getting into all of them but after completing this list with you… I dunno, I wanna keep having fun."

The server appeared with their food.

"I got you addicted to the wild side?" he asked with a grin.

She sucked her teeth. "I have to admit, it's fun. I guess… Would you want to keep doing this? Having as much fun as we can until graduation? Within reason of course, you're still on probation."

Lazarus nodded and raised his glass. "To modified bucket lists and fun."

Vassa grinned before she amended her list:

Vassa's Extraordinary Senior Send-Off

~~*1.Get totally wasted and regret nothing.*~~

~~*2.See all the tourist spots in San Francisco.*~~

3.Have an epic last Spring Break (In Progress!!)

~~*4.Do something completely wild.*~~

~~*5.Sneak into a party or event uninvited and pretend to be someone else.*~~

~~*6.Go on a date.*~~

Vassa dragged Lazarus down to see the "Welcome to Las Vegas" sign. Of course, he put the bunny ears behind her head, but it was an excellent picture. Rarely did she post pictures on social media pages anymore, but she posted that one with the hashtag: #bestvegastripeva

They were walking back into the lobby of the hotel as Jayden, Kiki, and Dara appeared.

"There you both are." Dara linked her arm with Vassa's. They didn't look too much worse for wear except for the dark circles under their eyes. "Kiki wants to go to a couple of boutiques we saw last night."

Vassa looked at Lazarus before Jayden motioned for him to follow. "I'm hungry. Let's go find something."

For the next several hours, she was dragged back down the strip from store to store. They were almost back at the hotel when a guy in plain clothes and a backpack claiming to be a club promoter stopped them. Vassa was going to tell him no thanks when he offered free entry into a club. Dara nor Vassa could answer before Kiki said yes.

"This is to Origin, one of the best clubs here." Kiki passed the flyer to Dara.

"How do you know it's a real club and not something sinister? Like drug trafficking?" Vassa asked as Dara passed the flyer for her to inspect. Dammit, her mother had gotten in her brain.

Kiki rolled her eyes. "You're too paranoid, live a little."

That night, they gathered all primped and pampered in the boys' room to begin their routine pre-gaming. Vassa decided not to overdo it like the nights before, opting for the cocktail in the can Lazarus bought for her.

This time Kiki gave the toast for the evening. "To a night we'll never remember."

"I thought Lazarus said that already." Dara grinned evilly.

Vassa shrugged. "It still feels appropriate for tonight."

Everyone was excited when they arrived at the Origin. Vassa had never been to a club, and she wasn't really sure what to expect in the slightest. The inside was electric. Cast in red light, it was both sinister and sexy. The place fed off the techno music and fast dancing. Vassa winced at the damp shoulders and bodies that brushed against her as they pushed through the dance floor. She couldn't even see the floor beneath them.

Jayden led them to the bar. Her opinion of clubs was dwindling as it was too loud to hear herself think. She let out a sigh of relief when she could sit and began trying to catch the attention of the bartender.

"Not too bad, is it?" Lazarus shouted in Vassa's ear.

Wincing, she nodded.

"What do I want? There's a drink I've never heard of," Kiki shouted as her eyes roamed the bottles.

Dara leaned across Jayden to speak to Kiki. "Something light. You had shots already!"

"What are you thinking of getting?" she leaned over and said in Lazarus's ear.

He rubbed his chin in thought, lips pursed. Over his shoulder on the other side of the bar, she noticed some girls eying him like there weren't a hundred other guys in the place. A burning sensation started in her chest. They ordered their drinks. Glancing at those girls, she saw they were still looking, and Vassa sucked in a breath. *Ignore them...*

Vassa had received her mojito when the music changed. Kiki squealed, grabbing her hand and dragging her to the dance floor.

"Wait! Take Dara!" Vassa tried to get out her grip, but Kiki was too strong. They got caught in the current of bodies and ended up in the center under the strobe lights.

Vassa stood with her arms pressed to her sides, unlike Kiki, who moved as if the music controlled her like a puppet on strings. "Relax and just dance!"

Kiki took her hands and tried to move Vassa from side to side. No one was looking at her, but she couldn't help but feel very aware of herself. She slowly mimicked Kiki's moves. Moving her hips, she swayed to the beat. The sequins on Kiki's dress caught the strobe lights, launching a rainbow into the darkness.

The song changed to one she knew, and she sang. Kiki grinned and jumped up and down, singing along with her. They tossed their hands up and before she knew it she was dancing, twisting, and turning. Vassa held Kiki's hands as they spun each other. Dara appeared and they opened their circle as she grinded to the music. They were all grinning, probably looking like idiots, but they didn't care. She felt an unknown part of her come out to play as she let her body go free. Vassa turned to their tables where they had left the guys. She got a glimpse through the bodies, and the smile fell from her face before she came to a stop.

The girls from the bar had made their move. Two surrounded Lazarus. One leaned in laughing with Jayden. One girl reached out and placed her hand on Lazarus's arm, her lips almost on his. She felt the urge to snatch someone's tracks out of their head when he pulled back and laughed before leaning in. Dara turned to see what had made Vassa stop dancing and she too stopped. Vassa looked at her and even in the dark lights she could see the flush in Dara's face. What was she upset about? Was she just as pissed about Lazarus as she was?

The music changed again, and Kiki was none the wiser as she danced. Vassa opened her mouth to shout to Dara, but she turned away and kept dancing. Vassa knew she should do the same, but she couldn't.

"I'm going to get something to drink!" Vassa shouted and pointed toward the bar.

She may have used more force than necessary to push people out of the way, but most were too drunk to care. At the bar she ordered a shot, hissing through the burn. She didn't bother with a chaser. Daring to look again, she saw that Jayden had disappeared with the other girl. That left one with Lazarus.

There was no need for Vassa to be jealous. Lazarus was interested in her only. That was obvious. Rubbing her face, she flagged the bartender for another shot. She didn't like this feeling, not in the least bit. What did she do, go over there and sit on his lap, make out with him in front of the other girl? Grab him by the ear like a deadbeat husband and drag him out of the club? Just start throwing blows? Oh, she did not know about jealousy and relationships.

Gathering her courage, she felt someone brush against her side. In the club's darkness, all she saw were his high cheekbones and dark eyes. He flipped his long hair back; she thought he was trying to be attractive, but to each their own.

"Do you want to dance?" he asked her.

Eyeing him, she looked back over at Lazarus and the girl before she nodded. The guy led her back into the thicket. The music had changed to old school club music. He looked like the scarecrow from *The Wizard of Oz* trying to dance. Limbs and hair just everywhere.

He danced like no one was watching and it encouraged her. They jived and boogied to the music, sometimes on beat and other times not. He danced and pointed to her. She tossed her head back, and it was an impromptu dance battle.

He did the Wop, and she couldn't help but laugh. Following along, they did all the old school dances they knew. The song changed to something slower; the guy moved in closer. Vassa wasn't sure what to do when his hands fell to her hips and he pressed his chest to hers. When she looked at him, his eyes were glassy as he smiled absently at her. *This dude is on drugs or drunk.*

His hands slipped lower, and she caught his hands and pulled them back up.

"Don't be a tease," the guy whispered, and she immediately felt uncomfortable.

She didn't respond because she felt a hand wrap around her waist. When she turned, Lazarus had a dark expression on his face.

"Mind if I steal her for a dance?"

He didn't wait for the guy to respond before he pushed through people into an open space. Pulling her into his chest, he drifted with the music. Licking her lips, she focused on a point out in the crowd as she clenched her fists.

"What happened to the girl you were with?" Vassa pressed her lips together. *I shouldn't feel jealous, but why am I jealous?* She felt him laugh. She didn't find it funny and stepped on his foot. *Hard.*

He hissed. "I don't know, probably dancing or kissing someone in here."

She decided not to respond. He pulled back and looked down at her. "Are you jealous?" There was a hint of a smile on his lips. Rolling her eyes, she would never in a million years admit that to Lazarus.

"No, I'm not."

"It's okay to admit it if you are," he said in a sing-songy voice.

She kept her lips shut. Taking her hand, he turned her in a circle and pulled her so her back rested against his front. "You're sure you don't wanna tell me?"

She turned slightly, glanced at him from under her lashes. *Just do it, don't be scared!*

Spinning on her feet, she closed her eyes and stood on her toes to press her lips to his. The music faded to a dull static as he pressed closer, neither concerned with keeping up with the dancing bodies around them. Vassa knew then and there he was what she wanted. They both pulled back with quickening breaths. Her lips parted slightly and her gaze traveled his entire body, taking in every detail of him. The way the strobe lights caught the blond of his hair, the faint sheen of sweat on his upper lip, and the way his chest rose and fell quickly. Lazarus held her stare, licking his lips he pressed closer, threading his fingers with hers. She could feel his excitement and curiosity rose within her.

"Come with me?" she asked with a soft squeeze of his hand.

He nodded, and she led him outside. The night air was a relief after the balmy club. She walked a few feet away from the club entrance to a dark corridor.

"Vee."

Her hand cracked against his cheek. Lazarus's mouth fell open. Blinking slowly, he shuffled forward as she grabbed him by the front of his shirt and stood on her toes. "Yes, I was jealous. I think I love you, jackass." Then she placed her lips on his.

She maneuvered his back against the wall and ran her hands up and down his arms, making him shiver. She blinked slowly, drinking in his chiseled features and expressive eyes.

Lazarus wasn't just the popular jock. It was his heart that captured her. That caring, silly, sensitive, and daring heart that trapped her. Vassa let herself melt against him with a contented sigh. When his tongue gently outlined her bottom lip, she parted her mouth and flicked her tongue against his.

She pulled back and her voice cracked. "Take me back to the hotel."

"God, yes," he said, crushing his mouth against hers.

CHAPTER EIGHTEEN

"SLOW DOWN LAZARUS, I'M WEARING heels!"

He didn't slow down; he went faster. Faces blurred as he pulled them through the crowd. She would have lost her shoe if he didn't come to a halt at the light. It felt like déjà vu, their reflection in the cars that zipped by.

Their faces said it all: eyes wide and faces flushed. His jaw set and lips pressed together. His hand tightened around hers. The light changed, and he darted across the street. Then he turned and, before she could stop him, scooped her up in his arms.

"Lazarus, what are you doing?" She wriggled in his arms, trying to get out. What if she was too heavy? His arms flexed to keep her steady.

"Stop wriggling or I'll drop you."

Vassa stilled and wrapped her arms tighter around his neck to prevent her backside from meeting the concrete. No one batted an eye at him carrying her down the street. They entered the lobby of the hotel and she forced him to put her down once they entered the elevator.

Pressing the button for their floor, she didn't turn around yet, but she could feel his eyes on her back. The small space only made her even more physically aware of just how close and alone they were. She had never felt this way about someone before. Hot, heavy, and antsy.

Her eyes danced partly because of the alcohol and partly

because of excitement. She backed up into the elevator panel as Lazarus advanced toward her. She licked her lips as her eyes traveled down his body.

Oh, my word.

She could see that Lazarus was… *Well,* he was working with something down there.

Her eyes flew up to his and then back down, then up again. Oh, gosh, should she stare? Ignore it? No, of course not for goodness' sake.

She clenched her thighs in response. She was sexy enough to cause this reaction? That empowered her more. Lazarus's intense stare made her stomach do that flip-flop feeling that she got on roller coasters. Her eyes closed as he stood in front of her, his head dipping toward hers, and he placed his hands on her waist.

She clamped her hand over his mouth, keeping him from kissing her. She blurted the first thing that came to mind, "I like your shirt."

Lazarus blinked and looked at himself. "Thank you?"

"I really like the color and the design, is that silk—"

He put a finger on her lips. "I would really prefer to kiss you."

Vassa nodded quickly, and he slowly removed his finger. His arms circled her waist, forcing her into him, and his hands slid down to caress her bottom. She placed her hands flat against his chest. To push him away or brace herself, she wasn't sure.

He grinded his hips into her front and she hissed out a breath, her nails sinking into his flesh. She was out of her body and he hadn't even done anything yet.

The kiss was tender but when she let out a soft moan, he pushed her into the wall, slightly hiking her leg up. Her dress was sliding up as she kissed him back eagerly, her hands running through his hair. Vassa inhaled shakily as her head hit the wall of the elevator. Lazarus kissed her neck on both sides, his tongue circling small patterns that had her shivering. He suddenly bit her neck and she squeaked, almost losing her footing as he grinded their fronts together. The ding of the elevator reaching their floor broke them apart.

On edge, in her room she threw the key card on the desk as she kicked off her shoes. Knocking the pile of clothes from earlier off the bed to the floor, she sat down. The only light in the room came from the streets and buildings below. Shadows passed over his form as Vassa braced her arms behind her and he knelt on the edge of the bed, causing her to slide.

Her nervousness was obvious, and he settled for gently running his hands up and down her arms as she gradually relaxed. He pressed soft kisses to her lips, then her neck.

"You can do more," she whispered to him.

He nodded before sitting them up. He reached behind her, finding the zipper of her dress and ever so slowly unzipping it. He pushed the straps of her dress off to the side. In her underwear, part of her wished she would have been wearing a matching set. Here she was, in a momentous life moment, and she was in mismatched bra and panties.

She would have to be content she wasn't wearing her grandma underwear and ratty bra. *Small wins.*

Instinctively, she moved to cover herself, but she didn't get a chance. Lazarus's eyes trailed her body. Was it too much fat? Gosh, maybe she should have done that cleanse with Dara? Her stubborn love handles. She hoped he couldn't see them. Were her thighs too big? They loved to pancake whenever she sat down.

"Open your eyes, Vee." His voice was hoarse and deep.

Her eyes fluttered for a moment before she met his gaze. His eyes looked black and wide, brimming with burning arousal like hers. He took a second to drag his gaze down the length of her half-naked body once more, now that he knew she was watching him. Her breath came audibly now, quicker and shallower than it should.

"You're absolutely perfect."

His hand touched her bare stomach and she jumped at the rough feel of his hands gliding across her skin. His fingers made small, mindless patterns as her eyes fluttered when his fingers dipped lower.

He propped himself on his side, facing her. Vassa bit her lip and gripped the sheets when his fingers ran along up her core and to the hem of her underwear. He gave her another look for confirmation, and she nodded.

She closed her eyes as he peeled the elastic band back and warmth pooled into her belly. He was going so, so slow. Wasn't it supposed to be clothing tearing, back scratching, and breaking the bed? Lazarus didn't seem in a rush; the anticipation was madness, pure unadulterated madness.

She wanted this more than her next breath. Daring to open her eyes again, she found Lazarus looking back at her, a silent, heated glint in his eye.

"Are you going to—"

His fingers brushed along her sensitive folds. Vassa jerked up, but Lazarus held her down. He didn't beat around the bush, rubbing circles around the sensitive bundle of nerves, and she stopped breathing. He removed his fingers and ran them through her soft curls before dipping inside. Her body was moving without her brain. She tensed and tightened up as his fingers came to her entrance and pushed. Vassa clutched his arm and whimpered, to stop or to encourage, neither knew.

Her soul left her body as he slowly slid his finger through the hot, slick folds of her steadily.

"How are you feeling?" Lazarus murmured.

Her hips writhed helplessly on the bed. Couldn't he see she was a mess? Her nails dug into his wrist as he drew the entire length of his fingers up against her bundle of nerves. She wasn't sure how he expected her to even answer that question.

"Is it okay for you, Vee?"

She winced when he pushed too deep, pain flashing for a second, and he pulled out, giving her a comforting rub. Was it good? Yes, yes, and God yes.

"Tell me," he urged when she didn't say a word. His fingers pulled up and began tracing slow, gentle circles around that little nerve again.

"Good," she breathed raggedly, arching her hips up as he touched her. "I feel nice."

Pleased, he returned to his strokes. A wave of heat made sweat break out over her body. She was close, and everything was getting tight. Her heart pulsed as her fingers flexed and gripped the sheets, her legs kicking out. She was sucking in air to stabilize herself, make sense of the moment.

Lazarus's strokes got faster, and her nails clamped further into his skin. She felt hot and pulsating, her moans a private symphony.

Then bliss stabbed through her. A desperate sound tore through her throat as her back arched and she twisted and turned to escape the sensation. Lazarus eased her back down. Her body jerked with aftershocks, leaving her exhausted.

She thought she was broken. *So that was it.* She tried to lift her head, but it fell back to the pillow. Each limb felt like a cement block as she blinked and focused on him. He tossed his shirt to the floor and his shoes followed. His fingers were fumbling for the belt on his jeans when she pushed herself up.

"Do you have protection?"

Lazarus's eyes went dumb for a second and she shook her head. "Lazarus."

He patted his pockets, dumping receipts and payout slips on the bed. Pulling out his wallet, he opened it and cursed.

"Stay just like this, I'll be back." He jumped up from the bed and she sat up.

"Where are you going?" She watched him reach down for his shoes; he tucked one under his arm as he slid the other on. Hopping up and down, he tried to tie his shoe.

He turned to her. "There's a convenience store in the lobby. I'll go down and be right back." He was still talking, not looking ahead as he slid his shirt on.

"Watch out!"

Lazarus smacked into the wall. Vassa covered her mouth with her hands and she moved to get off the bed to help him. "Are you okay?"

Grunting, he pulled his shirt down and shook his head and gave her a thumbs-up, grabbing her key from the desk. "Be back in stay right there. Don't move." He went back for the other shoe that had fallen to the ground before disappearing.

For a second, she sat there unsure what to do, and then she realized. Jumping up, she stumbled into the bathroom. Turning on the lights, she grabbed the band of her underwear and pulled it out.

Thank God he hadn't seen that area in the light.

The band snapped against her skin as she looked at herself in the mirror. She should probably trim the hedges. Rushing to her suitcase, she tossed her clothes to the side, looking for her razor. Once she found it, she rushed into the bathroom and got to work.

Five minutes later, she was perfect. She combed through her hair with her fingers. Should she put a hot comb to those edges that puffed up again?

Dabbing perfume here and there, she heard the key slide in the door. She turned off the light and did a running dive for the bed just as the door opened.

She quickly pulled the sheets back and slid under. Breathing hard, she placed her hand casually on her hip. Lazarus appeared, bag in hand. She flashed him a smile as he quickly shed his clothes and slid into the other side of the bed.

The kisses resumed as she let him undress her and position himself between her legs. She placed her hands on his shoulders, both to center herself and brace for impact.

"Relax, I can hear you thinking," Lazarus said.

He pulled back and licked his lips as he took in her naked chest. He held a bottle of lube. How could she forget that? Her fingers curled into the sheets as he leaned forward, kissing all over her body, starting from her neck, down to her shoulders, breasts, and belly. Her fingers curled into his hair as his mouth met her core. Her head hit the pillow and she moaned to the ceiling as his tongue lapped at her sensitive bud.

"Lazarus!"

He looked up at her and she broke eye contact, the connection too intense.

"Please," she croaked.

Her breaths were ragged as his fingers spread her drenched core. She heard the snap of the lube and felt cold before pleasure erupted. She was in awe of Lazarus's skills as he swallowed her moans, another wave of bliss settling over her.

He sat back, his skin flushed red. "Do you still want to do this?"

"I do. I'm ready."

"Tell me to stop if it becomes too much."

She lifted her legs and locked them around his waist. He kissed her cheek and then her nose. A breath escaped her as he rubbed her heat with the head of him. He threaded his fingers into her hair, bringing her close for a kiss as he thrust forward slowly.

The discomfort was there, not a feeling she was used to. She tensed and gripped his shoulders.

"Relax," he sighed.

She nodded and tried to relax as he pushed forward. Thankfully, she was more than relaxed by him, and his weight on top of her was comforting when he thrust forward. Vassa pressed her face into his neck and shuddered.

Her body instinctively moved with his. When he pulled back, his mouth hovered just above hers, their breaths mingled, and his eyes lowered. Lazarus's every sound and every movement were attuned to her. She felt beautiful in that moment.

Her arms circled his neck, pulling him closer, as his hips rolled deeper. She allowed him to teach her how to move, to pull sounds of pleasure from him. Sweat dripped down her face. He moved to his knees, sitting back on his haunches, and pulled her into his lap.

She let out a sob as pleasure radiated through every pore on her body. She contracted around him, loving the new position that hit a spot that made her legs shake. Their hearts raced together and Vassa's world focused to a pinpoint as everything got tighter, and tighter.

She didn't want to fight anymore. Relationships, people, none of that. Lazarus made her realize it as he looked so softly up at her, and she couldn't remember what could be possibly so bad about letting himin. At one time, Vassa had believed she couldn't trust anyone but herself. What would happen if she didn't have this moment with him, if she'd left him at the club with those girls? She wanted to give her loneliness to him, so she never had to deal with it again.

She rolled them to the side. Forcing Lazarus to his back, she resituated herself over him. A slow smile formed on his face as he looked up at her. Curling her hands into his, she rocked her hips slowly; Lazarus's fingers gripped her hips as he met her thrust for thrust. She was still scared to fully let him in. She didn't want to be hurt again. She couldn't be hurt again. But her walls had come tumbling down and he was storming her castle.

Vassa's heart thundered in her chest. Her hips sped up and she couldn't stop as her thighs slammed down. She met his gaze and saw the same vortex of pleasure there. Lazarus moaned again and his hips pushed harder into hers. She kissed him. Releasing an anguished whine into his mouth, she started to spasm, pulling him closer.

A low groan of satisfaction rumbled through his chest as she whimpered. He was able to ride out every twitch and spasm as he kissed her lazily.

"I love you too," he gasped.

Tears blurred her eyes. "Please don't hurt me."

Lazarus searched her face. Instead of waiting for his response, she pulled his face up to hers. His arms circled her waist and he pulled her down, turning her onto her back.

Running his thumb over her bottom lip, he gave her a huge smile. His kiss told her everything she needed to know.

A cry escaped her as he slowly wound her body up again.

Vassa's Extraordinary Senior Send-Off

~~1. Get totally wasted and regret nothing.~~

~~2. See all the tourist spots in San Francisco.~~

~~3. Have an epic last Spring Break (In Progress!!)~~

~~4. Do something completely wild.~~

~~5. Sneak into a party or event uninvited and pretend to be someone else.~~

~~6. Go on a date.~~

7. Get into graduate school

8. JUST HAVE FUN!

CHAPTER NINETEEN

THE DAYS THAT FOLLOWED WERE a blur.

They made the most of their time in the city. Thankfully there was no more running from guards or dine-and-dashing. Instead, they enjoyed sightseeing, kayaking, more drinking, and dancing. Spring break was almost over and everyone was trying to get in one last dance, one last memory, and one last kiss.

Touching her cheeks, she could tell they were pink, literal pink. She was smiling. No scowls or sneers. She felt… *airy.* It was something she hadn't felt in a while. Part of her didn't think this could happen. Being with Lazarus was different. They laughed together. Played together. He couldn't stop touching her now, whether it was a hug, his hand on her back, or holding her hand. He had hardly left her side since their first time together.

She let out a low whistle. "You clean up mighty well, don't you?"

"Better than my normal look?" Lazarus grinned, looking down at himself. He wore a buttoned shirt and black blazer.

He looked over the pale silk dress she wore appreciatively. Dara had demanded that on their last night in city they go to an upscale French bistro.

Holding out his arm like a gentleman, he did a little bow and she curtsied before they burst into laughter. The rest of the group was waiting downstairs for them.

"I love seeing you like this. Will I get this new Vee back home?" Lazarus asked once inside the elevator.

Vassa raised an eyebrow at him. "If you behave, I might."

"If I behave, huh?"

Lazarus moved in closer and Vassa grinned, backing into the wall. His hands circled her waist, leaving a trail of heat in their wake. She laughed as he dipped his head forward for a kiss and she stood on her toes to meet him.

Her eyes closed as their lips met. She could feel his smile as the kiss deepened, his hands traveling up and down her back. They missed the elevator ding signaling they'd arrived in the lobby, and she heard the snap of a photo and the clearing of a throat. They pulled away from each other to see Jayden, Dara, and Kiki looking amused.

"Hurry up, kiss, kiss! I'm hungry," Jayden grumbled, pulling at his tie.

Vassa's face flushed as Lazarus grinned.

Soon they were seated on the outside patio as the waiters handed them the menu. The Fountains of Bellagio were across the street from them and to their left was Las Vegas's Eiffel Tower. As the wine was poured, Vassa cleared her throat for everyone's attention.

"I think I want to do the toast tonight."

Everyone at the table looked at her with a strange expression. Lazarus took a sip of his wine and looked away.

"What? What's wrong with me making a toast?"

The waiter finished pouring Dara's glass. Dara gave Vassa a small smile. "There's nothing wrong with it. It's just I've never heard you do it. Ever."

The rest of the table nodded.

Vassa narrowed her eyes on Lazarus and he cleared his throat. "You'll do great."

She smoothed out her dress as everyone waited patiently for what she had to say. She picked up her glass. "I never thought I would be here sitting with people that I care so much about."

"As you know it takes me a while to warm up... but with all

of you it was effortless."

Dara patted her eyes and Jayden threw his arm over her shoulder, comforting her. Kiki grinned. Lazarus grabbed her free hand and squeezed it.

"There's nobody I would rather get kicked out of bars with or hold hair out of a toilet for. Thank you all for making this the best spring break ever."

They cheered as they toasted. Vassa smiled as the gang rolled into conversation. She patted her own eyes and let out a broken laugh as Lazarus rubbed her shoulder.

After dinner they found themselves walking down a sketchy street. Vassa pressed closer to Lazarus as she looked around. "Kiki, are you sure this is where we're supposed to be?"

Lazarus squeezed her hand as he frowned.

"Yes, this is where the show is supposed to be." Kiki turned around in her spiky heels.

Dara spoke up. "Bruno Mars is having a concert in *an office building*?"

Kiki had found someone on the street who was selling exclusive Bruno Mars tickets for a one-night only show.

"I'm not the one who scheduled this thing." Kiki threw her arms up and huffed.

"This is super shady." Dara sucked her teeth and held her clutch to her chest.

"We might get robbed," Jayden said under his breath.

Kiki led them down a small corridor. The corridor narrowed till they were down a few steps standing in front of metal door.

"We most definitely are getting robbed," Lazarus muttered.

Knocking, Kiki stepped back as the door swung open, narrowly missing her. A man that looked like a stereotypical Italian goon looked her up and down.

"Can I help you?"

Swallowing, Vassa took a deep breath. She hoped this wasn't going to end in a chase.

"We're here for the *show*." Kiki whispered the last word.

The man looked from her to the group.

"Tickets?"

Kiki rummaged in her purse and held up the tickets. The man snatched them and closed the door.

Everyone looked at one another before the door opened, and the man let them in.

"No cameras, cellphones, or video recording during the performance."

Kiki looked at the group before she stepped inside and the rest followed.

"I feel like we're going to either get murdered or inducted into a sex cult," Vassa whispered as she and Lazarus walked in last.

"A sex cult is not too bad," Lazarus whispered back.

Vassa punched him and he laughed.

It looked like an empty meat warehouse inside. The lights were dimmed. They had to take small steps to avoid bumping into any tables or people at them. The people looked normal, but most murderers and sex cultists did. They found an empty table in the center of the room in front of the makeshift stage. A waitress walked up to them, placing napkins down.

"See, not bad. Not bad at all." Kiki nodded as she took in the place.

"I wonder why he would have it here?" Jayden asked.

Dara shrugged. "They have a menu. So, it might be legit?"

Vassa picked up the menu on the table. Basic drinks and finger food.

"How much did you pay for the tickets?" Vassa asked.

"Ten dollars."

Vassa blinked several times and leaned forward. "Ten dollars? Ten dollars for Bruno Mars tickets?"

"Uh-huh." Kiki popped her lips.

"And that didn't worry you at all? Make you suspicious?" Vassa narrowed her eyes.

Kiki shook her head. "Nope."

Vassa's shoulders deflated.

Dara leaned across the table. "Why would someone sell you their tickets for ten dollars?"

The waitress came back with glasses of water. They waited until she was gone. Lazarus picked his cup up, inspecting the water. "Sex cult here we come."

Kiki shrugged. "The guy was in a hurry. He said he'll take whatever for it. I only had ten dollars on me. Pretty good deal."

"Pretty good deal to sell us to a cult." Vassa could feel a headache coming on.

"It's all about your perspective. If it is a cult, that could be a good thing," Jayden offered and Dara slapped him on the arm.

"Shut up!"

The table murmured an agreement.

"Hey, when he comes out singing "Uptown Funk" and you're losing your minds, know that I gave you all the experience of a lifetime." Kiki pointed to each and every one of them.

The room went dark. A light on the stage shone on the velvet curtains. They opened and out came a woman. A very elaborately dressed woman in a long ball gown with a split to her hip and elbow length gloves. Big hair, dramatic makeup, and comically proportioned breasts and hips.

"Is that a drag queen?" Vassa whispered and placed a hand over her mouth.

"Hello, and welcome to you all!" The drag queen extended her arms in a flourish.

"Yes, a drag show! Much better than Bruno." Dara grinned.

The drag queen reached into her cleavage she pulled out a fan and begin to fan herself.

"I'm Blanca and tonight, get ready for an event of a lifetime..." The curtains opened up and Blanca stepped to the side.

The girls at the table cheered and the guys laughed when, there she was, the queen herself, *Beyonce.* Or at least a Beyonce impersonator. Vassa had to admit, she couldn't tell the difference.

The first chords to "Crazy in Love" began to play and the lights went crazy. Kiki started to cheer and whistle as two background dancers walked on the stage.

"This is better than a sex cult." Lazarus laughed.

The performance began, and the energy that radiated from the stage was contagious.

The lights beat, and the music jumped as a pole descended from the ceiling, the scalper tickets an issue from the past. When the Beyonce impersonator came down from the stage and neared their table, she headed straight for Lazarus.

Vassa wished she could record the blush that spread across his face as fake Beyonce began to dance near him and sing to him.

"You have some competition Vassa!" Dara wiggled her eyebrows.

Lazarus made sure to give her a generous tip before she moved around the room. The rest of her performance was a blast. Once she was done, they cheered as the next performer appeared. Kiki might have done right this time.

After the show, Kiki and the others wanted to hit up one last club on the strip. Vassa wasn't in the mood to party but followed along anyway. She was sitting on one of the couches in the club nursing a glass of water when Lazarus appeared next to her. "Come with me."

Vassa didn't say anything. Taking his hand, she followed him out of the stuffy building and they ended up back on the main strip. It felt good to just walk in silence and see the flashing city lights and people. In just a week she had gotten used to the performers on the street, the Vegas girls, and occasional party bus filled with screaming passengers.

They arrived back at the Bellagio's Fountains. A small crowd had formed to wait for the next show. Vassa leaned against the railing, watching the water ripple. She felt Lazarus's eyes on her.

"What are you thinking about?" His voice was soft.

Vass sighed and looked out at the water. "If I'll be any good."

"Good? At what?" Lazarus asked.

The water it rippled from an invisible force she couldn't see.

"Being a girlfriend, being with you. I mean I don't know what to do. Now do I have to call you every day? Wait for you to go to class? Share my location and post about you all time? I mean I'm going in blind." The words fell out all at once and she felt embarrassed she said something. Of course, her overthinking had to get in the way of a perfectly good evening.

Lazarus was silent and she turned to look him full on.

"I mean I could be trash. I would hate to make a mistake, I can't make a mistake with you." She clenched her fist and her brows dipped.

"I'm sorry, I shouldn't have said this. I just want to do this right. It doesn't help that we're graduating soon, what are we going to do about that? Honestly, what are we going to do—"

Lazarus pulled her into his chest. Sucking in a deep breath, she let his cologne and Irish Spring soap relax her. Seconds later he pushed her hair behind her ear as she looked at him from under her lashes.

"I'm just scared. What happens when Alexa finds out? Is this gonna start some more mess?" Vassa bit her lip.

Lazarus blinked slowly. "I'm not scared."

"You're not?"

Lazarus shook his head. "No."

Vassa dipped her head now, embarrassed she had told him she was going to fail.

"We're going to take it one day at a time. Don't worry about it or put any pressure on it." He cupped her face, his thumb tracing her bottom lip. "I know what we have will last a very long time. All you have to do is believe."

Vassa smiled at him and stepped closer, her arms circling his shoulders. In a routine that she had now become used to, he bent down for her lips to meet his. His blazer bunched under her fingers as she gripped him. She allowed herself to melt into him just as the chords to "Viva Las Vegas" began to play. The crowd gathered around and began clapping as the lights flashed on, and Vassa settled into the possibility of what could be, and the peace of the present.

Subject line: Countdown to Commencement!

Are you ready, Vasilisa?

Graduates can now reserve their cap, gown, and tassel for commencement. If there are any questions, please email or visit the Office of the Registrar.

Robert Peña
Degree Audit and Graduation Adviser
Office of the Registrar,
Pacific Grove University

Light rain drizzled outside, lulling Vassa to sleep. Rubbing her face, she blinked several times before rereading the email. It had been a couple of weeks since spring break. It still felt hard to get into the groove of everyday life. She had received her first acceptance letter for graduate school. It was for PGU's creative writing program, but Vassa wasn't interested in staying here. That was a safety. She still had enough time for the rest to roll in.

The studio was slow today. Reaching into her pocket, she pulled out her bucket list:

Vassa's Extraordinary Senior Send-Off

~~1. Get totally wasted and regret nothing.~~

~~2. See all the tourist spots in San Francisco.~~

~~3. Have an epic last Spring Break (In Progress!!)~~

~~4. Do something completely wild.~~

~~5. Sneak into a party or event uninvited and pretend to be someone else.~~

~~6. Go on a date.~~

7. Get into graduate school

8. JUST HAVE FUN!

She had done it; she'd almost completed her bucket list. Only a few months ago this list had been just a hope and a prayer but now, it was reality. What was something fun she could do today? Lazarus had influenced her more than she realized, because she was ready to skip out on her work duties just to be with him.

She had sent a text to Dara earlier asking if they were still on for grabbing sushi that night. Nothing. That had been the routine lately. Dara was spending more and more time hanging out with this Suri chick from her class and God knows where else. It was always Suri in their apartment. Or Suri's dorm. *Suri, Suri, Suri.* A bit of fear crept in. That's how Alexa and Theresa's relationship had started. "Just a friend from class," then everything went to hell.

She couldn't lose Dara now, especially when New York was so close for them, but she decided to look on the bright side. Dara wasn't Alexa. She also knew Dara was working hard for a gallery opening in the next week.

She texted Lazarus.

Wanna have a movie night? Or go back to Green Apple?

It took him almost ten minutes to respond.

Can't, busy.

That was it? No explanation? Vassa didn't want to be the clingy girlfriend and know where he was all hours of the day but... her stomach felt uneasy. First Dara, now him. Granted, Lazarus was trying to prove to his brother that he could be trusted now. She had to trust him too.

Her phone vibrated with an incoming text message from

Oscar. Clicking on it, she read:

Hope you had a fun spring break! Let's meet for coffee again?

Did she have to tell Lazarus about this?

It wasn't like she was dating Oscar; he was a friend, and they had gone out to coffee before. He said he was busy too. That was fine, right?

She replied.

Totally… Actually, are you free for sushi tonight?

She wanted to know what stories he had written lately. They had talked a little during break and workshops were next week. She wanted to read what story he wrote next. Oscar's reply was instant.

You read my mind.

Vassa told him the place to meet. Forty-five minutes later, she was shutting down the studio and on the bus heading to Maki Magic Sushi Bar. Oscar was waiting outside.

Oscar set his book bag on the ground and she asked him, "Tell me, what did you do for spring break again?"

"Nothing as fun as Vegas."

Vassa laughed and they exchanged stories. He had gone back home to San Jose. She avoided the more intimate moments of spring break, but she included the pimp brawl and surprise drag show.

Oscar held his stomach as she grabbed a bowel of edamame floating by.

"You should write a short story about that."

"I don't know…"

"It would entertain! You can say it at Word Slam."

Vassa gave him a look. "You don't let up do you?"

Oscar shrugged. "I can be persistent."

Leaning over, she unzipped her bookbag. Pulling out a notebook, she flipped it to a page and handed it to Oscar. He gave her a curious look before he took it. "What's this?"

"Something for Word Slam." Vassa's heart raced and she focused on her food as he smiled and took the notebook. She had workshopped her work in groups many times before, but this time she was nervous. Relief came when he smiled or nodded. When he set the notebook down, she bit her lip. "Something wrong?"

Oscar leaned back in her chair. "Why do you think something is wrong?"

"It's been a while, I'm rusty."

"It was perfect."

"The description was excellent? The sentences didn't sound amateurish?" Vassa rattled off.

Oscar shook his head and tapped his finger on the page. "Besides the odd grammar issue, I think this would be great at Word Slam. It's completely unique."

Vassa pursed her lips. "Are you serious? You're not just saying that?"

"Of course not."

Vassa's phone went off, and it was Dara:

Sorry, can't. With Suri and the gang. Let's meet up later.

Vassa sighed and set her phone down.

"Are you okay?" Oscar asked, reaching for his water glass.

"Yeah, I'm fine. I know this poem needs some work, but I'm excited too."

Oscar grabbed another tray of sushi. "Why did you stop coming to Word Slam again?"

She took a sip of her drink and thought about Alexa being there. Or if any of her goons were still lingering. She didn't know what she would do if she was face to face with Alexa again. A part of her wanted some closure, an explanation of why it got so toxic so quick. Another part of her felt it was better the way it was.

"Oh yeah, I haven't seen her lately. That is not something you should worry about. Let your writing speak for you and everyone will listen."

Oscar was right. Wasn't the biggest middle finger success?

"I just have to get you into our writing group…"

Vassa laughed as she nudged him. "Fine. I will be a part of the writing group and perform at Word Slam. Satisfied?"

Oscar rubbed his hands together. "Absolutely. Next Saturday is our writing group. I'm excited to have you there."

That made her ask, "Will Melinda be a part of the group?"

Oscar blushed, and she grinned as he took a sip of his drink. "She will."

Vassa grinned. "Oh I need to know this story."

"It's nothing!"

Vassa knew it wasn't just nothing.

A few nights later Vassa was lying on her bed. No fun had happened and she was feeling despondent. Then there was knocking on the window.

Vassa looked up from her notebook. Lazarus was crouched at the window with a paper bag in his hand. She rushed to the window and opened it. He stepped inside, placing a kiss on her lips as he held the bag like a trophy. "I have some great news."

Happiness spread in her chest. "What? Why can't I have it?" Vassa reached for the bag and he held it over her head.

"I went ahead and reached out to Mario. He wants me to submit an application for the internship at his company."

Vassa gasped and he nodded.

"It's only a start. That means I really need to make that website. I want to step out on the best foot possible."

"Lazarus!" She launched herself at him and he spun her around.

"I'm know! I'm nervous and I don't want to mess this up." She managed to pry the paper bag from him. It was more donuts.

"You won't! Are you going to tell Harvey yet?" Vassa munched on a donut and Lazarus shook his head. She sighed. "*Lazarus.*"

"I want to be able to shove it in his face. That I have a chance. Then… I didn't tell you everything."

Vassa bit her lip.

"Another reason I wanted this so much was because Harvey took control of my finances."

She blinked rapidly, "What? Then in Vegas-"

"Money from working with Gideon. That's why I need this Vee."

She had strong opinions on that, but if he had a plan, she would respect it.

"Since I have such good news, I think it's time we go on another date."

Vassa looked down at her pajamas. "I'm not ready! Let's work on your website and resume…"

Lazarus waved her off. "You can wear pajamas. People may stare at you funny, but wear what you want."

"Lazarus what you just said is more important, not to mention you have another test soon."

He sighed dramatically and snatched the donuts from her. She protested and he held it above her. "Let's celebrate, can we do that?"

Vassa agreed. She couldn't say no to his puppy dog look. He placed a kiss on her temple. Ten minutes later, she was dressed and in his car. Lazarus kept up conversation for most of the ride. It was an hour after they had left that she became suspicious. She was just about to ask him where in the world he was taking her when she saw the sign. "Santa Cruz Boardwalk?"

She bounced on her heels as he parked the car, and they headed for the gates. She pointed at people sitting in the ski lift above. "Can we do that?"

Kids walked by with giant bears and cheap toys. Lazarus and Vassa passed by gift shops selling park merchandise and she squealed as birds swooped past her head to eat dropped food on the ground.

"What should we do first?" Lazarus shouted above the screams of riders on the pirate seesaw.

"You might be right; this could be better than studying."

"You like it?" Lazarus grinned.

She nodded and heard the ringing of a ride. "Let's do the Cyclone."

She pulled him toward the line. It was a standing ride. All the riders piled in, holding the bars on the wall for stability. Then the platform lifted and spun like a tilt-a-whirl on crack. She screamed and laughed as the lights of the boardwalk blurred in front of her.

She looked to her left and Lazarus's face was green and sweat poured down his face. That made her laugh and hold her sides. She almost couldn't breathe as he groaned. The moment they were off the ride, he ran to the garbage can and vomited.

"Don't puke everything up, we have a bunch of more rides to get on!" She patted him on the back and cackled. It felt good not to be the one puking for a change. Lazarus's chest heaved up and down as she led him toward the Fireball. If he thought the Cyclone was bad, then this ride was hell.

They went on ride after ride. She had pegged Lazarus as an amusement park guy but his permanent green appearance convinced her otherwise. Having pity, she navigated him to the arcade and carnival games. Nothing was catching her eye until he stopped her at a shooting booth. The goal was to hit the moving ducks in order to win the big bear. It was a stereotypical couple's thing to do and her inner romantic went crazy when he insisted on winning her the bear. He went to pick up the gun as Vassa pushed him to the side. She had this. The attendant started the game and she lifted the rifle to her shoulder.

Closing one eye she fired, missing. She counted it toward never holding a gun before. She lifted the gun up again. Missed. Lazarus snickered and she glared at him. Determined to prove him wrong, she let off shot after shot, but once the minute was over, she had only managed to hit two ducks.

"Sorry sweetheart, better luck next time." The attendant reset the game.

Vassa pouted, setting the gun on the counter. Lazarus came up and took it. "Let me show you how a professional does it."

Firing, he hit the duck on the first shot. Lazarus smirked, and she rolled her eyes at him as he focused back on the game. The next shot? Missed. She snickered, and it was his turn to glare. He leveled the gun again and shot and missed. He began shooting wildly and she had to look away as the BB beads flew everywhere. By the time the game had ended, he had to admit defeat.

"What happened?" she asked innocently.

He poked his tongue out at her. He slapped money on the counter for another game. "I got this, don't worry."

Vassa got comfortable as she watched him try again. Twenty minutes and thirty dollars later, and Lazarus was hogging up the game, a line forming behind them. She tried to get him to leave, but he refused. "You're going to get a bear."

He missed again. Vassa looked at the small crowd behind them with a sorry smile and tapped Lazarus on his shoulder. Lazarus slammed the gun on the counter and went to pay again. "Another one!"

"Lazarus, little kids want a turn," she hissed under her breath and ducked her head when she made eye contact with an impatient father and antsy kid.

He ignored her and lost again. She thought he was going to lose it when the attendant took pity on him and handed him the bear. "I got other people in line man."

Lazarus smiled proudly as he handed her the bear. She dragged him away from the booth and pointed to the Sky Glyders. The bear was seated between them as they watched the sun setting in the distance. Vassa swung her legs back and forth as she looked down on the people below. The musical roar of the boardwalk dimmed as they sat with their thoughts.

The Glyder shuddered to stop, swaying. Vassa craned her neck to see what had caused the ride to stop but she couldn't see anything from this distance.

"Did you like the date? How does it rank on your list of dates?" Lazarus leaned back, rocking the contraption.

"Considering this is my second one ever, great. If we leave out you paying thirty dollars for a two dollar bear, it was memorable. I'll cherish it forever." She squeezed the bear.

"It's the principal" was the only explanation he gave. The wind whipped his hair around and he ran a hand through it. He blinked slowly, both exhausted and content at the same time.

Vassa tucked a strand of hair behind her ear. "The bucket list is almost complete."

Lazarus smiled. "Really? So, we did it?"

"You have fulfilled your end of our deal."

The wind picked up, and she shivered. Lazarus sat up and, unzipping his heavy jacket, shimmied out of it and put it around her shoulders. Less than three months ago, she was just sitting at her job wondering how the semester was going to end. Now she was on dates and accomplishing things.

"We just need to keep having fun and I need to get accepted into my graduate program. Well, I got into the PGU program." The suspense was killing her not knowing if she got into those other top programs. That would be a big fuck you to Tom and the other elitists.

"Congrats, Vee. You want to go to New York City, right?" Lazarus licked his lips and she had to stop herself from squirming. Why did he have to look so good?

"That's one place. I could end up in Iowa."

She just wanted to be in a place where she could write and read and be with other amazing writers. "Gosh it will be perfect being around other people who love writing." Vassa let the vision play out in her head.

"I'm excited for you. I know you'll get in." Lazarus placed a hand on her thigh and gave it a squeeze, but there was something in his expression that caused her to pause.

"Something wrong?" she asked softly.

Lazarus leaned back, rocking the glider. "What if you don't get in? Would you mind staying here? In California?"

Vassa raised an eyebrow. "I'm going to get in, that's no question."

"You should always have a backup plan."

Vassa shook her head. "I don't need one. I know I'm getting into NYU or Iowa."

She had been preparing for four years for this moment. They were silent and Vassa looked at him. His jaw was set. "What about this Mario guy? That's great right?"

He didn't immediately respond. Then he made a face. "Yeah, but it's no guarantee. What if nothing works out, what if I don't get either. I'm left being the family fuck-up and my father—"

"Oh my God! Lazarus, that's not possible. You've done the work that's required. You've changed." He shook his head and she scooted closer to him and took his hand. "Nothing beats a failure but a try. Even if you don't get it, you tried. That's enough. *Your father will be proud.*" Vassa said through her teeth.

"I'm not expecting much out of it. Thoughts that I'll still be the same no matter what happens keep echoing in my mind... I was thinking of something else." Lazarus turned to her. "I can come to New York with you. Anywhere really."

Vassa pulled away from him. "What?"

"If I take the job with Harvey, they have a New York office," Lazarus said and Vassa pursed her lips.

"Lazarus, you don't wanna be in that office. How long do you think you'll last? I don't want you changing your plans for me, or to take you from your family." Lazarus and Vassa stared at one another and he cleared his throat.

"I'm not changing my plans—"

Vassa shook her head. "It sounds like you are. I want you to do what makes you happy overall. You like being around people and parties. Event planning can be something you're great at and you have an opportunity in front of you. Following me to New York will just make you resent me in the future. Stay here and find out what happens with this job." Vassa said.

"It makes me happy to be with you! You're rejecting that?" Lazarus pulled away from her.

She said nothing; she wanted to, but she wasn't sure what to say. She wanted to finish this relationship and possibly see where it went, but they hadn't discussed anything yet. She also didn't want him changing his plans because she had gotten involved in his life, at least if that wasn't what he truly wanted to do.

"If you got accepted to New York, you don't want to try to make this last? Long distance?" Lazarus balled his fist.

She bit her lip and Lazarus broke their stare, not attempting to put his arms back around her. The ride began again and Vassa's heartbeat slammed in her ears. She still couldn't say anything when they were escorted off the ride and made their way back through the boardwalk.

In no time, they were back on the road heading to their apartment, both in their own worlds. He stopped the elevator at her floor. She began to leave, ready to leave the awkwardness between them, but she turned around and fisted her hands in his shirt, bringing him toward her.

The same warm and tingling feeling still came over her when their lips connected. Her fingers curled into his jacket and their lips parted and clasped onto one another, till it grew greedy and he was the one to break it.

Her eyes slowly opened, and she sucked in air. Her eyes searched his, looking for any lingering anger or disappointment. Lazarus's face was impassive. Dammit, she couldn't tell.

"I'll see you later," Lazarus whispered. He stepped back into the elevator and she watched the doors close.

The apartment was silent as she entered. Vassa glanced in

Dara's room to find it empty.

She really wished Dara was here right now to help her through this.

In less than a minute she had changed into her pajamas and lain down in the bed.

For hours she tossed and turned, but her mind wouldn't shut off.

When she sat up, the clock read two in the morning.

"I could come to New York with you."

He wanted to come with her. Sweet and she loved that but she couldn't just say yes. Changing his plans for her? She couldn't see Lazarus outside of California. She could see him staying here. With two-point-five kids, all blond and blue eyed, with a golden retriever and a wife that did Pilates. That was his future.

She would teach freshman writing and rhetoric to pay the bills, all the time submitting manuscript after manuscript to publishing houses from a shoebox apartment with her cat, eating old Chinese food. That was her future.

They were too opposite. Night and day. Popular and outcast. He was every literal thing she would and could never be. How would they work outside of those titles?

It could work, long distance isn't bad.

She turned on her back, staring at the ceiling. What was she waiting for?

She took a deep breath before tossing the blanket to the side. Slipping her feet into her bunny slippers, she went to her notebook from the night before with Oscar. She climbed up to Lazarus's window. It was unlocked. He was in bed, on his back with one arm crossed over his face and a bare foot sticking out the side of the blanket. She gave herself one more chance to back out.

Vassa pried the window open and slowly lifted it. Lazarus didn't move an inch as the old window croaked and groaned. Pulling the sheets back, she revealed his bare chest and black boxers.

Lazarus stirred as she settled in. When her cold body

touched his, he moved his arm and blinked slowly, his eyes unfocused. "Vee?"

"Read this in the morning. It's my poem for Word Slam. Will you come?"

He blinked slowly and nodded. "Of course."

She leaned over him and pressed her lips to his. He didn't react immediately. Then she felt him lift slightly, curling his right arm around her waist, pulling her closer. His other hand attempted to run through her hair, but her bonnet blocked him. He pulled back and frowned before snatching it off and tossing it to the floor. As her hair fell to her shoulders, he tangled his fingers in it, angling Vassa's head the way he preferred and returned to kissing.

Now she knew how to move with him. How to let him know what she liked and to give her more. Vassa felt his teeth graze her bottom lip, and she opened slightly as his tongue met hers, and he released a low groan of pleasure. His fingers traced back and forth on her lower back, leaving goose bumps in their wake.

"Lazarus," she tried to say but he turned them and she was lying on her back. Her arms circled his shoulders. No, she wanted to be on top.

Remembering a scene in a movie, she tried to turn him on his back. She overestimated how much force and space she needed because he went flying off the bed to the floor with a thump and a curse.

"Oh, my God! Are you okay?" she asked and sat up on the bed, crawling over to the side to peek at him.

He looked partially dazed and blinked at her. He tried to hold it in, his shoulders shaking before he burst out laughing. Embarrassed, she started to laugh too. He sat up, rubbing the back of his head. Vassa moved to the side as he returned to his spot on the bed. "I'm sorry, you don't have a concussion, do you?"

Lazarus laughed. "A well-deserved concussion."

Trying again, slowly, she placed her leg over his waist, settling into his lap. His kisses trailed down her neck and to her collarbone. She grabbed the back of his hair, forcing his head back. Lazarus chuckled low and let her manhandle him how she pleased. Grabbing the hem of her shirt, he pulled it over her head.

They were desperate and soon he was sliding within her. Letting out a helpless groan, Lazarus pulled himself out and buried himself to the hilt inside her.

Vassa didn't think she would ever get used to it. Her body jerked and she sighed, settling into him as her eyes fluttered shut. She matched him thrust for thrust until any semblance of rhythm broke and they jerked wildly against another.

"Yes. God, yes." She fell apart, with him close behind, pumping wildly into her before shouting his own release. Lazarus collapsed on top of her, but shifted slightly to the side on his elbow so he wouldn't crush her. Her limp legs hung over his back and one of her arms hung loosely off the side of the bed. She wanted this warmth to last, but realized they would soon have to untangle their limbs and go into the world. Then what?

CHAPTER TWENTY

WORD SLAM WAS PACKED.

The last time Vassa was here, there were only about twenty people in the room. Tonight, students filled every corner. Lazarus and Vassa walked in together, his arm over her shoulder.

Her eyes roamed, looking for Alexa and Theresa as Lazarus forced her to stop and talk to some of his friends. She gave his friend a tense smile. *Is Alexa here?*

"Have you met Max before? He plays on the team and gonna take the leadership mantle after I graduate. Can't hit the ball worth a damn, but the team should survive." Lazarus looked from Max to Vassa with a grin.

"What! You're a liar." Max playfully punched Lazarus.

The guys laughed and Vassa laughed briefly before looking around. Pressing down her skirt she tried to get her heart to return to a normal beat. *I'm really here after so long.*

Lazarus shook Max's hand and they began to look for an empty seat when Oscar appeared. "Vassa, you're here!"

She sighed in relief.

"Are you ready? Did you finish the poem?" Oscar looked from her to Lazarus.

Vassa grinned and nodded. "Oscar, you remember Lazarus, my boyfriend."

Oscar led them to a couch he had saved. Memories of freshman year flooded her mind. She had snuck in from outside with

Alexa and Theresa and they clustered in a group with snacks, snapping and cheering for the poets they could relate to, wiping tears away from the poems that made them cry. She had wished she could be a writer like the ones who presented.

The lights dimmed as Oscar left them and stepped onto the makeshift stage. Everyone clapped and cheered. A few late stragglers ran in. Vassa looked around. She didn't spot Dara anywhere. Where was she? She sent her a quick text.

Word Slam's starting. Where are you?

"Thanks for coming to Word Slam. We have some outstanding performers on the agenda tonight." Oscar snapped and the rest of the room followed.

Lazarus squeezed her side and placed a kiss on her forehead. "Are you ready?"

"I feel like I'm going to pass out." She let out a shaky breath and relaxed into his arms.

"You got this Vee," Lazarus whispered.

Oscar called the first performer. Vassa recognized him as Tom. *Boo!* When Tom was done, she clapped for him, even if she didn't care for him. Vassa looked back out to the crowd. So far, no Alexa, Theresa, or Dara. She was probably just running late. There was no need to worry. Dara knew how important this was for her.

Oscar called the next performer up. This one was livelier, including music. Lazarus was getting into the scene now, snapping and audibly responding when something resonated. Performer after performer took the stage. She recognized some people from her classes, those she passed in the halls.

Oscar called her name. This last performance would be hard to follow. "Now I want to welcome a friend of mine. I know she's gonna rock it, come on up Vassa!"

Lazarus screamed in her ears, temporarily deafening her. All eyes were on her as she stood up. Forcing herself to move her limbs normally, she was in a daze as she made it to the stage.

Oscar gave her a thumbs up before stepping to the side. She tapped the mic. "Hi, I'm Vassa—"

Everyone responded by saying hello.

"I haven't done this in a while. I made a promise to a good friend and to myself." She scanned the crowd and continued, "What I'm about to read to you is a long overdue letter to myself. If it wasn't for Oscar encouraging me to show my work again" —she turned to him and he smiled— "or for Lazarus, for never giving up on me." She swallowed and made eye contact with him.

"You have been the most insistent, relentless, and kindhearted person I've ever come to know."

"That's my girl!" he shouted. The crowd laughed at that. She playfully rolled her eyes. "You taught me courage. To let loose. No matter what, you're going to do awesome. I'm grateful for being with you."

Sniffing quickly (she would not cry on this stage) she dropped her shoulders and took another breath before she recited the poem. The words flowed and for a moment, she felt outside her body. Excitement and nausea twisted up. A high fell over her. *God,* she missed performing.

The crowd cheered once she was done. Grinning, she high-fived a couple of people as she exited the stage. Oscar gave her a thumbs up as he went back to emcee the crowd. She fell back on the couch as Lazarus brought her into his arms.

"That was amazing, Vee!"

Her heart pounded in her ears as she looked around. A few people around them congratulated her on the performance.

I did it, I really did it!

Lazarus was talking in her ear, but she was on a permanent high and she couldn't process what he was saying. Sitting up in her seat, she looked around at the faces of the crowd. Vassa hadn't realized how much she missed this, the energy and feedback from the crowd. She didn't understand why she had stayed away so long.

Alexa.

Vassa stiffened. Was she here?

Sitting up in the seat, her eyes scanned for those familiar brown eyes. She looked at face after face, but none of them were Alexa. A strange feeling sat in her stomach. Was it disappointment? Relief? With the bucket list and this performance, she wanted to prove to Alexa that she had gotten past their drama.

"Vassa?"

She turned to come face to face with Theresa.

Sucking in a breath, she thought she would fall out seeing her nemesis. She was the reason that everything went to shit with Alexa. Her emotions were torn. Should she grab her by the hair and start walloping? Walk away and ignore her?

"Theresa?"

Always impeccably dressed, she wore a stylish outfit and her hair was pinned back in an elegant chignon.

"Yeah, how are you?"

Vassa didn't think that encompassed everything that transpired between them.

"What are you doing here?"

Silence stretched between them and Theresa picked at imaginary lint on her skirt. "Alexa suggested it."

Right, things always came back to her.

"Oh," Vassa said and Theresa licked her lips.

"She transferred you know?"

Vassa's arms hung loosely at her sides. Her eyebrows furrowed as she tried to understand. "What?"

"A month ago," Theresa said and Vassa felt a knot in her stomach. No longer would she be tormented by their memories but gloat that Vassa could do better than her. Alexa wasn't here. She realized she didn't need her here.

Closure. That's what Vassa had wanted this whole time.

An explanation of why Alexa did what she did. An apology or grovel would be a nice add on but she would never get that. Her friendship with Alexa was over. Vassa was fine with that. She couldn't let the ghost of Alexa control her any longer. It was time to lay that chapter in her life to rest.

Resting back in her seat, she listened to Lazarus chat on happily as she watched the next performer. She felt a warm sense of security wrap itself around her that wasn't Lazarus. Something in her clicked together in that moment, and it was confidence and strength.

Vassa felt her phone buzz with an incoming email. Coldness devoured the warmth inside her when she saw it was from Iowa State, one of the top writing programs in the country, with her admissions decision. Lazarus sucked in a breath and they both looked at each other.

"Read it," he said.

Her fingers shook as she clicked the email.

> Dear Vasilisa,
>
> Thank you for your interest in the MFA program at Iowa State. We received many interesting and excellent applications, only some of which we were able to accept this year. We reviewed your application very carefully and note several strong features. There is rigorous competition for entry into our graduate program and your application was not among those that we were able to accept.
>
> We encourage you to apply to other graduate schools and we wish you every success with your studies and beyond.

Vassa set the phone down on the table gently, her arms hanging loosely at her sides. Lazarus was talking again, consoling her, but she couldn't hear anything as her mind shut down.

Rejected. She had been rejected.

She stood up and Lazarus's hands fell from her. She ignored him calling her as she walked toward the exit, disrupting the current performer. She ignored the curious looks from others as Lazarus hopped over people to follow her. The world darkened. Vassa wanted nothing more than to walk to the ocean beach, into the water, and never return.

This shirt itched like hell. As he fixed his tie, his phone chimed with a text message.

Be on time, professional, and clean.

Harvey had been riding him all morning. There was nothing he could do but grin and bear it. It would be over soon enough. He replied:

I'll try to not appear too wild. Should I leave my tiger with the receptionist?

Harvey's response was instant.

Haha, asshole. Be there.

Lazarus grinned as the window opened. Vee was holding a plate covered in aluminum foil. She was wearing a T-shirt of his. He was still worried about the night before. He had never seen her shut down like that. The entire walk home she said nothing, moving like a zombie. She didn't even glance at him when she walked into her apartment. What hurt most was that when he came down to her window, she'd locked it.

"I've come with a thank-you gift," she said. Crossing the room in her slippers, she offered the plate to him. He looked at it.

"Is it poison?"

Vee made a face, "No, fool."

"Rat droppings?"

"I guess you'll have to find out. Trust me, I've seen enough crime shows. I know how to make you disappear without leaving a trace."

Lazarus laughed and uncovered the plate. There were donuts there, in alternating sizes and thicknesses. He held up one that looked absolutely pitiful and it broke and fell back on the plate.

"I'm rusty at baking, but it should be edible,"

Vee watched him as he lifted the donut and bit half of it. Nodding as he chewed, he licked his lips.

"This is delicious, babe." It wasn't. It tasted like ash, but he wouldn't tell her that. Not when she was looking up at him with wide eyes.

Vee grinned. "I'm glad I destroyed the batter like, five times before I got it right."

He cleared his throat, forcing the rest of the donut down.

"What are you thanking me for?"

Vee sighed before she turned to his bed and fell on it, looking at the ceiling. Lazarus followed her, lying down next to her as he turned his head to face her.

"For supporting me at Word Slam. I couldn't have done it without you."

He grinned as he tugged on her curls. "You don't have to thank me for that."

"I do. If you weren't there… I don't know."

"Have you talked to Dara?"

A dark look passed over her face. "I don't want to talk about that."

Lazarus decided not to say anything. "What about that college?"

"Lazarus." Vassa closed her eyes. Her fingers curled into the blankets and he sighed.

"Just listen to her. It could've been a mistake—"

"Lazarus, I don't want to go there right now, okay?"

He dropped it, but he could feel the tension dripping off of her. Vee placed her hands on his cheeks and he closed his eyes and leaned into her touch. Her fingers traced his bottom lips. "Where are you going in a suit?"

Lazarus kissed her. They pulled apart slightly before he pressed his lips to hers again and again before she stopped his hands from sliding farther.

"Lazarus, focus."

Lazarus blinked a few times. "What?"

"Focus!"

Lazarus leaned back as he looked at her. How many times had he imagined being with her like this? How he wanted to keep moments like this in their future.

"A job interview."

Vassa blinked at him. "Job interview? You didn't tell me about that."

Right. He was going to last night, but was distracted. Lazarus leaned over and pressed a few kisses to her neck before he pulled back.

"Harvey set it up." Lazarus leaned down to kiss her again when she pressed a hand to his mouth.

"Hold up. Roll up your tongue."

Vee sat up. "Harvey's company? The one where I embarrassed myself spilling deviled eggs on the vice president of marketing?"

"Sales actually, Harvey's VP of marketing."

Vee cut her eyes at him, and he raised his hands in surrender. "Lazarus, I thought you said—"

He sighed before he sat up. "It's fine."

Vee shook her head. "Is this about what I said on the glider? I was stupid. Of course, I want us to stay together. What does this job have to do with anything because you wanted to go with Mario—"

"It's not that. What happens when I meet your parents? I can't be like Gideon. Just being a hippie out in the plants all day—"

"Nothing is wrong with Gideon. You love him!"

Lazarus shook his head. "Of course I do, but I'm not making a hundred thousand a year with a fleet of men at my bidding. I need to prove to you, Coach Maverick, Harvey, and Gideon I can be responsible. You want to write and I want to do that for you. I want you to have everything."

"I don't need you to provide me anything."

Lazarus ignored her. "I told Harvey I'd go to the interview. It's for a unique position: brand manager."

Vee blinked. "I thought you were going to do the internship. I thought—"

"This is what I want."

This was what he wanted. Once he had enough money, he could always switch to something else. Do his dream then. It wouldn't matter if he delayed it. He knew it. Vee's shoulders dropped. "Great, that's great."

Lazarus scooted closer to her, playing with the edge of his shirt she was wearing. "This is my shirt."

Vassa looked down at it, then to him with a sheepish grin on his face. "Is it? I thought it was mine..."

He gave her a look before he pulled her to him. She let out a squeak as he positioned himself over her, pulling the shirt higher.

"I should repossess it then, shouldn't I?"

Vassa giggled as she tried to pull the shirt down. "You're going to an interview!"

Lazarus pulled her shirt up and tossed it to the floor. He kissed her shoulder and trailed down to her chest and to her nipples. Her fingers curled into his hair. When she pulled him back up to her, he made love to her again. He couldn't help himself. He used her touch as both an anchor and reassurance. Taking her high and hard, their climax crashed over them and left them both shuddering and gasping. His warning alarm went off and he managed to get his clothes back on and stumble out of his apartment on time, opting out of a tie altogether.

"You're late."

Lazarus stepped off the elevator onto the floor of Fit Energia. Centered right in the middle of the financial district, the lobby was overwhelming, the logo and protein bar plastered all over the walls.

"I guess you can't forget who you work for, huh?" Lazarus muttered, looking at the posters of the protein bar.

Harvey was in his usual attire, a crisp suit with cufflinks. His hair slicked back and eyes cold he groaned. "You're not wearing a tie?"

Lazarus looked down at himself.

"I, uh, forgot."

"Whatever, just fix yourself up and let's go."

Lazarus followed him past the receptionist's desk. The office was loud. People walked with stacks of papers down the hall. Some were on calls and others gathered around their desks for small meetings. Harvey led him past more rows of cubicles, most of the people focused on their computers, barely sparing him a glance. *I guess that'll be me soon.* They arrived at the door to an office.

"Now try not to embarrass me again."

Lazarus raised an eyebrow, but said nothing. Knocking on the door, they heard a reply and stepped inside.

The office had large windows with an impressive view of the Bay Bridge. An executive desk sat in the center, and Adrienne looked up before standing.

"Adrienne." Harvey smiled. The annoyance was completely gone, masked with a professional expression.

"Harvey. And this must be Lazarus. It's good to see you again. Thankfully, there's no food around us." She offered her hand to him.

Lazarus took it, deciding not to comment as he could feel Harvey's eyes on the side of his head. She pointed to the chair in front and Lazarus sat. When Adrienne wasn't looking, Harvey gave him a threatening look.

"I'll leave you to it then." Harvey smiled at Adrienne and gave Lazarus one last look before leaving.

The sound of the door closing enveloped him and suddenly he felt warm. Rubbing his sweaty hands on his pants, he cleared his throat as she sat down and looked at him.

"Let's begin, shall we?"

"Of course." His voice sounded high-pitched. He cleared his throat. "Of course."

Opening a notebook, she lifted a sheet of paper.

"I have your resume. I see some good experience here. Can you tell me what your five-year goals are?"

Lazarus's mouth was dry. He let out a sigh.

"I'm taking it one day at a time."

Adrienne made a face and Lazarus quickly countered. "You know, I like to keep my options open. Flexible and willing to adapt to change but I'm hoping to become part of a team and mission that drives me to do my best."

Lazarus cleared his throat again as she jotted down notes.

"So that means you're open to chance and opportunity?"

"Yeah, uh, yes that. Exactly."

Lazarus gripped the sides of the seat.

"What do you know about our company?"

Lazarus closed his eyes. Why couldn't he think of anything besides that they sold protein bars? Every shred of information that he ever heard Harvey talk about vanished from his mind.

"I, uh, know that it's energy bars. Athletic enhancements for athletes. You see I'm an athlete myself..."

"Oh really?"

"Yes. Pitcher for my university. You probably know that as an athlete, our energy is the most important factor of all. Finding something that..." Lazarus's mind went blank as he tried to think of something. "Yeah that's it."

Adrienne raised an eyebrow at him and she wrote down some notes.

"Would you like some water?"

"Yes, please." Lazarus said.

Adrienne reached to pour the water from a pitcher that was nearby.

"Tell me, what challenges have you had either in your past positions or school that you worked with a team to solve?"

Adrienne handed him a glass of water. Lazarus downed it before making a gesture for more. She obliged him.

"When I'm faced with a problem, I typically start by doing research or looking at examples of how this problem has been solved by others. I talk to friends and other players I trust." Lazarus felt himself relaxing. "From there, I'm able to decide which approach works best for me and my team and get their feedback."

This was great. If he talked about what he knew, he wouldn't sound like too much of an idiot.

"We recently had a game for my baseball team, but our new shipment of equipment was delayed. I called several local equipment stores in the area and asked them to hold enough for our team. I had it shipped to our university within two days for free."

Adrienne looked impressed and Lazarus thought this situation might not be an extreme loss.

"That's amazing. Can you tell me more about your leadership on the team?"

"Yes, well—" Lazarus set the glass back on the edge of the desk, and it tipped over, the water soaking Adrienne's desk and all her notes.

"Oh!"

"Let me get that!" Lazarus snatched the other papers on the desk to try to sop up the mess. The ink on the papers smeared into an unreadable blob. Lifting the soaking papers, Lazarus rushed them to the nearest trash can.

Lazarus looked at Adrienne. Shock was written all over her face.

Harvey was going to kill him.

She had only been in the art gallery for fifteen minutes and was already on her second glass of champagne. Vassa knew she probably shouldn't even have been here tonight, but Dara offered an olive branch and asked if she would still come. Even though she totally skipped out on her Word Night with no explanation. No matter how pissed Vassa was, Dara was still her best friend, and she wanted to support her in any way she could.

Pictures of design students' work lined the walls of the swanky gallery located on the marina that boasted a full view of the bay and Golden Gate Bridge. Patrons admired the stacked sculptures strategically scattered within the gallery. Vassa looked at a picture of what she thought was a pumpkin or squash with tentacles. There was no sign of Lazarus yet, even though she had seen a few members of the baseball team. It hurt her to know that he didn't trust her enough to be honest with his feelings about his father. She knew that it was hurting him, but he wouldn't discuss it with her.

She sent him a text message:

I'm here. Where are you?

"Everything okay?" Oscar asked.

It was a last-minute decision, but she invited Oscar as well. She thought he would enjoy the artwork and wanted someone to talk to for the night while Dara was on duty, mingling with folks in the gallery.

"Yeah, everything's fine."

The gallery owner was supposed to deliver a special speech. Oscar stood beside her and looked at the painting and both tilted their heads.

"Art is subjective, I know, but I'm not sure if the art is showing the artistic vision."

Vassa looked at him. "That's a pleasant way of saying it."

Oscar took a sip of his champagne. "Your feelings about the art?"

"Looks like tentacle porn."

He laughed. "I have to agree there."

Her mind wandered to Dara. She could see her over on the other side, yet Vassa couldn't get herself to go over there. Why couldn't she just apologize? They had a slight argument about her missing Word Night, and over the past few days, everything seemed to be all right but Vassa knew it wasn't.

"Should we move on?" Oscar asked and she nodded. Vassa looked at her phone again. There was a text from Lazarus,

Be there soon.

What did that mean? They moved to the other side of the room where there were more abstract statues. A tall one, mimicking a weeping willow, was made of recycled plastic. Next to it was a live person, dressed like a marble statue like the ones you find on the street that don't move no matter how hard you stare at them.

Oscar leaned down to her and said, "I wonder what training you need for that?"

"I know, right; what if you sneeze?" Vassa whispered.

Then she saw a flash of blonde out of the corner of her eye. Lazarus. She turned and smiled at seeing him. It had been less than a day, and she missed him already. She had taken a step toward him when she spotted Jayden next to him. Both were wearing frowns.

Oscar turned to see what she was looking at. "Is that your boyfriend?"

She nodded as Lazarus and Jayden crossed the room, and she opened her mouth to speak, but he beat her to it.

"Hey, Vee." His clothes were rumpled, and bags weighed heavily under his eyes.

"Vassa, merry meet." Jayden bowed.

"Merry meet to you," Vassa responded and turned her focus back onto Lazarus. He was still looking at Oscar with that frown.

"Where have you been?" Vassa inspected him as he shook his head. There was an unexpected coldness to him. The two stared at one another when tapping on a microphone broke their eye lock.

Jayden looked like he wanted to comment, but Lazarus shut him down and muttered, "It's nothing; I was busy."

"Lazarus, I know that isn't the truth." She frowned and crossed her arms, beginning to take his standoffish behavior personally.

Jayden cleared his throat. "Uh, Vassa, aren't you excited? Dara's told me she's moving to Toronto after graduation—"

The air left her body. *"What?"*

Dara was moving to Toronto? What about New York? Vassa's body went numb; why would she back out of their plan? After the fallout with Alexa, Dara knew how important it was for them to stick together after graduation. Now, she was abandoning her just like Alexa did. Lazarus moved to comfort her, and she backed away from him. *"Don't touch me."*

"Vee—" The outburst drew some attention, and Dara hurried over to them. She looked between the four. "What is going on here?"

Vassa turned her gaze to Dara. "I can't believe you."

Dara looked confused and then realization passed across her face. "There's an opportunity for me in Toronto—-"

Vassa crossed her arms, her body shaking with repressed anger. "Toronto? That's in freaking Canada the last time I checked, not New York City."

Vassa's voice rose, and Dara tried to shush her. She was briefly irritated. They had a plan— to move to New York together. They were supposed to be together, especially after the Alexa ordeal she knew how important it was to her.

"I was going to tell you—"

"When? On graduation day or the day that we're supposed to move in together?"

"Vassa, don't be dramatic. I was going to tell you. My professors recommended me for a graphic design fellowship there that would be perfect for me. I applied, sent off my application a month go, and was accepted."

Vassa wasn't listening to her right now. Of all the times she could have told her this, she chose this moment.

"You never answered my question. When we're you going to tell me? If ever?"

"When the moment was right—"

"When the moment was right… Do your parents know this?" Vassa echoed.

Dara looked down.

"They still don't know? Are you never going to tell them that you don't want to be a freaking accountant? How long are you going to keep up this charade? Just tell them; it's not that hard."

"You know how they are; they don't approve of the arts; I'll tell them when the moment is right."

"Just like you were going to tell me."

The girls were quiet. Vassa sucked in a deep breath. Closing her eyes, she counted to five before she released it.

"How could you say something like that?" Dara said.

"I don't know. You've already kept one secret. There must others. Don't tell me; I bet Suri already knew about this! This is Alexa all over again." Vassa threw her hands up in the air.

"Yes, she knows!"

Vassa couldn't help the anger burning in her chest. She was willing to overlook Dara missing Word Slam, not hanging out and studying with her, but it was the principle of the matter. Dara was her best friend. The one person who was supposed to know her inside and out. This feeling was like Alexa all over again. Vassa opened her mouth to respond when Suri appeared.

"Is everything ok?" Suri looked between them.

Offering a humorless laugh, Vassa slapped her hand against her forehead.

"Great. Why shouldn't you appear? *As if I don't see you enough already.*"

"What is your problem?" Dara stood up for Suri.

"You get a shitty attitude anytime she comes along." Vassa's muscles quivered. Planting her feet wide apart, she tried to hear past the pounding in her ears. Lazarus took a step toward Vassa, but she stepped away. He looked down at her, emotions swirling in his eyes. The same eyes she looked into didn't look like the eyes she had grown used to.

Vassa could only deal with one issue at a time. She looked at Dara and Suri.

"Why is she here? Why is she always here?"

Dara looked confused. "She's my friend; what don't you get?"

"You hang out with her all the time! She's in our apartment; you're texting her; you're calling her."

"Are you trying to tell me who I can be friends with?" Dara asked.

Vassa shook her head. "You were my friend first! My friend. Not hers. You're going to do what Alexa did to me before. All for her! You know what I went through with Alexa. And now, you're doing the same thing to me. You're leaving me and choosing her." Vassa pointed at Suri.

It took time for Vassa to warm up to Dara when they first met. It was almost six months later when she finally confessed everything, including her thoughts of self-harm after the bullying she endured. They had vowed to each other they would never turn their back on each other. Or that's what Vassa held herself to. Rubbing her temples, Dara shook her head slowly.

"Not to mention you didn't come to Word Night. You knew how much that meant to me!"

"Look, I'm sorry I missed it—"

"Sorry doesn't cut it!"

"I didn't make it because I got stuck in traffic with Suri to buy you a graduation present. I thought if I gave it to you, it would ease the blow a bit."

Vassa inhaled shakily and shook her head. She didn't believe that. "You know what? Have fun in Canada, and I hope to see what excuse you tell your parents. Maybe that you're going to be an accountant for the national parks? I'm not gonna sit around and let another friend humiliate me."

The words were out of her mouth before she could stop them. It was her fault she thought she wouldn't be hurt again by another friend. Dara stared at Vassa. The only sound was their heavy breathing as the entire room watched them. Vassa didn't bother to look at the gathering crowd. She wanted to get away and get away fast. She made it two steps when Lazarus grabbed her arm.

"Let me go Lazarus I want to be alone."

He shook his head. "Vee, c'mon; don't leave like this. Talk to Dara; I'm sure she'll—"

She retreated before he stopped himself. "This thing between us. Let's call it. Trust me. If you can't be honest with me about how you feel about your father, what is the point of us being together, huh? Trust, isn't that what you told me?"

His eyes grew impossibly wide, and his breathing grew shallow and rapid. "What?"

She shut her eyes as she talked through clenched teeth. "It's over, Lazarus. You did your job."

"No, Vee. Please."

"Go work for your brother's company. Make all the money in the world and be happy. I just can't right now. I can't think anymore."

"We can figure this out together."

Vassa turned to Oscar who lingered for a second before following her.

"I bombed the interview!" Lazarus shouted, but Vassa continued to walk. She turned from him, crossing her arms as she ran to the car Oscar was in. "Drive please."

She ignored the painful look on Lazarus's face as they drove away.

CHAPTER TWENTY-ONE

VASSA STOOD OUTSIDE HER CHILDHOOD home.

It wasn't bearable to stay in that apartment one more night. She packed her stuff and got on the first Greyhound back home. Stepping into the foyer, she took a deep breath of the familiar home scent, a mix of fresh linens and flowers. Sheentered the living room. A large, tan leather couch took up most of the room. The wooden coffee table was littered with magazines and her mom's nail polish. Dumping her bag onto the floor, she took the stairs two at a time before she pushed open the door to her old bedroom.

It looked exactly how she left it four months ago.

The same posters from her high school, all her stuffed bears and pillows. She changed into a pair of pajamas and slid into bed. As she closed her eyes, sleep refused to come. Flashes of Lazarus, Oscar, and Dara consumed her thoughts. She heard the incoming ding of an email from her phone on the bedside table. Reaching for the phone, she sat up in bed.

New York University.

She sucked in a deep breath. This was it. The time had finally come. Her heart was beating a steady rhythm against her chest. Her finger briefly hovered above the message. She just needed to do it. Instead, she couldn't.

Opening this email would seal her fate. She would graduate in less than a month and fly to the other side of the country to live her dream. Her parents would be in a different time zone. It would be difficult to come back and visit often. Her grandmother was getting older...

"You'll make it work, Vassa," she told herself.

Letting out a shaky breath, she nodded. Clicking the email, her eyes scanned the beginning contents.

> Dear Miss Vasilisa Blackwell,
>
> Regarding your application to the MFA in Creative Writing program at New York University we regret to inform you that we cannot offer you admission into this program. Each year, we receive numerous applications from extremely well-qualified candidates...

A knot formed in her stomach, and her ears rang. The phone slipped from her hand and onto the floor with a thud. Her chest rose and fell quickly. She placed a hand over her heart, trying to steady herself. Her thoughts swirled so quickly that it was hard to follow them. She had done everything possible to submit a worthy application. Letters of recommendation, writing samples. For months, *and months, and months,* she had poured herself into perfecting that application. Now, she was accepted into neither one of her top programs.

Where did I go wrong?

She bent over and placed her face on her knees; it was more than crying. It was the desolate sobbing that came from a person drained of all hope. She pressed her face farther into her knees, not caring if she could breathe. Her tears ran in streams, and her gasping wails echoed throughout the room. At that moment, she wished she had somebody nearby, someone to hold her, but she was all alone.

Lazarus rang the doorbell and took a step back. He could hear Gideon's ten-year-old dog, Riley, barking on the other side. The door opened up and Christie, Gideon's long-term girlfriend, stood there in a business suit.

"Lazzie!" Christie launched herself at him.

Barely past five feet, she was like a sister and now a successful stockbroker, he was always curious about how a serious and orderly person like Christie ended up with his lackadaisical brother.

"What are you doing here? Come in," Christie urged as she pushed Riley back from the door.

Lazarus picked up his bag and placed it on his shoulder.

"Did you just get in?" Lazarus asked as he closed the door.

Riley then jumped up, placing his massive paws on Lazarus' chest as he attempted to lick and slobber on his face.

"I missed you, too, Riley." Lazarus patted the chocolate lab. The old dog spent most of his days lounging around or farting himself awake than being an actual ferocious beast.

"Yes, and I could string your brother up. The place was a *mess as usual.*" Christie stressed the last part loudly as she walked to the back patio doors, and yelled at Gideon. Lazarus heard a gruff laugh in response.

Christie jerked her thumb over her shoulder. "The goof is back there."

Lazarus thanked her as he stepped outside the double doors with Riley on his heels. Gideon was on the patio with a sledgehammer in one hand. A decrepit fountain stood a few feet away.

"What are you doing?"

Riley left his side to run to Gideon. He looked up, wiping the sweat from his face and patted Riley.

"Christie brought a new fountain" —he pointed to a new fountain that was still wrapped in plastic— "but this one is still good. I didn't want to completely toss it, so I thought I could repurpose the stone."

Lazarus set his bag on the steps as he approached him, pushing his sleeves up. The sun beamed down on them brighter in Menlo Park than San Francisco.

"What's that look on your face? Either it's money or women. Or both." Gideon lifted the hammer smashing it on side of the fountain. A piece went sailing off, and Riley took off after it.

"Women."

"Ah. New girlfriend problems already? A rite of passage for a man." Gideon grinned. Lazarus rolled his eyes as he sat on the steps.

"What happened? She didn't break up with you yet, did she?"

That was a good question.

"It's undecided," Lazarus said.

Gideon grunted, "That's never good."

Riley came back with the discarded piece of stone, dropping it near Gideon's feet. He dug into his pocket and gave the dog a treat.

"You've barely been together for a month and angst already?" Gideon lifted the sledgehammer.

"Didn't you and Christie break up a week after you all got together?" Lazarus pointed to where he could hear Christie yammering on the phone.

"Those were simpler times." Gideon hit the fountain, and it cracked up the center.

"No, it wasn't!" Christie peeked her head out the door.

Gideon made a face. "I thought you weren't talking to me?"

"Who said I was?" Christie disappeared back into the house.

Lazarus looked at his brother. "Sounds like angst going on here."

Gideon shook his head. "Who told her to come back from New York early? If she didn't, she wouldn't have seen the mess." Riley walked toward Lazarus and laid down in front of him, groaned, and farted before closing his eyes for sleep.

"Anyway, tell me what's going on."

Lazarus started from the beginning, starting with the gallery opening and everything before that. Skirting over certain details, when he was done at some point, he was the one hitting the stone fountain to smithereens. Gideon had grabbed a ladder, plucking limes from his lime tree in the backyard.

"We need tequila," Gideon said.

Lazarus lifted the sledgehammer and smashed it into the final piece. Riley didn't flinch but let out another fart.

"We got to get you off the bargain chow." Gideon waved a hand in front of his face as he sat on the steps with a knife, plate, and tall bottle of tequila.

Lazarus dropped the sledgehammer to the floor and took a seat next to his brother. Gideon poured two shots and cut some limes before they clinked glasses, and tossed the liquid back.

"How was the interview?"

Gideon passed the bottle to Lazarus. "The interview? The interview sucked."

His brother shook his head, "Then I take it you didn't get the job?"

"I got it." Lazarus nodded as he looked at the bottle.

"So, you're going to be a marketing associate for an energy bar line?"

Lazarus shrugged. "Fitting."

"Why don't you end this farce and just talk to Mario? This is what you really want to do."

Lazarus glared at him. "Harvey's ecstatic."

Gideon looked at him in disbelief. "You're stupid—" his brother didn't stop with the harsh truth — "and you will be miserable."

His brother sighed and patted him on the back. "Dad loves you, Lazarus. The perfectly screwed-up, flawed mess that you are. He's always loved you; somewhere in your mind, you convinced yourself that you had to be perfect for people to accept you. Dad loves you how you are. Vassa will love you no matter what you do. And you're missing it because you have the dumb idea that you need to prove yourself. If you take the job with Mario, that will get your money back Laz."

"I'll tell you what's a dumb idea; that gnome." Lazarus pointed to the hideous creature a few feet away from them. It was turned to them. Staring. With cold, lifeless eyes.

"Yes. I hope it doesn't rise while we're asleep and bludgeon us all to death. Christie likes it, so it stays. You can try to turn the conversation all you want, but do what you want; don't say I didn't warn you."

"Stop it now, Lazarus, or you're going to end up like me or Harvey."

Lazarus blinked up at him. "You? What's wrong with you?"

Gideon looked down at him, and for the first time, Lazarus saw his brother as an older man, not just a guy to pal around with. "I was depressed. I was miserable trying to fit into what others thought was best for me. What Mom and Dad, Harvey and, the others wanted me to be. I was burned out and alone." Gideon's voice was like lead. "Christie left me, but I had to wake up. Don't make that decision when you're almost forty and everyone you knew and loved has moved on. Define your future for yourself and then deal with the consequences of your choices. Don't do it for someone else; do it for you."

Lazarus swallowed. "You're exaggerating."

"Probably; probably not. You don't need to be here talking to me. Riley, come."

The old dog got up slowly, following his brother into the house. Christie appeared in the doorway with her hands on her hips, frowning. Gideon opened his arms, and Christie hesitated before she eventually smiled and walked into his embrace. The couple kissed as Riley circled them before they disappeared farther into the house. Lazarus sat on the steps, watching as the lime tree blew in the breeze.

CHAPTER TWENTY-TWO

VASSA AWAKENED TO AT THE end of her bed. Cracking open her eyes, crusted from tears and makeup, she saw her mother, Eve, looking directly at her, concerned.

"Hi, Mom."

Eve cocked her head to the side. Her locs were piled on the top of her head, and she was in her workout gear.

"What are you doing home?"

"I just felt like coming home." Vassa evaded as plucked at the sheets on the bed.

Her mom gave her that look. Vassa's eyes were puffy, red, and swollen, her skin dull. She felt as if she had been tied to the end of a car and dragged down the street, face first. Eve asked again, and Vassa replied the same. Eve narrowed her eyes on her daughter. It was the look all mothers gave their children when they knew they were lying.

"Girl, why you lyin'? I came in here twice last night and you were dead to the world. We thought you were an intruder. FYI, you need to give notice when you make these unannounced pop-ups; your grandmother almost shot you."

"I'll make sure to give notice the next time in my crisis. I would hate for Grandma to carry the burden of knowing she sent her only grandchild to meet her make." Vassa lay back on the bed, clutching the pillow.

"It would really tear the family apart," Eve replied with fake sadness.

Vassa let out a pitiful laugh and pressed her face into the pillow before sitting up. She had no reason to try to lie to her mother.

"Can we make our super-sickening chocolate fudge shakes?" Vassa looked up at her mother pitifully.

Eve patted her daughter on her legs and stood up. Vassa saw her phone still on the bed from earlier. Grimacing, she took it and placed it in the bedside drawer then followed her mom down the stairs to the kitchen. Her mother reached into the cabinets for the sauce while she went to the freezer for the ice cream.

They moved in a quiet rhythm, just like old times.

Eve was in charge of putting the chocolate flakes around the rim of the glasses. Vassa used chocolate ice cream, rocky road, Moose Tracks, and every possible combination of chocolate ice cream they had in the freezer, tossing in a few peanut butter cups for "flavor." This shake was liable to put someone into a sugar coma. Vassa poured the shakes into two glasses and sat at the counter.

"NYU rejected me," Vassa's voice quivered.

She vowed she wouldn't cry again, but dammit, she did. The tears started to fall, and she wiped them away. Eve made a noise under her breath. Moving over, she set her shake down and wrapped her arms around her daughter. Rocking her softly, she rubbed her hair as she sobbed.

Eve leaned over and squeezed her thigh. "I'm sorry, baby; I know you wanted to get accepted there."

"That's not all of it," Vassa admitted.

Taking in a deep breath, she spilled everything to her mother. The list, the awkward party with Oscar's friends, the first rejection, and Dara. Of course, some parts she skimmed, especially the part about her and Lazarus in Vegas. Her mother didn't comment but listened the entire time. Vassa slurped her shake after she finished. Eve replied as tenderly as she could, "You fucked up."

Wide-eyed, Vassa looked at her mother incredulously. "Mom…"

Eve shrugged her shoulders. "You know I'm never one to sugarcoat things with you."

She wanted her mother to lie to her and tell her everything was going to be okay.

"I'm always going to be here and support you. No matter what, you know that? That requires me calling you out when you're wrong."

Vassa nodded, even though it sucked to hear.

"You need to let go of the past," Eve said softly.

Vassa looked at her and made a face. "I'm over what happened with Alexa."

"Obviously, you're not."

Shaking her head, she didn't want to think about everything that happened. Her friends or the people she thought were her friends. People she had invited to birthdays, holidays, and went on trips with. People she shared her dream with only for them to be secretly plotting behind her back.

"I'm past that she's gone now." Vassa focused her gaze on the floor.

Eve put a hand up to silence her. "You know how many people say that? People claiming things that happened to them as children don't affect them as adults. Or that heartbreak or rejection don't matter? Yet, people are walking around with childhood trauma, pining for the one who got away or trying to prove themselves to people who wouldn't give a shit if they dropped dead tomorrow."

Vassa mulled on that.

"You can't punish new people for the actions of those in your past. You want closure, baby, for the hurt she caused you. You may never get that, and you have to learn to be okay with not getting it. And you can't push people away because of what you perceive to be behavior like Alexa's," Eve muttered sympathetically.

"I don't try to."

"You're hurt. *Admit it. Own it.* Don't think it's ever a mistake to feel and love with all your heart. Sometimes, we love the wrong people, but that doesn't mean the love you gave was ever wrong. If people leave you, then it was meant to happen. Sometimes, we're friends with people for a season. Sometimes, a lifetime. It's up to you to accept the lessons they teach you when the relationship runs its course."

If she would have chosen better friends. If she known what she knew now, things would've gone a lot differently.

Eve continued, "You can't control what other people think and feel, baby. When Alexa decided to say those mean things about you online and whatever crap you young people do these days, it was just jealousy and immaturity. You were going somewhere, and she was threatened."

Vassa flinched as she replayed what went down. Those words and pictures were still all online, easily traceable.

"You were a great friend to her. She was your only friend in high school. You helped her, encouraged her, and were always there for her. Sometimes, we love and help the wrong people. It's a part of life. They weren't doing mean things simply to hurt you; it was a reaction to how you made them feel."

Vassa's brows furrowed. "How I made them feel?"

"It's not always who the person is but what they represent."

Vassa thought about it. "I made a mess of things with Lazarus and Dara; they no longer want to talk to me. I think it's better if I just cut my losses now and move on."

They would probably be off better without her. Lazarus would find a girl. He would go on to do something great because that was just in him. Dara would make amazing art and be uber-famous. They would all be living their dreams while she would be sitting back here, in a small town, figuring out her next move.

"That's the worst thing you can do. Even if they decide to no longer be your friend, you gave them closure by apologizing and speaking from your heart."

Would they even forgive me?

Her mother was right. Giving her mother a hug, she pressed her face into the chest that always provided the warmth and comfort she needed it most. "I love you."

Her mother squeezed her tighter. "I love you, too, baby."

After finishing their shakes, they ordered Chinese food and sat in front of the TV as they talked about the gossip of the town.

"So, you're telling me Victoria is having an affair with the mailman, whose wife is having her own affair?" Vassa looked at her mom in disbelief that she lived in a real-life Genoa City.

Eve picked up an eggroll and bit into, replying, "Yes,sir."

That's how Grandma Laura and her dad found them.

"What do we have here?"

Vassa gaspedand sat her wineglass down, laughing as she ran to her dad. God, she didn't realize how much she missed him. Tall, bald, and with those same brown eyes like her, he still smelled as she always remembered—woodsy with a hint of something spicy; she could never tell what it was.

"I missed you." Vassa burrowed her face into his chest. As he hugged her, he lifted her off the ground. She could have stayed there longer if not for the loud coughing next to him.

"Well, I don't get anything?" Grandma Laura mock-pouted.

Releasing her dad, she went to her grandma. All her favorite people in the world were in the same room. She just wished she could bottle them all up and take them back with her to San Francisco.

"Where were you all?" Vassa said.

Grandma Laura and her dad looked at one another before rolling their eyes upward. Vassa laughed, and Eve shook her head.

"What happened was a disaster," Simon began as Grandma Laura added,

"We went on an adventure!"

The two looked at one another and frowned. Simon's face told Vassa more than she needed to know.

"Simon; Mama," Eve said.

"It's not my fault, Eve, that your husband doesn't know how to dive to get the good wares at the flea market. Weren't you in the military?" Grandma Laura looked at him.

Simon rolled his eyes and crossed his arms. "I'm not fighting old women so you can score some secondhand must-have, Laura."

"You were fighting old ladies, Mama?" Eve was fighting a smile of her own.

"It's the flea market on a Saturday! Not for the faint of heart! I thought he—" Grandma Laura jerked a finger at Simon—"would be good muscle, but I had just as much of a chance with a limp noodle."

"Now, Laura." Simon gave her grandma one of his no-nonsense looks.

Vassa listened closely to the bickering between her dad and grandma as she settled deeper into the couch. Being home felt good.

CHAPTER TWENTY- THREE

"WHAT A PLEASANT SURPRISE! SHOULD I expect more of these?"

Lazarus was in Harvey's condo in SoMa. It was no surprise Harvey's apartment mirrored his lifestyle. Lavish. Modern appliances and all the latest technology could be found throughout the loft, located on the top floor of his building. They had a magnificent view of downtown as traffic whizzed down the street. Lazarus sat on the couch as Harvey stepped into the kitchen. Grabbing two water bottles, he passed one to Lazarus as he sat on the opposite side of the couch.

"Not if you still have this rock-hard couch," Lazarus said, opening the bottle. "Feels like concrete."

Harvey raised an eyebrow. "That was imported from Greenland. It's rare and native-made."

"That doesn't mean they can't add a little cushion for your butt?"

Harvey rolled his eyes. Lazarus took a deep breath as he tried to calm his nerves. It was time. He thought about what he practiced in the car on the way up.

"We shouldn't be focusing on that. I should be congratulating our new brand manager," Harvey grinned.

Lazarus took a sip of water as he steeled himself. Harvey was going to lose his shit. He tossed the script he practiced in his head, deciding it was better to speak from his heart even if Harvey didn't like what he had to say.

"I'm rescinding my acceptance." Lazarus exhaled and closed his eyes.

"What?"

He nodded and shifted forward on the couch. Setting the bottle on the coffee table, he clasped his hands. "I'm not taking the job."

Glancing at Harvey, Lazarus could see the confusion and anger swirled on his face as he ran a hand through his hair, disrupting his groomed look.

"Say that again?"

"I'm not taking the job. I'm taking the internship with Mario. If they give it to me."

Harvey glared at his brother. "You're throwing away a guaranteed job with excellent pay and benefits for a fantasy?" Realization passed over his face. "Stop joking, Laz, you're not doing that. You're working with me."

Lazarus bristled and shook his head. "I'm not. Adrienne already knows. By the way, I spilled water on her laptop, and she'll send you the bill."

The crackling of the plastic water bottle crunching under Harvey's grip filled the air. Slamming it on the table, Harvey now sat forward.

"What do you mean? How could you do that, Lazarus..." Harvey sighed and ran a hand over his face. "Do you know the strings I had to pull to get you in?"

"I know and I'm thankful, but it's not what I want to do."

"All the money I've spent for you to be at this school and you're about to waste your degree!"

"Harvey, it's not like that."

Harvey stood up. "Are you that selfish? After all the money I've invested in you. Dealing with you fumbling around for almost two years while trying to keep our family together..."

"Was it about helping your brother or you flaunting your money?"

Harvey's nose flared.

"Why are you asking me that? Of course, it's been about you."

Lazarus stood up. "I appreciate you, Harvey. You've always taken care of me, along with Gideon. Making sure I did my homework, got to school, providing anything I needed if Mom and Dad couldn't get it. I understand now; Mom was a wreck, and you loved us enough to rearrange your life for us. But all of that is over. I'm a man now. I've learned from you. You won't use your money against me or to shame me because you can't accept when it's time to step back."

Harvey's shoulders deflated, and softness replaced the ire on his face. Lazarus wasn't sure if they ever sat down and had a conversation about their family dynamic after their father's stroke and the toll it took on everyone. He always thought Harvey was difficult because he wanted to be. He didn't think about Dad's stroke and how that affected him. The pressure and sacrifice he endured to help his family. Harvey never confided in any of them, the strain it caused, but that could change.

"I know you don't approve of my decision. I'm not you, Harvey. I don't care if I get my accounts back at all," Lazarus stressed.

Harvey cleared his throat. "It's that girl; she's making you do this—-"

Lazarus shook his head. "It's far from Vee. If anything, she made me realize I need to find a passion that makes me want to get out of bed every day, *for myself.* Not just to take any job but find a mission worth my effort. I'm deciding this for myself, and you need to be okay with this. If not, it still won't deter me from pursuing *my* dreams."

Lazarus began to move toward the door. He felt good. Powerful even. If Mario couldn't mentor him or help get things set up, that was fine. He would figure everything out in time. He had time to discover himself.

"Lazarus!"

He stopped and turned around. Harvey walked toward him with a pinched expression. Lazarus clenched his fist, preparing for round two. He stiffened when Harvey pulled him into a hug.

"Follow your heart. I'll be here always," Harvey muttered.

A smile spread across Lazarus' face and he lifted his arms to hug Harvey back.

"Where is my brother and who are you?" Lazarus grinned.

Harvey stepped back and rolled his arms. "Get out."

"Love you, Harv."

Harvey nodded as Lazarus opened the door and turned. He leaned against the door as he inspected Lazarus. "I guess I feel love for you. Still trying to process how to show my face at work."

With that, Harvey shut the door in Lazarus's face. Laughing he placed his hands in his pockets, whistling as he walked away.

The living room and kitchen were empty, but the lights were on. The weekend went by too fast and Vassa listened for any sounds of movement as she walked down the hall to her bedroom. Dropping her bag in her room, she looked across the hall to Dara's bedroom door. The light was on underneath.

"Dara?" she called out as she knocked.

Waiting for a moment, she knocked again.

"Dara, are you in there I… I wanted to talk to you if that's okay?"

There was more silence.

"I know you don't want to hear from me, but I have to apologize."

She leaned against the door. "Remember when we met sophomore year and you asked me why my hair was pink? I had botched it, dyeing it burgundy after the Alexa situation. I was stupid, thinking people wouldn't recognize me and whisper as I walked past. You tried to help me correct it and we ended up totally frying my hair. We had only known each other for a few days, but it was like we knew each other forever."

Vassa shook her head and laughed. She didn't think her hair

would ever be the same again after that.

"I didn't tell you at the time, but the only friend I had left me so easily. You know people always say 'people come and people go', but it freaking hurts when the one you love the most abandons you. The effects of that hurt more than I realized."

Vassa crossed her arms.

"I was mean to you. I'm not even gonna lie about that. You would talk to me and I would ignore you. You kept coming back, inviting me to dinner. Doing those Korean face masks. Asking to read my writing. Bringing me those rice balls you like from Japantown. I couldn't figure out why you wanted to be my friend and why you wouldn't go away."

This wasn't so bad. She leaned back against the door as the memories flooded her and she felt warmth in her chest.

"You refused to stay away, and at some point, I let you in. You weren't like the others. You were just like me. It was the two of us and nothing else. Then you changed—"

Vassa slid down the door, crossing her legs on the floor.

"I… Uh, there's no way to say it nicely, but I panicked. We had been side-by-side through it all. Then, our New York plans changed. Lazarus and Jayden entered the picture. We began hanging out less and less. *Suri comes—*" Vassa took a breath. "The New York news, I could've handled it better. It felt like Alexa all over again. She pushed me to the side, and I thought you did that too."

Vassa tapped her fingers against her thigh. It was hard to say it, but she kept going. She needed to get this off her chest. Dara had said nothing yet, but she hoped she could hear how remorseful she was.

"I should have talked to you. I'm sorry. *I'm so sorry* and I understand if you never want to talk to me again. I was shitty and horrible on all accounts. You always supported me. With Oscar and my writing, and with Lazarus. I should have done the same for you. I will do the same for you."

Vassa wiped a tear that escaped.

"If you want to go to Seattle or Toronto or even the North

Pole, then I will support you with every bone in my body. I know you will be a brilliant designer."

She turned to the door and knocked again. "Dara?"

Vassa stood up and reached for the doorknob and turned it, stepping inside. *"I'll be damned."*

Dara's room was empty. An open textbook sat on her bed and her TV was on but muted. Stepping inside, she saw the flyer for Maki Magic sushi bar. She knew exactly where she was. Twenty minutes later, she was rounding the corner on Geary Boulevard. Peeking in the window, she spotted Dara sitting in their sushi bar, a pile of small plates piled up next to her and a half-empty bottle of sake.

The bell dinged above the door as she entered and she headed straight for Dara. Taking a deep breath, she pulled out the chair next to her.

Dara looked over her shoulder, and her eyes widened before she frowned and looked at the little sushi boats floating around. A few minutes passed before Vassa spoke. "Looks like you've been here a while."

A few pieces of sashimi and tempura rolls floated past on the rotating sushi bar.

"It's discount sashimi today." Dara looked ahead.

They watched as the chef effortlessly placed the rice and fish precisely on his workspace before rolling it together and slicing.

"I'm sorry," Vassa said.

Dara looked at her before grabbing a roll that came by. Vassa watched her mix her wasabi and soy sauce and take a bite.

"That's all you have to say?" Dara raised an eyebrow.

Vassa saw a salmon roll coming down and grabbed it. Reaching for her chopsticks, she said, "I did a whole spiel outside your bedroom door before I realized you weren't there."

A small smile went over Dara's face. "Is that so?"

"Yes. It was movie-worthy. Even shed a few tears; I could have won an Oscar."

"I want to hear this."

Vassa chewed. "You wanna hear it? Word for word?"

Dara raised an eyebrow and folded her hands across her chest, "Start from the beginning. And please, don't hold back on the groveling."

Vassa set her chopsticks down.

"I was stupid, inconsiderate, jealous, and a mess. You are the best friend anyone could have, and I can't imagine not having you around to watch trashy reality TV, getting drunk on wine, or day-dreaming about celebrities we won't ever meet. I fully support you being the best damn designer this world has ever seen, and I ask that you look into that big heart of yours and forgive me for the cruel things I said to you."

Dara watched her for a moment and rubbed her chin in contemplation. "You embarrassed me in public and hurt my feelings."

Vassa sobered up immediately. "I know. I shouldn't have done that—"

Dara held up her hand and Vassa stopped speaking.

"I would have never have done that to you." Dara turned to Vassa. "I shouldn't have missed your Word Night. Or our movie nights. It was wrong of me. I should have been honest about New York."

Vassa smiled. "I forgive you."

Dara nodded. "It's going to take me a little while to let go of this, but I forgive you. I wasn't the best friend you needed. I was shitty too; we both need space." To her surprise, Dara hugged her. "I feel you skipped some parts in the grand apology, but that'll do."

Hugging her friend closer. Vassa felt a weight lifted off her shoulders. Dara munched on the food. "I'm like totally scared, excited, and happy all at the same time about Toronto. I still can't believe it, you know?"

Vassa nodded and she thought about her rejection letter from NYU and Iowa. "You're gonna be amazing."

"Well, flights from Toronto and New York might not be that expensive, so you can visit or I can come to you. Be in the city that never sleeps?"

"I didn't get in."

Dara gaspeddropping her food. She placed a hand on Vassa's arm. "I'm so sorry."

Vassa revealed the rest. "I got rejected from Iowa State too."

Dara dropped the piece of edamame out of her hand. "Vassa, what are you going to do? This is what you wanted…"

Shrugging, she said, "It'll be fine. I got accepted here at PGU. I can stay or apply again next year. I'll work something out."

They watched the sushi boats pass quicker. With more elaborate sushi rolls on them, her stomach growled.

"Have you talked to Lazarus?"

Her stomach dropped at the mention of his name.

"Not yet but I will."

Just then, a deep-fried California roll came out, and they both reached for it. They laughed and Dara let Vassa have it. Splitting the rolls, Dara went for the sake she poured earlier. "Let's toast."

Vassa reached for her glass.

"To graduation and sushi!"

They clinked glasses. The alcohol burned as it went down. The girls fell into conversation as Dara continued gushing over her fellowship. She hoped Lazarus would be as forgiving as Dara. She didn't know what she would do if he wasn't.

CHAPTER TWENTY-FOUR

Subject line: Pick up your cap and gown!

It's time!

Stop by the library today to pick up your cap, gown, and tassel for commencement. Graduates that have RSVP'd to the ceremony will receive 4 guest tickets at the time of pick up!

Robert Peña
Degree Audit and Graduation Adviser
Office of the Registrar
Pacific Grove University

VASSA STOOD IN FRONT OF the café doors. She was here; she was doing it. She printed some poems and stories on nice paper she stole from her job and kept them in a folder against her chest. She was going to share her work with others. Oscar got his wish. It was writing group time.

"You can do it," she muttered to herself.

Stepping into the café, she was greeted by trays of baguettes and fresh sandwich bread sitting in the coolers near the entrance. A rack filled with bags of potato chips and a line of customers filled the entranceway.

"Vassa!" Oscar approached. "Just in time; everyone's here."

She followed Oscar to the enclave in the back. The tables were pushed together. and people were sitting around the table.

They smiled when they saw her, and she gave an awkward wave and sat down in the empty seat next to Oscar.

"We can get started."

Vassa placed her folder on the table in front of her. Looking around the table, she recognized a few people from class and some others she spotted on campus.

"You go first, Amy," Oscar said.

For the next thirty minutes, they went around the table, reading each other's work. At first, Vassa felt shy giving her honest feedback. Slowly, she loosened up. This group was much better than Tom and his minions. Time flew by and before she knew it, they even ordered some coffee and sandwiches and were currently debating the meaning of the wife murdering her husband for a monkey.

"Let's get to Vassa's story."

The table tried to calm down, but the table still teetered in excitement. Gulping her coffee once more, she picked up her story.

"It's something new I'm experimenting with, so I'm not sure how well it works yet..." she trailed off.

Everyone at the table watched her. The temperature spiked in the room, and she pulled at her T-shirt. Her hands shook, and she wiped her hands on her jeans before giving a shaky laugh. She didn't even feel this nervous at Word Slam!

Bracing herself, she began to read. She only stumbled over her words a few times but quickly found her groove. The noises inside the café faded into the background. As she read the final lines of the story, she set the paper on the table and looked up. She wished Lazarus could have been here to witness it. Daring a glance at Oscar, he clapped for her.

"Please, you don't have to," Vassa said.

The rest of the table joined in, and her cheeks burned.

"What do we think of Vassa's story?"

She held her breath and focused her attention on the table. This was the part she hated most about the workshops, but it also ignited her.

"I think the dialogue was humorous. The mom and grandma in the story were dynamic characters," someone said.

There was a murmur of agreement.

"It helped to serve the characterization of the characters and the journey her hero takes to achieve her list."

Vassa nodded as she took down notes.

"What wasn't working or could be improved?" Oscar threw out next.

There was a silence before someone said, "I want the ending to be really worthy of the character. She has been working in this yoga studio, but what about that guy who helps her? What happens to him?"

Oscar clasped his hands. "Anything else?"

Who said life couldn't become fiction? Vassa didn't feel like she was the crummiest writer in the world. She actually felt energized to edit and make her story better. They decided to take a short break. Oscar stepped away to answer a call. Sonya and Amy from earlier appeared.

"That was a really good story," Amy said.

"Great, actually," Sonya agreed.

Vassa nodded. "Thank you."

"You have to pitch it to some literary magazines. I know a few if you want me to send them to you," Amy said.

Vassa's eyes widened. "Really?"

"I have a few published out there."

Vassa nodded. She felt her phone vibrate in her pocket.

"Congrats Amy. That's an amazing accomplishment."

"You know, we're meeting up to have dinner on Thursday. Would you want to come with us? It'll be fun," Amy suggested.

"Really? Me?" Vassa said.

Amy and Sonya went on about the dinner, and they talked about pointless things before Amy had to use the bathroom and Sonya tagged along. Vassa reached into her pocket and pulled out her phone. Vassa read it and her stomach fell to her feet:

Dear Vasilisa,

I wanted to personally congratulate you on being admitted to Boston University's MFA program! I enjoyed your writing examples and am looking forward to helping you become an official student.

Office of Graduate Admissions
Boston University

Vassa couldn't breathe. The world went silent before she let out a scream that stopped the entire café as she jumped up and down. The only thought in her mind was *I got in! I got in!*

She needed to tell her Mom, Dara, and everyone. She needed to plan; she needed to—

What was she doing? There was only one person that she wanted to share this with. She had a plan and she was ready.

Professor Fernández's lecture was done for the day. With reminders about their final paper, Vassa closed her notebook and turned to Oscar. So far, there was no sign of hard feelings or anger for falling into a middle of a drama episode at Dara's art opening.

"Think you're ready for the final paper?" she asked excited to find Lazarus and tell him the news.

Oscar looked up from zipping his book bag. "I don't think I am, but I've faked it before."

They laughed and exited the classroom, and down the stairs out of the building.

"We can pick up or caps and gowns in the library. Did you want to come or…" Vassa trailed off.

"Sure, it's finally time, right?"

"Right." Vassa still couldn't believe that she was going to Boston with a scholarship.

The campus buzzed with activity, and it didn't look like they were the only ones heading for the library.

"Do you feel better?" Oscar gave her that look of pity she didn't want. She was already embarrassed by crying in front of him. She didn't want to bring it up again.

"Yes, no, maybe so."

Vassa crossed her arms across her chest. After coming back from the sushi bar with Dara, they had stayed up talking before she went to bed. She hadn't been able to sleep last night. She tried to listen for Lazarus's footsteps, but she heard nothing. Nor did she hear anything this morning.

"I have good news," Oscar said.

"What?"

"I'm staying at PGU for graduate school. A full ride plus being a teaching assistant, but that's not it. I can run Word Slam."

"Congrats Oscar! That's amazing," she smiled and shook his shoulder.

Biting her lip, she looked at the ground and then at Oscar. "I'm going to Boston."

Oscar's mouth dropped. "What?"

"Boston University with a teaching position."

To her surprise, Oscar scooped her into a hug, and she laughed as the people walking by gave them curious looks.

"That's amazing Vassa!"

Setting her on her feet, she pressed a hand to her heart.

"I'm sure. I want to thank you and apologize."

Oscar's brows went up into his hairline. "Apologize for what?"

"For being my friend. You gave me someone to talk to, someone I could relate to and share my writing with. It's something I never had before."

"Why do I feel like there's a 'but' at the end of your sentence?"

Vassa took a deep breath.

"I just wanted to let you know. Thanks for dealing with me, when I wasn't so nice. I realize now I didn't make it easy, and you were just trying to be my friend."

"Are you the same person I met three months ago?"

That was a good question. Was she still the same person she was before? No, she wasn't. If she kept this up, she hoped she would never be that person again. They grew closer to the library; her breath caught in her throat. Lazarus was coming out with Jayden by his side. They each held their graduation caps and gowns in one arm as Jayden clamped a hand on Laz's shoulder. Why did it feel as if years passed since she saw him? The guys stopped for a moment as Jayden pointed a finger in his face before hugging and Jayden walked away.

She opened her mouth the call him but no sound came out. Lazarus shifted the duffle bag on his shoulder before heading toward the baseball field.

"Vassa, are you coming?" Oscar turned when he realized she wasn't following.

She hesitated, "You go ahead. I realize I forgot a meeting I have."

"Are you sure?"

Was she sure? No. Absolutely not, but there was no time like the present.

Ten minutes later, she was back on the baseball field.

The baseball to the head hadn't exactly made her eager to go back. Country music played through the speakers as the players tossed balls back and forth. The coach shouted to the players and creeping to the banister; she tried to spot Lazarus.

Where was he?

Her eyes scanned through the players. She didn't notice before how many other players on the team were blond.

There he is!

He caught the ball with his right hand effortlessly before

tossing it back to his partner. His face was flushed, and the sun was glistening off the sweat just right and *lord*… She had to fan herself. *Pay attention!* Vassa found a seat closest to the dugout.

He was an excellent player, and she admired how he directed his teammates. They continued to practice for a while until the coach blew the whistle. They all jogged to him. She watched as he pointed and yelled at each one of them. Finally, the huddle broke. Some picked up loose balls and others headed her direction toward the locker room.

Lazarus headed her way before the coach called him back.

She wished she had super hearing. The coach smiled at him, placing a hand on his shoulder. Lazarus nodded before they shook hands. Holding her breath, her heart crashed against her ribs. His head was held down he seemed in thought as he passed her. She stood up.

"Hey… Lazarus!"

His head shot up, and he stopped for a moment. She smiled at him before he gave her a weary look.

"Lazarus, wait a second." The railing was blocking her from stopping him. Without thinking, she tossed her book bag over the railing and hauled herself over the fence.

"What are you doing? Hey watch—"

Her foot caught on the top of the fence and she went flying face first to the ground. If she had a lot of pride left, she might have felt some type of way about the incident. Pushing herself up, his hands circled her arms lifted her up, "Are you trying to hurt yourself on purpose?"

"It seems like every time I come in here, I get hurt," she joked.

A small smile crept over his face but it was gone just a fast, "You shouldn't plan it that way."

"That wasn't the plan."

Once he was sure she could stand on two legs, he took a step back. His lips were pulled into a fine line as he watched her. He wasn't walking away. That was a good sign, wasn't it?

"How are you doing?"

Lazarus shook his head. She missed his smile, and she would give anything to have it back in this moment.

"You're not here to see how I'm doing, are you?"

He wasn't going to make it easy for her. She deserved it.

"I came to apologize for what I said at the gallery." Vassa continued and looked at her hands. "I shouldn't have said the things that I did. I was hurt and angry."

Lazarus said nothing. A couple of baseball players walked up and called his name. He turned to them and smiled, doing the dude dap with them before they asked if he was going to come hang out with them on break. She waited awkwardly as they talked, one guy eying her with interest before Lazarus dismissed them and turned back to her.

"I'm sorry what were you saying?"

Vassa frowned before she crossed her arms across her chest, "You don't have to be a jerk about it."

"I'm not being a jerk."

"Yes, you are. I'm trying to apologize." She knew it would not be easy to apologize. She had hurt his feelings, but she had her own too.

"You're right. I just don't know if I need to be ready for you to leave me again?" Lazarus asked.

Vassa hung her head and stayed rooted to the spot, the breeze cutting the silence.

"You know I didn't mean it."

"You didn't mean it… Is there anything else?" Lazarus crossed his arms.

Vassa made a face, "I want to know how the interview went."

"You're not just here to come and let me down. To tell me it's better if we end it now?"

"That's not it," Vassa said.

They stood there in silence.

"Lazarus—"

"I don't want us to be like this," his voice breaking at the last word.

"Me neither."

There was more silence.

Lazarus scratched the back of his head. "I went ahead and made a website. Sent my application to Mario. He wants me to meet with him while he's visiting L.A."

Vassa's eyes widen. "You did? What about Harvey?"

"I told him I don't want the job. I gave it back."

"That's great. I'm happy for you." Vassa was surprise; she didn't think he was going to do it. In that moment, her heart grew two sizes bigger for him.

"Vee, it's fine. I was doing some thinking,"

Vassa lowered the cards.

"You were right. I allowed Harvey to manipulate me with the money. I don't care about that now, but deep down there was some fear about graduation. I was scared because I knew who I was here and not out in the world." Lazarus pointed around at them.

Vassa laughed. "Do you know how common it is? Every adult feels that!"

"It also allowed me to see you were right. We're going in two different directions. I don't know where this internship will take me. You're going to graduate school in New York."

"No, Lazarus, that's not why I came down here—"

"We finished the list. I'm passing the class. We did it."

This wasn't what she wanted right now in this moment. She wanted more. She wanted him to pull her back into his arms and tell her that everything was going to be okay. She wanted to be closer to him, hear him laugh, to tell him about the graduate school situation and more.

"I know I want you. I want us."

"I don't want to make you leaving any harder than it needs

to be." Lazarus took a few steps back and turned toward the locker room.

"Lazarus!" She called after him again and she ran to catch his arm pulling him to a stop. Immediately she circled her arms around his waist and clung to him. She didn't want to let go. She couldn't let go. She wasn't fully sure in her heart that he would come back this time.

They had changed positions now. He was the one walking away and she was the one begging him to stay. Life couldn't be this cruel to her, could it?

"You know I love you Vee. You'll be great," He touched the arms she had wrapped against his chest.

Peeling her arms from his chest, he turned around. She couldn't stop the tears from falling down her face, and he lifted his hand to brush the tears away. She closed her eyes at his touch and his thumb lingered on her cheek as she opened her eyes to look at him.

Dipping his head, his lips brushed hers before planting his lips firmly on hers. She curled her hands in his shirt, trying to keep him there just a little bit longer, but way too soon, he pulled her hands away from his shirt and took a step back.

"Bye Vee."

She didn't have the strength now to follow him again. She could only watch as the tears fell faster down her face until the entire world blurred before her. She held back a sob as she turned to get her book bag. The music from the speakers had long since stopped. It was just her and the gentle breeze. She couldn't leave this campus without letting him know she wanted to make long-distance work. She just had to make him believe that, too.

CHAPTER TWENTY-FIVE

"ARE YOU SURE ABOUT THIS? I don't want to end up in the hospital." Dara grunted as she tied the skate tighter around Vassa's ankle.

"We might. So, keep emergency services on standby just in case." Vassa looked over her shoulder behind the sheet that covered them. It was blazing cold in Golden Gate Park at nearly midnight, but this was the plan.

It took a lot to coordinate this. Some free meals. Some cash and a bit of bribing on her end with free yoga classes to convince the skaters to participate. Now, all that was needed was for Jayden to do his job.

"You think he's going to do it? He can can't he?" Vassa asked Dara.

Dara tightened the skate and sat back on her haunches.

"How many times do I have to tell you; yes they will be here. Jayden said if he had to hit him over the head, he would do it," Dara said.

"Hopefully, we don't resort to that." Vassa stood up, wobbling as she steadied herself. Looking down at her clothing, she extended her arms. "How do I look?"

It was eighties night for the skaters. Joining in, Vassa wore leg warmers, a leotard, and big, poufy hair. She looked like something out of a Richard Simmons workout video. She struck a pose and Dara whistled.

"Your ass is looking bomb in those tights."

"Thank you."

She heard people behind the curtain of their makeshift backstage. Voices began to rise and she looked at Dara. This was it. She took a few breaths.

Dara peeked around the curtain. "It's time."

"I think I'm gonna pee myself." Vassa reached for Dara.

The first note of Gloria Gaynor's "I Will Survive" played.

Dara pulled her to the curtain. Handing her the microphone, she squeezed Vassa's hands and said, "You can do this."

Vassa closed her eyes. She took a deep breath. She thought about the party, the way he danced with her. She thought about their trip through the city, trivia night, and going to sing karaoke. The way they studied, how he made her food that was absolute garbage and they had to go to the local pizza point down the street. Going ziplining, the dance in the club, their first time together.

It all culminated in this moment.

The chorus started, and Dara pushed her forward, rolling her into the center of the circle. Her arms out to steady herself. The entire crowd was looking at her. The skaters held glow sticks all around her as Lazarus stood there. His mouth opened in surprise. She could only imagine what he was thinking. Probably why she looked like Bambi trying to take his first steps. Her feet went out from under her, and the nearby skaters caught her.

"Thank you, thank you so much," she muttered to them.

With a hand over his mouth, he looked at her, shaking his head. The song continued and all the skaters danced. A bright light shone down on her, and she wasn't sure where that came from. Karaoke and skating sounded much better in theory than in reality. She raised the microphone to her mouth and sang the lines. She was off-key. She hit the line too hard. She stumbled over some words. In her nervousness, she sang one verse too early.

The skaters formed a circle around them. Their glow sticks made intricate shapes in the night. Lazarus hadn't moved, his eyes going from her to the skaters, to the audience watching them, and then back to her. She sang the last line, and one skater broke from the circle and pushed her toward him. She waved her hands out, almost falling as the force pushed her right into him and he caught her in time.

"I don't know what to think or say—-"

Vassa laughed. "Don't speak; let me. I love you. I'm sorry; I'm an idiot." Vassa spoke into the microphone as she looked at him. "I love the way you laugh, the way you tease me. When you steal my food when you think I'm not looking, or how you listen and let me rant. When you push me to try something new. How you taught me to trust again."

Her feet went out from under her again, and he caught her.

"Or how you always want to taste my food. But I love how you make me want to be better. I don't want to hold on to the hurt and pain if that means losing you. I'm sorry. I thought you would be like everyone else and leave me. I'm sorry I didn't trust you; can you forgive me and take a chance on me? On us?"

The crowd went silent. Her eyes were enormous as she looked at him and he took the microphone from her.

The tears came again, and she tried to push herself up in the skates, but she went back down again. He caught her and hauled her back up. The surrounding crowd cheered, but it was white noise to her as she stared into those blue eyes that completely had her body, mind, and soul. This time, she pulled his face forward and kissed him, releasing the longing, anxiety, and hurt she had felt. She kissed him with renewed hope, excitement, and trust.

"I love you, Laz."

He lifted his hand and used his thumb to wipe away her tear.

"I love you, too, Vee."

EPILOGUE

"LADIES AND GENTLEMEN, I AM *engulfed with the excitement this day has brought to us, and I welcome your new Pacific Grove University graduates!"*

Vassa moved her tassel from right to left as the entire auditorium erupted into applause. She, Vassa Blackwell, had endured four years of hard work, sleepless nights, happiness, sadness, and all the in-between to get to this moment.

She was a college graduate.

The graduates were the first to file out of the auditorium, and she looked around to catch a glimpse of Dara, Jayden, or Lazarus. It still felt surreal. Wasn't it four months ago she couldn't stand to be in his presence and now…? Now, he was her boyfriend, her love.

Outside the sun was high. The sweet fragrance of freshly cut grass, chirping birds, and cloudless sky made the perfect San Francisco day.

She was different. She was no longer going to hold on to the pain of the past. She would take full advantage of each day, filled with happiness, love, and the occasional guard chase.

"Vassa!"

Dara pushed through the crowd. How she did so in those staggering heels was a mystery, but she collided with Vassa. Embracing they cried and laughed, ruining the make-up they did this morning.

"We did it! We really did it!" Dara held her hands and jumped up and down.

"Did you think the day would ever come?"

Dara shook her head. "It couldn't come soon enough, but guess what—" Shaking Vassa one more time, she yelled in her ear, "My parents are fully on board with me going to Toronto for my fellowship! They're disappointed I lied, but they'll visit me once I'm settled."

That made Vassa feel ten times better. It looked as if they were all on the road to acceptance.

Dara shook her and her brain rattled. "Are you ready Miss Boston? You're going to be with the best of the best writers in the country! Fully funded and teaching your first semester!"

For so long, New York had been on her mind, but as Grandma Laura said, sometimes we have plans for ourselves, and life laughs at that.

Jayden appeared next to Dara. "We have fallen into man's construction of success, but it's a milestone nevertheless." Dara and Vassa rolled their eyes.

"Not today, babe." Dara patted him on the chest as he put his arm around her.

Vassa heard her full name shouted. Her mom was plowing through the crowd with a bouquet in hand with Grandma Laura and her dad holding balloons. "Oh, my baby! I've been waiting for this day forever!"

A flush crept across her cheeks as her mom kissed her face and pulled her into a hug. Thankfully the dress she wore wasn't too low-cut and her bouncy C-cups weren't on display. Eve continued to babble as Vassa's father pulled her mother back. "C'mon, Eve, let her breathe."

"This is my only child; we only get this once, and we're going to celebrate it right." Eve pouted and wiped at her tears.

Grandma Laura ignored Eve and stepped forward for a hug. "I'm so proud of you, honey. Not just for this," she whispered to Vassa as they hugged.

Squeezing her grandmother harder, they released and she could see Grandma Laura's eyes were misty as well.

"Grandma, you didn't bring the senior center, did you?" Vassa glanced around for older people with posters of her face. A flashback to high school graduation when Laura brought the senior brigade wearing T-shirts with her face on them made her shiver.

"Hush! Not this time. And you, too, missy; come give me a hug!" Grandma Laura brought Dara into a hug. Vassa's parents introduced themselves to Jayden. She felt an arm circle her waist and pull her into a hard chest.

"Congratulations, Vee."

Vassa closed her eyes for a moment, soaking in his voice. She didn't realize how much she loved to hear him say her name. Vassa twisted around to see Lazarus; he cleaned up mighty well. His hair was gelled back from his face, most likely Harvey's gel, and he wore a fitted blazer and chinos… chinos? He held a bouquet of two dozen roses in one arm.

"For you." He passed her the bouquet.

Taking the flowers from him, she circled a hand around his neck, bringing him down to kiss, but their hats bumping stopped them. They laughed as they tilted their heads to the side to kiss. She never thought she would be the one to kiss in public, much less in front of her family not even a foot away, but she didn't care.

She pulled away first. "Where's Gideon and your family?"

Just then Gideon, Christie, and Harvey appeared through the crowd.

"Vassa, always a pleasure." Gideon smirked as he handed her another bouquet of flowers. Then giving Lazarus a look opened his arms for a hug. Vassa laughed and returned it as Lazarus muttered under his breath.

Vassa then turned to Christie who gave her an embrace. "So nice to finally meet you!"

Harvey stood there with his arms folded behind his back and nodded. "Vassa, congratulations on achieving a huge milestone."

Looking at Lazarus, he gave her a squeeze and she turned to him.

"Thank you... Harvey."

"Derek and his kids are here but they had a bathroom emergency. Mom and Dad are talking to some friends," Lazarus explained, giving Harvey a lingering look. Vassa gulped. She was meeting his parents for the first time! She hoped she looked all right.

"I can't wait to meet them. Do I look okay?" Vassa looked down at herself. Her gown covered most of her outfit.

"You look beautiful."

She blushed. He was complimenting her a lot lately. They had talked about maintaining a long-distance relationship. It wasn't ideal but they decided they were going to be dedicated to seeing it through.

"I got better news," Lazarus said.

Vassa raised an eyebrow.

"I got the internship."

Her eyes widened and she shook her head. *"What!"*

"They want me to go out right away. I'll get to take a tour of the company, see how they operate and how the team functions. I'll be there for a year or more; I'm not sure yet, but it's located right next to Fenway Park."

Her mouth dropped and he smiled as realization hit her. He was going to Boston, with her.

"Are you sure?" she asked. They had a long talk about maintaining their independence in their relationship. No matter where they were in the world, nothing would come between them.

"It's gonna be a great experience. Can you handle waiting for me to make the big bucks?"

She launched herself back into his arm, and he caught her,

pressing her lips back to him. The kiss just wasn't a comforting one. It was a declaration, a promise, and an erasure of fear. She could feel his lips smile against hers, and he pulled her closer. The world ceased to exist, blurred and indistinct, and it wasn't until they heard the clearing of several throats that they parted.

"Mrs. and Mr. Blackwell." Lazarus wiped his lips and offered his hand.

"So, this is the boy?" Simon grunted. He looked Lazarus up and down.

"Dad..." Vassa gave him a look and Lazarus squeezed her side.

"Remember what I said, young lady. I don't want you bringin' no babies home." Eve pointed at her before smiling at Lazarus.

"He's a cute young thang. You better watch him around me!" Grandma Laura grinned. Lazarus's eyes widened, and he took a step back. Vassa was so embarrassed. Someone screamed and everyone turned to see Kiki charging through the crowd in her leather boots.

"I'm going to cry! You all graduated, I'm going to miss you both!" Kiki threw herself onto Lazarus and Vassa. Vassa and Lazarus's family looked at her in interest; they had yet to experience the bombshell that was Kiki.

"That means I now have Boston and Toronto to go to for some fun..." Kiki wriggled her eyebrows.

Oh no.

The families mingled as plans for the future and what to eat later began. She felt some movement from next to her, and it was Oscar.

"We did it," Vassa smiled and offered him a hug.

They had made plans with the rest of their writing club to keep it going online. With Oscar staying at PGU, she knew he was going to be an amazing teacher and Word Slam was in good hands. Oscar and Lazarus both sized each other up. Vassa looked at them worriedly but to her surprise, Lazarus smiled at him and reached out his hand.

"It wasn't easy, was it?" He looked at Vassa then Oscar.

Taking his hand Oscar said, "It wasn't."

"Can we can take a group picture? Now, everyone get together. Kiki you get in there too!" Eve called everyone's attention.

They bunched together with Lazarus and Vassa in the center. Lazarus held her close. Dara pushed in to her right. Jayden, Oscar, and Kiki squeezed in close on the other sides. Their families watched as her father held the camera up high.

"Everyone, say student debt!"

"Student debt!"

Everyone laughed as the camera flashed. Vassa glanced at the people around her. She was surrounded by everyone she loved and that supported her, and she was excited about the future.

CONNECT WITH ME!

You can connect with me on:
My Website: https://tiniamontford.com/
Facebook | Instagram | Pinterest | Tumblr: @tiniawritesbooks

Interested in listening to Lazarus & Vassa's entire playlist?
https://sptfy.com/itstartedwithaList~s

SIGN UP FOR MY NEWSLETTER!

Would you like to see deleted scenes, character interviews, new releases, and exclusive character art? Sign up for my newsletter, https://landing.mailerlite.com/webforms/landing/q4f2f5

ACKNOWLEDGMENTS

Ya'll... I can't even put into words these feelings I have typing my first acknowledgements page.

It's surreal, nerve-racking, amazing, confusing, and all in between. If I'm being honest, Lazarus and Vassa's story has been eight-years in the making. They've lived many lives: a high-school glee club (don't shame me here, haha), celebrities living in New York, best-friends to lovers then enemies to lovers then fake dating and a bunch of stuff that just didn't fit. My gut is churning with butterflies, and it feels as if I'm sending my first-born off to daycare. Can you imagine? My only baby, waddling inside to play with all the other children, and they don't look back to see me, crying my eyes out, snot and all, until they disappear from view. I can't coddle Lazarus and Vassa anymore. They belong to you, readers. I hope you cherish them as much as I do.

I want to give first thanks to God. He put it on my spirit to be a writer, but it was only through everlasting hope and faith that you're actually reading this book. He's taking me places I've never been before and I'm buckling my seatbelt up for the ride.

Grandma Jackie and Mom... Ya'll know. I don't even gotta say it. I know I ran ya'll crazy with this book, but your essences lives within these pages.

Priscilla... My O.G. from undergrad. It's crazy to think I just walked up to you that first week on campus and started talking about your tattoos, and now years later we're still friends. Thank you for reading this book when it was in its early-early stages and for being my inspiration for Dara.

Elizabeth Turner Stokes... I can't thank you enough for designing such a wonderful cover! You captured exactly the spirit of the book, and you're simply amazing! We haven't worked together long but I hope for more covers to come.

To my family and friends... Thank you so much for your

support! Especially my MFA Fiction cohort! I appreciate every share, pre-order, comment, and like that you've given me. You all pushed me to put my work out there and helped build my confidence as a writer.

ABOUT TINIA

Tinia (TUH-NIA) Montford is a Pisces who's a sap for romance, especially when there's (tons of) kissing. Loves eighties sitcoms and will consume anything with chocolate. She graduated from the University of San Francisco with a degree in English and Graphic Design.

She is a world traveler having climbed a volcano in Nicaragua, scaled Angkor Wat in the blistering sun, and roamed the Acropolis of Athens. Oh, she also dabbles in short stories occasionally.

If you can't catch her writing, you can bet she's overindulging on poke bowls, listening to the same four songs, or chilling with her adorbs doggie. She is currently pursuing her MFA in Fiction. You can find more information on her books on her website: http://www.tiniamontford.com